Out With
the Ex
In With
the New

BOOKS BY SOPHIE RANALD

Sorry Not Sorry
It's Not You, It's Him
No, We Can't be Friends

It Would be Wrong to Steal My Sister's Boyfriend (Wouldn't it?)
A Groom with a View
Who Wants to Marry a Millionaire
You Can't Fall in Love with Your Ex (Can You?)

Out With the Ex In With the New

SOPHIE RANALD

Bookouture

Published by Bookouture in 2019

An imprint of Storyfire Ltd.
Carmelite House
50 Victoria Embankment
London EC4Y 0DZ

www.bookouture.com

ISBN: 978-1-83888-248-8
eBook ISBN: 978-1-83888-247-1

Chapter One

Hi everyone!

So this morning I'm going to do a business make-up look. I know, it's not the most exciting thing ever, is it? But then, job-hunting isn't either, as you'll know if you've been watching this channel over the past few months. And if you're here because you've got a job interview coming up too, I hope it goes really, really well for you.

The whole corporate thing – well, it's not that corporate really, because that's just not me, but it's kind of low-key. Polished. Professional! That's it, professional. It's a look I've had to master over the past few months, because I've been going to a lot of interviews. A lot. I think today will be, like, the twentieth one. But it's all good experience, right?

And one thing I've learned along the way is that when you're attending interviews – or any business meeting, really – you need to look the part. What do they say? Dress for the job you want, not the job you've got. Or, to put it another way, fake it till you make it. And the same goes for make-up. I suppose if you were interviewing to be, I don't know, a receptionist at a modelling agency or something, you could be a bit more out there with your whole look, but for most jobs, you just want to look like someone they want to employ, and that means keeping things a bit subtle. You want them to go, "That's the girl with the amazing CV", not "That's the girl with the amazing blending skills". But at the same time, you want your make-up to last. Turning up for an interview with your nose all shiny and your mascara smudged is not a good look. Trust me, I know, because I've done it!

But that's enough waffling from me. I'm literally just going to show you what I do. Hopefully this look is going to work for me – I'm using my lucky Charlotte Tilbury lipstick that Jack bought me for Christmas – so keep your fingers crossed for me. And speaking of fingers, don't forget to give this video a thumbs up if you like it, and if you work this look for a job interview or an important meeting, let me know how you get on.

So, I'm going to start by applying my foundation…

"I'd like a bottle of Prosecco please," I said, when I eventually managed to fight my way through the throng around the bar and catch the barman's eye. "And two glasses."

It was all I could do not to say, "We're celebrating! I've got a job!" But I managed to stop myself, just like I'd managed to resist telling the guy in Pret when I bought a chicken sandwich, and the carriage full of people jammed in like sardines on the train, and the *Big Issue* seller when I bought my magazine, like I did every Friday. Although, come to think of it, it was just as well I hadn't told him. Crowing about my new gainful employment to someone who didn't even have a home would have been a massive dick move.

I'd told everyone else, though – well, everyone there was. I'd texted Mum. I'd texted Katie, Shivvy, Nancy and Olivia. I would have texted Stanley, only he's not great with technology, being a teddy bear.

And now it was time to tell Jack.

It was a Friday evening and the bar was packed with groups of office workers pouring pints of beer and glasses of wine down their necks as fast as they could, celebrating the end of the working week. It was the end of the month, too – payday, I guessed, because lots of the women had glossy carrier bags from Oasis and Whistles slung over the backs of their chairs. Soon that would be me, I thought, resisting the urge to skip with excitement.

Where the hell was Jack? I craned my neck, searching for him, glad for once of my height and the additional three inches lent to me by my smartest shoes. Finally, I spotted him at a table in the corner, his back to me, a pint of Guinness in front of him.

I just hurried over, clutching the sweating ice bucket to my chest.

"I got it! I got the job!"

"No way! That's brilliant, Gem, you must be really proud."

Jack stood up and hugged me, even though my top was damp from the ice bucket. I wrapped my arms around his neck and kissed him. He tasted of beer and a bit of cheese and onion crisps – the empty packet was on the table next to his glass.

"Have you been waiting ages? My train was cancelled so I had to wait for the next one and then there were no seats. It was grim."

"Not that long," Jack said. "So – tell me about the interview. Was this the advertising agency one?"

"No, doofus, that was yesterday." To be fair to Jack, I'd been for so many job interviews in the past eighteen months I'd almost lost track of them myself. Endless tweaking of my CV and my LinkedIn profile. Endless train journeys to London, expensive and fruitless. Endless emails starting, *We regret that on this occasion…* But it had all been worth it, because now, finally, I'd been given a chance.

"It's Clickfrenzy," I said. "You know – 'Winning the internet since 2010'? Their stories come up on Facebook all the time. I'm officially a junior writer. I start on the fifteenth. Just wait until you see their office – it's so incredibly cool. There's a popcorn machine and a coffee machine and a games room and it's right off Oxford Street."

"It sounds amazing," Jack said, easing the cork out of the bottle of Prosecco and carefully filling a glass for me.

"It is amazing!" I said. "Aren't you having any?"

"Maybe in a bit," Jack said, taking another sip of stout. "I've still got this. Anyway, cheers. Congratulations."

"I actually still can't believe it. My boss – how weird does it feel saying that? – Sarah, she's the MD, interviewed me, and I thought she'd do the usual thing of being like, 'We'll be in touch (not).' But she offered me the job straight away. She said they're growing so fast the challenge is getting talented people on board. She thinks I'm talented! I told her about my YouTube channel and made out like I was some social content guru, and I guess she must have believed me. She's super scary, though. Scary Sarah."

Jack didn't laugh. He was looking kind of thoughtful, staring down into his glass.

I said, "Look, I know this is huge. And it's kind of sudden – I was beginning to think it was never going to happen, and I'd have to carry on living with Mum and working in the bloody pub forever. But now it has – and it changes things for you, too, I guess."

"Does it?" Jack said.

I said, "Of course! It means I can finally move out of Mum's, and we can… you know. We can get on with life."

I didn't say it, but I knew he knew what I meant. *We can move in together. I can stop living out of a bag when I stay over at your flat. We can have a place of our own. We can move our relationship on to the next level, the way it's supposed to happen.*

I said, "I was looking at flats online, on the train home. We couldn't afford a place of our own, I don't think. But we could get a room somewhere together, easily. Somewhere with cool bars and shops and stuff. Somewhere like…"

I paused, thinking of the vastness of London. I didn't really know where. But I could picture it in my head: a sunny bedroom, maybe somewhere high up, with a view of the Thames. Or maybe not – I knew next to nothing about London but I was pretty sure that views over the Thames didn't fall within our budget. With a balcony, then, where we could have coffee and croissants on weekend mornings, before strolling hand-in-hand through cobbled streets, stopping at market stalls to buy bunches of tulips and cool vintage things, like people did in vlogs on YouTube. And I could film myself doing those things for my own vlog, which might mean I'd get some more viewers, because, as I had discovered, me putting on make-up for unsuccessful job interviews, serving pints in the Mason's Arms and trying not to have too many rows with my mother didn't exactly make for compelling content.

And Jack – Jack was surely ready to move on with life, too. To be honest, I'd found it – not frustrating exactly, but almost mystifying that Jack, to whom everything seemed to come so easily, didn't do more to make things happen. He'd gone straight from university to living in a flat his parents had bought as an investment and working for the software development company his dad owned, where he spent his days doing things to do with C++ and SQL and other stuff that made me glaze over a bit whenever he talked about it. If it was that boring to hear about, I sometimes thought, how boring must it be to actually *do*? But whenever he complained about it and I suggested that he could make a change, do something he was passionate about, he just said, "Yeah, maybe," and changed the subject. And because, after all, I wasn't exactly setting the world on fire career-wise myself, I hadn't pushed the issue.

Jack said, "Gemma. I handed in my notice at work today."

"You did? That's great. And how incredible that you did it on the same day I got this job! It's almost like you knew, or fate knew, or something. Now we can really…"

Then I stopped. I knew, right then, that I wasn't going to like what he was going to say. I wanted him to stop, but I knew I had to hear it.

I took a big gulp of my drink. It had gone a bit warm and flat while we were talking, and it tasted sour and not like a celebration at all.

I said, "Have you found something else, then? Or are you just going to take a break for a bit?"

Jack said, "I guess I'm going to take a break for a bit. If you want to put it like that."

I said, "A break to do what, exactly?"

Jack said, "I want to go travelling. I want to see a bit of the world, before I settle down."

Before *I* settle down, I noticed. Not before *we* settle down.

"Travelling where?" I said.

"Everywhere," he said. "I want to go to Dubai and see the tallest building in the world. I want to go to Thailand – I might try and find work in a diving school there. Then maybe India, Australia, Peru – I want to hike the Inca trail. And New Orleans, obviously. And New York."

"But you never said anything," I said. My voice sounded a bit wobbly, and even more squeaky than usual. "You must have been thinking about this for ages."

"I've been thinking about it," he said. "Obviously. Yeah, I guess I've been planning it. But I wasn't sure, and I didn't want to tell you until I was."

Then I heard my voice say the obvious thing – the stupid, inevitable thing. "But what about us?"

Jack said, "I love you, Gemma, you know I do. But I'm not ready for all the settling-down shit. I can't go and work every day in some fucking boring job I hate and save for a deposit and then save for a wedding and then have kids. I can't. I'm twenty-four. I've done fuck all with my life and now you want me to do all that and it just feels like more of fuck all."

I said, "I never asked you to do any of that stuff! I didn't!"

"Maybe you didn't," Jack said. "But I know it's what you want. Come on, Gemma, I've seen your Pinterest boards."

"What about my Pinterest boards?" I said. "So? I post recipes on them – it's not like I'm ever going to cook any of them. And pictures of what I'd like my living room to look like if I had a house that cost a million pounds, which is never going to happen, obviously. And I post… What were you doing looking at my Pinterest, anyway?"

"Wedding dresses," Jack said. "You had it open on your iPad, I couldn't help seeing them."

I said, "Look, all girls look at wedding dresses. It's theoretical. It doesn't mean anything. Not like buying a flight to the other side of the flipping world means something!"

I glared at him and he glared back. I could feel the row waiting to happen – if it hadn't already started – and our evening, which had got off to a pretty awful start, being irretrievably ruined. But then, I thought, if it was all over between us, what did it matter anyway?

I said, "How long were you – are you – going to go for, anyway?"

Jack said, "Six months, probably. Maybe a year. I'm not sure. But I'll come back, Gemma. I want to be with you. I really, really do. I'm just not ready for that kind of commitment just yet."

It was the straw I needed to clutch at – the promise that, even if he was on the other side of the planet, he'd still be my boyfriend. Call me a mug, but I grasped it.

"Do you really mean that?" I said. "What, like we'll still be together, even though you aren't here?"

Jack said, "Of course we will. I'll FaceTime you every day. It'll be almost like you're there. I want you to feel like you're having this adventure with me. I just wish you could be there in real life."

For a second, I thought, *Maybe I actually could. Maybe I could email Sarah and tell her I couldn't accept the job after all, or ask her if I could apply again in six months.* But then I remembered the long, depressing months of unpaid internships that were meant to teach me valuable skills and actually taught me how to make tea and call endless lists of telephone numbers to check that they were correct. I remembered the triumph and relief I'd felt when Sarah said, "We'd like you to start as soon as possible." And I remembered that I could barely afford a train ticket to London; I certainly couldn't afford a round-the-world flight, and Mum couldn't afford to treat me to one and then pay for places for me to sleep and food for me to eat and everything else I'd need for six whole self-indulgent months. Or maybe a year.

I felt the familiar sense of injustice, of resentment, of there being something horribly unfair about a world where everything was so easy for some people and so difficult for me. Then I remembered the *Big Issue* seller, and sternly reminded myself, as I did so often (and Mum did even more often), that in the grand scheme of things, I had absolutely nothing to moan about. But still, I couldn't help thinking how nice it would be to have rich parents like Jack did. Like Olivia did.

Then a horrible idea occurred to me, and as soon as it did, I knew that it was right.

I said, "Won't it be a bit... a bit shit, travelling on your own? Lonely?"

Jack said, "I'm not going on my own, Gemma. I'm going with Olivia."

"Of course you are," I said. I sounded angry, for the first time since he'd dropped his bombshell, and bitter, but I didn't care.

From the first day I met Jack, Olivia had been a constant presence. She was even *there* when I met him, having dinner with him in Lucio's, where I was working as a waitress during the summer holidays after my second year of uni (I was ignominiously sacked shortly after for throwing a bowl of minestrone soup over the chef when he pinched my bottom one time too many, which was totally worth it).

I assumed they were a couple – of course I did, the handsome, stocky man and the willowy blonde girl chatting and laughing together. So, when Jack lingered after he'd paid the bill and asked for my number, I said, "Fuck off, you've got a girlfriend."

And Jack had said, "That's not my girlfriend! That's Olivia."

And it was true – she wasn't his girlfriend and never had been. In some ways, it would have been better if she was. Because Jack wasn't just Jack; he was half of Jack and Olivia, bound to another girl by the ties of a friendship that had lasted since they were – well, basically forever.

Their birthdays were three days apart. Olivia's parents and Jack's parents lived next door to each other. They'd gone to the same baby music classes and the same riding school and been babysat together while their parents went out for dinner together. They'd even been on holiday together, for God's sake. And instead of hating each other, like most kids would surely have done with such close proximity imposed on them, they'd stayed best friends throughout their childhood, and when Jack and I started going out, they were best friends still.

Of course, when the closeness of their friendship became clear to me, I'd felt threatened. But Jack had laughed when I asked him if he and Olivia had ever… you know… had they? He'd said kissing Olivia would be like kissing his sister, if he had one. He'd said he couldn't imagine anything weirder or more wrong – and besides, he said, they didn't fancy each other. Not in the slightest, not even a tiny bit.

So I put my fears to one side. This wasn't as hard to do as it sounds, especially as Olivia made a huge effort to be nice to me.

And it wasn't hard to like Olivia – everyone likes her. She's got more friends on Facebook than anyone I know, and she actually stays in touch with them all, meets up with them and keeps up with what's going on in their lives. She kind of adopted me – inviting me on nights out with her mates, until Shivvy and Nancy and the rest of them became my friends too, giving me a ready-made circle of friends at home in Norwich that made up for the fact that I'd been a shy, uncool no-mates at school. She sent me flowers on my birthday. Recently, she'd listened to me complain about the misery of job-hunting and reassured me that I was brilliant, that something would come along eventually, that it was all meant to be and part of the Universe's grand plan for me (Olivia's a yoga teacher. She often comes out with zen shit like that).

But in spite of Olivia being my friend, I always knew she'd been Jack's friend first. Even though I'd been Jack's girlfriend for four years, I didn't know whether his first loyalty would be to me or to her. It had never really mattered – it had never been tested. Not until now.

I said, "So the two of you have been planning this together, and not said anything to me. You've done it all behind my back."

"Gemma, babe, please don't be like this," he said.

"Be like what? Be like your girlfriend, who was planning a life with you, who's found out you've had other plans all along?"

"There isn't an 'all along'," Jack said. "Please, Gemma, you have to understand. This has all been really recent. We only booked our tickets today. Liv only had the idea, like, last week. I mean, obviously I've been thinking for a while about stuff, about what I want to do, where I'm going…"

"Who you're going with," I said.

"Come on, Gemma," Jack said. "You know, if I could choose anyone in the world to go travelling with, to have this adventure with, it would be you. But…"

I said, "I could save up. They're not paying me much at Click-frenzy – it's a starting salary – but if I stayed at home for a year and saved like mad, I could maybe take some time off, like a career break. I could go with you then."

As soon as the words left my mouth, I regretted them. I knew what I'd said wasn't true. Not that I didn't want to travel, and see the world, and do it with Jack – but not like that. My idea of exploring wasn't remotely the same as his. He'd be quite happy sleeping in tents and in grotty youth hostels with filthy showers and maybe even bedbugs – evidently so would Olivia. But I wouldn't. There'd be nowhere to have a hot bath. The food would be weird. I wouldn't be able to make people who didn't speak English understand me. I remembered going to Glastonbury with Jack a couple of years before, and how much I'd hated it, even though I hadn't admitted as much to him and never would. This would be like Glastonbury, only with added foreign languages and probably even grimmer toilets, and it would go on for months and months.

Jack reached across the table for my hand, but I moved it away.

"I don't want to wait," he said. "We – I want to go now. It just feels right."

I could feel a huge surge of anger building up inside me. It wasn't fair – he was selfishly, casually doing exactly what he wanted to do, with no thought for me, my dreams and ambitions, the future we'd talked about having together. I wanted to accuse him of that, to demand to know why he thought that diving in Thailand was more important than me. But the words wouldn't come.

Instead, I heard my voice say again, even more pathetically, "But what about us?"

Jack said, "This isn't about us, Gemma. This doesn't mean anything about us. I love you. I'll always love you. When I come back, we can move in together, like you wanted. I just need to do this now, for myself. And you could come out to New York for Christmas – we think that's where we'll be then, anyway. And in the meantime, you can really focus on your new job. You're going to be so awesome at it."

As he spoke, he topped up our glasses with fizzy wine, then held his out towards me.

"Come on, Gemma," he said. "Let's drink to the future. To us."

And I clinked my glass against his and echoed, "To us."

Chapter Two

When I woke up, for a few seconds things felt just the same as usual. I opened my eyes and saw Stanley, lying next to me on the pillow where he always was. Beyond his battered furry body, I could see the dent where Jack's head had been, and I remembered that it was Saturday, and he always got up early on Saturdays to go to the gym. I saw greyish light making familiar patterns through the leaves of the lime tree outside my window. I could hear some eighties pop song blasting from the radio and Mum singing tunelessly along to it.

Then reality hit me like a brick. Jack was going away. Jack and Olivia. I remembered all the promises he'd made to me the previous night as we finished the bottle of Prosecco and then over the dinner he bought us to celebrate my new job, and later when we lay together in my bed. I'd found it so easy to believe that they were true when he was there, but now that he wasn't, doubt came rushing in to fill the space he'd left.

Long-distance relationships could work – I knew that. Katie and her boyfriend Matt had stayed together all through university, with Katie in Newcastle and Matt in Exeter, snatching weekends together and seeing each other in the holidays (admittedly, it all went horribly wrong shortly after we graduated, when we went on a girls' holiday to Ibiza and Katie shagged a barman. But still). Other people made it work too – of course they did, even though I couldn't actually think of any right this second. Jack and I would make it work. He'd promised.

But this was different. Jack and I wouldn't be seeing each other regularly. We wouldn't be able to have a routine of talking before we went to sleep every night, the way Katie and Matt had. I wouldn't know where he was or what he was doing, or feel connected to his life because I knew first-hand what it was like. He'd be seeing new things, meeting new people all the time. He'd be exploring the world, and he'd forget about me.

I remembered how I'd felt the previous morning, when my alarm clock had gone off and I'd known instantly that today was the day I was going for the interview at Clickfrenzy – full of excitement and apprehension and hope. I'd got what I wanted, but it didn't feel that way. It didn't feel like the beginning of my life as a grown-up – or if it did, I wanted nothing more than to be able to turn back the clock.

I picked up my phone and plugged in the earbuds to drown out the sound of Mum's singing, and went online to drown out my thoughts. I flicked through my Instagram feed, but I didn't post anything. I checked my YouTube channel and saw that some of my two thousand followers had commented on my video, saying I looked great and wishing me luck for the job interview. I knew I should reply, letting them know how well it had gone and how excited I was about it all, but I just wasn't feeling it.

I pulled the duvet back up to my chin, cuddled Stanley to my chest and closed my eyes. All I wanted to do was go back to sleep, and stay asleep until it was time to get ready for my shift in the pub, but I couldn't. There was a horrible taste in my mouth; the light was too bright. I needed to wee and I was hungry.

So, reluctantly, I got up. I had a long shower and washed my hair, but I couldn't be bothered to get dressed or put on any make-up (*Some kind of beauty vlogger you are, Gemma Grey*, I scolded myself). Instead, I put on fluffy slippers and my dressing gown and went into the kitchen.

Mum was on the sofa with her feet up on the coffee table, reading *Vogue*. She was wearing grey suede leggings and a drapey purple top, and she'd changed her hair. It had been a sort of ashy blonde yesterday; now it was chestnut.

I was used to seeing these overnight – or daytime, I suppose, strictly speaking, because they didn't actually happen while she was asleep – transformations. Mum used to be a model – not a supermodel or anything like that. I'm not going do a thing like, "You know Naomi Campbell? So, I'm her daughter." I mean, I don't think Naomi even has a daughter. But if she did, I'm not her. Anyway, Mum was an actual model, until she met my father and got pregnant with me, and then after Dad left she trained as a hairdresser, and now she manages her own salon. She's won prizes and everything. The only thing she likes better than experimenting with new colours and styles on her own hair is experimenting with them on mine. It means that, however down I might feel about my appearance generally, my hair is always fabulous.

I said, "Aren't those my leggings?"

Mum looked up. "Are they?" she said, ever so casually. "I must have put them in my wardrobe by mistake after I washed them. I could have sworn they were mine."

"Well, they aren't," I said. "They're mine, and they're dry clean only, so there's no way they would have been in the wash. I bought them last week at TK Maxx, they were, like, the bargain of the century and I haven't even worn them yet. So give them back."

"Oh, please, Gemma?" Mum said. "Can't I borrow them just this once? I've got a date and literally nothing else to wear. We're not even going for lunch, just a walk by the river and maybe a drink, so I won't spill anything on them."

"You're going for a walk by the river in those shoes?" I said, eyeing up her charcoal platform shoe-boots and making a mental note to borrow them at the earliest possible opportunity.

"It won't be far," she said. "And he said he's six foot two, so if he's lying he deserves to have me tower over him."

"Is this another Guardian Soulmate?" I asked.

"Match.com, this time," Mum said. "They're all a bit worthy on Guardian Soulmates. The last one I met was a vegan, as he told me within about five seconds of us meeting. So I was too embarrassed to order any food at the pub we went to, even though I was starving, and we just sat there crunching away on peanuts like Mr and Mrs Squirrel. He got one stuck in his teeth and the spark died, right then."

Reluctantly, I laughed. Mum's online dating stories are always entertaining, although I suspect they're often embellished for comic effect. She's been single for as long as I can remember, apart from when Cameron moved in with us for a couple of years when I was a teenager. I'm pretty sure it was my epic strops that scared him off, but Mum didn't seem too bothered when he left. It's like she doesn't mind being alone, but she does like meeting new people all the time. Weird as, right?

I said, "Want a coffee?"

Mum said, "No, I'm all… actually, yes, I'd love one. Thanks, angel."

I pushed the sleeves of my dressing gown back off my hands to fill the kettle. Even though it was a gorgeous, sunny day, I didn't feel warm. I wanted to go back to bed.

I made the coffee and took two mugs over to the sofa.

Mum said, "Did you and Jack have a nice evening? I heard you come in, but I was already half asleep."

"It was all right," I said. Then I sat down next to her and picked up my drink, clasping my hands around the mug with my dressing gown sleeves as insulation.

"He must be pleased about your new job," Mum said.

I said, "Yes, I suppose he is. Because I suppose he thinks it'll distract me from the fact that he's fucking off overseas for a fucking year with fucking Olivia."

I heard Mum give a little gasp. I looked sideways at her and watched while she composed her face from surprise to careful neutrality.

"That came a bit out of the blue, didn't it?" she said.

"I know, right?" I said dismally. "He told me last night. I was like, yay, new job, go me, and he was like, never mind that, see where I'm going."

Mum said, "Oh, Gemma. Does that mean the two of you are…"

"No!" I said. "He's going to come back, and then we're going to find a place to live together and… I don't know, settle down and stuff. That's what he says, anyway. He means it, right?"

I heard Mum take a deep breath and slowly let it out again, blowing on her coffee to cool it. I looked sideways at her again, but her face was still and unreadable.

"I'm sure he does," she said. "He loves you, Gemma. Anyone can see that. He's a decent guy, and he treats you well, and I've always liked him very much. But…"

"But what?"

"A year is a long time when you're twenty-four, Gemma. No, don't look at me like that. I know you think I'm patronising you, but I don't mean to. All I'm saying is, don't put your life on hold for him, because you never know what's waiting around the corner, for you or for him."

"What do you mean, don't put my life on hold?" I said.

"Just that," said Mum. "I know you've been talking about finding a place to live in London with him. You've been desperate to get out of here. You keep saying how you need your own space. And you're right – so do it on your own. Of course I love having you here, but commuting for four hours a day will get very old, very quickly. You'll make new friends in your new job, expand your horizons… make the most of the time he's away, instead of hanging about like some princess in an ivory tower. That's what I mean."

Mum had put down her coffee. Her hands were sort of twitching in her lap, as if they couldn't bear to be still. I'd noticed this before when she was thinking or giving advice – it's almost as if she's so used to doing it while cutting someone's hair, her fingers take on a life of their own and want to be doing stuff to a head that isn't there.

I said, "But I don't know if I want to do it on my own. It won't be the same."

"Gemma!" Mum said. "Feel the fear and do it anyway! I'll still be here. If whatever you do doesn't work out, you can come home, like you did after uni. But you need to follow your dream – Jack's following his, after all. Isn't he?"

"His and Olivia's," I said sourly.

"Well, quite," Mum said. "That girl… Anyway. You trust Jack, and that's a good thing. If you want to make this relationship work long-distance, the best thing you can do is show him what he's missing. You moping around, not changing, not moving forward, resenting him having this massive adventure – that's not the most attractive image for him to have in his head when he thinks about you, is it?"

"I guess not," I said.

"And that's not what you're like, anyway," Mum said. "Look at you! You're vibrant and brave and beautiful – even in that horrid rag of a bathrobe. Be those things without him, and then if – when – he comes home, you'll be even better at being them with him."

"I guess," I said.

"And what's more," Mum said, "that thing of yours – that video thing you do – I guarantee you he'll be watching that, because he cares about you and he'll want to know what you're up to. So let him see all the amazing things you're doing without him. Show him what he's missing. You catch more flies with honey than you do with vinegar, as my nan used to say."

"Maybe," I said. But I could kind of see what she meant, and as I thought about it, sipping my coffee, it started to make more and more sense.

"Christ, I'm going to be late for not-tall Tristan," Mum said. "I won't be gone long, but I expect you'll be at work when I get in. Take care, little lemon drop. Don't be sad."

She leaned over and gave me a kiss. Her hair swished over my face, still smelling of the chemical colour she'd put on it. It's the most comforting smell I know.

Chapter Three

Hi everyone!

So, it's Monday morning. Sadface! And it's raining – boo! But today is a big day for me for two reasons. First, it's my first day in my new job, which is why I am up, like, ridiculously early. I've got to get the train before seven o'clock, because it takes like two hours to get from Norwich to London. Ouch! I so need to find a new place to live. Anyway, the other thing that's happening today is also exciting, but exciting in a sad way. Jack's leaving tonight to fly to Dubai, and then going on to the next stage of his adventure in Thailand in a few days.

I'd be lying if I said I wasn't gutted. I'm gutted. I've cried loads about it – we've both cried, actually. But you know what they say – if you love someone, set them free. So that's what I'm doing. I'm going to go to the airport tonight after work and see him and the friend he's travelling with off on the start of their massive adventure, and then I'm going to start counting down the days until he comes back to me.

It's going to be tough, but I've got to put on my big girl pants – not literally, don't worry. I'm not working the Bridget Jones look today. My knickers are from Victoria's Secret – I think they were in the haul that I shared with you last week. Thanks for all the likes you gave that one, and remember, tell me in the comments or tweet me and let me know what else you'd like to see more of on my channel – and if you like this video, give me a big thumbs up!

Anyway. It's Monday morning, like I said – I said that, didn't I? – and I'm getting ready to go to work. It is chucking it down out there and it's really windy, brrr! But at least that means I get to use my giant umbrella – check it out, how cool is that? It's from this amazing shop on New Oxford Street that sells nothing but umbrellas – old school! Let's see if I can open it and show you… Ooops. Maybe not. Sorry, light fitting! It's meant to be bad luck opening an umbrella indoors, isn't it? My bad. Or did I make that up?

So as I was saying, wet weather and my hair are. Not. Friends. So on days like this, I normally try and nail frizz before it gets a chance to even start. A bit of serum through the lengths of my hair, then work a bit of curl cream through with your fingers, just kind of twisting each section a little bit to give it some texture and shape around my face, like so. Right.

Oh my God, look at the time! I've got to be out of the door in like ten minutes tops. So, I'm going to do my make-up really fast. This look takes literally five minutes: foundation, which I apply with my fingers. If I had more time I'd use a brush, but, you know – Monday! Tiny bit of concealer under my eyes – I had a massive night on Saturday for Jack's farewell, which I'll tell you guys about later on, and I'm still looking reeeeally tired. When I'm in a hurry, I love products that do more than one job – like this, *it's a lip and cheek stain, so I can just dab a bit on the apples of my cheeks, dab a bit more on my lips, and voila – done. Quick bit of eyeshadow, just in the crease to contour my eyes. Eyeliner flick – God, I hate doing this when I'm in a rush. Please let me not mess it up – there. Phew. Mascara, bit of lip gloss, and I'm good to go.*

Boots on, I've got my make-up bag, Oyster card, phone, keys – right, I'm going in! Or rather, out. I'm going out! I'll see you guys later on. Mmmwah – byeee!

It was a weird thing, I thought, snatching my camera off the chest of drawers and tucking it into my bag, how when I was filming, everything else seemed to kind of disappear. It felt almost as if there were real people watching me, people who cared about what I was going to wear on my first day in my new job, people who wanted to know whether my lip gloss was by Maybelline or Smashbox. People who cared about me. I knew that they were real, of course – they posted comments on my videos, followed me on social media, asked if I was okay if I hadn't uploaded anything for a few days. They weren't spambots, or anything like that. But when I was talking to them, it felt as if they were actually there in the room with me.

Okay, that sounds creepy. But it meant that I totally lost track of time, the way you do when you're having a good old chinwag with a group of mates. And on this occasion, it meant that I was going to have to get my skates on or be seriously late for work.

I did the ten-minute walk to the station at almost a sprint, threw myself on to the train with seconds to spare and narrowly made it to the last remaining seat ahead of a man in a suit, who gave me a death stare. I smiled sweetly back and took my phone out of my handbag. Now that I was sitting still, with nothing to do except skim-read my social media for the next couple of hours, all my worries came flooding back.

What if I fucked up at work? What if they all hated me, and Sarah called me into her office at the end of the day and told me she'd made a terrible mistake? And Jack – tonight would be the last time I'd see him for months and months. The thought made me feel all hollow inside, as if the space inside my heart that I kept for him had been torn open and left empty. It made me want to cry, but I'd cried so much in the past two weeks I was sure I didn't have any tears left. Maybe that's what the hollow feeling was, I thought – a reservoir of tears that had been soaked up by a succession of soggy tissues, my pillow, Jack's shoulder and Stanley's fur.

I forced my thoughts away from Jack, away from crying, because if I thought about it I'd end up doing it, and checked my YouTube channel. The video I'd posted the previous day, showing off the new clothes I'd bought for work (actually, in the interests of full disclosure, some had been bought and others had been acquired during a stealth raid on Mum's wardrobe while she was out), had been viewed almost a thousand times and had fifteen comments. I read them all, responding to the messages wishing me luck for my first day in my new job, answering the few questions about my purchases and admitting the "borrowing" from Mum.

Most of the people commenting were familiar names – people I'd got to know over the two years since I set up SparklyGems (I know. It seemed like a great idea at the time), and even though none of us had ever met, they felt like friends. Some of them were vloggers too, mostly unsuccessful bottom-feeders like me who'd got all excited when we hit a thousand subscribers and then despondent when we seemed to stick there and our dreams of being followed by millions withered and died.

I spent the rest of the long journey chatting online to them, watching their videos and posting comments of my own, and by the time the train snaked its way on to the platform at King's Cross I'd forgotten all about being nervous.

But when I got to Clickfrenzy HQ and realised that I was actually going to have to go up in the lift and face whatever unknown terrors the day had in store for me, I felt sick with apprehension again. I signed myself in at the reception desk, which was guarded by a suited man with a moustache – half receptionist, half bouncer – and walked reluctantly to the lift.

At least I was the only person in the lobby, which meant I'd have eight floors on my own to compose myself and check my make-up on the way up to the office. I stepped in, pressed the button for the Clickfrenzy floor and turned to the mirror. But just as the doors were closing, I heard hurrying feet on the marble tiles outside and a voice called, "Hold that, please!"

Shit. It was Sarah. I considered letting the door slam shut, leaving her to wait for the next lift – but what if this one stopped on multiple floors on the way up and hers didn't, so we emerged at the same time on the eighth floor, and she knew it was me who hadn't opened the door for her? The thought was too cringeworthy to contemplate. Hastily, I pressed the button and the doors parted again.

Sarah stepped into the lift. I wondered anew how someone so tiny could be so imposing – even in her five-inch stiletto heels, she was shorter than me. Her make-up was heavily, immaculately applied. Her hair was expensively highlighted and styled in the kind of messy, beachy waves that I knew must have taken at least half an hour and a small ocean's worth of sea salt spray to achieve. She wore leather trousers with over-the-knee boots, and didn't look like a twat in them, even though it was the middle of summer. She impressed and intimidated me in equal measure.

She gave me a look that was a bit like, *who the hell are you*, and then she recognised me. "Gemma! Welcome to Clickfrenzy, it's great to have you on board."

"Thanks," I said. "I'm really excited to be here."

"I'll just find Jim, who you met at your interview, and hand you over to him. He'll show you where everything is," she said.

The doors opened and we stepped out into the huge office, where ranks of iMac-covered desks stretched off into the distance.

"The writers are down the end," she said. "And this is Daisy, who looks after our reception desk. Daisy, this is Gemma, who's joining the team today."

I muttered a shy hello, then followed Sarah all the way to the back of the room, noticing how face after face turned to glance at us, then returned to staring at the screens. The room was totally silent, except for the tap of computer keys and a background hum that I supposed must be air conditioning, fans keeping the servers cool, or a mixture of the two.

"Here we are," Sarah said. "I'll hand you over to Jim."

Half an hour later, I'd been shown around, introduced to what felt like hundreds of people whose names I was sure I'd never remember, and shown where the loo was and where to make coffee (I was desperate for caffeine, but too intimidated by the space-age machine to make any). I'd been assigned a desk at the end of a group of eight, next to a girl called Emily. I'd been given my email address, shown the company intranet and read through a load of stuff about annual leave and grievance procedures. I'd spent a few minutes staring in bewilderment at a huge leaderboard that seemed to show whose stories were getting the most hits and shares online, and wondered if my name would ever appear at the top, and what would happen if it remained at the bottom.

No one seemed to be taking any notice of me. Did no one ever talk to anyone here? How did people know what to do? Everyone was focussed on their screens, only occasionally someone would stretch up and peer over the top, looking to see whether someone at the opposite end of the room was at their desk, looking a bit like the meerkats in that ad everyone was obsessed with a few years back. I watched as someone at the next-door pod of desks got up and walked the length of the office, returning a few minutes later with a tray carrying mugs of tea and coffee and distributed them, apparently without being asked. *God, I could murder a cappuccino.*

Then a message popped up on my screen: *Team meeting in ten. Coffee?*

I realised that I'd entered a world in which everyone was online all the time. Everyone was communicating constantly – they just did so digitally. *This is going to suit me rather well,* I thought.

A few minutes later, cappuccino in hand, I stood up and followed my new colleagues back past the ranks of desks, though a door and into a meeting room furnished with a sofa as well as a normal table and chairs, a fridge full of soft drinks and a popcorn dispenser. Still in silence, everyone took their seats around the table.

I looked at the other faces: Jim, with his sandy hair gelled into a pompadour. Emily, with her glossy dark ponytail and thick-framed glasses. A girl with an amazing Afro, whose name I couldn't remember. A chubby guy in a Bart Simpson T-shirt who I thought was called Tom. Three other girls down at the end of the table, all scribbling in notebooks. I'd be seeing them every day – I'd get to know their names and their habits and how they liked their coffee. Some of them might even become friends. But for now, they were all entirely strange and terribly intimidating.

"Right," Jim said. "Morning, all. Everyone here? Then let's crack on. First, a warm welcome to Gemma, our new starter."

"Hello, Gemma," everyone said, and I felt my face turn scarlet, praying that he wasn't going to ask me to say a few words about myself and feeling almost dizzy with relief when he didn't.

"Right, on to some housekeeping."

Jim talked a bit about plans for the summer staff picnic, reminded us that we'd all need to get our August holiday dates booked ASAP, and assured us that the recent problems with the lifts seemed to have been sorted out. He gave us all a bit of a lecture about the importance of sticking to the coffee machine cleaning rota. He updated us on the forthcoming speaker event with a big cheese from Facebook, which had been postponed and would now take place next Wednesday.

"Now, let's talk a bit about some of the stories we're working on. Ruby, you've been doing your CrossFit diary. How's that going?"

"Um, not so great, to be honest," said one of the girls at the end of the table. I made a mental note: *Ruby, blonde hair and braces.* "I went to the first class, and it legit made me cry. It really did. I almost threw up it was so hard, and the next day I literally couldn't get out of bed. And then last week I had really bad hayfever, so I thought I'd better give it a miss. So today is week three, but I'm really busy. I'm not sure whether I'm going to be able to get away in time this afternoon to…" She looked around the table. "Okay, okay, I'll go. Jeez, you lot. It's like living under the Nazis."

"No one even said anything, Ruby," the girl with the Afro said.

"You didn't have to, Hermione," Ruby said. "You just judged me with your judgey faces."

"We'll look forward to reading about how it goes," Jim said. "So, Hermione, what's happening in politics?"

"Brexit's still a massive thing, obviously," Hermione said. "And we're continuing our series of columns by experts analysing what the impact of an Out vote would be. And everyone's still talking about Donald Trump, but I kind of feel like we've done him to death. You know, the wall thing, *The Apprentice* – it's all feeling a bit old."

"Especially since he's never going to win," Emily said.

"Well, obviously he won't win," said Tom. "I mean, like, duh. As if."

"Yes, anyway," Hermione said. "We did an in-depth comparison of his and Hillary's policies last week, so I thought it was time for something a bit more light-hearted. A separated-at-birth thing. People who look more like Trump than Trump does. But I got as far as Biff Tannen from *Back to the Future* and then I got stuck."

"He is a bit special-looking, isn't he?" Jim said. "Any ideas?"

"He looks an awful lot like Mussolini," Emily said, and I wondered what on earth Mussolini had looked like.

"Grumpy Cat," said Tom.

"Chewbacca," I suggested, then blushed again.

"Boris Johnson," said Ruby. "Only with better hair."

"Brilliant," Hermione said, scribbling away in her notebook. "Thanks, guys."

"Good," Jim said. "Spot anyone else who looks like a power-crazed Oompa-Loompa, let Hermione know. Callista, any celebrity gossip to share?"

"Everyone's totally obsessed with sideboob," said Callista from the opposite end of the table. "It's, like, the fourth most searched term on Google at the moment. So I'm doing a gallery. So much for my feminist principles."

"You can do celebrity feminists next," Emily suggested.

"Emma Watson," said Hermione. "Serena Williams. JK Rowling. Florence Welch."

"That should redress the balance a bit," Jim said. "Tom, what's happening in lifestyle?"

"Fried chicken," Tom said. "Now that burgers are, like, totally over, it's all about chicken. So I thought I'd do a roundup of the best."

Judging by Tom's bulging T-shirt, he took his research seriously.

"I'm not sure that's really got the Clickfrenzy edge," Jim said. "Remember, our stories aim to take a sideways look at life. Maybe something a bit more out there?"

"Obviously, we've passed peak burger," Ruby said. "But they're still a thing, and people are doing weird shit with them. Crimes against burgers. I went on a date last week with this guy who turned out to be a raw food freak, and he took me to a place that did a raw burger. Literally raw mince between two pieces of lettuce. How gross is that?"

"What did it taste like?" Tom asked.

"God, I don't know! I had a salad. Obviously."

"I'm sure I saw a tweet the other day about a ramen burger," Hermoine said. "You know, with noodles instead of a bun. It looked foul."

"Horsemeat burgers," Jim said.

"I thought Tesco didn't do those any more," Emily said.

"No, but there's a place at Borough Market that does," Jim said. "Proper, legit horsemeat, not, you know, horse pretending to be beef."

"Aren't doughnut burgers a thing now?" I said.

"Cronut burgers, surely?" Callista said. "Doughnuts are so 2015."

"Right, I'm sure you'll have fun with that one, Tom," Jim said.

"I might just, like, research them online." Tom looked downcast.

"You do that," Jim said. "Any more story ideas to share? No?"

There was silence around the table.

"Okay," Jim said. "Gemma, we'll start you off on cats."

"Cats?" I said.

"You know," Tom said, sticking his fingers out at the sides of his face. "Miaow?"

I laughed. "Yeah, I do know what they are. Honest. But what about them?"

"Cat stories get clicks," Hermione said. "You know, the internet is basically, like, made of cats."

"And there are more than six billion cat pictures online for you to choose from," Callista said.

"They get more views on YouTube than any other video category," Emily said helpfully. *They certainly get more views than my vlog*, I thought, but I didn't say anything.

"You've heard of the cute cat theory of digital activism, right?" said Tom.

"Of course," I lied. "But I've forgotten what it is. Is it…"

"Anyway, never mind about that," Tom said, and I suspected that he had no more of a clue about what the cute cat theory of digital activism was than I did.

"So we generate a lot of cat posts," Jim said. "You'll need to create at least one story a day. It could be a listicle, or a collection of images, or a quiz. Whatever you like. But remember, the goal is contagious content."

"Right, I get it," I said.

"Cool," Jim said. "Put something together and let me know when you're ready to run it past me. Any other business?"

I looked around the table. Everyone shook their heads, so I shook mine, too. Then we all stood up, gathered our notebooks and coffee mugs, and made our way back to our desks.

By the time half past five came, I'd looked at more pictures of cats than I ever thought I'd see in my life. Cute cats and cross cats. Sleeping cats and pouncing cats. Cats that looked like loaves of bread and cats that looked like bagels. Cats that looked like pin-up girls and cats that looked like Hitler.

Don't get me wrong, I like cats as much as the next person. But the knowledge that, for the foreseeable future, I'd be doing nothing else, every day, except finding pictures of cats and thinking of amusing captions for them, was daunting to say the least.

Still, I thought, I'd survived my first day. I hadn't made any awful mistakes. Jim had seemed happy with my first article ('25 Reasons Why Your Cat is Cross', since you ask). I'd made a round of coffee without getting muddled or spilling any. And now it was time to go to the airport and say goodbye to Jack.

But no one was leaving. Around the pod of desks, my new colleagues were still transfixed by their screens, tapping furiously at their keyboards, as they'd been all day. I checked the company intranet – the hours were definitely half past nine until half past five. Why was no one going anywhere? I was new; there was no way I could be the first to leave.

Surreptitiously, I checked my phone. Jack and Olivia had posted a selfie of themselves on the train with their backpacks. I felt a lump swell up in my throat and determinedly swallowed it. I couldn't cry – not here. But I needed to go – I needed to say goodbye to Jack, to feel his arms around me one last time and hear him say again how much he loved me and would miss me.

I read the email he'd sent me with his flight details again, even though I knew it off by heart. Their departure time was nine o'clock, which meant they'd need to check in by seven thirty at the latest. I'd have plenty of time to get there if I left soon. But I couldn't leave yet.

I tucked my phone into my bag and tidied my desk – not that there was much to tidy, just a pack of Post-it notes and a tube of hand cream. I looked around. No one was moving. *Come on*, I willed them. *Come on! Don't you have homes to go to?*

Then Tom said, "You're wussing out of that CrossFit class, aren't you, Ruby?"

Ruby said, "Oh shit, is that the time? I was totally engrossed in Joe Wicks's… er… plank technique. I guess I've missed it."

Tom said, "Bollocks! It's just down the road. You'll get there if you leave now."

"Oh, I don't know," Ruby said. "I should really…"

Tom flapped his elbows and made clucking sounds.

"Okay, fine!" Ruby said. "I'll go. But if I don't come to work tomorrow because I've got stuck in the bath and drowned, I'm blaming you."

I watched with mounting impatience as she saved her work and shut down her computer. A split second after she stood up, I stood up too.

"See you guys tomorrow," Ruby said.

"Have a good evening," I said, and legged it towards the lift as fast as I could.

As soon as the Tube train emerged from the tunnel at Baron's Court, I got my phone out of my bag. There was no message or missed call from Jack.

On my way, I texted. *There as soon as I can. Wait for me!*

I checked his Instagram. There was another picture of him and Olivia, this time posing in front of an illuminated departure board at Heathrow. *Shit.* They were there already.

I willed the train to go faster, but of course it didn't – in fact, as the gaps between the stations got longer and longer it seemed to go slower and slower. It was ten to seven.

Heaps of time, Gemma, I told myself. *Relax. You'll be there soon. You'll have five minutes with him, that's long enough to say goodbye.*

I closed my eyes and tried to make myself breathe deeply as the train passed through station after station. But I couldn't relax. I abandoned my seat and stood by the door, shifting from foot to foot. Only a couple of stops to go.

Then, at Hatton Cross, instead of the doors beeping and closing again, they stayed open. I looked at my watch; so did everyone else in the carriage. Someone sighed and someone else tutted.

"Ladies and gents, this is your driver," crackled a voice over the PA system. "We're just being held here for a short time at a red signal, in order to regulate the service. We'll be on the move shortly."

I don't know what his definition of "shortly" was, but it wasn't the same as mine. It seemed like an eternity before the train set off again – an eternity during which I calculated the time I'd have to say goodbye to Jack decreasing from five minutes to three, then to two. And that was assuming I was even able to find the place where we'd arranged to meet, in front of the WHSmith in Terminal Five.

The rest of the journey felt a bit like an out-of-body experience. At last, the doors opened and I sprinted out, turning the wrong way at first, then getting my bearings. At twenty-seven minutes past seven, I skidded to a halt outside the newsagent, my breath coming in croaky gasps and my top clinging clammily to my perspiring back.

Jack wasn't there and nor was Olivia.

I looked at my phone. He'd sent a text. Just one text. *Sorry, babe, we couldn't wait. They were calling our flight to check in. I'll ring you.*

My hands were sweating so much that my phone almost slipped through my palms on to the floor. I gripped it tightly, as if it was an unexploded bomb, and checked Instagram again. Jack hadn't posted anything new, but Olivia had. It was another selfie of her and Jack, holding glasses of champagne.

Through security! she'd written. *Dubai, here we come! #Adventure!!* She'd posted it half an hour earlier.

Chapter Four

Hi everyone!

So this is a haul video – but with a difference! I know you all love watching these and I love watching other people's, whether they're about fashion or beauty or… well, anything really! You can't go wrong with a bit of retail therapy. Anyway, this past weekend I've been spending loads of time and even more money in Ikea, TK Maxx and Zara Home – I fricking love Zara Home, don't you? And I've got so much amazing stuff to show you, and I'm going to go through it all in just a minute. But first, I've got some really great news to share with you all.

I couldn't help feeling optimistic as I stepped out of the Tube station into the sunny street. It was a gorgeous July day – although it had chucked it down with rain earlier, now the sun was shining and everything had that washed-clean feeling. The leaves on the trees were bright, acid green against the blue sky. The red buses looked extra red. Even the air seemed to sparkle.

I looked approvingly into the windows I might pass every day on my way to and from work. There was a bakery claiming to use organic, stone-ground flour and specialise in paleo cakes, wafting a delicious smell out on to the pavement. There was a nail bar where I imagined going for manicures that would motivate me to stop biting my nails. There was a greengrocer where I could buy vegetables to make fresh, healthful meals – and an M&S Simply Food, which, if I was being honest, I knew was more likely to become my dinner provider of choice.

Okay, there was also a rather run-down-looking council estate, prefab blocks of flats surrounded by a car park bristling with 'No Ball Games' signs. But even that, I noticed, was surrounded by a hoarding promising that it was due to be redeveloped and replaced by shiny glass-walled high-rises with private gardens, a residents' gym and even a noodle bar. The artist's impression showed couples sitting on their balconies drinking coffee and nibbling croissants, just as I'd imagined Jack and me doing.

It was two weeks since Jack and Olivia had left. I'd emailed every day to tell him how much I missed him, and sent him links to my YouTube channel every time I posted a new video. My resolution to vlog every day wasn't going so well, though, partly because between work, four hours every day on the train to and from Norwich, and rushing off after work and during my lunch hour to look at various rooms to rent, I just hadn't had time. Of course, Jack was busy too – his Instagram was full of pictures of Dubai, then Bangkok, then Koh Tao, where he was working in a diving school and Olivia was doing a yoga retreat.

Knowing that he hadn't waited to say goodbye had hurt almost more than the fact of his leaving. But, I told myself, it was partly my fault – I'd been late, after all. If he'd missed his flight because of me, it would have been unforgivable. He'd explained in an email written from his seat in Premium Economy class that Olivia had been really stressed about being late, and her stress had infected him, and they'd seen the length of the queue to get through security and panicked. So I'd put my hurt to one side and replied saying that I understood.

And when he didn't send me another email for five days, I wrote to him saying I understood that too, and how it must all be so exciting that I'd, like, totally understand if he didn't have the time or the headspace to reply. I did understand – but I didn't like it. Not one bit. Just a month before, however badly everything else in my life was going, I could think about Jack and feel happy. Now, thinking of him just made me anxious and sad. It was a strange feeling – a kind of shifting of reality, like stepping on to a pavement and finding it covered with ice, and the next thing you know you're on your arse in the snow and people are laughing at you.

But now wasn't the time to worry about Jack. I needed to find number forty-seven Manwood Close. The name made me giggle, and cringe a bit, but hey – a stupid-sounding address was a small price to pay for a place of my own. I turned a corner, and the roar of traffic from the main road died away. The street was lined with plane trees and pretty Victorian houses. I could hear a magpie cackling away somewhere above me. I wished I'd brought my camera so I could film how lovely London looked and explain how lucky I felt to be here and why I felt deep down that this, the fifth room I'd looked at, might just end up being home.

Mind you, I'd felt like that about the others, too. The one where the 'large double bedroom' was so tiny that the door couldn't actually open, and the 'fitted wardrobe' was a 1980s monstrosity built around the head of the bed, its peach-coloured doors listing on their hinges. The 'relaxed, friendly, houseshare' where the smell of weed hit me in the face like a fist as soon as I walked in. The one where the advertised room turned out to be accessed through another bedroom, whose occupant was snoring thunderously in bed surrounded by crusty socks. The one I thought was perfect until the girl showing me round cheerfully introduced me to her pet tarantula. *This has to be okay*, I told myself, *I can't go on spending every single evening trailing around London, and every single lunch break trawling the Gumtree website and sending text messages*. I took my phone out now and reread the ad.

Two double rooms available in Hackney house, shared with owners, for six to twelve-month let. We're a young, professional couple looking for single people, women preferred. Close to transport, all bills and Wi-Fi included. Text or WhatsApp Hannah or Richard…

Okay, the monthly rent was high – far more than I'd budgeted for. But I'd find a way to manage. It wasn't like I'd be going out much, anyway. And this was exactly the sort of street I imagined Jack and me living on, one day. I quickened my pace, hurrying towards number forty-seven, determined to make a good impression by being exactly on time. *This has to work*, I told myself. *This is definitely, totally The One.*

A few seconds after I carefully tapped the chrome knocker – hard enough to be audible, not so hard as to be rude – the door opened.

A man and a woman stood in the hallway, looking at me. There was a quick, assessing pause while I looked back at them.

Then the woman said, "Gemma? Come in. I'm Hannah, and this is Richard."

I followed them through to the back of the house, realising I had just passed the first in a series of tests. The kitchen was immaculate and smelled faintly of baking. There was a bunch of yellow roses in a white china jug on the table, which was covered with an oilcloth printed in pastel stripes. Everything looked new, and everything was spotlessly clean.

It sounds weird, I know, but Hannah and Richard looked clean, too. I know everyone is, really, apart from little kids who've been playing in muddy puddles and people who sometimes sit next to you on the bus and you're too embarrassed to move away, but they seemed to radiate freshness.

Hannah had long, very straight red hair and porcelain skin with a scattering of freckles. The hand she gave me to shake was cool and soft. Richard had an immaculately trimmed beard and shiny conker-brown hair. They both looked like they spent a lot of time ironing their clothes, and Richard's shoes gleamed with polish. I'd never met anyone who'd actually admit to polishing their shoes before, and certainly not anyone who ironed their jeans. I remembered a quiz Emily had written for work – 'You Know You're Normcore When…' – and wondered if they were early adopters of the trend.

"So, Gemma, tell us a bit about yourself," Richard said.

Stage two of the assessment centre, I thought.

I cleared my throat. "Yes, of course. So I've just started a job in London – I'm a writer for a new media company – Clickfrenzy, you might have heard of them? And I'm living with my mum in Norwich at the moment, which is fine but not ideal, obviously, with the commute and everything. So it just feels like the right time to make a new start."

"Do you know the area at all?" Hannah asked.

"Not very well," I admitted, but I didn't admit that I'd chosen it on the basis of a Google search: 'coolest places in London'. My new start, my new life, if I was going to succeed in my goal of showing Jack what he was missing, depended on my being able to vlog about on-trend coffee shops, vibrant street markets, quirky boutiques and, hopefully, achingly hip cocktail bars where I would hang out with admiring men and fabulous friends. Okay, I hadn't actually met any of them yet, but that was just detail.

"We're still exploring it ourselves," Richard said.

"We've only just moved in, you see," Hannah said. "And it's obviously a bit of a stretch financially, hence renting out the rooms. Every little helps, doesn't it?"

I remembered the rent they were charging for the room, which to my mind wasn't little at all. But I said, "Yes, of course it does," then added sycophantically, "It's a gorgeous house."

"Isn't it?" Hannah said. "We were so lucky to get it, we never thought we could afford Hackney."

"When we first started to save for our deposit, it was still really gritty round here," Richard said.

"Or vibrant and cosmopolitan, as I prefer to think of it," said Hannah.

"Yes, darling," Richard said. "But now it's up and coming. Especially now they're knocking down that dump of an estate."

"Actually, it's more upped and come," said Hannah. "So we thought that we were completely priced out, and then this place came on to the market."

"It was a total wreck," said Richard. "And it still went to sealed bids. We had to do everything: rewire, overhaul the heating system, new windows, new roof…"

"And since we were doing that we thought we might as well do the loft too," Hannah said. "It adds so much value."

"As will the side return extension, when we get around to doing it," Richard said. "But that won't be for a couple of years yet."

I thought, *They're only a few years older than me, but they act like they're ancient. Would this have happened to Jack and me? Did it happen to everyone? Surely not.*

"But when we do, I'll be able to have my dream kitchen," Hannah said. "With a utility room and integrated appliances and a boiling water tap."

"When we discuss these things, Hannah-banana," Richard said, "it would be helpful if you could retain at least some semblance of a grip on reality."

It was really weird – for a second it was like they'd forgotten I was there. Richard didn't sound angry – he'd even reached over and given Hannah's cheek a little pinch that looked quite affectionate. But her face went suddenly still and even whiter. I couldn't care less about damp-proofing and side returns, and I didn't know boiling water taps even a thing to aspire to, but clearly, whatever they were, they were a bone of contention between my would-be landlords.

Then I remembered that I was meant to be impressing them, and making them like me enough to offer me one of the rooms – which, if what I'd seen of the house so far was anything to go by, would be Buckingham Palace standards of luxury compared to what I'd seen before – and that meant contributing something to the conversation, as opposed to sitting gawping at the two of them and wondering what it was about integrated appliances that had made Richard look fleetingly furious and Hannah briefly frightened. I remembered an article I'd read at work that morning: '20 Things People Say About London Property That Make Us Wish They'd STFU'.

"You've got to get on the property ladder before the bottom rung is out of your reach," I said.

"Exactly," Richard said, and Hannah nodded, visibly relaxing.

"Would you like to see the room now?" she said.

I followed them upstairs, half-listening to Richard's running commentary about double-glazing and penetrating damp. The house was beautiful. The room they showed me was big and airy, with a window that overlooked the garden. The bathroom, compared to the mould-ridden horrors I'd seen earlier in the week, was a haven of white-tiled luxury.

Then Richard said, "We're up in the loft, of course, and we've our own en-suite. You and the other lodger will be on your own on this floor."

That settles it, I thought. *So what if they're Mr and Mrs Weird?* They wouldn't be able to overhear me when I recorded videos in my bedroom, and that was the biggest selling point of all.

"It's lovely," I said. "When were you looking for someone to move in?"

"As soon as, really. We've got five more people coming round this evening," Richard said. "And more tomorrow – nine, I think."

"Eight," Hannah said. "The nurse and the accountant cancelled, but the trainee police officer is coming round first thing, remember?"

I was up against some stiff competition, I realised. Clearly only pillars of the community need apply for this couple's spare bedrooms.

"But we're hoping to make a decision before the end of the week," Richard said.

"Would you like a cup of tea?" Hannah said.

I gave myself a mental high five. Clearly, I had managed to pass another stage of their test, even though no one had told me there was going to be one, or what texts I needed to study.

I followed them downstairs again and sat in the immaculate kitchen and heard about Richard's job in the City and Hannah's as a primary school teacher. I made interested noises when they showed me about a zillion photos on Richard's tablet of the house before and during its renovation and talked about ceiling roses and floor joists.

"The plastering was the worst," Hannah said. "The dust gets absolutely everywhere. I've been mopping the floor constantly since we moved in and every day there's more."

"Hannah-banana is extremely house-proud," Richard said. "One of our priorities in choosing who will be sharing our home with us is that they treat it with the same respect we do."

I said, "I know just how you feel. It's one of the reasons I'm so looking forward to having my own space – so I can make it all serene and homely. Not that I'd paint the walls or anything, but just – you know, soft furnishings and things. Although it's homely already, of course."

They exchanged a glance that told me I had scored another point.

"And what do you do outside of work?" Richard asked.

Hannah said, "I mean, we just want to make sure that people are a good fit for us. In terms of your social life and things."

I said, "Obviously, I'm hoping to get to know more people in London once I'm living here. But my boyfriend is off travelling at the moment, so I won't be having guests overnight or anything like that. I spend quite a bit of time online."

I considered telling them that I would be spending most of my evenings in my room, alone, filming videos. But even though I knew that was probably exactly what they wanted to hear, I couldn't quite make myself say it. I felt oddly shy about it – embarrassed, even. Although for the people I knew online, making YouTube videos was a totally normal thing to do, lots of other people just didn't get it. When Mum walked into my bedroom the first time and saw me filming, she completely freaked out. I think she thought I was making amateur porn or something. Even when I pointed out that firstly, I had all my clothes on and secondly, if anyone wanted to get their rocks off watching me talk about eyelash curlers and stippling brushes they were most welcome to try, she remained deeply suspicious of the whole thing for a long time. It's an age thing, I guess – either you've grown up with YouTube being a thing or you haven't. And Hannah and Richard were just old enough for me not to be sure which group they'd fall into.

"Thanks for coming round, Gemma," Hannah said at last. "We'll be in touch as soon as we can."

"Look forward to seeing you again soon," Richard said, and I felt a little surge of hope and excitement. They liked me!

I said goodbye and walked out into the sunny evening, and began making my way back towards the station. On the corner was a shop I hadn't noticed before, with a blackboard outside that said, *The Daily Grind – East London's best coffee. Vinyl records. Cycle repairs. Free Wi-Fi.*

I looked in through the window. The place was seriously stylish, with battered wooden floorboards and face-brick walls hung with vintage movie posters. There was a mixture of comfy sofas, small round tables and tall benches surrounded by long-legged metal stools. I imagined myself coming here on a Saturday morning, meeting friends for brunch or sitting alone and working on my laptop, as I could see several people doing. I imagined bringing Jack here, when he came home, and them knowing my name and my regular order, and him being impressed by the coolness of the area where I lived and, by extension, me.

Lured by the smell of coffee, I went into the shop and joined the small queue at the counter. I noticed a pile of leaflets with pictures of the estate I'd passed, printed with bold red capital letters. *Save our homes! Save our community! Save the Garforth Estate!* I read. I picked one up, glanced at the dense type inside, then put it down again.

I was going to get home so ridiculously late anyway, I might as well text Mum and tell her I wouldn't be back for dinner, and grab something to eat here. There were two guys taking orders and making coffee, one of them shortish and gingerish, the other tall and dark. As I waited to get to the front of the queue, I watched them.

The ginger guy seemed to be in charge; the other one looked like he was new on the job, and his first day wasn't going too well.

"Skinny chai latte, madam?" He handed a cup to the woman at the front of the queue.

She sniffed the plume of steam emerging from the vent in the lid and said accusingly, "This is coffee. I asked for chai."

"So you did. Then where…"

"I think that one's mine, mate. Cappuccino with an extra shot?"

"Cappuccino with an extra shot, yes. So this must be the chai latte… Wait. Maybe it's this one. Never mind – I'll make them both again. I'm so sorry – these are on the house."

While he sorted out the muddle, his friend sprang into action and started taking orders.

"Espresso, please," said the man at the front of the queue.

"Would that be Guatemalan, Brazilian, Colombian or Rwandan?" asked the ginger guy.

The customer looked bewildered. "Um… what would you recommend?"

"Depends on your taste, sir. All our coffee is fair trade and sustainably sourced. The Guatemalan is a light roast, with notes of honey and cinnamon. The Brazilian is darker, richer – more of a morning coffee, I feel. The Colombian is mellower. And the Rwandan is our special this week – it's got notes of raspberry jam and raisins, with molasses on the finish. Really excellent stuff."

"I'll go for the middle one," the customer said, clearly in the grip of choice paralysis.

I could sympathise – who knew ordering coffee was suddenly so complicated? I studied the blackboard while I waited. It listed the usual lattes and cappuccinos, alongside a load of things I'd never heard of. Cold-brewed coffee. Nitro coffee. Pulped natural coffee. I made a mental note to suggest to Tom that he do an article about all this, if he hadn't already. He could call it '15 Signs We've Reached Peak Coffee'.

"One Colombian espresso," the ginger guy said. "And for you, madam?"

"Coffee and tonic, please." Clearly the woman ahead of me in the queue knew what she was about – or maybe not, if coffee and tonic was anything like as horrible as it sounded.

The other guy – the tall one – seemed to be getting his act together after his shaky start. *Bless him*, I thought, *he must be a student, scrabbling to get together a bit of extra cash to spend in the pub. Or an out-of-work actor. Or someone like me just a few weeks ago, working for minimum wage while waiting for his big break.* Anyway, the coffee confusion was over, and the woman who'd ordered the chai latte and the man who'd ordered the extra shot cappuccino were carrying their drinks to their tables, mollified.

And I could see why they hadn't been able to stay cross for long. The tall guy was actually quite hot, with the most amazing blue eyes that seemed almost too pale for his tanned skin. His teeth were very white and straight when he smiled – which seemed to be most of the time. He was a bit older than I'd thought at first – a couple of years older than me, I guessed, so not a student. Unless he was doing a PhD.

"What can I get for you, madam?" he said, and I realised I'd been staring at him and speculating about him instead of deciding what I wanted to order.

"Oh my God, I'm so sorry," I said, blushing furiously. "I was miles away. A cappuccino, please, and… um… avocado on toast."

His smile really was distracting – I don't even like avocado. Normally I'd have ordered a grilled cheese sandwich, but somehow I couldn't bring myself to reveal my embarrassing lack of culinary sophistication.

"Oat milk? Almond milk? Coconut milk?" he said.

"Am I allowed normal milk?"

"Of course you are – but if I don't ask, I get in trouble with Luke. He doesn't approve of unreconstructed coffee. Although our milk isn't ordinary; it's high-protein milk produced specifically for coffee."

"Seriously?" I said. "What, like, is it made from special coffee cows?"

"You'll have to ask Luke," he said. "Probably. It's organic, I know that much. And unhomogenised, whatever that means."

The queue behind me was building up a bit, and I saw the guy glance anxiously over at his boss, so I said, "Wow, that's really interesting. And thanks."

"We'll bring your food to your table as soon as it's ready," he said, and I paid and went to find a place to sit.

Ten minutes later, I was crunching my way through my dinner – which was actually really nice, in spite of the avocado and weird seedy wholemeal toast – and checking my social media. Someone had linked to a vlog I'd done about exploring shops in Soho during my lunch break, and I'd gained two hundred new followers since the weekend, which was pretty amazing. My latest post on Clickfrenzy ('This Cat Was Separated From His Dog Bestie For Two Years. Their Reunion Will Make You Cry Actual Tears') had twenty thousand likes on Facebook. Jack had posted loads of pictures of fish on Instagram, but I didn't want to see fish – I wanted to see Jack. I clicked over to Olivia's feed, and then froze, my finger hovering over the screen.

This was weird. Where just the day before there had been a flood of images of Olivia doing downward dogs on the beach in a bikini, the fruit platter Olivia had eaten for breakfast, Olivia's feet in flipflops showing off her immaculate primrose-coloured toenails, now there was nothing. Just a blank screen with the message, *No posts yet.*

She'd blocked me, and I had no idea why.

Chapter Five

"Are you sure you don't want me to come in?" Mum said, making a move to open the car door.

"No!" I said. "I mean, no thanks, Mum, it's really sweet of you to offer and thanks so much for driving me here, but I can manage. Honestly I can."

I thought of the bulging blue Ikea bags filled with clothes and my recent homeware purchases, my backpack stuffed with yet more clothes (some liberated from Mum's wardrobe), my laptop and camera bags, and Stanley perched on top of it all in the boot of the car. Managing was going to be a bit of a challenge, but we were parked right outside Hannah and Richard's house and it was unlikely that the few steps to the front door would wrench my arms out of their sockets. I was feeling awkward and nervous enough about moving in without Mum fluttering around wafting scent and looking far more glamorous than any mother had any right to look. I love her, obviously, and mostly I'm proud of her, but sometimes she does have a way of making me regress to being a sulky teenager and this was one of those times.

"Well," Mum said, "if you're sure? Then I suppose I'll say goodbye."

She pushed her sunglasses up on to her head, sniffed and ran a finger under her eye.

"Mum! For God's sake. I'll only be two hours away on the train. And there are these things called phones. You know, you can send text messages with them and everything."

"What, you think I'm going to miss you?" Mum said. "I can't wait to have the flat to myself again and not have you banging on the door as soon as I've got into the bath and leaving crumbs in the butter. You'll have to clean up your act when you're living with this Hannah and whatshisname – from what you say they won't put up with that kind of thing."

"I have lived away from home before," I said. "I survived three years of uni, remember, without getting an ASBO."

"I know, I know," Mum said. "You're a grown-up. I hadn't forgotten. This just feels so… Never mind."

She shut up, to my relief – if she'd said anything more I reckon I might have cried too. I undid my seatbelt and gave her a brief hug.

"I'll call you soon, okay?" I said.

"Okay, sweetie," Mum said, pushing her sunglasses down and sniffing again. I got out of the car very quickly, took a deep breath, manhandled all my stuff to the front door and tapped the knocker.

Hannah opened the door almost straight away, as if she'd been hovering behind it.

"Gemma!" she said. "Welcome. Welcome home, I guess. Wow, that looks heavy. I'll get Rich to give you a hand upstairs. We're in the kitchen. Amy, the other lodger, arrived this morning so we thought we'd wait for you and then all have a little chat and get to know one another. Take your time, get settled in – I'll stick the kettle on. Rich! Gemma's here."

Richard appeared from the kitchen and there was a bit of an awkward tussle while he tried to take the heaviest of my bags and I tried to insist that I could manage, which I let him win because I knew I couldn't really. I followed him upstairs into the back bedroom that was going to be mine – was mine already, I supposed, since I'd transferred three months' rent into his account (a loan from Mum – the last one I'd ever need, I promised myself). We put my stuff down and I immediately started to worry about leaving scuff marks on the spotless mushroom-coloured carpet or staining the new pale grey mattress.

Richard didn't immediately turn to go back downstairs, but stood in the doorway, more or less filling up the space that was there, and looking at me.

I looked back, trying to get a sense of this man whose home I'd be sharing. He was okay looking – no Jack, just an average, pleasant-looking guy in his early thirties. I noticed again how tidy – almost formal – he looked; even though it was a Sunday, the bits of his face that were outside the precise lines of his beard were as smooth as if he'd just shaved. He was wearing a blue and white striped shirt tucked into his very clean jeans, with a brown leather belt. The sleeves of his shirt were rolled up and his arms were brown and strong – I'd noticed the lean swell of muscle between his watch and his sleeve when he carried my bags up the stairs.

He smiled at me and I smiled back. He had a bit of a gap between his front teeth – it was the only thing about him that wasn't all squared away and perfect. But there was something else about his smile that wasn't perfect – it was a bit too lingering, somehow. He kept looking at me a bit too long, and his eyes did a sort of leisurely up-and-down assessment of me, stopping at my chest for longer than they should.

I said, "Thanks for helping me. I'll get my stuff sorted and come down."

Richard said, "Sure." He stood in the doorway for a few more seconds, then turned and went away.

I unpacked my clothes into the wardrobe, arranged my make-up collection on the dressing table and put the framed photo of Jack and me next to the bed. I draped my new fairy lights over the headboard and made the bed with my new duvet cover, sheets and pillowcases, and propped Stanley up against the pillows. I went to the bathroom and put my toiletries into the half of the cabinet that wasn't already filled, taking the opportunity to have a bit of a snoop at Amy's stuff and discovering that she used macadamia oil on her hair and owned a set of fluffy fuchsia pink towels and an impressive collection of Bobbi Brown skincare.

Then I couldn't think of anything more to do, so I said to Stanley, "Cover my back, I'm going in," and went.

Hannah, Richard and Amy were sitting around the kitchen table drinking tea out of spotty pastel-coloured mugs, evidently chosen to match the tablecloth. Or perhaps the tablecloth had been chosen to match the mugs. The teapot was pale pink and the spoons had mint green handles. The door was open to the garden and I could see a perfect green rectangle of lawn and a rose bush in a stone pot. It was all so immaculate it was almost creepy.

"Amy, this is Gemma," Hannah said. "Gemma works in new media; Amy's training to be a police officer."

Amy stood up and held out her hand for me to shake. Her nails were painted white, with silver glitter on the tips. Her hair was a mass of sleek braids twisted together into one chunky plait. She was wearing a denim mini skirt, a Hello Kitty T-shirt and silver gladiator sandals. Honestly, if you'd asked me to describe the person least like a trainee police officer in the whole world, it would probably have been Amy.

"Hello," I said. "I love your nails."

Amy said thanks, and that it was nice to meet me, then she sat down and took another sip of her tea. She seemed totally poised and calm, not like me – I felt all untidy and ungainly in this pristine house, as if the milk jug might jump into my hand and then on to the floor at any moment, and it would be my fault.

Richard said, "Well. Now that you're both here, Hannah and I just wanted to run through a few housekeeping things."

He reached behind him and handed us each a sheaf of A4 printouts, held together with plastic binding combs.

"We just wanted you both to know from the outset where everything is, and how things work," Hannah said. She sounded apologetic – almost embarrassed. "I mean, it's just going to be easier if we all understand what's expected."

I flipped through the pages and saw PDF printouts of the operating manuals for the washing machine, dishwasher, coffee maker and cooker. A whole page was devoted to the broadband, how it worked and who to call if it didn't. All four of our email addresses and mobile numbers were in there. There was a list headed 'Guidelines' that ran to more than fifty points, from how often to clean the crumbs out of the toaster to what to do if the carbon monoxide alarm went off.

My face must have given something away, because Amy caught my eye and winked.

Hannah said, "I'll put the kettle on again, shall I? Would you like a tea, Gemma? There's Earl Grey, peppermint, chamomile and vanilla, lemon and honey – take your pick. I'm a bit obsessed with tea. And would anyone like some cake?"

From a shelf next to the fridge, she produced an Emma Bridgewater tin, levered off the lid and lifted out a cake piped with pink and white icing saying, *Welcome, Amy and Gemma*.

So of course then there was no way I could say that I preferred coffee to tea, and no way of saying no to the cake – although when is saying yes to cake ever a problem? We drank our tea and ate our cake (with actual cake forks, for real), and Hannah talked us faux-casually through all the pages of the book of rules.

When eventually we got to the end, and we'd all had a second slice of cake and declined a third, I said, "Would anyone like… I mean, shall we pop out for a drink, maybe?"

Hannah looked at me like I'd suggested going down the local Satanic temple to slaughter a few kittens.

"I'd love to," Richard said. "But, you know, school night. We have a team meeting at eight on Monday mornings."

"And I'm on earlies this week," Amy sighed. "In fact, I was about to head up to bed."

And so, over the next few days, I discovered that, far from finding myself in a real-life season of *Girls*, I'd moved into in London's most sedate houseshare. Hannah only seemed to go out to the local primary school where she worked and to her Stitch and Bitch knitting group on Wednesdays. Richard's job kept him at the office until after seven thirty almost every night, and glued to his laptop most of the weekend. Amy's shift pattern meant that she was rarely home when I was, and her idea of a fun time seemed to be kicking the shit out of her fellow tae-bo enthusiasts at the gym.

Don't get me wrong – they were the perfect housemates in many ways. No one came home pissed and threw up in the sink. No one tried to get out of doing their share of the chores. No one had screaming rows. No one ever even opened the fridge, for God's sake, without asking whoever else was there if they wanted a glass of orange squash. They were the Stepford Wives of the housemate world.

Still, getting home night after night and finding the house empty and quiet except for Hannah listening to Radio Four in the kitchen and painstakingly preparing some gourmet feast for her and Richard's dinner, and then setting the table with flowers and candles and waiting for him to come home so they could eat it together, didn't exactly make for a welcoming vibe.

At first, I tried engaging her in conversation while I made my own food (toast, mostly. I love toast – toast with peanut butter, toast with jam, toast with cheese – it's all good. But that doesn't necessarily mean I want to eat it every single night of my life). But she seemed reluctant to be engaged with. She always answered my questions about how her day had been and what she was cooking perfectly politely, but she never asked me anything back and I got the sense that she would far rather be alone with *The Archers* or *Front Row* or whatever it was she was listening to.

So I took my toast up to my bedroom and ate it while looking at videos on YouTube, and after a few days I gave up trying to chat and just said, "Hi," and, "See you later."

*

And so it was that, a week and a bit after I'd moved in, I was up in my room, alone, a plate scattered with crumbs by my feet, realising that my plan of showing Jack, through the medium of YouTube, that I was leading an enviably fabulous life was pretty much dying on its arse.

"I need to have more fun, Stanley," I said.

Stanley regarded me steadily though his plastic eyes. I knew perfectly well that he didn't care about fun – he was perfectly happy just chilling in my bedroom, elderly bear that he was.

"I should make a video," I said. "But I've got nothing to say."

I'd done concealer and contouring – not that well, admittedly. I'd done strobing. I'd even tried Kim Kardashian-style baking, except I think I must have got it wrong because it made me look like a panda. My viewers thought it was all great, but I couldn't see Jack giving even a fraction of a toss about whether a brush or a sponge was a more effective applicator for highlighting concealer.

I needed to up my game. Maybe I could learn to cook – get some tips from Hannah. After all, don't they say the way to a man's heart was through his stomach? Although if this were true, Jack would end up marrying the waitress from our local Nando's. I'd take my plate downstairs anyway, I decided, as instructed in the Book of Rules: *We would prefer you not to consume food and drink in your bedroom. However, if you do, please remove all used crockery immediately.*

I followed the delicious smell down to the kitchen and slotted my plate in the dishwasher. Hannah was standing by the cooker, stirring determinedly away at something in a pan. There was a big bowl of salad on the table, glossy green leaves and slivers of red onion shining with dressing. It looked good. It looked like it had vitamins in it.

I really do need to sort out my diet, I thought. I've always been skinny, but since I'd moved out of Mum's and wasn't getting even the occasional benefit of home cooking (which, in Mum's case, generally meant a few roast vegetables chucked on top of some couscous), my skin had gone to pot.

I considered stopping and trying yet again to chat to Hannah, but then I heard Richard's key in the front door and changed my mind.

"I'm off upstairs," I said. "See you later."

"See you later," Hannah said.

I went back to my room, but before I could close the door I heard Richard say, "What's cooking, my little domestic goddess?"

Hannah said, "It's only risotto, with the rest of the chicken we had on Sunday and some pea purée."

"And most of a pack of butter, if I know you," Richard said.

Hannah gave a little laugh. "Well, it wouldn't be risotto without butter, would it?"

"Not that I mind," Richard said. "More of you to love."

"What?" Hannah said.

"More of you to love," Richard said. "Look at those lovely curves. Mmmm."

Ick. Pass the brain bleach, I thought, ducking inside my room and closing the door.

I lay back down on the bed and picked up my phone, reflexively flicking through my social media for the thousandth time that day.

I responded to new comments on my vlog and Instagram. I posted a picture of Stanley lying face-down on the bed and made a joke about him having been on the vodka. I liked a few friends' posts on Facebook. I retweeted a link to the new Pixiwoo video – not that Sam and Nic needed any help from me, with their two million followers versus my four thousand.

Then I checked my email, and literally as I watched, a message from Jack landed in my inbox. It didn't have a title. I tapped and read, and as I read I felt my whole body growing colder and colder.

It didn't start with *Hey babe* or *Hi Gems*, but just with *Gemma*. So at least I knew right from the beginning that what I was going to read would be about as welcome as a slug in Hannah's salad.

I'm sorry, but I can't do this any more. I don't think it's fair on either of us to pretend we're still together when we're not. You're a great girl and we've had some amazing times, but I think we want different things at the end of the day. We've grown apart – not just since I've been away, but before that. That's partly why I decided to go travelling – I needed some space to think about things and find myself. And it only seems fair to let you get on with your life instead of waiting for me. Hope you're loving London and your new job – bet you'll nail it. You were always way smarter than me.

Then he'd added – of all fucking things – a winking emoji. And then a postscript. *Borneo is sick. You'd love it here.* And then another. *Liv says hi.*

As if, I thought. *Liv* – Olivia – had blocked me on social media. After four years of friendship, she'd said bye in the most definitive way possible. And now, I was convinced, I knew the reason.

I clicked through to her Instagram feed, feeling all trembly with shock and anger. I was still blocked. *Fine*, I thought – *block me all you want, but duh, a five-year-old can get around that.* Which was probably true, but your average five-year-old isn't reeling with shock from being unceremoniously dumped by their boyfriend. It took me three goes to create a new account, because I kept mistyping the password and I had to create a new email address because it seemed to know exactly who I was and kept bouncing me back to my normal account. Eventually I cracked it, but it didn't feel like a success at all.

I lay there for a long time – well, more than a minute, although it felt like years – looking at my phone, knowing that what I was going to see would hurt me even more than Jack's email had, but that I was going to go right ahead and look anyway. It felt inevitable – it felt necessary. It felt bloody horrible.

I picked Stanley up and tucked him under my arm for comfort, and then I searched for Olivia's username and found her straight away. I didn't need to scroll through her feed to find what I was looking for, because she'd already changed her profile pic.

It was a selfie of her and Jack, lying on their backs on a beach somewhere. Around their faces, in the sand, one of them had drawn a massive heart with their initials in it. They weren't looking at the camera – they were looking at each other, their noses almost touching and their hair intertwined. Jack's hair had got loads longer in the four weeks they'd been away, I saw, and the sun had bleached it a bit. They both looked so fucking happy it made me want to die.

I love yoga, travelling, and most of all my favourite person in the world, Olivia's profile said. *Together on the adventure of our lives #forever.*

And so that was that. I knew that no amount of begging, nothing I could do – not even booking a flight out to Asia and flinging myself into Jack's arms and pleading with him to realise he'd made a mistake – would make him change his mind. Olivia must have wanted to be with him the whole time he and I were together – maybe even before – and now she'd got her wish. She was there with him, with the beaches and all the freedom of travelling, and I was left behind, abandoned, rejected and alone.

I cried for a long time. But crying when you're on your own is hard, especially when you're trying to do it silently. There was no one to give me a cuddle and pass me tissues, no one whose kindness would set me off sobbing all over again. No one to talk to.

I could ring Mum, or Katie. But I knew that however sympathetic they were, they'd be thinking, *Yep, I saw that coming a mile away.* I knew they'd think that because I'd seen it myself – I just hadn't allowed myself to acknowledge it.

And then I thought, *I do have people I can tell. A whole internet of people who've been in love and been hurt and will listen.*

I picked up my phone and opened the camera app. I looked a mess – my eye make-up all smudged and my nose bright red – but I didn't care. I started to speak.

Hi everyone. This is a bit of a weird video but I guess I just need to talk. I'm really, really sad right now, and I might not even post this, but – yeah, I need to talk. You don't have to listen – I'll totally understand if you don't. So, Jack, my boyfriend, just dumped me. I know – big deal, right? Everyone gets dumped. Lots of people dumped multiple times. Maybe it gets easier with practice, like doing that flicky eyeliner thing. I don't know. But it really hurts right now, because you see, I thought we were going to be together forever. At least, that's what he told me, and I believed him. What a mug, right? But this isn't about self-pity, not really. Although, obviously, I am feeling extremely sorry for myself right now. I'll get over that, I expect. But what I'll never get over is the way he did it. We were together for a long time – four whole years. One sixth of my life. We talked about stuff – all kinds of stuff. Important stuff. Stuff like falling in love. Like having a future together. Like giving each other the freedom to follow our dreams. Like the things we could forgive and the things we couldn't. And I was always pretty clear that I couldn't forgive being cheated on. I guess some girls can – maybe they can look the other way and pretend it doesn't matter, or maybe say things like, "He always comes back to me," and, "It's like going out for a burger when there's fillet steak at home." Well – newsflash – I'm not a piece of meat. I'm a person. I deserve to be treated decently. I understand that sometimes people grow apart. I know forever is a hell of a long time. Maybe I should have realised what was going on when he decided to go travelling without me – that it was the beginning of the end, that he wanted to spread his wings, or find himself or whatever it was he wanted to do. Or shag someone else. But I didn't. Because he said he wanted to come back and move in together and that he wanted to be with me – that word again – forever. Maybe he even meant it at the time. I've got no way of knowing. So, yeah, I'm really hurt. And I'm also really… really angry. When someone does something to you… when someone you love and trust does what Jack did to me, I think it's understandable to come over a bit bunny-boiler. And that's how I'm feeling right now. I know I ought to be shrugging my shoulders, sending him good thoughts, and telling myself that living well is the best revenge. Maybe one day I will. But right now, I want Jack to feel every last little bit as shitty as I do. And not only that – I want his whole life to be shitty. I want it to rain on his wedding day, and then the bride to change her mind at the altar and leave him standing there looking like a dick. I want Norwich City to get relegated this season, and next season, and the one after that. I want his bag to get misrouted to Nairobi every time he boards a plane. I want him to never notice dog poo in the street, and step in it. I want his chips to always be just a bit underdone, so they still taste of raw potato in the middle. I want him to get software update messages every time he's doing something important, and then forget his password. Yes, I am bitter. Am I going to spend the next ten years stalking him and making his life a misery? No, I'm not. Because I'm actually a nice person and, besides, that would be weird and not leave me any time for shopping. So why am I telling you all this? I don't know, really. I guess because I'm over this thing that when a person gets dumped they've got to be all, "Look at all the fucks I give!" and go off and do a dragon boat race or whatever, when all the time they're dying inside. Because that lets the person who's done the dumping, who's taken the feelings of someone who loves them, looked at them for a bit and then gone, "You know what?

I don't really care," and stomped all over them – by pretending you're not hurting when you are, you let the person who's hurt you go, "She's better off without me. It was tough, but I did the right thing. Aren't I brave and noble?" I know what people are going to say now, because I've said it to my friends. People mean well when they say it, and they're right, but it doesn't actually help. They say, "See, Gemma? He's a cowardly, selfish git! He was all along! Haven't you had a lucky escape?" And then of course they totally contradict themselves when they try and offer you a crumb of hope by saying, "He'll come crawling back, just you watch. He'll realise what he's lost and regret it forever and ever." Maybe Jack will. Maybe he won't. I can't even comfort myself with that prospect at the moment, because to be honest I don't know if I would want him back. All I can think right now is that I want this not to have happened. I want to hit the back button and land on the page where we were before, when we were happy and thought we'd be together forever. The thing is, when you're the one being dumped and not the one doing the dumping, you don't get to prepare for it. You don't get to spend days or weeks or whatever thinking, "Hmmm, maybe this relationship has run its course, actually. Maybe it's time I shagged someone else." I haven't had time to adjust my feelings like he has. So however abjectly shitty I feel, I haven't got to the point where I no longer love him. And that's the worst thing about having just been dumped. I still love Jack.

By the time I finished talking, my voice sounded all scratchy and my throat hurt with the effort of not crying. My arm hurt, too, from holding my phone up over my head. Even now, I thought, I cared about Jack seeing my best angle. That thought made the lump in my throat swell and burst out in a massive, choking sob, and the tears I'd been holding back for so long started to flow again. I lay down on the bed and gave myself up to crying – not that I had any choice; I couldn't have stopped it for anything. I cried for ages, as quietly as I could so Hannah and Richard wouldn't hear me. Then I realised that they'd have heard me talking, recording the video for Jack – and all the other ones I'd made over the past few weeks. *They must think I'm dangerously mental*, I thought.

An image sprang into my head of Hannah and Richard lying in bed together, discussing me.

"There she goes again, talking to her imaginary friend."

"Is she? I can't… Oh my God, yes, you're right. What's she saying?"

"I can't hear. Shall I put a glass against the door?"

"No! Don't be daft. But she's… Do you think she's, like, all right?"

"She's not on the phone, you can tell – it's just, like, one long monologue."

"She's properly mad, isn't she? Should we lock away the kitchen knives?"

The thought was mortifying, but also funny. I found that my tears had stopped and, to my surprise, I felt a bit better. I pulled off my work clothes and put on pyjamas and a dressing gown.

For a moment I thought about plugging my phone into my laptop and playing the video back, maybe editing it a bit. But then I told myself, *No, Gemma. You decided to do this – have the courage of your convictions and do it.*

So I did. I logged into my YouTube account and I posted the video, and then, without even bothering to wash my face or clean my teeth, I crawled under the duvet, took Stanley in my arms and fell asleep.

Chapter Six

In romantic novels, heartbroken heroines sleep fitfully, if at all. They toss and turn, ideally between silk sheets, and wake the next morning looking wan and haunted. I didn't, though. I slept so deeply I don't think I moved all night, so I woke up with Stanley still cuddled in my arms and a crick in my neck. I felt as if I had a hangover, although obviously I didn't.

First, there was a moment when I didn't know what had happened – the first few seconds of consciousness when I thought that everything was okay, that life was still normal. And then, with a sickening crash, memory returned and realisation hit. Jack had dumped me. Jack was in love with Olivia. I was going to be extremely late for work. My phone must have died during the night, so my alarm hadn't gone off – a glance at my watch told me it was almost nine o'clock.

Not thinking or caring about where my housemates were, I dashed to the bathroom and showered so quickly I barely had time to get wet. I threw on a dress and flipflops and ran down the stairs two at a time, stuffing my things into my bag as I went. I'd do my face on the Tube and charge my phone at work.

I'd only just had time to clean my teeth – I certainly didn't have time for coffee. I dashed Past The Daily Grind, sniffing regretfully at the blast of warm, spicy fragrance that spilled out of the door. Red-haired Luke was outside having a fag, and he called out a good morning to me, but I could only gasp, "Late! Can't stop!" as I hurried onward to the station.

It was nine twenty-nine when I finally arrived at work, sweaty and dishevelled but with my make-up at least vaguely in place. Tom and Ruby were waiting for the lift, chatting animatedly about something. When they saw me their conversation stopped.

"Morning," I said.

"Morning," they both said, but they didn't meet my eyes.

I felt my face growing hotter. Perhaps I was all-too-obviously not okay. Perhaps I'd messed up my eyeliner when the train pulled out of a station and smeared it over my cheek. Perhaps they thought I was late and flustered because I was doing the walk of shame after hooking up with someone the night before. I glanced surreptitiously at my reflection on the way up to the fifth floor; I was puffy-eyed and looked tired, but my layers of highlighter and concealer had done their work adequately, as far as I could see.

"Have a good day," I said, stepping out on our floor.

"Yeah. You too," Ruby said, and I could have sworn I heard Tom snigger.

Walking to my desk was the weirdest thing. I was feeling a bit strange anyway – knackered and spacey, as if the floor might suddenly tilt like one of those fairground rides, and tip me off my feet. The hollow of sadness still filled my insides, and I knew that tears weren't far away. I'd have to spend the day lying low, find a story to work on and do so as quietly and efficiently as I could, until the time came when I'd be allowed to go home and get into bed and cry some more.

Obviously, I wasn't at my most focussed. But I couldn't be imagining the swivel of one pair of eyes after another towards me as I walked the length of the office to our pod, nor the way everyone's gaze seemed to slide away from mine if I glanced in their direction, nor the wave of silence followed by almost-silent whispers that followed me.

Reaching my desk felt like reaching the end of a swimming pool after a length under water. I dropped my bag and flopped into my chair with an audible exhalation.

Emily was there already, a web page open on her screen, headphones in her ears. She glanced up when she saw me and actually blushed.

"Hi Gemma." She removed the earbuds.

"Hi," I said. "Is it just me or is it, like, really weird in here today?"

Emily gave me a strange look. "You've seen your social media, right?"

"No." My mouth felt terribly dry, as if I'd tried to eat three cream crackers at once. "My phone's dead. Why? What's happening?"

"I think you need to look," Emily said. "I'll get you a coffee."

I nodded mutely, switched on my computer, fumbled in my bag for my phone and plugged in the charger. I knew, already, what must have happened – but I didn't know how, or the full extent of it. People must have seen the video I'd uploaded. But how? My YouTube channel wasn't private, but it was tiny – no one except my few thousand followers ever watched it. No one at work had ever mentioned it, and nor had I – not since my interview with Sarah weeks before. Unless you searched for my name, there was no way you'd come across any of my posts among the millions of others that were uploaded every day, all over the world.

While I waited for my computer to whirr to life, I glanced at Emily's screen. She didn't have the Clickfrenzy tab open; she was on Boredcubed, one of our main competitor platforms. She was looking at a headline that shouted, 'This Girl Just Got Dumped, And Her Reaction Is EPIC'. And underneath it my face was silently moving, mouthing the words I'd said last night.

I pressed the power button on my phone and waited while it started up. My hand was oddly steady, although inside every bit of me felt as if it was shaking. For a moment, my phone's screen looked just the same as usual, its icons floating serenely over the photo of Jack and me on my twenty-third birthday. That was going in the trash, I thought. Then, one by one, little red tags started appearing. I had new notifications from Twitter, Facebook, Instagram – it was just like the feeling I'd had walking through the office: the sense that eyes were watching me, people were discussing me, only this was online, not in real life, there were far, far more people, and they didn't know me or care about me.

I swiped my phone's screen until I found the YouTube icon and tapped it. I didn't want to know what I'd see there but I knew there was no point putting it off.

Just the other day at work, some expert from Google had come in to give us a talk about managing social media disasters. As a lowly writer of stories about cats, I was pretty sure such responsibility would never fall to me, but it had made sense to show willing and, besides, I'd seen massive platters of cheese and bowls of biscuits being carried through to the boardroom. Whoever said there's no such thing as a free lunch didn't work in an up-and-coming new media business, that was for sure. So anyway, I'd gone along and listened to case studies about Rio Ferdinand promoting Snickers bars and #AskELJames, and it had all been very interesting, and one thing I'd taken away from it (along with a massive wedge of Brie which I'd wrapped in a napkin and stashed in my bag, then forgotten about until a week later) was that if you suddenly find yourself the laughing stock of the internet, you can't just ignore it.

So I had to look. I had to see what people were saying about me, and decide what I was going to do about it. I'd already decided, actually. I was going to delete the video and delete all my accounts. I was going to do the social media equivalent of hiding in the loo until everyone had gone home. Then I realised the impossibility of erasing what I'd created. The genie was out of the bottle. Boredcubed's three million subscribers had seen me in my bedroom, crying and ranting about my unfaithful boyfriend. People would have posted my video on their Facebook walls and Twitter feeds and Tumblr blogs.

"Once it's out there, it's out there forever," the guy from Google had said in our lunchtime seminar.

My YouTube channel took a few seconds to load on my phone. I squeezed my eyes shut for a second while I waited, trying to force a deep breath down into my tight chest. Then I opened my eyes and looked at the screen.

Last night when I went to bed, I'd had three thousand subscribers. Now, I had eighteen thousand. As I watched, the number jumped to twenty thousand, then up again. People had commented, too – loads of them.

I let my eyes slip down the list of comments as my finger scrolled up the screen.

*You're amazing, Gemma. You just said what we all think when
we get dumped. Hope you feel better soon – he's not worth it.*

*You're gorgeous and he's clearly a loser. Chin up – you deserve
better.*

*You're so brave to have posted this, and so honest. Well done
– and don't stop vlogging. The camera loves you.*

And so on. As I skimmed through them, I felt my face growing
hotter and hotter, and the urge to cry growing stronger. But this
time, it wasn't tears of misery and mortification I wanted to shed,
but of – not happiness, exactly. But you know the feeling you get
when something bad has happened and your best friend touches
your hand and asks if you're okay – that, times thousands. I felt
like I was being hugged by a bunch of strangers who liked me
and cared about me. It was completely freaky and weird, but it
was nice, too.

Just then, I did feel the friendly brush of fingers on my shoulder,
and Emily put a steaming cappuccino down next to me and said,
"Are you okay, Gemma?"

Predictably, her kindness tipped me over the edge. I felt tears
streaming down my face, and dug in my bag for a tissue.

"I'm okay," I said. "Just… how the hell did this happen? And
have you seen what all these people are saying? Everyone's being,
like, really nice. I don't get it."

"How the hell did what happen?" Emily said. "The video go
viral? Someone shared it and then someone else did and… come
on, Gemma. You know all this stuff."

"I do, obviously," I said. "I just thought – I mean, my vlog's so tiny. I never get new followers. Even when Tanya Burr retweeted me once, it didn't make this much difference."

"Because you haven't posted anything that's resonated like this before," Emily said. "I don't want to be rude or anything, but there are loads of people doing make-up tutorials and stuff. This is kind of different."

"Different? I guess it is. Shit, Emily, this is the worst thing that's ever happened to me."

I sipped my cappuccino. It was true – I was mortified. I felt more stupid and more exposed and more embarrassed than I ever had in my life before. But still, amid the horrible, crawling sense of shame that made me feel like my whole body was blushing – the way you feel in those nightmares where you're in Primark and you walk out of the fitting room and you've forgotten to put your clothes back on (it's not just me, is it? Or is it?) – in spite of that, there was still a hint of happiness. Of pride, almost. That what I'd done, even though it was such a massive mistake, had been enough to make so many people like me and care about me, and maybe feel less alone themselves. That it had, as Emily said, resonated.

"Look, Gemma," Emily said. "I know this must feel really embarrassing right now. But it'll blow over. These things always do. Chloë Sevigny once liked a photo I posted on Instagram and I got a load of new followers overnight. It was insane. But most of them have unfollowed me now. Tomorrow's chip paper, innit?"

"I suppose so," I said. But I found my eyes drawn back to my phone. Every few seconds a new notification flashed up from Twitter or Instagram telling me I had a new follower, or someone had posted a link to my video saying how much they related to it, wishing me well, or even, randomly, saying how much they loved my hair or my make-up.

Katie and Nancy had sent me messages on Facebook, but I couldn't face reading them – what if they took Jack and Olivia's side, and were angry with me for shaming them so publicly? I pushed my phone aside and blacked the screen, but even as I turned to my computer and started scouring the web for posts to include in the listicle I was compiling ('20 Cats Most Likely To Achieve World Peace'), I kept seeing my own name, my face, even quotes from my video flashing up on my feed.

It made it almost impossible to focus, even on kittens curled up on top of babies.

After gazing at my screen for over an hour and managing to write just a handful of words, I gave up and braved the long, long walk to the kitchen for a glass of water. Once more, I was conscious of my colleagues' eyes following me. I couldn't help tugging my skirt down, as if I was worried about it being caught in my knickers, even though I knew it wasn't. My feet felt far too big for my body. I could feel sweat snaking down my back, even though the office was as cool as a Frappuccino. And, of course, when I reached the kitchen, there was Sarah, firing a second shot of espresso from the machine into her cup.

I shot into reverse, but it was too late – she'd seen me. Actually, it was more like she'd smelled me coming, or divined my presence by some sort of sixth sense, because she didn't even look up from the stream of coffee.

She just said, "Good morning, Gemma."

"Good morning, Sarah," I parroted like a six-year-old.

The coffee machine gave a final gurgle. Sarah slid her cup – it was one of the special ones, reserved for client meetings, which mere mortals like me were forbidden from using on pain of a telling-off from Anthony, the office manager – off the metal drip tray and inhaled the steam like I imagine wine connoisseurs must do during the process of getting utterly shitfaced. I wanted to leg it – I really did – but now she'd acknowledged me I felt I had to wait for permission to leave. And besides, my legs appeared to have lost the power to move.

Sarah lifted her face from her coffee and said, "Would you like a drink?"

Hell, yes, I thought, *a double vodka and anything would go down just brilliantly right now*. But I said, "I just came to get a glass of water."

Sarah nodded. She reached into the fridge and took out a bottle of water (also normally reserved for clients – it was the water cooler for the rest of us), and handed it to me.

Before I could stammer out a thank you, she said, "Next time you decide to break the internet, please let us know in advance so we can get the clicks, not those clowns at Boredcubed."

Then she winked at me, and swished away to her office.

When I left work that afternoon, I didn't go straight to the Tube station. Instead, I walked up Tottenham Court Road, past the vast construction site that would eventually become the new Crossrail station but for now was just a massive, fenced-off hole in the ground, the streets around it thronged with bewildered tourists and frustrated commuters. I found a photography store and bought a little tripod with a special clip to hold my phone, and a selfie stick as well. I even found myself looking longingly at the high-end video equipment and lights – but even if I could have afforded them, I hadn't actually decided what I was going to do – had I?

Then I went to Boots and bought a load of make-up, including some magic light-reflecting cream that promised photo-perfect, airbrushed skin. Because obviously I'd want to look my best for the viewers I wasn't even sure I wanted.

When I got home, I chucked all the carrier bags under my bed. I didn't want to think about what I was going to do, and I certainly wasn't ready to actually do it. I looked at my phone and saw that, as Emily had predicted, the flood of tweets and subscribers was easing off. I knew that if I ignored it, it would slow to a trickle and stop. But people were asking about me, wondering why I hadn't responded to any messages, wanting to know if I was okay. A few people were even suggesting finding out my address and sending the police round, in case I'd 'done something stupid'.

I had, that was for sure. And now, somehow, I was going to have to deal with the consequences – but I didn't know how. I found myself pacing around my bedroom – which was a challenge because it was only about six paces from the door to the window – sitting down and then standing up again, unable to focus on anything. I went downstairs and made myself a couple of bits of toast with peanut butter and sat in front of the telly, but when I tried to eat my throat closed up. Then Hannah arrived home from her knitting group, shortly followed by Richard arriving from work.

"All right, Gemma?" Richard said.

I said, "Yeah, good thanks. You?"

"I bought takeaway," Hannah said, dumping a greasy carrier bag on the table. "It's buttermilk-fried chicken – seriously good. Want some?"

The smell made my stomach rumble, but at the same time I felt a bit sick. I shook my head.

"Sure?" Richard said. "It's really good."

"So good," Hannah said around a mouthful of batter.

"Thanks, guys," I said. "I ate earlier." I hoped they wouldn't spot my uneaten toast in the bin. "Think I'll head for bed, actually. I'm knackered."

At least my flatmates appeared to be oblivious of my new-found fame – or notoriety – I thought, closing my bedroom door. The carrier bags under the bed seemed almost to rustle with anticipation. *Come on*, they said. *You bought all this exciting new kit. Aren't you even going to look at it?*

I thought, *I'll just look. See how it all works. Maybe try the magic blurry make-up stuff.*

And so, an hour later, I found myself with a full face of slap applied, perching on the bed with Stanley on my lap, looking up at the camera. Last night, I'd spoken into it without a second thought – but that was then. Now, I was acutely, terrifyingly conscious of the world that waited out there beyond my phone's expectant screen. *You can edit it, Gemma*, I soothed myself. *You don't even have to post it at all. Just have a go, see whether it works.*

I licked my lips, which were sticky and sweet with gloss, and squeezed Stanley closer.

"Hi everyone," I said.

I don't know how long I spoke for, but it felt like ages. When I started, I said that I didn't know what I was going to say, but once the words began to come, they just didn't stop. I explained that I hadn't meant my video to go viral, and that when I realised it had, all I wanted to do was delete it. I almost did, I said, but then I saw all the lovely things people had said about me – people who I'd never met in my life and never would – and I felt that to do so would somehow be a betrayal of them.

I told them how they'd made me feel: like when you're at a gig and somehow find yourself lifted up and crowdsurfing, held aloft by the hands of strangers, supported and safe, but exhilarated too. Or, on a more humdrum note, like when you go to the corner shop to buy a can of Coke and you realise haven't got enough cash and their card machine's broken, and the person behind you says, "Don't worry, love," and gives you 10p. Or when you're wearing new shoes and you trip and fall over while you're walking past a big group of teenagers, and instead of pissing themselves laughing at you and taking photos of your knickers to post on Snapchat, they come rushing over and ask if you're okay and help you to your feet. (All those were things that had happened to me, which I'd forgotten all about until I started trying to describe what today had been like, and then the memories came flooding back.)

I said that I hadn't been sure about posting again, and that I still wasn't – I was going to record a video, though, and watch it back, and see how I felt. I wanted to be sure, this time. And I wanted them – whoever they were, however many of them there were – to know that I wasn't sure, right now, while I was speaking. And then I realised I'd used the word "sure" about ten times in one minute, and I started to laugh, because it was all so earnest and stupid, and there I was baring my soul when I didn't even know if anyone was going to see me doing it.

Then I finally got round to the point, which was that, really, I'd been a dick – I'd done the emotional equivalent of accidentally releasing a sex tape (does anyone ever actually release sex tapes accidentally? Or is it always some calculated publicity stunt, or an angry ex wanting revenge?), and instead of mocking and vilifying me, the internet had been nice to me. I still couldn't quite believe it, I said. It made me feel all warm and fuzzy and happy, this surprising proof of the kindness of strangers.

So, I said, I wanted to say thank you to every single person who'd posted a message of support, and everyone who'd told the people whose messages hadn't been supportive not to be mean. Oh, and by the way, I said, a lot of them had asked me if I'd heard from Jack. I hadn't. And then I said I was going to have to stop talking or I'd cry, and I felt that the internet had seen more than enough of me crying already and I didn't want to make a habit of it. So I said goodnight.

And then I stood up and switched the camera off. My legs felt wobbly and strange and my throat was as dry as sandpaper. The house was in darkness – Richard and Hannah must have gone to bed, although I hadn't heard their feet on the stairs passing my door on the way to their bedroom up in the loft. I really, really hoped that would mean they hadn't heard me talking, either.

I went to the bathroom and cleaned off every scrap of make-up and brushed my teeth. I filled a glass with water from the tap over the basin and took it back to my room. I unclipped my camera from its stand on the chest of drawers, downloaded the video on to my laptop and pressed play, careful that the sound was turned down low.

I was surprised by how okay I looked. My bedroom was tidy-ish. The fairy lights sparkled prettily over the headboard of my bed. I was in focus. My skin looked smooth and a bit glowy. My hair covered my ears. I even sounded quite good – even though my voice sounded strange, as it always does when you listen to yourself on a recording, it was less squeaky than I'd feared, perhaps because I'd cried so much over the past twenty-four hours. I changed the lighting slightly to make everything look brighter and less yellow, and I deleted the bit at the beginning where I was saying, "Hello? Hello?" like an idiot to check that my camera was actually recording, and the bit at the end where I got up and pressed the button to make it stop.

There wasn't much else to do. I could have cut out the bits where I stumbled over my words and umm-ed and err-ed, and the bit near the end where my voice went all wobbly and I had to wipe away tears and do a massive, gross-sounding sniff, but I didn't. I uploaded the video, and this time, I deliberately chose the option that would make it public. And then, for good measure, I went on Twitter and told my followers what I'd done.

Chapter Seven

Hi everyone!

So, first of all, thank you so much for all your lovely comments and likes on my last video – I can't tell you how much it means to me. The last few days have been really, really hard, but I kind of feel like I'm not alone. Every time one of you reaches out and says you're thinking of me, or you're going through something similar, or whatever, it feels like a lovely little virtual hug. You are all, like, truly amazing.

So today I thought I'd talk about something a little bit different. As well as everything that all of you have been doing to make me feel better – to make me feel a bit cherished and supported – there are other things I've been doing for myself too, to help put a smile on my face and also just look after myself a bit. Because when you've gone through a break-up, it's so easy to just wallow in it, and that doesn't do anyone any good.

But before I start, some of you might be thinking, "What the actual frick is this girl doing with a teddy bear? Is she seven?" Well… Part of me can't believe that I'm about to introduce the world to my teddy, but that's exactly what I'm about to do. Even though he hasn't learned how to use the internet yet, he gives truly awesome hugs, and he's been here for me through all my tough times for twenty-four years. I can honestly say I don't think I'd be brave enough to make these videos at all without him here by my side, and if that makes me look stupid – hey, it won't be the first time! So, everyone, meet Stanley. Stanley, gimme a high five!

For once, I was up and ready for work way earlier than I needed to be. I even had time to paint my nails, which were looking distinctly the worse for wear – the orange gel polish I'd put on a week ago was growing out and chipped around the edges. I'd go downstairs and do it in the kitchen, I decided, and while the new polish was drying I'd have a proper breakfast – eggs, maybe, or some of the organic seedy granola I bought in the health food shop on the high street and hadn't yet got around to opening.

Also, I could check my YouTube channel and see how my new video was doing. I'd wanted to look the second I woke up, but I hadn't. I hadn't even checked my email. It was weird – part of me was eager to know whether people had seen it, liked it, commented on it – but a far bigger part was frightened that, after how kind and lovely my followers had been the first time, the tide would now turn. Maybe I'd been boring? Maybe I'd looked and sounded stupid? And anyway, what possible reason could anyone have for caring about me, my life and my relationship woes? Most probably, the people who'd commented on the first video would simply ignore this second one and move on to whatever new thing the internet had to offer them today.

If there was one thing I'd learned at Clickfrenzy, it was that you couldn't count on your audience being loyal. And if there was another thing I'd learned, it was that consumers of online media had the attention spans of particularly fickle goldfish. Anyway, I'd wait until my nails were painted and my breakfast made, I decided, and then wake my phone up and find out the worst (or, I secretly hoped, the best).

As it turned out, though, I didn't get to have a leisurely appraisal of my social media over breakfast, because when I got down to the kitchen, Amy was there. And she wasn't alone.

"Morning, Gemma," she said. "Er… This is my housemate, Gemma. Gemma, this is Kian."

"Hi," I said.

"All right?" Kian said. He was leaning against the kitchen counter drinking tea, looking as comfortable as if he was in his own home – more comfortable than I felt in the house, if I'm being honest, and it *was* my home. It was Amy who looked awkward and a bit shy – well, you do, don't you, the morning after the first time you bring a new boyfriend home. Although anyone who brought Kian home would be perfectly entitled to punch the air and go, "Yes – result!" because he was quite seriously hot – about six foot two of pure muscle, with a buzz cut and a jawline Zayn Malik would be proud of.

But then I took another look at the two of them, and re-evaluated my take on the situation. Amy was wearing her gym kit. Kian was wearing trackie bottoms and a T-shirt. And okay, maybe after you shagged someone for the first time, you'd make him a cup of tea before heading out for a run. And maybe he'd have gone on your date, or whatever, in his loungewear. But it didn't seem all that likely to me.

"Kian goes to the same gym as me," Amy said. "We arranged to meet up this morning for a workout in the park when I finished my night shift, and he came back for a cuppa."

"And now I need to head off," Kian said. "I've got work to go to, unlike some people who get to kip all day."

Which I thought was a bit off, given that Amy had been working all night. But she didn't seem to mind – she laughed and stuck her tongue out at him, and he reached out a hand as if he was going to caress her face, but then ended up just chucking her under the chin.

"Nice to meet you," I said.

"Likewise," Kian said. "I'll see myself out." He rinsed his mug in the sink and put it on the dish rack to dry, picked up his bag and headed for the door, then stopped, turned back and said to Amy, "I'll WhatsApp you, okay?"

We heard the front door carefully close, then Amy sort of squeezed her arms around herself and gave a delighted little shiver.

"Sorry, Gemma," she said, although she didn't look sorry at all. "That must have been a bit weird, coming down for your breakfast and finding him here."

"It's fine," I said. "No worries at all. I was just going to do my nails, though, which might have spoiled the mood a bit."

"Oooh, were you?" Amy said. "What colour?"

"Just this." I fished my nail varnish out of my bag. "It's like a greige – I thought it would go with everything but now I'm not sure I'm loving it."

Amy looked at it. It would be fair to say she looked askance at it. "No," she said. "Not loving it either. Want to use some of mine? I've got loads, and I'm only allowed boring clear at work, so I only get to do mine properly when I'm off, and then I only get to wear it for a couple of days, which seems kind of pointless."

"Cool," I said. "Thanks. I'll stick the kettle on."

A few seconds later, I heard Amy's trainers come pattering back down the stairs and she plonked a huge make-up case full of nail polishes on the table. I'm not lying – there must have been at least seventy bottles in her horde, plus loads of cuticle oils and quick-drying sprays and undercoats and other bits and pieces whose function I could only guess at.

"How long have you got?" she said.

"An hour, maybe? Normally I have zero time in the mornings, but I woke up early."

"Cool!" Amy said. "I'm going to go crazy. Do you mind?"

I briefly weighed up the value of a healthy breakfast against having really amazing nails. The nails won easily.

"So," I said, ever so casually a few minutes later, when Amy's head was bent low over my hands so that it would be easy for her to avoid meeting my eyes if she didn't want to. "Kian seems nice."

The brush moved smoothly over my nail, an even coat of aqua varnish following it.

"You think?" Amy said.

"Yeah! I mean, he's fit, obviously. But you know that."

"Oh my God," Amy said. "I've fancied him for ages. I thought he'd never, ever notice me. The gym's full of these really hot girls – why would anyone pick me?"

I opened my mouth to say that of course they would, Amy was gorgeous – the way you instinctively do, even when it's not true, although in her case it totally was. But she carried on talking before I could say anything.

"And then the other morning I was doing bench presses without anyone spotting me, which you shouldn't do really, because it's dangerous and you can drop the weight on yourself. But I thought, whatever – I wasn't lifting anything really heavy anyway, and I know what I'm doing. And he just came over and put his hand under the bar, like this—" She gestured, sending a splatter of nail polish off the brush and on to the stripy oilcloth. "Oops. Fuck. Hold on."

She saturated a cotton ball with acetone and carefully blotted the stain away. "Just as well there's a cloth on there. Rule twenty-four, isn't it: 'This is your home, but it's ours, too. Please treat our belongings with as much care and respect as you would your own.'"

We met each other's eyes and both started to giggle.

"I know, right?" I said. "Anyway, go on about Kian."

"So he helped me with my workout, and we got chatting, and he said, as it's so hot out, why didn't we meet up in the park and train together sometimes. And I said I'd love to, but it was hard with my shift patterns, and he said that was cool, because he works weird hours too. So we met up this morning and we had such a great time."

"Wicked!" I said. "So, do you think you'll see him again?"

"Who knows?" Amy said. She looked up at me again, and her dark eyes were full of doubt. "The thing is, Gemma, I'm totally shit at relationships. I just seemed to get it wrong when I was a teenager, over and over. So I said to myself, no more. I'll focus on my career and get that sorted, and then maybe everything else will fall into place."

"Maybe everything is falling into place now, though," I said. "Maybe things will work out between you two. Or maybe they won't – maybe it's just, like, a dry run? After all, you've only seen him at the gym and then met up with him this morning and had tea, right? It could be the beginning of something, or it could be nothing at all. Don't stress – just go with it."

"I know," Amy said. "You're totally right. I shouldn't be stressing about it – but that's what I do. You don't, I can tell. You're totes sorted, with the love of your life coming back to marry you once he's finished travelling."

Her words shocked me as much as if she'd thrown a glass of cold water in my face. For a while, thinking about her and my nails and how much time I had before I really, really needed to leave and go to work had made me forget about Jack. And even before that, the total weirdness of talking to the internet about how I felt had somehow insulated me from what was really going on.

But now I was made aware of my situation as harshly as if it had only just changed. I'd told Hannah, Richard and Amy that Jack was off travelling for six months, maybe a year, and that when he got back we'd be looking for a place together. That was true, then. Now it wasn't. Now I was single, unequivocally so – dumped and dealing with it in a terribly public way that suddenly seemed also to be terribly stupid.

I wanted, briefly, to confide in Amy. Her hands on mine felt safe and gentle. She'd trusted me enough to tell me things about herself that were private and important. But then I heard Richard and Hannah coming downstairs, laughing at some private joke. Quickly, Amy pulled a piece of kitchen towel off the roll and put it underneath my hand before misting a film of cold spray over my nails.

"There you go," she said. "They'll dry really fast now."

I'd been so engrossed in our conversation that I'd barely concentrated on what she'd been doing. Now I looked, and felt my face spread into a delighted grin. My nails were an even pale blue, except every alternate finger was painted with a perfect, puffy white cloud.

"That's so fucking insane," I said, just as Hannah said, "Pfft, it really stinks in here."

The moment of closeness between Amy and me had evaporated as quickly as acetone.

I said, "Oh my God, I need to rush or I'll be late again. Thanks for the incredible nails."

Amy said, "No bother. I should get some sleep." And she gathered up her collection of manicure stuff and headed upstairs.

Hannah said, "Earl Grey or English Breakfast, Rich? And do you want eggs or porridge?"

I wasn't early any more, but I wasn't too late to stop for a coffee at The Daily Grind. I'd got used to chatting to Luke and his assistant while I waited for my order, and the assistant seemed to be getting used to the job, too. He didn't mess up so many orders now, and he was starting to recognise his customers – when he saw me, he grinned and said, "Cappuccino and an almond croissant?"

"That's right," I said, smiling. Whatever his reason was for needing to work there, I really hoped he'd stopped fucking up and wasn't going to get the sack.

He handed me my drink and I handed him a tenner, but instead of putting it in the till he paused and looked at me.

"Is your name Gemma?"

I thought, *How does he know?* Then I remembered my video, and that just a couple of days before, it had felt like the whole of the internet knew my name. I wished I could disappear into the glossy wooden floorboards.

"That's me," I muttered.

"You do YouTube videos, right? Make-up and stuff?"

"I – yes, I do. A bit. Hardly anyone watches them, though. How did you…?"

He laughed. "I recognised your voice, then I realised I knew your face, too. My niece loves your videos. I was at my sister's place over the weekend and she made me watch about five of them back-to-back, then she went off to her mum's bedroom and put loads of make-up on. My sister went absolutely mental. Zara's only eleven."

"Oh my God," I said. "I'm so sorry. I mean – that her mum was cross. I didn't want to be a bad influence."

He shrugged. "I told my sister she's going to have to get used to it. Zara's growing up, after all. Would you mind if I took a selfie of us for her? She'd be so excited."

I hesitated, then I thought, *What harm could it do?* I was putting my image online almost every day – what difference would one selfie for an eleven-year-old girl make? So I said yes, and he came out from behind the counter and we put our faces close together and he took a photo on his phone.

"Thanks," he said. "I'm Raffy, by the way."

"Gemma. But you knew that. Nice to meet you, anyway." I fumbled my coffee and croissant into one hand so I could shake his with the other. It felt awkward to greet each other formally when we'd just been close enough for me to smell him – his hair had a faint fragrance of coffee.

"I'd better get on," I said, seeing the queue behind me building up.

"Have a good day," he said. "See you later. And thanks."

"That's okay."

As the door swung shut behind me, I heard one of the other customers say, "Who do you think she is, then?"

"No idea. She's tall enough to be a model, but…"

Then the door closed and I couldn't hear any more. I wasn't sure I wanted to.

I spent my lunch break reading back through the comments on my vlog, and reading new ones for the first time. Alongside all the sweet, supportive messages, there were more and more questions. Although they were all different, they were also all the same.

What do you do when you've been dumped?
How do you mend a broken heart?
How do you make yourself get out of bed in the morning when all you want to do is pull the pillow over your head and cry?

And the problem was, I didn't know the answer. Although I'd had my fair share of rejections and minor bust-ups, I'd never had my heart broken because, before Jack, I'd never been in a proper relationship. And now that I had, I'd responded in the stupidest way imaginable, and that appeared to have started a chain of events I could never have predicted. I got out of bed in the mornings because if I didn't, I'd lose my job and then I wouldn't be able to pay the rent – but that wasn't exactly groundbreaking advice to pass on to the people who'd asked, and nor was it enough to fill more than about sixty seconds of YouTube time.

As for mending a broken heart – well, mine wasn't mended by any means. But the shock of finding myself suddenly known to several thousand people on the internet had been pretty effective at distracting me from it. But again, as relationship advice went, "Dumped? Pro tip: try making a twat of yourself online, because that will make you feel even worse!" was probably not the kind of wisdom Dear Deirdre would dispense.

So I turned from my YouTube channel to Google and searched for 'getting over a break-up'.

There was no shortage of advice out there; the problem was that a lot of it couldn't really be made to work in the context of fifteen minutes of me talking to a camera in my bedroom.

The best way to get over a man is to get under another, seemed to be a popular axiom. Which was all very well, I supposed, but although I was grateful to my viewers for all their kind words, I wasn't grateful enough to go out and pull some random stranger and shag him on camera.

Get out in the fresh air and work up a sweat, were the bracing words I found on another forum. *Exercise releases endorphins, the feel-good hormones that are guaranteed to leave you with a smile on your face and roses in your cheeks. And, when you're ready to start looking for a new relationship, you'll be toned, glowing and looking better than ever.*

I thought of Amy, and how she coped with the stress of her job by going to the gym. And how that was where she'd met Kian, who was certainly a potential boyfriend even if he wasn't an actual one yet. Exercise – a good idea, certainly. But I wasn't sure I was ready for the internet to see me scarlet-faced and sweaty, barely able to breathe after jogging round the block. If I was going to embark on a fitness programme, it would need to be kept private for the time being.

Have an evening in with your besties, curled up on the sofa watching cheesy movies and eating popcorn, another site counselled. *Yeah, right*, I thought. Until recently, my best friends had been Jack and Olivia, which kind of ruled that one out right away, even if it weren't for the fact that Hannah would freak out if I dropped popcorn behind the sofa cushions.

Then I remembered what Mum used to say back in the day, a long time ago, when Dad was still living with us and they'd had one of their epic and horrible rows. She'd emerge from her bedroom, her face perfectly made up to conceal any trace of tears, dressed like she was going to a party. She'd pick up her car keys and toss them from hand to hand, and say, "I'm off out, Gemma. When the going gets tough, the tough go shopping."

So, that evening after work, I went to Oxford Street. Later, when I set my phone up on the tripod to record my video, I was surrounded by bags and boxes. I hadn't shopped randomly; I'd planned my haul carefully to include everything the heart-broken dumpee could possibly need to make herself feel better. And as I removed each item carefully from its packaging and held it up so the camera could focus on it, I remembered Mum teaching me how retail therapy worked.

"So when you're getting over the end of a relationship," I said, "one of the hardest things is being able to have a good night's sleep.

I've found that, anyway. I've been having the most vivid dreams – I think the worst are the ones where Jack and I are still together, because then I wake up and we're not, if you know what I mean. Scented candles are great for helping you to relax and unwind before bed – I just love this one, it smells like… I don't know, a bit like walking through a pine forest, only with a bit of wild flowers in it, maybe. But you can't burn candles while you're asleep. No. Fire risk! So I also bought this gorgeous pillow spray. It's lavender, but not, like, nana-lavender. And tonight, I'm going to spritz some of that around my room and hopefully I'll sleep beautifully.

"And speaking of beauty. Some of you have asked about my skincare and make-up routine, and while I really appreciate all the lovely, lovely things you've said, I can promise you that I give myself a lot of help with that, because tears and sleepless nights do not make anyone look good. So here are a few of the magic potions I've discovered…"

I presented item after item to the camera, starting with the eye-depuffing serum. There was a pair of high-heeled over-the-knee boots that I'd bought, I said, because they'd make any woman feel like a goddess. There was gorgeous silk lingerie that the broken-hearted should buy and wear (although, I hastened to add, it didn't have to be expensive), because even if no one else would ever see it, you would, and you'd know you were wearing it and feel amazing. There were snuggly pyjamas for those nights when all you want to do is feel comfy and cosy. There were herbal teas to make you sleep and other herbal teas to uplift you. There was even a handbag that cost more than my monthly rent, because, I said, "If there's one thing that will get you taken seriously, it's a serious bag. Know this!" And I winked at the camera.

Finally, I said, "All this stuff is great. Every single thing I've shown you guys tonight, I love. But the best things don't have to cost anything – like my gorgeous nails that my good friend Amy did for me thing morning. Look." I held my hands up to the lens and waited for them to come into focus. Amy wouldn't mind me referring to her as a friend, I hoped, even though we hardly knew each other. I needed people to see – to believe – that I wasn't friendless as well as boyfriendless – and anyway, the chances of Amy ever seeing the video were, like, microscopic. "They're so pretty, and every time I type or use my phone or wash my hands, I think of Amy and remember that she cares about me. So thanks, Amy, and thanks all of you for watching. I'm going to make a cup of sleepy tea, drink it in a bath with my lovely soothing bubbles and maybe a face mask, and then go to bed, and hopefully I'll have the best sleep ever. And I hope you do, too. Night-night."

I switched off my camera. Then I carefully packed all my purchases back into their bags, making sure the receipts were there too. If I hurried, I'd be able to return every item to the shop where I'd bought them in my lunch break tomorrow and still have time for a sandwich. And if I was lucky, my credit card company wouldn't know I'd bought a thing.

Over the next week, things at Clickfrenzy returned to normal. People stopped following me with their eyes as I walked to the kitchen or the loo. Emily stopped asking me how I was in a concerned way in the mornings, and reverted to just asking how my evening had been. When I got into the lift at the same time as Sarah, she commented on how many hits my latest cat post had got, not how many my 'So my boyfriend dumped me' vlog had. I began to realise that in a world where people obsessively followed the new, the trending, there was no headspace for thinking about last week's viral post.

But I didn't stop vlogging. I posted three more videos. I'd spent ages analysing other people's channels, looking for tips and ideas, and discovered that 'What's in my handbag?' posts were a thing. I couldn't imagine why – the idea seemed as dull as it was bizarre. But then I watched a few and realised how strangely addictive it was to see a stranger sorting through a jumble of Oyster cards, lipsticks, packs of stale chewing gum and spare knickers. So I upended my bag on to my bed and sorted through all the junk that was in there and talked about it. The photo of Jack, which I'd carried everywhere with me for years, I buried at the bottom of the pile and didn't show.

The next evening, I made another. I called it, 'A letter to my teenage self'. In it, I talked about how I'd always hated my height and my sticky-out ears and my knock-knees, and how jealous I'd been of the popular girls who were permanently surrounded by laughing, gossiping friends. I said I wished I'd known then that their confidence was only a veneer – that underneath, they were just as wracked with self-consciousness and doubt as I was. I said that your teenage years are the time when you find out who you are, but it's sometimes hard to actually know, because who teenagers are changes all the time. I told my viewers to surround themselves with friends who were kind and true and made them laugh. I reminded them that it's not what you look like that counts, but who you are inside. (When I was a teenager, I knew as surely as I knew the earth wasn't flat that that wasn't true, but maybe if I'd believed it I'd have minded less about my ears and my knees.) I finished by talking a bit about how I wished I'd known not to be pressured into things like smoking and drinking at parties, and how if you're worried about peer pressure you should talk to an adult you trust. But when I played it back, that bit seemed embarrassingly prissy and worthy, so I edited it out.

The third one was about nourishing yourself in body and spirit, and it took some serious research. I downloaded a book about mindfulness and read it on the Tube on my way to work. To be honest, I've never been the most spiritual person and a lot of it didn't really make sense to me, but I could kind of see the point of living in the moment, especially when you're going through a tough time emotionally. So I talked about that, and about the little daily blessings that are bestowed on us all every day, like being smiled at by a stranger, or seeing a rainbow, or the guy in the coffee shop forgetting to charge me for my paleo carrot and cashew muffin and then giving it to me for free when I pointed out his mistake (I wasn't entirely honest about that. It was actually an almond croissant that Raffy had forgotten to charge me for). I bought a pretty little notebook, which I showed the camera while I explained that I used it to write down five blessings every day. This wasn't strictly true either, but it seemed like such a lovely idea that I resolved to start doing it, which made it almost true. If I remembered, of course.

I also talked a bit about healthy eating, and how when you take care of your body, your immune system is so much better at coping with stress and your mood is lifted. I waited until Hannah and Richard had gone to work and took my phone downstairs into the kitchen, and bunged a load of kale, apple and avocado into the blender with some ice cubes and coconut water. Then, after

I'd removed the Post-it note that said, *Please don't put hot liquid in this machine*, I filmed it all going round and round. I filmed myself pouring it into a glass and taking a sip, but then I had to stop recording while I spat it out. It was so disgusting I could still taste it even after my coffee and almond croissant.

Chapter Eight

Over the next few weeks, I became more and more confident that things at Clickfrenzy had returned to normal. If any of my colleagues watched my vlog, they said nothing about it. I friended some of them on Facebook and followed them on Twitter and Instagram, but apart from occasionally sharing one another's posts, especially the work-related ones, we pretty much ignored one another on social media. There seemed to be a kind of unwritten rule about it. If I knew, thanks to ill-judged ranty tweets, that Emily had had a row with her mum or that Ruby had complained to her beauty salon about an inept Hollywood wax ("Third-degree fanny burns! WTAF?" There was no accompanying picture, thankfully. There's too much information, and then there's much, much too much information), I knew better than to say anything about it in the office.

At home, it was different, but also the same. Hannah had set up a Facebook group that we used for things like Amy keeping us up to date on her shift patterns and Hannah letting us know when British Gas were coming to read the meter but, by common and unspoken consent, we all had each other on limited profiles. I still didn't know whether my housemates even knew I had a vlog.

Given Hannah's obsession with Radio 4 and the fact that Amy was almost always at work, at the gym, asleep or, more recently, out with Kian, I thought it was likely that they didn't have a clue and wouldn't have cared anyway.

That was fine with me. But my vlog was taking up more and more of my own time. Responding to comments, sharing other people's posts, editing videos – it was all beginning to feel a bit like a second job. And more than that – a second life. I began to feel like I knew the people whose comments I replied to, whose own videos I shared – they were part of a world, a community, that I was just starting to understand and feel a part of. And that worked for me, in a way, because my first life wasn't exactly thrilling. Without Jack, and with my friends in Norwich a short enough, but still inconvenient and expensive, train journey away, keeping in touch in real life was getting harder.

I didn't go to Nancy's birthday drinks, because they were on a Thursday night and I knew I'd miss the last train back to London and even though I could have stayed over at Mum's, packing an overnight bag and being hungover and knackered at work the next day seemed like too much hassle. I replied to Katie's texts, but with so many other messages to answer, my replies were cursory, and I sensed an increasing narkiness in hers. When Shivvy said she was coming to London for a weekend and asked if she could crash at mine, I said no, partly because I didn't want to ask Hannah if it would be okay and see her thinking it wasn't but saying it was, but also because I knew from my second, stealth Instagram account that Shivvy had been posting endless likes and comments on Olivia's posts saying how made up she was that Olivia and Jack were so happy together and having such an amazing time.

Not that I was bitter or anything but… well, I was. Go on, admit it, you'd be bitter too if you were me.

But anyway, then, two things happened that I hadn't expected.

The first thing happened when I was at work.

It was my turn to do a coffee run for the content team, so, as was customary, I took everyone's orders and headed for the kitchen, repeating over and over in my head, *Latte for Jim, peppermint tea for Hermione, builders' tea for Tom…* knowing that by the time I got to the kitchen I would almost certainly have forgotten and would have to go back and repeat the process.

As it happened, though, I didn't even make it as far as the kitchen, because when I passed the reception desk Daisy said, "Gemma! God, I'm glad to see you."

"I never knew you felt that way," I said.

"Don't be daft! Look, this arrived for you, and now you can take it yourself instead of me having to cart it all the way to your desk."

She gestured to a large cardboard carton next to her chair, all wrapped up with red and white 'fragile' tape and with my name printed on the label.

"Been shopping?" Daisy asked. "Is it anything exciting?"

"I've got no idea," I said. "I can't shop – it's a week until payday and I'm skint. I wasn't expecting any deliveries. God, that's heavy!"

I carried the box back to my desk and carefully slit the tape. A mass of packaging came billowing out – foam worms that reminded me of the puffed corn crisps Jack loved, even though they made his fingers smell of synthetic cheese for ages. I scooped some of them out and found an envelope with my name on it. There was a card inside.

Dear Gemma, I hope you don't mind us contacting you at work – we didn't have an address for you but managed to find you on LinkedIn with a bit of detective work! We are Original Organics, a new company specialising in all-natural pampering products for people who love giving themselves bit of TLC. We really hope you enjoy trying these few samples – please do get in touch and tell us what you think.

I pushed more of the foam worms aside and reached into the box. It was full of stuff. Scented candles, soaps, body lotion, three different reed diffusers… *I couldn't get through all this if I spent the rest of the year in the bath*, I thought. The smell was lovely – a mixture of floral freshness and a deeper, muskier scent that reminded me of how Mum used to smell when she came back from one of her spa days. It was also filling the office – I could see people turning around and hear them muttering, "What's that? Can you smell that?"

Hastily, I closed the box and resealed it with random strips of Sellotape.

Tom said, "When you're finished stinking the place out with your shopping, Gemma, any chance you could make our tea?"

The parcel from Original Organics might have been the heaviest delivery I received that month, but it was by no means the only one. A couple of days later, a hamper of herbal tea arrived at the office. I took a few teabags home to try and left the rest in the kitchen. Then a PR company sent me a load of make-up and nail polishes. Then a salon contacted me on Twitter offering to do my nails for free (I politely declined, because Amy had done them over the weekend, a French manicure with glittery tips and little diamanté embellishments, and I couldn't imagine any professional making them look more fabulous).

I didn't know what to do about it. At first, I was giddy with excitement at the flood of lovely, free stuff arriving for me. But soon it began to be a running joke. "Here's another haul for you, Gemma," Daisy would say. I muttered that it was samples for my vlog, and gave things to my colleagues, which felt weirdly like paying them for their silence about it. I gave the nicest of the nail varnishes to Amy; I took a few candles to the charity shop after I'd filmed myself smelling them and saying how fab they were, and asked Hannah casually whether she'd like the others, pretending that they were samples from work – which in a way they were. I even took a bunch of the pinker, sparklier, more age-appropriate stuff to Raffy at The Daily Grind to pass on to his niece, and received an adorable hand-drawn thank-you card in return (from Zara, not from Raffy. That would just have been weird).

But it all didn't feel right, somehow. I felt obscurely guilty every time another package turned up, as if I was getting freebies under false pretences, or getting them with an expectation I wasn't able to meet. I was new to this vlogging malarkey, but I was learning fast – I'd seen how quick viewers were to accuse someone whose biggest fan they'd been the day before of selling out if they dared to appear even slightly commercial.

I didn't want to sell out – I wasn't vlogging to make money. I wasn't even sure why I was doing it, but I knew that I wasn't quite ready to stop. Now that I was gaining new subscribers every day, I wanted to see what would happen if I carried on – how far it could take me, how big it could get. I felt like I was achieving something for myself. In spite of how public it was, I felt like I had a secret.

Then the next week, I checked my bank statement. I know, I know – as a responsible adult I should have been doing so on a regular basis. But I'd been avoiding looking, because I knew exactly what was there to see – a whole lot of nothing, since I'd withdrawn my last fifty pounds, which was going to have to last me until payday. But I had a sudden attack of the Fear – what if some direct debit that I'd forgotten about had gone through and I was overdrawn? And what about the council tax bill, which had arrived the previous day? I was avoiding Hannah and Richard even more than usual, in case they wanted me to pay my share early for some reason.

So, feeling slightly sick, I logged into my online banking and went through its elaborate security checks. And then suddenly I didn't feel sick any more – I felt elated. YouTube had paid me forty-five pounds. Forty-five! It was hardly anything, really, I knew that. It was nothing compared to the riches I'd dreamed of accumulating when I set up the channel to enable monetisation, all those months ago when I'd had visions of becoming an online superstar. But it was actual, real money I'd earned from people watching me – or rather, from watching the ads they had to sit through before my videos.

I celebrated by going out in my lunch break and buying a Krispy Kreme chocolate truffle parcel, sugar-laden snacks being sadly under-represented in my deliveries of free stuff.

When I got back to my desk, I was greeted by an email from an unfamiliar address.

Hi Gemma, I read.

I'm reaching out to introduce myself, and hopefully to arrange to meet up for a coffee and a chat. I'm with Ripple Effect, a talent agency specialising in new media, and I'm a huge fan of your blog. I'd be really excited to speak with you about possible ways we could work together. Do call me and let me introduce myself in person.

It was from someone called Sloane Cassidy.

That afternoon, I found it harder than ever to focus on the online antics of cats. I kept reading and rereading Sloane Cassidy's email and gazing at my bank balance. I waited for Sarah to go into a meeting, leaving her office empty so I could sneak in and make my call in private.

I'd imagined finding out a bit more about who Sloane was and more importantly what on earth had possessed her to get in touch with me, but I'd reckoned without her forceful personality, and by the time I ended the call five minutes later I'd agreed to meet in my lunch break the next day at Ripple Effect HQ, which was just down the road from the Clickfrenzy office in Soho. As soon as I ended the call, I began to wonder if I was making a massive mistake.

Back in my bedroom that evening, I tried on just about every garment I owned in an effort to find the perfect, elegant yet edgy, effortless yet immaculate 'I go to meetings like this every day' outfit. Needless to say, my wardrobe failed to produce such a thing, and nor did the pile of clothes I found under my bed.

I tried on my favourite white skater dress with slightly battered pink Converse, but decided that it was too short to be even vaguely meeting-appropriate, and the shoes made my legs look like golf clubs. I put on the pencil midi skirt I'd worn to my interview at Clickfrenzy, but I couldn't find the top I'd worn with it – and then I remembered that I'd put it in the tumble drier and shrunk it beyond salvaging, so my lucky outfit was no more. I couldn't wear leggings or jeans – I just couldn't, not without abandoning my self-respect altogether and losing what little fashion-cred I had.

When in doubt, crowd-source, Gemma, I told myself. So I put together four vaguely appropriate looks, Instagrammed myself wearing them, asked my viewers to vote on the best one and went to sleep.

I made my way to my meeting with Sloane Cassidy the next day wearing white trousers that were meant to be ankle-skimming but I was sure looked as if they were just too short, together with a stripy T-shirt and a scarf with poppies on it, which I hadn't managed to tie in a way that didn't look stupid, however many video tutorials I watched.

The first words Sloane Cassidy said to me were: "Oh my God, you got your viewers to dress you! Gemma, that's just too adorable."

It hadn't occurred to me that she might check my channel and see if I'd uploaded anything overnight. I felt my face turn bright red, which at least matched not only the stripes on my top, but also the scarlet feature wall of the meeting room into which she ushered me.

"I'm just so psyched to meet you," she gushed. "Have a seat, make yourself at home. We want all our talent to feel right at home here. Help yourself to candy."

There was a huge bowl of jelly beans on the table. Apart from them and the wall, everything else in the room was white. I felt utterly foolish, as if I'd dressed to match the decor, and wished I'd thought to do a Google image search and see what the place I was going to actually looked like.

Sloane, in stark contrast to me, looked immaculate. She was wearing a stark little black dress that made her waist look tiny and her bottom look smaller than I suspected it actually was. Her shoes were black too, with sky-high heels that had that geometric thing going on, so they looked like they'd been attached to the shoes upside down, and I knew that however simple they looked, they had cost a fortune. Her glossy dark hair was twisted up on top of her head and held with a silver chopstick thing in a style that looked effortlessly simple, but I knew would have required straighteners, curling tongs, back-combing and half a can of hairspray to achieve. Likewise, she was working a 'no make-up make-up' look that takes at least a dozen different products and about six brushes to get right.

"What can I get you to drink?" Her accent was American – or maybe Canadian, I couldn't tell. "Tea? Coffee? Juice? Soda?"

"Just a glass of water, please," I said, and she picked up the white telephone on the table and said, "Could we have two waters in meeting room one, sweetie? Oh – one of each, I think. Why not?

"Now, Gemma. SparklyGems – I love that name, it's so cute – tell me all about yourself."

So, after taking a too-big gulp of fizzy water that almost came out of my nose and made my eyes stream, I did. I told her about starting the vlog, hoping, like so many people, that I'd become the next big thing, and how when I hadn't, my enthusiasm had waned and the frequency of my posts declined. I told her about Jack and being dumped and the video going viral. It felt weird confiding stuff like this to a stranger – but it wasn't as if anything I said was news to her. She'd even known what I was going to be wearing before I'd walked through the door.

"And you have how many subscribers now?" she asked, even though of course she already knew that, too.

"Thirty-eight thousand," I said. "At least, that's how many I had this morning. It keeps changing."

"It keeps growing, you mean! And other social channels – where else do you have a presence?"

I told her about my Twitter and Instagram feeds. "I don't post much, though. Just to tell people when I've uploaded something new."

I didn't tell her about Clickfrenzy and the cats, even though my articles on there got far more hits than all my videos put together.

While I talked, she nodded enthusiastically, occasionally tapping a note into her tablet.

"Right," she said. "Now, I'll tell you a little more about Ripple Effect and what we do here. When Megan, our founder and MD, started the business, it was a modelling agency. Have you done any modelling at all? No? I thought, with your height… Anyways, Megs soon realised that there was this huge, exciting pool of talent out there in new media, people creating content in a way we've never seen before. She figured there was massive potential there – a way to harness the passion and the energy not only of the creators, but of their fans, too. But you're not here for a history lesson, right? The point is, we're here now, and we work with some of the biggest names in the business."

She gestured to the wall – not the red one – where a selection of naturally posed yet carefully retouched photos hung in white frames. A stunning blonde girl running through a field with a golden retriever. A black woman with an impossibly perfect, toned body, grinning at the camera as she did a bicep curl. Two cute boys who looked like they must be identical twins.

"You must recognise most of our other clients," she said.

"Some of them. I… I'm new to all this. I watch other people's videos, but mostly they're the ones like me, who aren't famous."

"You guys," she breathed. "You're just amazing, you know? I never stop being amazed by the level of creativity, the ability to just come up with awesome, original ideas all the time."

"I don't think they're necessarily original," I said, blushing. "I mean, I don't think I've done anything that other people haven't done, really."

"But it's the way you do it," Sloane said. "There's something about you that appeals to viewers, else you wouldn't be getting the hits you're getting after such a short time. But I didn't bring you here to make you all big-headed! I brought you here to talk about how we can work together to tap into your talent and maximise your potential. And, I hope, start getting you a good income from this."

"I got my first payment yesterday," I admitted. "It was tiny, but I'm really excited about it."

"Rightly so! But once you become even better known, we can open doors to even more lucrative opportunities."

She talked a bit about endorsements and product placements and merchandise and affiliate links until I began to feel as if my brain was about to seize up. I knew that people made money from

YouTube, that vlogging could be a business – of course I did – but I had no idea of the complexity of it, the idea that someone might be willing to pay me for having a particular brand of oat milk in my fridge. Except I didn't drink oat milk, and it wasn't my fridge, it was Hannah and Richard's. It felt as if Sloane was talking about somebody else, not me.

She must have noticed me glazing over, because she said, "But that's all far in the future! For now, I'd see my role as helping and supporting you, being a listening ear, and most importantly, plugging you in to a network of people like yourself, so you can collaborate and share ideas – and share viewers, too. We believe, here at Ripple Effect, that the whole is greater than the sum of the parts. Am I right?"

"Yes, of course," I said.

"Anyhow," she said. "I've talked enough, and I hope I've given you plenty to think about. We'd love to represent you, Gemma. But I don't expect a decision today – or even next week. This is your career – take your time, talk to your friends, your mom… get back to me whenever you're ready."

"Thanks," I said. "I'll do that." But I already knew that I was going to say yes.

I realised I was being dismissed. My head was buzzing with about a zillion more questions I knew I needed to ask, but I couldn't think what any of them were right now. My mouth was dry in spite of the water I'd been sipping, and my palms felt at once clammy and sticky.

"Oh, wait," Sloane said. "Take this." She pulled a bright yellow envelope from her squashy leather document holder and handed it to me. "We're throwing a party next week, for the launch of the

Berry Boys' new book. You should come along. Meet the gang. Our parties are legendary."

And with that she showed me out.

Over the past few weeks, while juggling what had begun to feel like a whole bunch of separate lives, I'd found myself falling into a new routine. In the evenings after work, I'd stop off at The Daily Grind and spend a couple of hours there with my laptop, drinking coffee, editing a video ready to post and responding to comments on the last one. There were more and more of them, more people were liking my content and I had more subscribers, too. As the numbers crept upwards and I began to dream of getting to six figures, this process was taking longer and longer. I spent more time editing my videos, because I knew that they were being seen by more people – and I never stopped hoping that, maybe, Jack was watching my channel. That, maybe, he'd see the details I posted about my life and realise what he was missing, realise that it was me he wanted to be with and not Olivia.

I even allowed myself to indulge in fantasies in which he posted a picture on Instagram of himself in an airport somewhere, with his backpack on his back but no Olivia by his side, saying something like, *You know when you wake up one morning and realise you've made the biggest mistake of your life? #Cominghome.*

But he never did, and eventually the fantasy became more of a habit than a hope – a habit I tried without success to break. And so, one Wednesday night at The Daily Grind, I drank the cold dregs of my coffee, snapped a picture of the empty cup and posted it on my Instagram account. *Editing fuel! Look out for a new video on my channel later on tonight.* Then, knowing I shouldn't, knowing I wouldn't see the post I longed for, I clicked on Jack's feed.

It was full of images of him and Olivia. Them holding a surfboard and laughing like maniacs. Them outside the Sydney Opera House. Them sharing a giant ice-cream cone. Them constantly laughing or kissing or sometimes both at once. It was like when you pick a scab you thought was healing, but discover the wound underneath is still a raw, bleeding mess.

I quickly clicked away, and went on Facebook instead. And then I noticed a weird thing. Facebook's weird anyway, right? You see things like Nancy being on holiday in the Maldives, and realise you'd totally missed the run-up to it. You see that the dorky guy you were at school with whose friend request you only accepted for the lolz has somehow gone and got himself In a Relationship with some beautiful, successful woman, proving once and for all that life is full of strangeness. But one thing you don't do is actually count your friends, because that would be tragic. But even so, I was quite sure that I had ten or twenty fewer than the last time I'd looked. I searched for Olivia's name and, sure enough, she'd defriended me. So had Calliope, her best mate. So had Shivvy. Katie hadn't, but I could tell when I looked at her feed that she'd changed her settings so I couldn't now see things I'd been able to see before.

I tried to make myself not cry, but I couldn't. The screen went all blurry and massive tear splatted down on to my trackpad, making the cursor on my screen jump.

"Hey, Gemma." I hadn't noticed Raffy appear next to me with a cloth and a spray bottle. He squirted cleaning fluid over the next-door table and wiped it. "Are you okay? I'm sorry. Daft question. You're not okay."

I tried to laugh, but it didn't sound right. "I am, really. It's just… Looking at pictures of my ex and his new girlfriend. And loads of people I thought almost liked me have culled me on Facebook. I know, it's like I'm fifteen. But it hurts. I'm such a dick."

I attempted the laughing thing again, but this time it came out even weirder and ended on a sort of hiccup.

Raffy picked up my coffee cup. "Hold on one second," he said. "I'm just about to close up."

I snapped my laptop shut. "Oh God, I'm so sorry. I've been sitting here ages. I've totally lost track of the time. I'll head off home."

"If you want," he said. "Only, I was going to say… we keep a bottle of bourbon behind the counter, strictly for emergencies. This looks like it might be one."

I thought about going back to Richard and Hannah's house, and the carton of carrot soup I'd been going to microwave for my dinner. I thought about going up to my room afterwards and the video I was going to post, and how I wouldn't be able to stop myself from scrolling through Jack's Instagram feed again and again, torturing myself with what I saw. I thought what a stupid idea it was to have a private lock-in in a coffee shop with a bottle of bourbon and man I hardly knew.

"You know what? I think it is an emergency," I said.

"Don't go anywhere," Raffy said. "I'm on it."

"So yeah, I got dumped. Your little niece will probably have seen me looking stupid talking about it on YouTube. I expect I swore and stuff and your sister's going to hate me. But what's so shit is that I thought I was making him jealous of my amazing life, when actually my life isn't amazing at all. All I've got is a rented room in a house with a pair of right weirdos, and my job that I thought was going to be so awesome is all about finding pictures of cats. Not that there's anything wrong with cats. They're cute and everything, but – sorry, I'm rambling."

It was half an hour later, I'd had two – or it might have been three – shots of bourbon, and I was rambling like a good 'un. I'd told Raffy how Jack had ended our relationship with a curt email, how I'd seen the picture of them together and realised that Jack's relationship with Olivia had pre-dated the end of his with me.

"Ramble away," Raffy said, splashing more whisky into our glasses.

"I thought that if I vlogged all the time, he'd think I had this perfect life. But my life's not perfect. It's boring and a bit shit – all I do is go to work and write stuff to make people click, because the Google metrics say they will. The other day I made a smoothie with kale, to show how into being healthy I am. I fucking hate kale. And I buy clothes and then take them back to the shop the next day because I can't afford them. None of it's even real. I'm a fraud."

I sniffed loudly and took another gulp of my drink. "Sorry," I said.

"Don't be sorry, Gemma." Throughout the time I'd been talking – ranting, more like – and caning the bourbon, Raffy had been sitting opposite me, his elbow on the table and his chin in his hand, barely moving except to top up our glasses and to push his hair back off his forehead. His face was very still, as if his attention was focussed entirely on me, but when he smiled it suddenly came alive, his teeth and eyes bright and somehow warm, even though their colour was cold.

I said, "I am sorry. I've wanged on and on about me and not asked you anything about you."

"I'm just the guy who works in the coffee shop," he said, his amazing smile flashing out again and lighting up his whole face.

"Obviously, I know that," I said. "But why?"

"I like coffee," he said. "Even though I'm shit at taking orders. And I like my mate Luke, and I offered to help him out when the girl who was working here went home to Madrid, because I wasn't doing too much else at the moment. And I like talking to people."

"Having people talk at you, more like," I said.

Raffy shrugged and said, "That too. All part of the service."

I said, "I just need to go to the bathroom. 'Scuse me."

Standing up, I realised I was actually quite pissed. I had to concentrate hard to walk in a straight line to the loo, and when I looked at my face in the mirror as I washed my hands, I realised I looked quite pissed, too. My nose was all shiny where my foundation had rubbed off and there were massive black smudges of mascara under my eyes. Even my hair was a mess. I repaired the damage as best I could, thankful that the 'what's in my handbag' vlog had involved installing a fully equipped make-up bag that definitely wouldn't have been there before. I wished I'd thought to include toothpaste, but I hadn't. Or condoms.

I made my way back to the table where Raffy was waiting. He wasn't tapping away at his phone, as most people do when they're left alone for ten minutes. He was just waiting. He looked like he was thinking, and I wondered if he'd been thinking about me.

I sat down again, this time on the chair next to him instead of the one on the opposite side of the table.

"Raffy," I said. "Do you think I'm pretty?"

He laughed, then his face settled into seriousness again. "Gemma, I don't know your ex – this Jack bloke – but I can tell you one thing with absolute, one hundred per cent certainty. Your relationship ending had precisely fuck all to do with how you look. Okay? So don't even go there."

"No, but…" I said.

"Gemma, you're fishing. But if you insist, I'll tell you something else. Even if Olivia looks like – I don't know, like Emma Watson or someone – that still isn't what this is about. And don't go thinking it is, because that way madness lies."

I said, "What about you?"

"What about me?" Raffy said. "Do I look like Emma Watson?"

"No!" I put my elbow on the table and tried to prop my chin on my hand, as Raffy had done, and look at him alluringly through my eyelashes. But my elbow somehow slid off. I took another sip of my drink, but the glass was empty and Raffy didn't fill it again.

"I'll fetch you some water," he said.

"Have you got a girlfriend?" I blurted out.

"Nope." He put a jug of water on the table between us. I couldn't help noticing that, although he'd appeared to be drinking at the same rate I had, he was walking quite straight, unlike me. I sloshed water into our glasses, and rather a lot went over the table.

"No girlfriend? Why not?"

"I was seeing someone, a woman I worked with, until about six months ago. It didn't work out. No big deal."

I reached out and brushed my fingers over his arm. It felt nice – hard and smooth and warm.

"Where do you live?" I asked.

Raffy said, "Here. In the flat above the shop. They're between tenants, so I'm squatting here for the moment."

I said, "Can I see?"

Raffy stood up again, and I stood up too, but somehow my feet weren't where they were supposed to be, and I found myself tipping and almost falling. He put out a hand to save me, and I clutched it, then put both arms around his neck. I felt his arms around me, and the length of our bodies pressing together. Up close, I could smell his hair – it smelled of shampoo and coffee. Because I was wearing high heels, my eyes were almost level with his and I could see their colour, a pale greeny-blue like glass. I could feel his breath on my cheek, warm and quick.

I closed my eyes, waiting for the moment when he would kiss me. But it didn't come.

"Gemma," he said gently, "I think you need to go home."

Chapter Nine

I was having a dream about drinking water. A huge glass of water, cold from the fridge. Or maybe it was Sprite – sweet and fizzy and wonderfully wet. I drank and drank, but I was still thirsty. It was the thirst that woke me up, and I would have given anything to go back to sleep. My mouth tasted foul, my head was pounding and my stomach was churning.

I curled up tighter under the duvet as memories of the night before came crashing back. Any hope I might have had about Jack changing his mind and coming back to me was gone. And I'd told Raffy about it – my God. A virtual stranger. I'd cried. And I'd got drunk. And – fuck. The duvet wasn't sufficient to bury my mortification – I pulled the pillow over my head, too. I'd made a pass at him. A massive, stupid, drunken pass.

And that wasn't even the worst thing. The worst thing was that he'd turned me down. He'd walked me home and given me a hug and waited until the door had closed behind me, and then he'd gone home. I remembered the expression on his face as he gently untangled my arms from around his neck – sympathy and slight, carefully disguised amusement.

Jack didn't love me. Raffy didn't want me. And I didn't blame either of them one bit.

"Oh my God," I said to Stanley, my words muffled by the pillow. "I am the world's biggest dick. No contest. I tried to hook up with the poor guy, and he doesn't even fancy me. I'm totally going to have to find somewhere else to buy my coffee now."

I turned over and gingerly peered out at the morning, then checked my phone. It was half past six – too early to get up, but I knew I wasn't going to be able to get back to sleep. I scrolled quickly through the comments on my vlog, then checked my email and my calendar, and said again, "Oh my God. Oh fuck. The bloody Berry Boys party is tonight. Do I have to go, Stanley?" My teddy regarded me silently from the pillow. "Yes, of course I do. But I definitely, definitely don't want to. Everyone there will know one another. They're 'the gang'. But Sloane said I ought to go, and I don't want her to know what a wimp I am. And I could do a vlog about it, I suppose. But I won't know anyone. And I've got nothing to wear. And I've got the worst hangover in the history of the world, ever. Aaaargh, I don't know! What am I going to do? And who are the Berry Boys, anyway?"

Stanley was no help. Reluctantly, I got out of bed and dressed for work. I'd leave it in the hands of fate, I decided – I'd go to Topshop in my lunch break, and if I found something to wear that cost less than my remaining YouTube money, I'd go. If not, I wouldn't.

I knew as soon as I stepped off the escalator at five minutes past one that the shopping gods had made their decision. For once, I wasn't going to have to rifle through rack after rack of dresses that all turned out to be too short, or looked fine on the hanger but then had some weird thing wrong with them like a belt that wasn't in the same place as my waist or a corsage that sat right over one of my nipples. There, hanging right in front of me on a sale rack, was a pale pink midi dress with cutaway straps and a low back. It was gorgeous. It looked like it would cost a fortune but was exactly forty pounds. It even went with the silver flip-flops I was wearing. And so what if my black bra was completely unsuitable to wear with it – I'd just leave it off. For once, my flat-chestedness was a blessing instead of a curse.

"You shall go to the ball, Gemma," I told myself in the mirror, not caring that it sounded more like a threat than a promise.

I changed in the ladies' after work, topped up my make-up and made my way to the Tube, feeling increasingly nervous. I'd tried to snatch a moment to look at the Berry Boys' channel, but I'd only glimpsed a couple of lads wearing masks running after each other brandishing water pistols and laughing uncontrollably. Then Jim came and asked me a question about my 'Cats 1, Dogs 0 – See 21 Felines Totally Nailing It' story, and I'd got caught up with work for the rest of the afternoon, so I was none the wiser.

On the Tube, I pulled the invitation from its yellow envelope and read it again.

They've taken YouTube by storm with their pranks, challenges and crazy collabs. Now, the twins who took over the internet have arrived in print. Join us at Wishy Washy for the launch of Two *– the summer's zaniest read.*

The rest of the invitation was taken up with details of the venue – Wishy Washy (housed in a disused launderette, obviously) was a bar so tooth-achingly cool that even I had heard of it. I tried to go there once with Jack, Olivia and some of their friends when we were on a night out in London, but we got turned away at the door with barely a glance. At least that meant I'd be able to find it without having to shamble along staring at the map on my phone like a tourist.

There was no steely out-of-work model guarding the door tonight. Two friendly guys about my age, one with a massive beard and the other with his hair twisted into a topknot, welcomed me in with barely a glance at my invitation. For a second I thought, *Are they the Berry Boys?* But there had been no beard poking from under either mask in the few seconds of video I'd seen.

I stepped inside and paused for a moment, tucking my sunglasses into my bag and waiting for my eyes to adjust to the darkness. There was a faint but distinctive smell of freshly washed laundry in the air – could it be left over from the place's former incarnation? That wasn't possible – they must pipe it in somehow. Then I saw the lines of sheets and pillowcases hanging from the ceiling – presumably some staff member went to an actual launderette every few days to put them through a boil wash and top up their scent.

The room was already full of people, standing around in groups chatting and drinking. Almost all of them had a glass in one hand and their phone or camera in the other, and were filming their conversations. I wondered whether taking out my own phone would make me feel less out of place, but I couldn't quite bring myself to do it – I was sure I'd be clocked as a newbie and a fraud straight away.

Instead, I made my way to the bar and pretended to be engrossed in the menu for a bit. All the cocktails were laundry-themed too – it was seriously cool. For a moment, I imagined texting Jack and telling him about it, and then I remembered that that wasn't going to happen, not now or ever again. God, I wished he was there right now. I wished anyone I knew was, even Olivia. I swallowed the sense of loss that welled up inside me and forced myself not to mind. I had to move on – I had moved on. I was here, wasn't I, an invited guest in this most fabulous of places? I didn't need them, I told myself. I didn't need anyone. But I knew it wasn't true.

"I'll have a Whiter-Than-White, please," I said to the barman. A few minutes of measuring, shaking and squeezing later, he was done. Drink in hand, I turned to make my way into the crowd and try and locate Sloane.

Then I paused.

"Oh, and my friend asked me to get a drink for her, as well," I said. "What would you recommend?"

At least now people see me with a drink in each hand and think that I must, obviously, know at least one other person there. Or that I was a degenerate alcoholic, of course.

"What kind of thing does she like? Fruity? Maybe a Fast Spin? Or something longer? A Pre-Soak? Or the Energy-Saver is alcohol free."

"I'll go for a Pre-Soak," I said. I watched as he scooped ice, measured coconut milk, added dashes of various spirits, stirred and shook. I willed it to take forever, but of course it didn't. I now had the requisite two drinks, and I'd run out of excuses.

The room had filled up some more while I was at the bar. I stepped tentatively out into the throng. I couldn't see Sloane anywhere. But there, I was sure, was the stunning black woman I'd seen in the photo on Sloane's wall. She was surrounded by chattering friends, juggling her camera and a bottle of sparkling water as she gestured and laughed. She looked impossibly confident and self-possessed.

And there, leaning against the wall, talking into an actual, proper camera, not one of the small ones that almost everyone else seemed to have permanently welded to their hands, surrounded by microphones and lights, was… No. It couldn't be. There was, like, literally no way I was in the same room, breathing the same air, as Harry Styles. Even though I was totally over my teenage crush on him, this was epic. It was immense.

I was so transfixed by the sight of my former hero that I forgot to look where I was going. I took another step forward, heard a voice say, "Ouch!" and felt an icy wave of Pre-Soak splash down my front.

"Fuck! Can't you look where you're going?"

I tore my eyes away from Harry and towards the person who'd spilled coconut-based cocktail all over my brand new dress.

"I was looking where I was going," I lied. "You stepped right out in front of me. And look what you've done to my dress."

"Hmmm, yes," he said. "Nice."

I glanced down and realised that the icy cocktail had made the thin satin cling to my skin, and I wished I hadn't been such a complete idiot as not to wear a bra. I averted my eyes from my chest and, to his credit, so did the man I'd collided with.

"Sorry," he said. "My bad." And he smiled a smile of such self-effacing charm that I couldn't help smiling back. Even though it was so dark, even though Harry Styles was just a few feet away, I couldn't take my eyes off him. It was as if there was a spotlight trained on his head.

He was only a bit taller than me. But lots of guys are shorter, so any bit is a bit worth having. He was wearing what I guessed would have been proper black-tie gear, only the shirt was unbuttoned to reveal a white T-shirt underneath, and the bow tie was undone too. I could see a tattoo snaking over his collarbone from the top of the T-shirt. His hair was golden-blonde and seemed to reflect what little light there was as dazzlingly as his perfect teeth.

Then he said, "But I haven't thanked you. You brought me my drink." And he took the Pre-Soak out of my hand and sipped it. "Yummy."

I thought about trying to defend my imaginary friend's right to her cocktail, but decided against it.

"It's a Pre-Soak," I said. "Appropriate, in the circumstances."

I saw him try not to look at my dress again and succeed, then fail. I felt a quick, delicious surge of power.

"They ought to do a cocktail called a Dry-Clean-Only," I said.

"They probably do." He drained the glass. "You've finished yours. Let's go and find out."

He headed off into the crowd and I followed. But then a weird thing happened. People seemed to close around him like iron filings around a magnet, and I was distant enough to be excluded from the force field. There were two people between him and me, then six, then I bumped into a table and had to go around it, and I lost sight of his golden head in the gloom.

It was fine. I'd make my way to the bar and find him there, and if I didn't, I'd go home, satisfied that I had actually talked – even flirted – with a stranger. But then, heading towards me, I saw the familiar smiling features.

"Gotcha." I reached out my hand and clasped his. But, instead of the grin of acknowledgement I'd expected, I was met with a look of total bewilderment.

"Hello," he said.

"Hey," I said. "Come on, let's go and get that Dry-Clean-Only."

And then I looked again, and I realised that somehow, the bow tie had magically tied itself again. The tattoo had vanished. The smile that had lit the room was dimmed like it had been replaced with a low-wattage, eco-friendly bulb.

"Sorry," I said, "I thought…"

I stumbled away, bewildered. I wasn't used to drinking any more. A few shots of whisky the night before had knocked me sideways. And now I was hitting on random men for no reason at all. I was even – no. This couldn't be happening. I was seeing double.

"Augustus," a voice laughed in my ear. "Step away from the girl in the pink dress. I saw her first. And anyway, she literally doesn't know who we are."

Belatedly, I realised. I looked up and noticed for the first time the huge poster above the bar: the cover of the book everyone was there to help launch. It was the same bright, stinging yellow as the invitation, with the word *TWO* in huge letters at the top, and at the bottom in slightly smaller letters, *By Gus and Charlie Berry, aka the Berry Boys.*

The rest of the cover was taken up with a photo of a man's face, only it was split in half down the middle and if I looked hard, I could see that the two halves didn't quite match up, although they almost did. The same way the faces grinning down at me were almost exactly the same, but not.

"I so do," I said. "Everyone does. You're properly famous."

"YouTube famous," Gus said. "Not quite the same thing."

I looked closely at him, trying to imprint in my mind the things that made him different from Charlie. I'd been caught out once; I was determined not to let it happen to me again. Making a fool of myself once a night was quite enough – more than enough. There was Charlie's tattoo, obviously. Gus's hair was a bit longer, styled into a high quiff while Charlie's was a slick short back and sides. Gus was slightly taller, Charlie slightly broader shouldered. But they were tiny differences. If you ran into one of them in the street and the other wasn't there, chances are you'd find yourself saying, "Hey Gus!" when it was Charlie, or vice versa.

"Anyway, we know who you are," Charlie said, interrupting my inspection of them. "Don't we, Gus?"

"Of course we do," Gus said. "Gemma Grey. Not properly famous. Not even YouTube famous. But people have noticed you."

"No wonder," Charlie said, "in that dress."

I took a big gulp of my drink, hoping the icy cocktail would somehow stem the flood of hot colour I could feel creeping up my neck. "So, tell me about your book," I said.

"It's the hottest read of the summer," Gus said.

"It's a hilarious look at the madcap lives and stratospheric rise to stardom of two of YouTube's most successful creators," Charlie said.

"It gives you all the low-down on what we get up to when the cameras are off."

"Plus never-heard-before goss about your favourite celebs."

"Hilarious pranks and gags for you to try at home."

"Fashion and gaming advice."

"And blank pages for you to fill in and make the book your own."

"Or so we're told," Charlie said.

"We didn't write it, obviously," said Gus.

"We've read it, though," said Charlie, as if this was a major achievement.

"Well, I read the front half," Gus said.

"And I read the back. Because, teamwork."

"But, to be fair, it did only come out today. And Sloane says it's good."

"And if Sloane likes it, that's cool with us."

"And it sold more copies pre-release than any other book published this year."

"Or this century. Or something."

I'd followed this rapid-fire exchange like someone watching a game of ping-pong, mutely gawping as the conversation bounced between them, waiting for there to be an opportunity – or a need – for me to participate. But now it seemed the point was over – who had won, if there was even a winner, I couldn't tell.

"Gemma needs another drink," Charlie said. "And so do I."

"Go get one then," Gus said.

"I'll go," I said. "What would you like?"

"You aren't going anywhere," Charlie said. "You're going to stay with me, and I'll tell you all the insider goss about your favourite celebs. You won't even have to read the book. How lucky are you?"

I laughed, not knowing whether to be amused or shocked that they were so staggeringly indiscreet about the work attributed to them.

"Who did write it, anyway?" I asked.

"Guy called Jamie Fletcher," Charlie said. "He's a journalist. Writes for *Heat* magazine. He's here somewhere. Go on, mate, get Gemma and me a drink."

Reluctantly, Gus sloped off to the bar. Charlie draped his arm around my shoulder and leaned in close. I could smell his aftershave – it was something citrussy and sharp.

"So, who do you want to hear about? Go on, ask me anything. I know everyone here."

"Since you knew me, I guess you do," I said.

"You're different," Charlie said. For a second, our eyes met. His were a deep denim blue, framed with long lashes so dark and feathery they looked like they'd been applied in a salon. Then he looked away again. "You're new."

I felt a little lurch of disappointment. Was he only talking to me because I was an unfamiliar face in what I was beginning to suspect was a highly incestuous world?

"Okay, then, tell me about the girl over there, dancing – the one with the blonde hair and the amazing legs."

"Maddie," Charlie said. "She's got a fitness channel. All about her yoga and raw food diet. She went out with Gus for a bit, but he finished it because she's so incredibly boring. She used to turn up at the flat with all her food for the day in Tupperware boxes and then she'd spend all the time looking at her watch waiting for it to be time to eat again. Nice girl, though."

"And him? Over there by the bar on his own?"

"Glen Renton," Charlie said. "My God, you really are new to this, aren't you? Glen's got, like, eight million subscribers. That's more than a million more than us. Everyone fucking hates him, though."

Before I could ask why, Gus reappeared with our drinks. "One Power Rinse, one Mangle," he said, handing them over. I looked at him and Charlie again. They were so similar – yet there was something entirely different about them. Like a pair of very beautiful shoes, a left and a right. No – like those mask icons that people use to represent theatre, totally identical, except one's happy and the other sad. Charlie was all cheer and energy; Gus wasn't. There was something subdued about Gus, a restraint, as if he was keeping an important part of himself firmly battened down. But for me, the difference was far clearer and more visceral. I didn't know why, but I knew it for sure: I fancied Charlie and I didn't fancy Gus. And that was a good thing, because it was Charlie's arm that was still casually draped around my shoulders.

"I'm going out for a fag," Gus said. "Coming?"

"Okay," Charlie said. "Don't let Sloane see you, though."

I didn't say anything. I waited for Charlie to move his arm from around my shoulders, which I'd take as my signal that our conversation was over and it was time for me to leave. But he didn't, so I let myself be guided back towards the door. Gus hurried ahead of us, extracting a pack of cigarettes and a lighter from the pocket of his dinner jacket as he walked.

He pushed open the door just as one of the doormen said, "I wouldn't go out that way if I were you, mate."

But it was too late. The street, which had been empty and silent when I arrived, was now heaving with people – mostly, from the brief glance I was able to get, teenage girls. I could hear a babble of excited chatter, which turned instantly to screams of excitement.

"There's Charlie!"

"There's Gus!"

"Oh my God, it's actually them!"

"Gus! Charlie!"

A hundred camera flashes exploded; Charlie's arm dropped off my shoulder as if I'd suddenly become radioactive. Gus shot backwards, almost knocking me off my feet and spilling my new drink, fortunately not all over me. The door slammed shut.

"Fuck," Gus said.

"Someone must have leaked the venue details," Charlie said.

"Where the hell is Sloane?" Gus said.

"Right here." She appeared behind us. "I see you guys have met Gemma. Cool."

"It's fucking madness out there," Gus said. "Every fourteen-year-old in London's camped out outside the door."

"Yeah," Sloane said. "No idea how that could have happened. I guess someone must have seen Harry leaving and put it out on Twitter." She looked pleased, I thought, and not entirely surprised. But I had no opportunity to analyse her expression.

"We could go out there," Charlie said reluctantly. "Sign some books. Give them some selfies."

"No fucking way," Sloane and Gus said at the same time.

"It's too dangerous," Sloane said. "Without proper crowd control, those kids are going to get hurt. It's a health and safety nightmare."

"What about my fag?" Gus grumbled.

"You'll have to wait for that," Sloane said. "We're going to have to smuggle you out of here. There's no way you'll get out the front and now they know you're here they won't leave until gone midnight."

"Gemma's coming with us," Charlie said. "Unless you have to be somewhere else?"

I thought about playing hard to get, pretending I had another, even better party to go on to. I thought about work the next day, and the three cocktails I'd drunk already without any food. And then I thought about how Charlie's body had felt holding me against him, the echo of fragrance I'd smelled on his skin. I remembered how everyone in the room had turned and watched us as we walked towards the door. "I… No, I don't have to be anywhere," I said.

Sloane looked at me, a cool, assessing stare. "Right. Great. We'll get all three of you out then. Give me five."

She disappeared into the crowd. Charlie, Gus and I finished our drinks and waited. A couple of people I didn't recognise came over to say goodbye and thanks for the invites, and film themselves doing so. Gus removed the unlit cigarette from his mouth when the cameras were on him, then put it back afterwards.

Then Sloane reappeared. "Right. One baseball cap, one fedora, two pairs of shades, one parka. I borrowed this lot from the staff here – I'll pick them up from The Factory tomorrow. And one Berry Boys T-shirt. Hiding in plain sight, right? Who wants what? Gemma doesn't need a disguise; no one will recognise her. Not yet, anyway," she added, almost under her breath.

After a brief tussle over who got to wear the fedora and parka and who'd be stuck with the T-shirt and baseball cap, which Gus won, we were ready to escape.

"Uber back to The Factory?" Sloane said.

What's she talking about? I wondered. But before I could ask, Gus said, "It's only half nine. I want to go on to Shoreditch House."

Sloane's eyes narrowed. "Now, Gus, you know you can't…"

"Calm down, Sloane. Just for a couple of drinks. I'm not going to fall out of there at three in the morning with coke on my tie."

"That's what you said last…" she stopped. "All right. Charlie, promise you'll make sure your brother's on best behaviour."

"I don't want to go to Shoreditch House," Charlie said. "I want to go home with Gemma. If Gemma wants to come. Do you, Gemma? You'll love The Factory. We can watch Netflix and chill."

"Netflix and chill?" I burst out laughing. "Do you think I've been living under a rock?"

Charlie blushed, and I liked him even more. "We've got a hot tub on the balcony," he said.

"I want to go to Shoreditch House," Gus said, as petulantly as a child.

I said, "Maybe if the guys left separately, people wouldn't be so likely to recognise them. If they're watching out for twins, I mean."

"Good thinking, Batman," Charlie said.

"Yes," Sloane said. "Good call. Right. You two head off, and I'll go for a drink with Gus. Just the one, mind."

Gus agreed, looking mutinous at the idea of being chaperoned on his night out, and Charlie and I left the back way, through the kitchen, pausing only for a selfie with a Romanian waitress who almost dropped a tray of glasses when she saw him, and climbed into the waiting cab.

Now that we were alone, I felt suddenly shy with Charlie, and I sensed he felt the same – or maybe it was his brother's absence that rendered him silent and awkward. Maybe he could only function as part of a double act, I thought, looking across the expanse of leather seat to where he sat biting the skin around his thumb and alternately looking out of the window and staring at his phone.

We said nothing to each other the whole journey, which is not quite as bad as it sounds, because it was one of the shortest cab rides I'd ever taken in my life. Normally, I'd have walked and not given it a second thought, or jumped on a bus if my shoes were hurting. But in Charlie's world, you got a cab, even if it only took five minutes.

"The Factory," the driver said.

"Cheers, mate," Charlie said, opening the door and swinging his long legs out. For a moment, I considered asking the driver to take me home, or tapping the Uber icon on my own phone and asking him that way. But then Charlie appeared on my side of the car and opened the door for me, and offered me his arm to help me out, his sweet smile in place again, and I was lost.

"Welcome to The Factory," he said. "Manhattan-style loft living in the heart of east London. It used to be a factory that made – stuff, I can't remember what. Buttons or something, probably. It's a landmark architectural development, appaz. That's what the estate agent said anyway. Come on up."

I followed him into the lift and he pressed the button for the third floor. Clearly, Charlie Berry took the same approach to walking up stairs as he did to walking along streets. I was going to tease him about it, but there wasn't time; the lift opened, we stepped out and Charlie unlocked a bright orange-painted door.

"My God," I breathed, stepping in. "It's huge." The polished concrete floor spread ahead of me for what seemed like miles. In the distance, I could see a group of sofas, a dining table and chairs, and a space-age kitchen. The exposed brick walls were hung with massive canvasses splashed with brilliant colour. Mismatched industrial-style light fittings hung from the steel beams. There was camera equipment everywhere: lights, tripods, reflectors and other things whose purpose I could only guess at.

"So this is where the magic happens?" I said, trying to sound off-hand and not a bit impressed. But Charlie seemed impervious to my sarcasm.

"Like it? We sometimes skateboard around," Charlie said. "Gus wants to get a Swegway."

"Maybe a bicycle would be better," I said. "Or a season ticket for the commute between the door and your computer."

He laughed. "Anyway, let's have a drink. And I'm starving, aren't you?"

I realised I was. And although I knew I shouldn't have any more to drink, I wanted to take the edge off the sudden rush of nervousness I felt. I followed Charlie across the expanse of floor to the kitchen and watched as he opened a glass-fronted fridge and took out a bottle of champagne. Then he opened the freezer and looked gloomily inside.

"Fucking fish fingers," he said. "That's all me and Gus ever cook. Fish finger butties."

"I quite like fishfinger butties," I confessed.

"So do we, obviously. But I can't kiss you if we both taste of fish."

How entitled was he, I thought, assuming that I was going to kiss him. And then I realised that it was in no doubt – I'd come here, hadn't I? I'd let a man I'd just met bring me home. Obviously, I was going to kiss him – and kissing would only be the start of it. And at that moment, I didn't care whether that was sensible, or safe, or what he'd think of me afterwards.

I watched his strong brown hands unwrap the wire cage from the top of the champagne bottle and pull the cork out with an easy twist. He took two glasses from a cupboard and said, "Since there's no dinner, shall we have a go in the hot tub?"

I remembered my black bra, which was stuffed into my handbag and anyway had a massive hole in it where I'd poked a thumbnail through taking it off, and my nude cotton pants, which were totally invisible under clothes and totally hideous without them.

"I've got nothing to wear," I said.

"Oh," Charlie said. He looked briefly flummoxed, then he peeled the yellow Berry Boys T-shirt off and chucked it over. "Why don't you put that on? I won't look."

He took the bottle and glasses in one hand and opened the door to the balcony, letting in a rush of warm night air and traffic noise. "I'll be just out here."

I hesitated, then slipped off my dress and draped it over the red suede sofa, put on the T-shirt and followed him.

The balcony was almost as huge as the living room, surrounded by plants in pots and open to the night sky. A haze of steam rose from the blue water where Charlie lounged, his body hidden by bubbles.

"Hello," he said.

"Hi," I said. I put one foot into the hot water, then the other, then lowered my body in. The T-shirt billowed absurdly around me, and we both laughed. "Guess I won't be doing any swimwear special vlogs."

"Guess not," Charlie said. "Although if I had to choose someone to model a Berry Boys T-shirt, it would be you, right now."

He handed me a glass of fizz and we clinked and drank. I let my legs drift in the water, and they drifted inexorably towards his. I felt my foot touch his naked thigh, and then his hand reached down into the water and began caressing my ankle. I took another gulp of wine – my throat felt tight and my breath was coming faster, as if I'd been dunked under the water and just come up.

"I'm glad you came, Gemma," Charlie said. "I didn't think you would."

"Don't girls always, when you invite them?"

"I hardly ever do," he said. "Like I said, you're different."

It's not true, said the sensible part of me. *He's telling you what he thinks you want to hear. He must bring girls back here all the time. He must have girls camping outside every club he goes to, wanting him to take them home and show them his hot tub.* But I didn't want to believe that, and the gentle, teasing pressure of his fingers on my leg made me not care anyway.

I looked at his lean shoulders rising up out of the water and longed to brush the droplets from his skin. His hair flopped down over his forehead, whatever products he'd used in it no match for the steam. He pushed it back and I wanted to touch it too. My foot found his chest and slipped down over the hard muscle of his stomach. Jets of water were pummelling my body as firmly as hands; I wanted to feel his actual hands touching me everywhere.

"What are you thinking?" he asked.

"I'm thinking you're too far away," I said.

And then with a rush and a splash we were kissing each other, our glasses abandoned on the floor, my hair floating in the water like seaweed.

I'd never snogged anyone in a hot tub before. Maybe people who've had more practice know a graceful and elegant way to do it, but I didn't, and Charlie didn't appear to, either. We slipped off the seats and got water in our mouths. The sopping wet, too large T-shirt kept getting in the way. It was awkward and hilarious and sexy as hell.

"Come on," he said eventually. "Let's go inside."

He took my hand and we stepped out of the water and back into the flat, and stood dripping on the concrete floor, our bodies pressed together. It was his touch, not the rapidly cooling, sopping wet fabric against my skin that made me shiver, but he said, "You'll catch cold."

I said, "No, I won't." I peeled the T-shirt off and dropped it on to the floor with a loud splat. I started to giggle and couldn't stop, and then I was kissing him again, kissing him and laughing and gasping with pleasure as he touched me.

"What about Gus?" I managed to say. "What if he…"

"They won't be home for ages," Charlie said. "When Gus says one drink he means five, and Sloane will do what he wants."

He pulled me down on to the sofa and we kissed some more, and I reached down and touched him through his soaking wet boxer shorts and heard his groan.

"I haven't got…" I said. "Have you…?"

"Bedroom," he said. "Don't go anywhere."

I lay back and watched him hurry across the room, his legs slightly too long for his body, almost gangly, his skin smooth and tanned. He came back a few seconds later, stepped out of his underwear, snapped on a condom and took me in his arms again. I closed my eyes, loving the way our damp bodies felt together, waiting for his kiss.

"Gemma," he said softly. "Is this okay? Are you sure?"

I opened my eyes and saw my smile reflected by his, his beautiful eyes crinkling at the corners. He had a dimple in his right cheek, another thing that made him different from Gus, different from anyone – unique and perfect.

"I'm very sure," I said.

Half an hour later, we lay together listening to a church clock somewhere strike midnight, our skin drying and our breath returning to normal.

"I think we've ruined your sofa," I said, looking at the dark, wet imprint of our bodies on the suede.

"Doesn't matter," he said. "We'll buy a new one. Or Sloane will tell the interior decorator to."

"Just like that?"

"Yeah, why not? We didn't choose any of this stuff – we wouldn't have a clue how. You should have seen the place where we lived before. It was a right dump. This is pretty cool though, don't you think?"

"It's amazing," I said. Then I trailed my finger down his torso, lightly, from throat to groin. He shivered. "You're amazing too."

"How's your heart?" he asked.

"My what?" I could still feel it beating hard in my chest, but it was returning to normal. "I'm not going to have a coronary, if that's what you mean. Although it was pretty close there at one stage."

"I don't mean that! It being broken, I mean. Your vlog…"

"Oh, that." I paused. If I could see inside myself, into whatever part of me my feelings were kept in, what would it look like? Different from how it had looked that morning, for sure. I'd imagined that there was an emptiness somewhere, a Jack-shaped wound that would never heal. But I couldn't feel it now. I felt sated, happy, a bit drunk and very hungry. "I don't think it's broken any more."

"Good." Charlie kissed me again, stood up and padded over to the fridge for another bottle of champagne. "I'm bloody ravenous now, aren't you?"

"Seriously, legit starving," I said. "I'm even willing to risk a fish-finger sandwich."

"No way," he said, splashing wine into our glasses so the bubbles almost fizzed over the edge. I knew I should tell him to stop, I'd had enough, but I didn't. "I'm trying to impress you, remember? We'll order in."

"Won't everywhere be closed?"

"Nope," he said, reaching for his phone. "Well, most places will. But I have a late-night delivery app. What do you fancy? We can have pizza, curry, noodles, hot dogs or all the above brought to our door in half an hour."

"What a time to be alive," I said.

Chapter Ten

I woke up in my own bed, alone. For a second everything felt normal – just like it had the previous day. Then, just like it had the previous day, the full weight of my hangover descended. But there was one important difference: yesterday, I'd felt rubbish – not just physically, but sick with remorse and shame. Today, I didn't. I sat up in bed and saw, next to my handbag, the goody bag from Charlie and Gus's launch lay, a jaunty yellow reminder of the night before.

I tipped its contents out on to my duvet. There was a copy of *Two*, signed in a black Sharpie scrawl with Gus and Charlie's names. There was a sparkly cherry-flavoured lip gloss. There was a yellow T-shirt just like the one I'd worn in the hot tub the night before. There were a few make-up samples from a brand I'd never heard of – presumably some vlogger who'd just launched her own product range and was hoping to piggyback on the Berry Boys' success. There was a colouring-in book and a pack of crayons.

I looked at Charlie's face on the book cover. "Well, that was fun," I said aloud. "I guess I won't be seeing you again."

And the weird thing was, I didn't really care. As I showered and got ready for work, snatches of the night before kept resurfacing in my mind: eating hot salt beef sandwiches in Charlie's bed with him (expect they weren't hot by the time we ate them, because we had sex again first), drinking more champagne, kissing and giggling and eventually falling asleep, tangled together under his dark blue sheets. Pinging awake at five in the morning, woken by the crash of the door as Gus came home from wherever he'd been, still a bit drunk and knowing I needed to get home to my own bed. And Charlie, half asleep, summoning an Uber to take me away. *The Uber of shame*, I thought. But I didn't feel ashamed at all – each piece that came together to make the puzzle of the memory just made me smile.

I'd pack up the goody bag again and take it to Raffy at the coffee shop to give to his niece, I decided – I couldn't carry on avoiding him forever, after all.

But when I got to The Daily Grind, Raffy wasn't there. Luke was alone behind the counter, and when he saw me he said, "Cappuccino and an almond croissant, is that right?"

The thought of hot milk and marzipan made me feel a bit sick. I shook my head, pressing my lips together.

"Could I just have a Diet Coke, please? And… I brought this for Raffy. For his niece, at least – for Zara." I handed over the yellow bag.

Luke said, "Cheers. I'll pass it on when I see him."

The queue was building up behind me, and I wasn't sure how to ask when that would be, or where Raffy was. So I just said thanks and paid for my drink, and went to work. I drank my Diet Coke at my desk, washing down two paracetamol I found in my drawer, and immediately felt a bit less queasy. But now my hangover had abated, I remembered the advice I'd read online, about how the best way to get over a man was to get under another one. I remembered Charlie asking me how my heart was, and realising that it didn't appear to be broken any more. So that had worked, at any rate. But what about my feelings for Charlie?

As I searched the Twitter and Instagram for images to use in my article ('30 Facts Every Single Cat Owner Knows Are True'), I tried to work out my feelings. Charlie was cute – seriously cute. Even with my limited experience (limited enough, in the interests of full disclosure, to be counted on the fingers of one hand. And I wouldn't even need to use my thumb) I could tell that he was seriously good in bed, too.

Well, that's just tough, Gemma, I told myself firmly. *You're never going to see him again. You've got to pull up your big girl pants (the fugly ones you were wearing last night, the ones you dropped so happily on the floor) and face up to it. You were just the latest in a long, long line of girls who fell for the disingenuous Netflix and chill line and ended up sharing Charlie Berry's hot tub, his bed and his late-night takeaway. No wonder he was so relaxed about replacing the sofa – he's probably caused irreparable water damage to enough of them to keep the local British Heart Foundation shop stocked for years.*

But my silent telling-off did nothing to take the shine off my memory of the evening. It had been fun – the most fun I'd had for ages. I remembered Charlie's smile and it made me smile too. At lunchtime, I went and sat in Soho Square and watched as many Berry Boys vlogs as I could fit into an hour. At the end of each one, I told myself I must stop, but then found myself pressing play again.

I watched Charlie riding a skateboard around the apartment, just like he'd said he did. I watched him and Gus tasting a load of random sweets they'd brought back from a trip to Seoul, grimacing and laughing and marking them out of ten. I watched them trying to follow yoga videos on their balcony, groaning and laughing and falling over. I watched Gus go out and get Charlie a latte and put salt in it instead of sugar, and Charlie wincing and laughing and spitting it out.

I went back several years, right to the first videos they'd posted on their channel, and saw a much younger Charlie and Gus singing along to One Direction videos and playing computer games together. Their hair was different then; Charlie didn't have a tattoo; they filmed in their bedroom in what I presumed was their parents' house instead of in the palatial flat.

I was astonished at the sheer volume of material they'd created over the past five years. There was hours and hours of it – and I now knew all too well that even more hours would have been spent editing and uploading it all. It made me realise for sure what I'd begun to suspect: I was too late to the party. People who had really successful vlogs, massive ones, like Charlie and Gus, had been doing it for ages.

It was time to face facts: I might get a few freebies delivered to the office, a few hundred people might give my videos a thumbs-up, but unless I was willing to work at it for hours and hours, for years and years, I'd be the YouTube equivalent of that not-very-talented hopeful who gets booed off the stage in the first round of *The X-Factor*.

So I returned to my desk and my cats, and when Sloane tried to call me later in the afternoon, I didn't answer. I didn't answer her next call either, and I deleted her voicemail without listening to it.

When I got home that evening, Amy was in the kitchen eating beans on toast and drinking tea.

"Guess what?" she said.

"What?"

"I passed my course! Top of the class. I'm an actual police officer."

"Amazing! Clever you. We should go for a drink to celebrate."

"Even better," she said. "Richard and Hannah are going away for the weekend, so I'm planning a party. I've sent out invites on Facebook – I'll add you to the group, too, if you're free this weekend?"

Was that really such a good idea, I wondered, imagining hordes of people turning up and spilling red wine on the cream sofa, smashing glasses, painting graffiti on the walls… but then I remembered that we were responsible grown-ups, and anyway Amy would never commit such a rookie error as to make her event public on social media.

"I'm writing a note to drop round to the neighbours," she said. "How does this sound? 'To celebrate completing my police training course, I'm inviting a few people over for drinks this Saturday. Please bear with us if there's some loud music – we won't carry on too late. And feel free to drop round and say hi.'"

"It sounds like, 'Don't call the police – I *am* the police,'" I said.

"Exactly!" Amy laughed. "So you must invite some mates, too."

I thought of Olivia, and all the times we'd organised Halloween parties, movie nights and barbecues together. I remembered planning a fancy-dress party for Jack's twenty-first. He'd gone as Simon Cowell, his hair all bouffy with mousse and his trousers pulled up too high, and I'd even persuaded him to let me give him a fake tan, which he'd scraped off over the next few days when he shaved, so the stubbly bits of his face were paler instead of darker than the rest. It looked ridiculous and we laughed about it for ages. I'd persuaded Mum to dye my hair blonde for the first and only time in my life, and scoured the local charity shops until I found a floor-length sequinned dress that Amanda Holden would have been proud of.

Well, neither Jack nor Olivia would be invited to Amy's party, that was for sure.

I thought of Emily at work, who was maybe, potentially, a friend. But she wasn't really one yet, and asking her round on a Saturday night, at short notice, when she'd almost certainly have plans, would be running a serious risk of looking weird.

I thought of Charlie, then pushed the thought firmly aside.

"Maybe," I said.

Then I helped Amy deliver a few copies of her carefully worded note through the neighbours' letterboxes, and we watched *The Great British Bake Off* together and painted our nails, and it was all really companionable, until Hannah and Richard came home and we both drifted up to bed even though they hadn't finished the technical challenge yet.

"I'll just show you where the stopcock is," Richard said.

"And the folder with the operating instructions for all the appliances is in the drawer under the microwave," said Hannah. "I cleared the filter on the tumble dryer yesterday, so it should be okay, but if it starts to smell at all hot... Did you check the smoke alarm battery, Rich?"

"Just last week," Richard said.

"I'll check it again," Hannah said. "And here's a list of emergency numbers." She placed a laminated A4 page on the table. "My mum and dad are in Basingstoke so they're closer to hand than Rich's, but they play golf on Saturdays so if they aren't available you can ring Rich's brother. And I've put the numbers for the fire service and the emergency plumber and the police…"

"Hannah," Amy said, "I am the police."

She caught my eye and we both looked away again quickly, stifling giggles.

"Oh." Hannah coloured slightly. "Yes. I suppose you are. I'm sorry, I know I'm stressing, it's just that…"

"Don't stress," I said. "Honestly. We'll look after everything, I promise. If there are any problems at all we'll let you know. Don't worry about anything, and have a great time in…"

"Lesbos," Richard said.

"Fab," said Amy. "I've never been there but I've heard it's gorgeous."

"Amazing beaches," Hannah said. "And olive oil and ouzo."

"And ancient monuments," Richard said. "It's fascinating from a historical and archaeological point of view. And geological, too – it has one of the world's most perfect examples of a petrified forest."

"I hope you're not going to want to spend the entire five days looking at churches and fossils, Rich," Hannah said. "Remember, when we went to Tunisia, you promised…"

"We spent two days looking at Roman mosaics," Richard said. "Two days! It wasn't nearly enough."

"It was two days too many for me," Hannah said. "This time I want to actually relax, not spend hours wandering around ruins when I could be lying in the sun. Please, Rich."

There was a pause. The atmosphere had suddenly, subtly changed. Amy and I looked at each other again, but this time we didn't feel like laughing.

Richard reached out and patted Hannah's bottom, then the pat turned into an affectionate pinch – at least, it looked affectionate, and Richard was smiling. But, for a second, Hannah looked as if she was about to cry.

"Don't be silly, Hannah-banana," he said. "If you want to waste your time lying on the beach, I won't stop you. I hope you've packed your sunblock."

"I'm sure I have," Hannah said. "But I'll just check in my bag…"

"There's no time." Richard glanced at his phone. "Our cab will be here in two minutes and if you start unpacking you'll never get your case to close again. Typical woman – we're going away for a long weekend and you've packed six bloody bikinis."

"They hardly take up any room," Hannah objected, and I could see her point – her little wheelie suitcase looked a perfectly normal size to me.

"Anyway, I hope you have a wonderful time," I said. "We'll text you tomorrow if you like, just to let you know everything's all right."

Richard's phone buzzed and they got their stuff together in a final flurry of key-gathering and boarding-pass-checking.

"Right," Hannah said. "We're off. See you girls on Tuesday."

Amy and I waited in silence for a few seconds after the front door closed.

"Those two," she said. "Fricking weird, right?"

"Fricking weird," I said. "Listen, this party – are you sure it's all going to be okay? Because if anything went wrong…"

"It's all going to be fine," Amy said. "Come on, let's go down to the off-licence."

By early afternoon, we'd stocked the fridge with cans of beer, bottles of cheap wine, tubs of dip and enough sausages and burgers to feed an army (or, I supposed, a police force). The kitchen table was laden with packets of buns and crisps, paper plates and the huge pack of napkins I'd insisted on buying in case of red wine spillage. Amy had made a massive bowl of coleslaw and I'd baked some rather wonky cupcakes. The barbecue was ready to be lit and Taylor Swift was playing on the stereo.

"I think we're good to go," Amy said. "I'm off to shower and change."

I surveyed the room. Even with all our party supplies, it was immaculate. I felt a horrible pang of guilt.

"We're going to have to smuggle all the empties into the neighbour's recycling," I said. "If they find out…"

"They won't find out," Amy said. "Honestly, we're doing nothing wrong. They didn't even say we couldn't have a party."

"No," I said. "But that's just because they didn't know we were going to. If we'd asked…"

But then I heard the bathroom door close and the shower start to run.

I went upstairs and sat on my bed. I was sure Amy's friends were all just as sensible and responsible as she was – or at least, as I'd thought she was until this madness had overtaken her. I didn't want to be a party pooper. And I didn't want to spoil the new friendship that seemed to be growing between Amy and me. I'd stay sober, I decided, and try to make sure the mess didn't get too out of hand. After all, it was just a little barbecue for a few of my housemate's friends.

I reached for my make-up bag and spilled palettes and brushes out on to my dressing table, then found my eye drawn irresistibly towards my camera. I hadn't posted a vlog for ages – at least, that was how it felt. It had only been a few days, really. But in the meantime, I'd had my meeting with Sloane. I'd spent the night with Charlie. I knew how silly I'd been to dream of being a YouTube star one day, and how remote my chances were of ever achieving anything in that strange, glamorous and exclusive world.

But still, I realised, I missed it. I'd started to enjoy my little chats to my camera and to the people who'd eventually watch the videos when I posted them. And they were missing me – I'd seen loads of comments on Twitter asking where I was and when I would post again, and replied vaguely to a few of them saying I was very busy at work and would be back soon. I knew that if I never posted again, they'd unsubscribe, unfollow and forget me – but I didn't really want that to happen.

I switched on my camera.

Hi everyone.

It's been a while, I know, and I'm sorry. So much has been happening, and maybe I'll tell you all about it another time. But for now, I'm getting ready for a little party my housemate is having. It's such a gorgeous day, so we're going to have a barbecue in the garden. My legs are, like, really white, otherwise I'd have worn shorts. (To be perfectly honest, they're a bit hairy as well as

being white.) So I'm going to wear the trusty maxi dress I got from
Primark a couple of years ago. Is it just me, or do you also have
this thing with maxi dresses where you buy one every summer (or
two, or even three) and then there's only about one day a year
when you can actually wear it? So you end up with a wardrobe
full of the things and then when it's sunny like today, or you're
going on holiday or whatever, you look at them all and you're
like, eeny meeny miny mo…? Just me then. Anyway, I totes heart
this dress – it's white and floaty with a bit of broderie trim, and
hopefully I won't spill ketchup all over it. I'll put my hair up – this
is just a sort of messy bun, with a bit of sea salt spray in it to help it
hold – and I'm just going to put on a bit of BB cream, bronzer…

The act of getting ready, of talking about getting ready, was oddly
soothing. By the time I'd finished, edited the video (which, as
always, took way longer than I expected) and posted it (after two
false starts because, as always when I was in a hurry, the broadband
connection dropped and I had to do the whole thing over again)
my worries about Hannah and Richard, and what horrors would
ensue if they found out what we had done, had melted away.

I went downstairs, poured myself a glass of wine (I wasn't going
to get pissed, I told myself, but not drinking at all, all night, was
too big an ask) and found Amy and Kian in the garden.

Soon, more and more people began to arrive. Someone brought
a bottle of Pimm's and we raided Hannah's herb garden for mint.
Someone else brought a massive cake with a Metropolitan Police
logo iced on it, putting my dodgy cupcakes to shame. Amy's sister

brought her guitar and played 'I Really Like You' totally beautifully, and a few of us sang along less beautifully. It was all very civilised, and I felt quite guilty that I'd been worried, but relieved that my worries had proved unfounded.

As the day turned to evening, though, I realised that it was Amy herself I should have worried about. I'd never seen her drink before, and although she occasionally mentioned having been to the pub with colleagues, I'd never seen her drunk. But now she was clearly determined to make up for all those months of long shifts and hard work and not knowing whether she was going to be among the few to make the grade.

She laughed and danced and chatted and ate, but mostly she got cheerfully shitfaced, and by ten o'clock, when just about everyone had left, her cheerfulness suddenly deserted her.

I came downstairs from the bathroom to find Amy, Amy's sister and Kian in the kitchen. Amy was holding the salad bowl and sobbing her heart out.

"I forgot about the coleslaw," she said. She had to say it a couple of times before we understood. "I made it specially and I forgot it in the fridge."

"Babe, it doesn't matter," Amy's sister said. "Everyone's had an amazing time. We're all so proud of you."

"Does matter," Amy said. "It's Nan's special recipe and I wanted everyone to try it and I forgot."

"Love, you're knackered," said Kian. "Come on, you need to go to bed."

"I don't want to go to bed," Amy said. "No one's going to bed until we've eaten all this fucking coleslaw. Right?"

Amy's sister and I looked at each other and I saw her mouth twitch in just the same way Amy's did when she was trying not to laugh. It was an enormous bowl and absolutely full of the cabbage, carrots, celery and apple I'd watched Amy painstakingly shred that morning.

"We'll have it tomorrow," I suggested, even though I knew that Amy would be in no state to face cold, mayonnaisey vegetables the next morning. "Or we can save it for Hannah and Richard, like a welcome home present."

Amy started to laugh, although she didn't stop crying. "Rannah and Hichard," she said. "What a pair of nutters. You know, I'm fucking sure he…" Then she paused, and her face turned a weird shade of khaki.

"Babe?" Amy's sister said.

"Are you okay?" Kian said.

"Going to be sick," Amy said, suddenly not slurring at all.

Then lots of things happened at once, but seemingly in slow motion, like the reverse of when I speeded up a make-up application video to make it less tedious. Amy dropped the bowl of coleslaw on the floor. It was plastic, so it didn't break, but its contents splattered everywhere. She made to run for the stairs and the loo, but slipped in the mess and went flying, hitting her head on the corner of the marble worktop.

Then, as abruptly as it had slowed, time returned to normal speed. Amy was lying on the floor in the ruins of her salad. Kian, Amy's sister and I were looking at her, horrified. I thought, *She didn't put beetroot in it, did she?* and then I realised.

"She's cut her head," Kian said, squatting down and carefully moving Amy's hair out of the way.

"Jesus," Amy's sister said, looking at the rapidly spreading red stain. "Do you think…?"

"A&E, definitely," Kian said. "I'm a first-aider at work, and head wounds always need to be looked at."

"Right." Amy's sister did a brief hand-flappy dance around the living room before finding her handbag and her phone. "I'm calling a cab. We'll take her."

Kian found some ice in the freezer and a clean tea towel in a drawer and did his best to staunch the blood that was oozing, slowly but persistently, from Amy's head. Amy's sister stood looking down and saying, "Oh my God. Oh my God," with none of Kian's imperturbability. I just stood, numb with horror.

I was still standing there like an idiot when the taxi arrived and the two of them bundled Amy into it, assuring me that they'd text and let me know she was okay. After they'd gone I stood a bit more, surveying the carnage.

As parties go, as I said, it had been pretty civilised. The barbecue was still smouldering in the garden, and would need to be scooped out and cleaned in the morning. There were paper plates and glasses scattered about, half-eaten hot dogs and crisp crumbs to throw away. If I took the whole clearing up thing seriously, I might even pick the bits of cucumber out of the flowerbeds, where people had chucked them out of their Pimm's glasses.

That would all have been fine.

But this was something entirely else. The kitchen floor was a morass of mayonnaise, soggy cabbage, the water Kian had spilled from his bowl of ice and – horrifyingly – blood. All the blood. My flip-flops and the hem of my long dress were splattered with it. It was like a scene I might have written in one of my little horror stories when I was a teenager, except I wasn't worried about the Slender Man coming to get me – I was worried about our landlords, who'd trusted us to look after their home and who we'd betrayed.

I didn't know what to do. Well, I did, of course – I knew I was going to have to sort all this out, because Amy wasn't there to help. But for now, I was paralysed by the enormity of the task. I went out into the warm, dark garden and fished the last beer from the bucket that had been full of ice earlier and was full of water now. I sipped it, staring into the embers of the fire. I tweeted, *OMG. Carnage. #sendhelp*. Then a few minutes later I realised how stupid that was, and deleted my tweet. I leaned forward and rested my cheek on my knees, staring at my pretty silver toenails and my ruined dress, and started to cry.

I was still crying when I heard the crash of the door knocker.

Chapter Eleven

"Oh fuck," I said aloud, jumping to my feet. "If that's Hannah and Richard, they are totally, legit going to kill me, and I won't blame them."

Then I remembered Hannah checking her handbag that morning, making sure she had her keys and then looking again a minute later to make even surer. It couldn't be them. They were in Greece, drinking ouzo on a balcony overlooking the Mediterranean, or exploring some ancient monument in the dark, if Richard had his way. Then I thought, *What if they got mugged on the way to the airport, and their bags, passports and keys stolen, and they'd just managed to make their way home?* I felt a flood of cold dread, the way I imagine it must feel to do the ice bucket challenge. I walked quietly through the house and stood by the front door, wishing there was a peephole so I could see who was on the other side. I waited, but I couldn't hear anything at all. Then the knocker crashed again, making me almost jump out of my skin.

I was going to have to answer it – there was nothing else for me to do. Besides, I thought, it was probably Kian, or Amy's sister, coming back with news of Amy.

But it wasn't. When I opened the door, there stood Charlie and Gus.

I don't even want to think what I must have looked like, in my dirty dress, gawping open-mouthed at them.

"How did you get here?" I said stupidly.

"Uber, obviously," Gus said.

"We stalked you," Charlie said. "Our fans do it to us all the time. They watch our videos and look on Google Street View to work out where we live, and then they turn up at midnight wanting selfies."

"But they don't get past the concierge," Gus said.

"We started with your coffee shop," Charlie said. "The Daily Grind – you've vlogged about it, and you've filmed yourself walking there in the mornings. So once we found it, the rest was easy."

"Unfortunately it was closed," Gus said, "so we couldn't even get a coffee. But that's okay, because you were just about to put the kettle on, weren't you?"

"Gemma's got more important things to do than be your personal barista, mate," Charlie said. "She needs help, remember? She tweeted."

I said, "But I deleted that tweet, like, straight away."

"Yeah," Gus said. "We saw. Charlie's been glued to your feed all day, but that's the only thing you posted apart from one lousy five-minute vlog. You're going to need to raise your game, Gemma."

"What happened at the barbecue?" Charlie said, suddenly serious. "Are you okay?"

I said, "You'd better come in and see."

I led them through to the back of the house, and the three of us stood in silence and looked at the chaos of Hannah and Richard's kitchen. I felt my eyes sting with fresh tears, and sniffed loudly.

"Blimey," Gus said. "Do you always invite Lindsay Lohan to your parties?"

I started to laugh, but the laughter quickly turned to tears, and the next thing I knew Charlie's strong arms were around me and I was sobbing into his shoulder.

"My flatmate got pissed," I said, when I'd recovered enough self-control to actually talk and blown my nose on the wad of paper napkins Gus handed me. "And she fell and hit her head, and her boyfriend's taken her to hospital, and our landlords are away and they don't know we were even having a party, and I feel so terrible about it, and… well, look."

"I'm looking," Gus said. "Impressive night's work. Just as well we came over, isn't it, mate?"

"Definitely," Charlie said. "Right, we're going to need bin liners, bleach, a mop, Marigolds…"

"We don't want to spoil our manicures," Gus said.

I opened the cupboard under the stairs, where Hannah's enormous hoard of cleaning products was stored. There was a Post-it note on the inside of the door that said, *If you finish it, please remember to replace it or add it to the shopping list*, with a smiley face underneath. I felt a fresh wave of guilt.

"Bloody hell," Charlie said. "Not only do you invite LiLo to your parties, you're renting a room off Kim and Aggie. Why didn't you say?"

"What's all this stuff even for?" Gus said. "Baby oil? Kinky."

"It's for polishing the stainless-steel splashback," I said.

"Yeah, I bet that's what they tell you," Charlie said. "Dirty bastards. Right. I'm going in." He pulled on a pair of yellow washing-up gloves and chucked another to Gus. "Why don't you stick some music on, Gemma? I need tunes while I work."

"Like a brain surgeon," Gus said, gloving up. "Scalpel, sister!"

"Look, you two…" I said. "I mean, it's so sweet that you came over…" *Sweet or creepy*, I wondered? But I didn't have time to analyse it. "But you really don't have to do this. You really, really don't."

"Someone's going to have to," Charlie pointed out, "and since we're here, it may as well be us. We can't take you out clubbing if you're going to be fretting about the state of your kitchen floor all night, can we?"

"Anyway, we're awesome at cleaning," Gus said. "Our mum always made us do chores. She brought us up to be new men, didn't she, Charles?"

"She did indeed," Charlie said. "With our steam mops, we will smash the patriarchy!"

"So you see, Gemma, you really ought to be glad we stalked you, and not anyone else," Gus said. "You wouldn't get this level of service from Thatcher Joe, would you now?"

I could see that resistance was going to be futile – and besides, I didn't actually want to resist. It was taking a bit of time to sink in, but Charlie was here – actually here, in my home. It wasn't the romantic reunion I would have imagined, if I'd allowed myself to imagine there being a reunion with him at all, ever, but here he was. His smile was at least as dazzling as I remembered. His hair even shinier and blonder; his blue eyes even more sparkly. The bits of his arms that I could see between the gloves and the sleeves of his brilliantly white T-shirt were lean and muscly, and I couldn't help remembering how they'd felt around my body.

"Well, now you put it like that…" I said, pulling on a pair of gloves of my own and making a mental note to stock up on new ones. "Let's crack on."

It took us two hours, but at last, at one in the morning, the house was restored to its pre-Amy's-party condition. Every last glass was washed, dried and put back in its place. Gus had chucked water on the coals and cleaned the barbecue. We'd filled two black rubbish bags and three clear recycling ones and stashed them, furtive as burglars, in the neighbour's wheelie bin. We'd mopped the kitchen floor until it gleamed, and you wouldn't notice the tiny bloodstain on the grouting unless you knew it was there. Gus even polished the splashback with baby oil and said, "Look, it comes up a treat," waving an e-cloth in high camp style.

I'd received a text from Amy's sister telling me that Amy had had two stitches in her head and was fine, but she was taking her back to her place for the night, and asking whether I was all right, and I'd been able to reply saying that she should tell Amy not to worry, I had everything under control. I didn't mention that that was only thanks to the timely intervention of the Berry Boys, YouTube's hottest double act. Apart from anything else, Amy's sister would almost certainly have no idea who they were.

"Well," Charlie said at last, peeling off his Marigolds and pushing back his hair. "Looks like our work here is done."

"Thank you both so, so much," I said. "Honestly, you've been so totally amazing. I don't know what to say."

"Any time you need us," Gus said, "just beam the Berry-signal into the night sky. We'll see the feather duster lighting up a passing cloud and arrive in the Berry-mobile."

"Bruce Wayne doesn't have Uber, that's what cramps his style," Charlie said. "The Batmobile's instantly recognisable. We can do our good deeds in secret."

"You know what?" Gus said, a delighted, wicked smile lighting up his face. "No one knows we're here. Not even Sloane. I haven't been on Snapchat for four hours."

As if compelled by some hidden force, both of them pulled their phones from their pockets and, with identical gestures, pressed and swiped the screens to life. With identical expressions of intense concentration on their faces, they scrolled and tapped. I watched for a moment, feeling suddenly superfluous and forgotten, then took out my own phone and scrolled and tapped too.

There was no further update from Amy's sister. There were a few comments on my YouTube channel from people saying they hoped I'd have a fun night. *If only they knew*, I thought. There was nothing more. It took me a couple of minutes to get my social media curation up to date; Charlie and Gus looked like they could be at it for hours.

"Holly's at the Queen of Hoxton," Gus said. "Fancy a drink?"

"Is Glen there too?" Charlie said.

"Dunno," Gus said.

"Wanker," they both said together. Then they both pocketed their phones again and looked at each other.

"Right," Gus said. "Shall we?"

All at once, the mood of cheerful, almost manic camaraderie had melted away. Charlie and Gus were a unit again, and I wasn't part of it – I was excluded from the magic circle, a newbie, an interloper. Even though it was my home they'd descended on, I felt like an outsider. I had no idea whether their plan to go drinking included me or not, but I suspected it didn't. And even if it did, I was in no fit state to go anywhere near the Queen of Hoxton without a shower, a change of clothes and half an hour in front of the mirror, and I knew without having to ask that they wouldn't be willing to hang around while I got ready.

"There's still some wine in the fridge, if you'd like a glass," I said pathetically, knowing even as I said it that Amy's choice of Blossom Hill white Zinfandel would cut no ice with the Berry Boys.

Charlie looked at Gus, and Gus looked back at Charlie. I had no way of interpreting whatever wordless conversation they were having, and it didn't matter anyway. They'd decide regardless of what I wanted to do.

Then Charlie said, "I'm knackered. Cleaning's fucking hard work – I'd forgotten. And anyway – the Queen of Hoxton? Meh."

I couldn't begin to read the expression on Gus's face. He looked just the same as he had a minute before, casually smiling, but his blue eyes seemed just a little more opaque, his smile a little less carefree.

"Right then," he said. "Bat-Uber for one it is. Unless you want to head back to the flat?"

I saw Charlie hesitate, and knew I shouldn't say anything at all.

"I'll have that glass of wine, if you're still offering, Gemma," Charlie said, turning the laser beam of his smile on me.

"Course," I said, relief and excitement making me tingle all over. "We've got four bottles to get through, because I'll have to destroy the evidence before Hannah and Richard get back."

"Piece of piss," Charlie said, opening the fridge. "Augustus? May we tempt you with a splash of Blossom Hill?"

But Gus was already looking at his phone. "Four minutes," he said. "I'll wait outside and have a fag."

"Okay," Charlie said. "Laters, then."

"Laters," Gus said.

I said, "I'll see you out."

I walked with him to the door and we stepped out together. It was still warm, but a thin drizzle was falling, glossing the pavement and enveloping the street lights in a misty halo.

"Gus?" I said.

"Mmm?" His eyes didn't move from the small screen. "Here he is now. Mohammed in a Škoda Octavia."

"Listen," I said. "Thanks so much for everything tonight. Really, thank you. You were amazing. I'm so grateful. I…"

"No worries," he said. "Laters, Gemma." I watched as he opened the car door and swung his long legs into the seat, and I heard him say, "Yeah, The Factory, thanks mate."

Then Charlie's warm, strong arms encircled me from behind.

"How about that wine then?"

I turned around and looked at him, and the sight of his bright eyes and almost-but-not-quite smile made me smile too.

"I'll open it," I said. "Do you mind if I… I need to shower quickly."

Charlie reached out and stroked my cheek, then both his hands were in my hair and his mouth found mine. "You so don't," he said.

*

I dreamed I was watching one of Charlie's videos, but it didn't make sense. Every time I went back to the beginning again, he said something different. His face kept swimming in and out of focus and his voice was all weird and distorted. I tried to force myself to concentrate, to figure out what he was talking about, and gradually his words joined up into sentences.

"So guys, this is just a short video to tell you about an important thing that's happened to me. Lots of you know that Gus and I launched our first book last week, which was absolutely awesome and probably the most challenging, exciting thing we've done together. The launch party was last Wednesday, in London, and so many of our friends were there to support us. It was a totally amazing night. I'll add a link for those of you who want to buy the book.

"But anyway, what I want to do is tell you something that happened to me a few weeks ago. Or rather, *someone* who happened to me. Guys, I've met a girl. A really beautiful, amazing girl called Gemma."

My eyes snapped open. Charlie was sitting on the edge of the bed, his back to the window, filming himself on his phone. He was wearing his jeans, but no shirt, and the morning light illuminated the smooth, hard planes of his body, which I could so clearly remember touching. His hair was sticking up and he needed to shave – my own face felt raw where his stubble had scratched my skin as we kissed and kissed.

I stretched, still not properly awake. We'd slept all tangled up together and my body felt pleasantly achy.

"Gemma's a vlogger too – you might know her channel, but in case you don't, I'll put a link to it too. She's incredibly talented, and as I may have mentioned, she's also amazing and beautiful. And I'm sure you guys will meet her later on, but for now I need to get showered and dressed and get some coffee on. Mmmm, coffee," Charlie said. Then he put down his phone.

"Good morning," I said.

Charlie bounced over to me and wrapped me up in a massive hug, kissing me and rubbing his sandpapery skin over my cheeks and shoulders. I reached up and hugged him back, pressing the length of his body against mine, feeling us wanting each other again.

"No time for that now, young lady," Charlie said. "Come on, you need to get up and get dressed. Sloane's on her way."

"Sloane? What? Why?"

"You don't mind me giving her your address, do you? It seemed easier than meeting her at home."

"Of course I don't mind," I said, although I wasn't sure that was actually true – thank God Richard and Hannah were away. "But what's she coming for?"

"I'll tell you while we shower," Charlie said. "So long as you promise to wash my back for me."

"I'll wash all of you, if you like," I said. And so we very nearly weren't ready when we heard Sloane's knock at the door.

"Good morning, you gorgeous pair," she said, sweeping in and heading straight for the kitchen as if she'd been to the house a thousand times before. "I've got cappuccinos, muffins, croissants and fresh OJ – that's a seriously good coffee shop at the end of your road, Gemma."

Sloane was wearing what I presumed was her version of weekend casual – a retro halter-neck dress with tiny white hearts printed on a red background. Her lipstick was bright red too, and she was wearing red shoes with high cork platforms. I'd just dragged on a pair of jeans and a vest top with no bra, my hair was wet, I hadn't had time to put on any make-up and I was worried I still smelled of sex.

Sloane opened the cupboard where the plates were kept, getting it right first time, arranged the pastries and dished out the coffee.

"Now," she said. "Let's get down to business. But first – oh my God, you two! You are just the most adorable couple I have ever seen."

I said, "I'm sorry, Sloane, I just don't understand. I mean, what's happening?"

Charlie said, "I haven't actually had time to explain to Gemma."

"You haven't?" Sloane arched one perfectly shaped eyebrow and I saw her take in my dishevelled appearance. I realised she knew exactly why Charlie and I hadn't had time for explaining or being explained to. "Well, it has all happened rather suddenly. The pics were only posted on Twitter last night – I have no idea why they waited, but they did. There were two: one of you two together at the launch, and one of Gemma leaving The Factory the next morning. You really do need to be more careful, you know. But anyway, there's no harm done, we just need to manage it all quite carefully."

"Manage what?" I said.

"This situation." Sloane sipped her coffee and broke off a minuscule corner of blueberry muffin. "Help yourselves. These are low fat, allegedly, not that either of you need to worry about that."

"Thanks," I said. A few minutes ago, I'd been starving, and planning on seeing if there were any sausages left for us to have for breakfast. But now I didn't feel a bit hungry. "Anyway – manage what?"

"It's the fans, you see," Charlie said. "I mean, they're great and everything, but they're all, like, really young."

"Charlie and Gus have an obligation to be positive role models," Sloane said. "Not only from a moral point of view, but contractually, too, as we discussed when we signed the deal with Pepsi. And that means being responsible and sensible in the way they conduct themselves publicly."

"No falling out of nightclubs," Charlie said.

"As I keep having to remind your brother," Sloane said.

"No smoking," Charlie said.

"And, of course, no Coca-Cola," said Sloane. "And no…" She paused and looked at me again, and again, I knew exactly what she meant. I felt a horrible little twist of shame inside me that hadn't been there before. What Charlie and I had done had been fun, joyous, beautiful even. It had never crossed my mind that anyone would think there was anything wrong with it. That twelve-year-old girls needed to be shielded from it in case they picked up something dirty.

Charlie said, "Basically Sloane thinks we should live like Trappist fucking monks."

Sloane laughed. "Oh come on! You know I don't! But you've got your careers to think of, and if you stop thinking about them occasionally – understandably, because you want to go out and have fun – I don't. It's part of my job to make sure that your reputation isn't blemished, and that your fans and your sponsors aren't let down."

Charlie said sulkily, "I haven't let anyone down."

"Of course you haven't!" Sloane said. "I think it's absolutely wonderful that you and Gemma are an item. You're so cute together, this will be a real boost to your career – and yours too, Gemma, we can discuss that in more detail later on. But for now, we just need to make sure we play this correctly. Am I right?"

I sipped my coffee. I could feel a bubble of resentment rising up inside me. This was the first morning I'd spent with Charlie. We ought to be in bed together still, listening to music, having sex again, maybe watching something on Netflix and ordering a takeaway, and then having sex again. Not sitting in a meeting about how our relationship needed to be managed. Not when I hadn't even known we had a relationship until now.

"Is all this actually necessary?" I said. "I mean, can't we just, like, go out? If we want to? Like normal people?"

"You can!" Sloane said. "That's exactly what I'm so excited you're doing! But it's so important to avoid damaging your image, your reputation – and this means you as well, Gemma, because you also have a career to think about. Which is why I suggested to Charlie earlier that he… er… backdate the beginning of this."

"Basically, Sloane thinks we should say we've been going out for a few weeks," Charlie said. "And now we're ready to go public about it."

"But isn't that…" I began.

"Slightly disingenuous?" Sloane said. "Maybe. But come on – anyone can see you two were made for each other. It's like you've been together for months, even if you haven't. Just look at you." And she put her head on one side and beamed at us as if she was Mary Berry and we were a cake that had just won the Showstopper Challenge.

"I'm not announcing anything unless Gemma's cool with it," Charlie said. "If she's not, we can leave it out there and I'll take whatever hit I have to take."

I thought, *I'm really not cool with it.* I liked Charlie – I liked him a lot – but I hadn't expected us to be catapulted into relationship territory so soon. I was over Jack – I was pretty sure I was, anyway – but that didn't mean I was ready to start seeing someone else just yet. It had all happened so quickly that I hadn't had time to think it through properly. Just the day before, I'd thought I would never see Charlie again. And then he'd turned up at my door and… well, thinking things through hadn't exactly been my top priority.

Then I thought, *But what will happen if I say no? What if I really had caused damage to Charlie's image, to the Berry Boys brand, to Gus, who hadn't even done anything wrong? What if not wanting to be his public, back-dated girlfriend meant I couldn't see him again?* I looked over at him and saw his still blue gaze on me, his face concerned and serious, and I realised I did want to see him again, see all of him again, lots of times.

"I'm cool with it," I said.

Sloane stood up, brushing crumbs off the front of her dress. "Amazing! Totally awesome! Right, then. Gemma, why don't you go and get yourself ready, and Charlie, you and I can have a look at the footage you recorded earlier and give it a quick edit, and get something out on Snapchat. Then we can film the two of you out and about today – nothing formal, just having fun together. I thought the zoo, a picnic in Regent's Park – I'll pick up some food at Selfridges while you're looking at the polar bears or whatever. And then you could go for a wander round Camden Market. Just a lovely day out, all very natural and unstaged. You'll need your camera too, Gemma – people who see Charlie's post will go straight on to your vlog so you'll need to get a video up too."

"Okay," I said. There didn't seem to be anything else I could say. I went upstairs and put on some make-up, half-listening to Charlie and Sloane's conversation as I swooshed bronzer on my cheeks and curled my eyelashes. Then I put on a maxi dress – my collection was seeing more action in this weekend than it had for months – packed my camera and reported back to the kitchen.

Chapter Twelve

When I pushed open the door of The Daily Grind two days later, it took me a few seconds to realise that something was different. My brain was so full of everything that had happened, everything that had changed, and was still changing, that I'd barely noticed the walk from the station. Having only had four hours' sleep the previous night hadn't helped – my eyes were scratchy and sore from staring at my computer screen all day, and now I was going to have to do a bit more staring, because I had thousands of new tweets and comments to respond to.

But the scene inside the coffee shop brought me up short. The tables had all been pushed to the sides of the room and chairs arranged in rows. All the chairs were full, and people were standing two-deep against the walls. In front of the bar, there were four more chairs, with people sitting on them who I didn't recognise. A woman was standing at a microphone, but I couldn't hear what she was saying because her words were drowned in a storm of clapping. There was a man with a camera – a proper camera, not like the small hand-held one I used for my vlogs – filming the scene.

I paused, bewildered, then noticed the posters that had been stuck up on the walls and a massive banner on the bar: *Save the*

Garforth Estate! it said, in massive orange letters on a green background – the same colours and font that had been used on the piles of leaflets I'd seen before. I realised I'd inadvertently gatecrashed a meeting, and shot into reverse – I'd have to go home, and do the stuff I needed to do there instead.

Then I saw Luke and Raffy standing by a table of leaflets in the corner. Raffy raised a hand in a half-wave to me, mouthed, "Stay," and gestured to a free spot next to him. Sure that everyone must be watching me, wondering who the hell I was and why I'd barged in late, I made my way over as quickly and quietly as I could, leaned against the wall and listened.

"They want to take our community from us," the woman at the microphone was saying. "They want to knock down the homes where we've lived – some of us all our lives – and replace them with luxury flats. They want to sell them for three-quarters of a million pounds to investors who won't even live in them, who know nothing about our lives and our area.

"I've lived in Hackney for forty years," she went on. "When I moved here with my mum and dad, this area was poor. And if I'm being honest, it was dead rough. You couldn't walk the streets at night. But we were just glad to have a roof over our heads, a home we could afford. And gradually, together, the local people worked to make this a safe, happy place to live. We have jobs locally, our children go to school here. The people living on the estate keep the local library going, the local children's centre going – if we go, all those things will go too. It's not just bricks and mortar, it's the heart of our community they're trying to destroy."

Then she stopped, and said, "Thank you," and a fresh roar of approval came from the crowd as she sat down, and a man in a grey suit stood up.

"Who are they?" I whispered to Raffy.

"That's Alethea Ayoola," Raffy said. "She's chair of the residents' association. And this is Gordon Lavery, the local councillor, who didn't expect to have such a fight on his hands."

The cheers turned to boos, which were frequently renewed as Gordon Lavery muttered about bringing investment to the area, the priority being to rehouse residents as close by as possible ("Like where? Stevenage?" shouted a heckler in the back row) and the percentage of affordable homes and key worker housing that would be incorporated in the new development ("Yeah, with a poor door," said the heckler, to whoops and applause).

I listened with increasing fascination. I heard people saying that if they had to move, they wouldn't be able to afford the cost of commuting to their jobs, and didn't know if there'd be work where they were moved to. I heard a woman say that if she kept her son, who had autism, in the school where he was thriving, she'd have to spend two hours every day ferrying him there and back across London, and that would mean giving up her job. I heard a man say how he'd scrimped and saved to buy his council flat fifteen years ago, and the price the developer was offering him for it wouldn't buy a rabbit hutch nowadays.

I listened, and I remembered seeing the billboards when I'd first gone to see Hannah and Richard's house, how impressed I'd been by the vision of glass towers and manicured gardens that would replace the scruffy estate. I remembered Richard describing it as a dump, and how, privately, I'd agreed with him. Now, hearing a woman almost break down in tears as she described moving into her flat as a young bride, and raising her three children there, and how moving would feel like a desecration of the memory of her husband who'd died last year, I found myself not agreeing any more.

At last, Alethea Ayoola stood up to speak again.

"I want to thank everyone who's come here tonight," she said. "Even those who we disagree with – those who are wrong, and prepared to let grasping developers have it all their way, and do a land grab of our homes. I want to thank Luke McInnes for the use of the venue." (There were rousing cheers at this, and Luke went a bit pink and nodded modestly.) "And most of all, I want you, Mr Lavery, to know that we're not going to take this lying down."

With much scraping of chairs, the meeting broke up. Luke shot behind the bar and started making coffees. I could hear people talking about decamping to the local pub to plan their next move over a pint. Soon, Raffy and I were alone in our corner.

"I have to…" He gestured at the disarray of the room.

"I'll give you a hand," I said.

Together, we carried tables and chairs back to their normal positions. It was surprisingly difficult, because everything had to be moved away from where it was in order to get it back to where it needed to be, but of course there was nowhere to move it to because something else was in the way.

While we figured out the puzzle, Raffy told me how Luke had got involved with the campaigners and offered to host the meeting.

"He's always been a bit like that," Raffy said. "When we were at uni, he was always involved in some big issue or other. I think he feels guilty, because his family are loaded and everything's always been easy for him. So he loves a good cause. But he doesn't just dip into things, he really gets stuck in."

"He's certainly stuck into this," I said.

"That's for sure," Raffy said. "I guess maybe he feels guilty – he saw the opportunity to start a business here, and it's doing really well, but he knows that this place is part of what's changing the area, and not necessarily for the better. He reckons if you're not part of the solution, you're part of the problem."

"And what about you?" I said. "Are you part of the solution, too?"

"I'm just doing the heavy lifting," Raffy grinned. "And I guess I like seeing how things work, how stuff happening makes other stuff happen."

I couldn't help it, but when he said "heavy lifting", my eyes were drawn to his arms, brown and muscular in his stripy shirt. His chest looked like it was muscly too, like he spent some serious time in the gym. So different from Charlie, who was lean and slim, almost gangly. I remembered waking up with him, reaching out for his body, and the memory made me shiver and smile.

"So how are things with you, anyway, Gemma?" Raffy said. "How's the vlog going? Still baring your soul?"

"It's going really well, actually," I said. "This weekend's been totally mad. I've got loads of new subscribers – more than I ever, ever thought I'd have. Sloane – my agent – thinks I'm on track to hit half a million this month. It's awesome, but it's – I don't know. A bit scary, too. Daunting, I guess. So I guess I'll be baring my make-up bag a bit more and my soul a bit less."

"But that's amazing," Raffy said. "You know, it must put you in a really powerful position. Being able to influence so many people."

I thought about that for a second. "Maybe influence them to try different make-up, or drink green smoothies. It's no big deal, really. I'm not changing the world, or even a bit of it, like that woman today was."

"Yeah," Raffy said. "She's a great campaigner. But how many people were here tonight? A hundred and fifty? A hundred and seventy-five maybe. And maybe one of them was a journalist from the local paper, and maybe one works for a local radio station, and maybe a handful of them have big Twitter followings. If she had a platform like yours…"

"But the people who watch my platform don't watch it for stuff like this," I said. "They want to know about my clothes and my hair and my boyfriend…"

I stopped. Raffy looked at me curiously. "Boyfriend?"

I felt a blush creeping up my neck. "Yeah, that's kind of what's changed everything. I've got together with this guy – I met him at a vlogging party thing – and he's got a massive following. So now lots of them follow me too. It's really weird."

"I see," Raffy said. "That's great. I'm pleased it's going so well."

I pushed the last chair into its proper place and looked around the room. Everything was back to normal, but it was too late for me to settle down and start working – the last customers were leaving and Luke had turned off the coffee machine and was wiping down the bar.

"I should go," I said.

Luke said, "Thanks for helping out, Gemma, I really appreciate it. Your next coffee's on the house."

"Thanks," I said.

"We're all meeting here on Saturday morning," Luke said. "Doing a leaflet drop around the area, if you fancy helping out."

I thought of the lie-in I was already longing for, even though it was only Tuesday, and the four vlogs I'd promised Sloane I'd upload before the weekend, and Charlie's promise to call me and see me soon. I looked at Luke's open, smiling face and Raffy's, suddenly still and not smiling.

"I'd love to," I said. "I'll try, but I'm pretty busy." And I knew, even as I said the words, that it wasn't going to happen.

"So, yeah, it was total chaos," Amy said, tipping tuna out of its can into a bowl and squirting mayo over it. "Just like you'd expect from A&E on a Saturday night. But eventually I got seen and they stitched me up – look."

She pushed her hair aside and showed me the shaved place on her head.

"That looks really sore, you poor thing," I said.

"Yeah, well, I was so out of it at the time, I hardly knew what they were doing," she said. "My head hurt like crazy the next day, but that was mostly hangover. What am I like? I'm totally mortified about it, and I'm so sorry you got left with all the clearing up."

"It really wasn't a problem," I said, "and it was so sweet of you to get me flowers. You didn't have to do that."

It was the first time I'd seen Amy since the drama of Saturday night. I'd arrived home from The Daily Grind to find a big bunch of pink roses on the kitchen table and, at first I'd thought they might be from Charlie. Then I noticed that Amy was hovering anxiously around, and read the card.

"You want some of this?" She scooped tuna mayonnaise on to a piece of toast and grated cheese on top. "I've made loads."

"I'm good thanks. I'm going to make myself a salad in a bit." I remembered the stern advice Sloane had given me about modelling healthy living, and thought without enthusiasm of the ingredients I'd picked up at Whole Foods in my lunch break. I'd filmed myself filling a basket with micro herbs and sprouted pulses, so there was no going back now.

"So was it really bad? The state of the house, I mean?" Amy took a huge bite of her tuna melt. "God, that's so good."

"It was pretty bad," I admitted. "Your poor coleslaw – what a waste! But it was okay, because the weirdest thing happened."

I told her about Charlie and Gus turning up and rescuing me in my hour of cleaning need. I didn't tell her how they'd found the house, or who they were, or mention the newly official nature of Charlie's and my relationship.

"So he's your boyfriend?" she said.

"I guess he is," I said.

"Is he the one you were with the other night, when you did the walk of shame home at five in the morning? I was just getting ready for my shift and I heard you come in."

"That's him," I said, ducking my head in embarrassment. But Amy didn't seem to care.

"Cool. Where did you two meet?"

"At a work thing," I said. I thought how much I'd like to tell the story to someone, to describe Charlie's flat and the hot tub and how surreal the whole night had been, and unburden myself about how ambivalent I still felt about it all. But I couldn't – I'd promised Sloane that I must stick to the party line: that Charlie and I had met by chance several weeks before, when we'd both been arriving for appointments at the Ripple Effect offices. So although I wasn't lying to Amy, I wasn't telling her the full truth, either. She was fast becoming a friend, and my instinct was to trust her, but I couldn't be sure. The ink on my contract with Ripple Effect was barely dry, so to speak, and I was determined to be on my best behaviour.

"Right." Amy stood up and slotted her plate into the dishwasher. "I'd better make a move – I'm on shift in half an hour. I might stay over at Kian's tomorrow – he's on nights this week too, and we can't go breaking the rule about no gentleman callers, can we?" She winked at me, and I knew she knew I'd already broken it.

"They're meant to be getting back tonight, aren't they?" I said.

"That's what they said. Therefore, I'm out." Amy shouldered her bag and headed for the door. "Thanks again, Gemma, for what you did. It was immense. We should go for a drink sometime, me and Kian and you and your Charlie."

"I'd love that," I said.

I waited until she'd gone, waited five more minutes, then hurried upstairs and fetched my camera. I'd done extensive Googling of superfood salad recipes earlier and although none of them were exactly appealing, they were certainly quick to make.

"So, it's Tuesday evening now," I told the lens, "and I've got all my wonderful, nourishing ingredients ready for my dinner. Charlie's busy tonight so I'm all on my own, which means I get to have girl food. You know how it is!"

Since when did food even have a gender? I wondered. But Sloane's instructions had been clear.

"Why don't you have a quiet, girly night in tonight, Gemma? I'm off to Birmingham with the boys for a book signing, so take it easy, make a healthy dinner, put on a face mask, go to bed early with *Glamour* magazine. It'll be great if they can see you're a fan – I might approach them about doing a shoot with you in a few months."

"I'm making a dressing with lime juice, peanut butter and honey," I said. "I know it sounds weird, but it's really yummy and high in protein too. If you have a nut allergy, there are loads of delicious seed butters available too. I particularly like pumpkin, but you can get hemp, sunflower – all sorts. But I'm going for good old fashioned peanut butter tonight."

I showed the camera the label on the jar, making sure the Whole Foods bag was visible in the background too.

"We'll start getting you product placement deals very soon," Sloane had said. "But it helps if you show you're amenable to that sort of thing. And obviously, keep telling your viewers about the products you already use and love."

"And to give even more protein power to this, I like adding a few sprouted grains. You can grow your own, and I quite often do, but I've been a bit short of time lately." I gave the camera a coy smile, "So I bought these in."

Thank you, Google, I thought. Until today, I hadn't known sprouted grains even existed. Or seed butter, either. I thought hemp was like skunk, only milder.

"I'm just going to tumble these into a bowl with some kale and radicchio leaves – I just love this, it's the most gorgeous colour." It was. How it tasted, I had yet to discover. "And I'm going to mix the dressing through, and then I'm going to do something to make it even tastier and add more goodness."

I pulled another pack out of the brown paper bag and held it up to the camera, hoping I didn't look as dubious as I felt.

"Everyone loves halloumi cheese, right? I do, anyway." And Jack did, too. I felt a sudden pang of nostalgia for the nights we used to spend at our local Turkish restaurant, gorging on grilled cheese, bread and dips, so we had no room for the enormous lamb kebabs he always insisted on ordering too. "But the problem is, even if you're not avoiding dairy, it's really, really high in salt. So tempeh makes a great alternative. This is made from organic soy, and it's flavoured with seaweed, so it's got a great savoury flavour with not too much salt."

I slit open the package and a block of what looked like wet polystyrene slid out on to the chopping board.

"That looks absolutely fucking bogging," I said, before I could stop myself. Shit. But I'd have to edit the video anyway – no lasting harm was done. "It looks a bit weird, I know. But when you slice it up and sauté it in a little olive oil, it's really delicious."

It took me ages to work out how to work the fancy induction hob, which I realised I'd never used before. It looked like pretending to be a health food fanatic might actually force me to acquire some cooking skills, and that would be no bad thing. But given how much the ingredients for my simple, solitary supper had cost, it might bankrupt me first.

I carried on chatting to the camera as I finished assembling my salad, finally saying, "So there you have it. Organic leaves, sprouts and tempeh with a lime and peanut dressing. I'm going to have a glass of cold-pressed apple juice with this – I always dilute it fifty-fifty with sparkling water, because it is very high in sugar." Not as high in sugar as the Coke I was longing for, I thought. And that was totally off limits now – thanks to Charlie's contractual obligations it was Pepsi or nothing. I hated Pepsi even more than organic cold-pressed apple juice.

I sat down on the chair Amy had recently vacated, plate in front of me and glass by my side. "Bon appetit," I said. Then, at last, I was able to switch off the camera.

Five minutes later, I was still staring morosely at my salad in between checking my YouTube channel. As I'd said to Raffy, it had all gone a bit mental since I'd posted the video of Charlie and me on Sunday. Actually, it had all gone *completely* mental. I had more than a hundred thousand followers on my vlog and fifty thousand on Twitter and Instagram. More than three million people had watched us on Charlie's second channel as we laughed at monkeys, admired flamingos, ate smoked salmon bagels on the picnic blanket Sloane had purchased for the occasion, kissed each other in a rowing boat and strolled around market stalls, our tasteful wicker picnic hamper having been stowed away in Sloane's car.

The numbers were so mind-bogglingly, frighteningly huge that my mind sort of shied away whenever I tried to think about them. But they were nothing to the numbers of subscribers Charlie and

Gus had on their main channel, and Sloane was what she described as "quietly confident" that this was "only the beginning" for me.

When I was with Charlie, or when I was talking to the camera, there was no chance to think about it all. When I was at work, it seemed so remote, so utterly alien, that it could be happening to someone else. When Sloane was there, the sheer force of her personality erased my doubts. But now I was alone, the enormity of it all descended, weighing me down with a strange, formless apprehension.

I speared a bit of tempeh with my fork and ate it. To my amazement it wasn't too awful, and the peanut butter dressing was actually quite nice. But I couldn't summon up the enthusiasm to carry on eating. I poured my apple juice down the sink and switched the kettle on.

Then I heard the front door open, a sort of scraping crash, and Hannah's voice say, "Oh bugger."

I hurried through to the hallway. Hannah was pulling two suitcases backwards through the door, and one of them had tipped over, upsetting the little table where we all left our keys.

"Do you need a hand?" I said.

"Please," she said. "Richard had to go straight from the airport to work – there was some crisis with one of the servers. So I've dragged this lot from Gatwick on my own."

She turned around, and I couldn't stop myself from saying, "Jesus Christ, what happened to your face?" even though it was obvious what had happened.

"I know, right?" Hannah said. "I forgot my sunblock. It was so stupid of me – I was sure I'd checked. But then the pharmacy didn't open until after we needed to leave for our tour of the petrified forest. And I'm such an idiot, I thought, petrified forest, trees, shade... As if! We were out in the sun all morning and I got fried. Fortunately, temples and things are cool, and I bought some factor fifty the next day, but that was it for me lying on beaches."

"That looks really sore, though," I said. Her fair, freckly skin was tomato-red. Big patches were already peeling, with raw, new skin showing through. "Come on, let's take your bags upstairs. I'm sure I've got some stuff somewhere that might help."

It was simple enough carrying Richard's case up to their room, but it was still pretty heavy. I wondered why she'd manhandled both bags on the Tube instead of getting a cab, but it was none of my business, so I didn't ask. I just left the bag outside their door, went up to my own bedroom and found a tube of aloe vera gel I'd been sent in one of the PR company hauls and almost forgotten about, and took it back to Hannah.

"Here you go," I said. "It's probably too late, if I'm being honest, but it can't do any harm."

"Thanks," Hannah said. Even her smile looked painful, making new bits of damaged skin detach from her cheeks.

"No worries," I said. "I'll just clear up downstairs, then I was going to go to bed. Would you like a tea, or anything?"

Hannah shook her head. "I'm going to have a shower and go to bed, too. I'm still feeling a bit weird. It wasn't much of a holiday, to be honest. What a numpty."

I looked at her for a moment. She didn't look like someone who'd just got home from a weekend away with her boyfriend, all glowing with sun and sex and feeling a bit guilty about having eaten and drunk too much. She looked bloody miserable. If I'd known her better, I would have wanted to give her a huge hug and make her tell me what was really wrong.

But she said, "Thanks for helping with the bag, Gemma," and turned away. I saw a flake of dead skin drift off her face on to the carpet as she pushed back her hair.

"Okay," I said. "Hope the aloe stuff helps. Sleep well."

I left her there, cleared up the remains of my dinner, and spent a couple of hours in my room editing my video. It might have been, as Sloane had put it, disingenuous, but I was pleased with it, and uploaded it well before midnight.

Stanley in my arms, I fell asleep almost as soon as I turned out the light, but then I was half-woken again by the sound of Richard's feet on the stairs. I turned over, pulling the duvet over my head. Amy was right. Those two were fricking weird.

Chapter Thirteen

I didn't see very much of Hannah for the rest of that week, and I didn't see Amy or Richard at all. When I left for work the next day I took an overnight bag containing a couple of changes of clothes. I went to Boots in my lunch break and bought a toothbrush, razor and deodorant, and at half past five I left the office and went back to The Factory, not home to Hackney.

I felt oddly shy, finding my way to the apartment block from the station, turning up on my own and announcing myself to the concierge – the two nights I'd spent there before, I'd arrived with Charlie in a cab.

"Hi," I said, hovering at the reception desk.

"Good evening, madam. What number, please?"

"Three D."

"And your name, madam?"

"It's Gemma. Gemma Grey." I remembered what Charlie had told me about groupies turning up and being turned away again, and felt an absurd rush of fear that that was going to happen to me, even though I'd spoken to him on WhatsApp just that morning and I knew he was expecting me.

But after phoning and saying, "I have Gemma Grey downstairs," the concierge waved me through to the lift without demur.

The lift swooshed open and I stepped out, feeling my heart beating harder, as if I'd walked up the three flights of stairs. I was going to see Charlie. Charlie was my boyfriend. I was going to hang out with him for the evening, and then I was going to go to bed with him. A totally mundane night, then – but still new, thrilling and a bit nerve-wracking.

I paused outside the door, steeling myself to knock. I could hear music coming faintly but clearly through the orange-painted wood – a violin, something classical, I supposed. My musical knowledge didn't extend much beyond whatever was in the top forty, but I knew this was something special, haunting and sad. I waited and listened for a bit longer, then I saw the CCTV camera in a corner and imagined the concierge downstairs watching me, wondering why the hell I was loitering in the corridor instead of going in, and I imagined Charlie wondering where I was, coming out to find me and seeing me standing there like a total plonker. So I raised my hand and tapped on the door. The music stopped immediately, and a few seconds later the door swung open.

"Hi, Gemma," Gus said.

"Hi," I said. "Sorry – did I interrupt something?"

He shook his head. "Come on in. Charlie's not here. He's been on a shoot all day – I guess it dragged on, they usually do. They only wanted one of us – maybe they're on a budget and planning to clone me in in Photoshop – so we tossed a coin and he lost. Can I get you anything? Drink? Coffee? Pepsi?"

"Just a glass of water, please." I wanted to tell him he needn't go to any trouble, I knew where the fridge was and I could help myself, but then I thought that would probably be even more presumptuous than having him wait on me. So I followed him across the endless floor to the group of sofas and sat down (the red suede sofa appeared to have either been replaced or somehow restored to its former glory).

Gus handed me a bottle of fizzy water and a glass. "Ice?"

"This is great, thanks."

"No worries." He opened a beer, opened his laptop and sat opposite me, staring silently at the screen. I took out my phone too and checked my email and social media.

We sat like that for five minutes, then ten, and the silence became more and more oppressive. I wished Charlie was there. I wished I could go and wait for him in his bedroom, but I knew I couldn't – I knew how important it was that Gus should, if not actually like me, at least unbend a tiny bit.

"You can put your music back on, if you like," I said. "I heard it from outside. It was beautiful."

"Mendelssohn," Gus said. "You don't know much about classical music, do you?"

I laughed. It sounded as stagy and awkward as it felt. "Absolutely nothing. I'm a total philistine. I can name every number one One Direction have had, though."

"Piece of piss," Gus said, but he was at least looking up from his screen now, and there was an expression on his face that might, eventually, become a smile. "They've only had five."

"Yeah, well," I said, "that's five more than Mendelssohn."

The almost-smile defrosted another degree. "True. But if you knew anything about music, you'd know what you heard back then was shit."

"Oh," I said. "I thought it sounded lovely. What was wrong with it?"

"That was me playing," Gus said. "And I'm shit."

"Shut up! There's no way you can play the violin like that."

"Shitly? I can, and I do."

"Okay, we've established that I'm a philistine and know nothing about music," I said. "But I do know what shit violin playing sounds like, because my friend Katie used to play – or rather, her parents made her, when she was a kid, and then she sometimes did at parties, if she was pissed enough. It sounded awful. Like a cat trying to open a tin of cat food with its teeth. Worse than that."

Now Gus smiled properly – in fact, he almost laughed. "So why weren't you made to learn the violin when you were a kid?"

"My Mum wasn't bothered by stuff like that," I said. "So long as I was happy and got a few GCSEs, she was fine. And she had other stuff going on, anyway. But the point is, Katie never sounded anything like you, even though she did exams and stuff, she said."

"Yeah, well." Gus grimaced. "I'm competent. Just barely. But not good enough."

"Good enough for what?"

"To play professionally. I thought I was Mr Big Swinging Dick at school, and I went to college thinking I was going to be this incredible concert violinist, and then…" He stopped.

"Then what?"

"I realised I wasn't. And I'm not into being mediocre at stuff, and I'm not into not making money. So teaching kids to saw their way through 'Amazing Grace' in some shit comprehensive wasn't an option."

"Is that why you started vlogging?"

"Me? Fuck no. That was Charlie's idea. I'm just his bitch."

"But you enjoy it, don't you?" I said. "You must do. I was watching your videos the other day – there are so many of them. You look like you're having a great time in them."

"Yeah, well…" Gus said. "Do you watch much porn? People look like they're having fun in that, too."

I definitely didn't want to have a conversation with Gus about porn, I decided. Not now and probably not ever. "But it's great, isn't it," I said, "how passionate people are about your channel? How many subscribers you've got, and everything?"

Gus laughed – or it may have been a cough. It was a short, mirthless sound that started and ended somewhere in his throat and didn't seem to reach his mouth at all. "Yes, they certainly are passionate. Hey, it's a job. It beats stacking shelves in Poundland. You'll see, now that you and Charles…"

Then he paused, turned and looked towards the door. "And here is Charles now, if I'm not mistaken."

Less attuned to the sounds of the flat than Gus, it took me a moment to recognise the sound of the key in the lock, but then I heard it, and heard Charlie's voice calling, "Hey, you!"

I jumped up and hurried to meet him, pushing aside the realisation that I'd found out more about Gus in the past five minutes than I knew about my boyfriend.

"Gemma! You're here already." Charlie pulled me into a hug, and I hugged him back. "Has Gus been looking after you?"

"Of course," I said. "He gave me a glass of water. We were chatting about music."

"All terribly civilised," Charlie said. "We'll have to do something about that." He slid his hands under my top and stroked my back, and I felt something melt inside me. His hair smelled different from usual, and I noticed it was styled differently, too, presumably by whoever had done it before his photoshoot.

"So how did it go today?" I asked.

"Okay," Charlie yawned hugely. "Tedious, having like a million stylists and art directors and make-up artists pawing at me all afternoon. They're all great people, it's just…"

"You look different," I said. "What did they do to you, besides the hair? Oh my God, you've had your eyebrows plucked."

"Threaded," Charlie said. "And it hurt like fuck. Worse than when we did that vlog about waxing our backs. I don't know how girls do it. They dyed my eyelashes too, look." He fluttered them at me.

"You look like Bambi," I said. It was true – and not unsexy. But then I couldn't think of anything about Charlie that wasn't sexy.

"So, what's the plan?" he said. "Want to go out, have a couple of cocktails and some food? See a movie?"

"We've got work to do, remember?" Gus said. "We're scheduled to post a video on the main channel tomorrow."

"Oh, right. Yeah. I guess we do. What's it going to be, then?"

I followed Charlie back to the other end of the room and sat next to him on the red sofa. Gus was still staring at his laptop screen.

"Condom challenge," Gus said.

"Awesome," Charlie said. "Guess my new barnet isn't going to look so good after that."

"What's a condom challenge?" I said.

"You'll find out soon enough," Gus said. "We can do it out in the hot tub."

"Gemma can do it too," Charlie said. "Two vlogs for the price of one. I hope you brought a bikini, Gemma."

I hadn't. I had the skirt and vest top I was wearing, a dress in my bag for work the next day, and a satin camisole and matching French knickers, which were the closest thing I possessed to seductive nightwear.

"Gemma can wear a Berry Boys T-shirt," Gus said. He was still looking at his laptop screen, but I was sure I caught a glint of blue as he glanced at me under his eyelashes. I wondered how much Charlie had told him about our first night together.

"Every time I see you two I end up getting soaking wet," I said.

"Fnar," Charlie said, and he and Gus laughed. I joined in, blushing even more.

"Right," Gus said. "I'll do the dropping, you provide the head."

"No fucking way!" Charlie said. "We'll toss for it."

"Fine." Gus rummaged in his pocket and produced a coin.

"Heads," Charlie said.

Gus tossed. "Sorry, mate."

"Come on! Best of three."

"Tails again."

"Best of five!"

"Jeez, what are you, six years old? Deal with it. Suck it up. Not literally, or you'll choke. You can drop when Gemma's the victim. Okay?"

"Okay, fine," Charlie said. "I'm having a beer first though. You switch the hot tub on."

Half an hour later, we were all standing around the hot tub in the warm evening sunlight. Charlie's camera was set up on its tripod, focussed and ready to go. Charlie and Gus were wearing board shorts and flipflops. I was wearing the now-familiar yellow T-shirt and the ballet flats I'd worn to work. I wished the T-shirt was longer – it only just covered my bottom – but at least I had a bra on this time. Still, I resolved to stay out of the camera's view for as long as possible.

"In you get, Charles," Gus said. "Sooner we get started, the sooner it'll be over. Remember, that's what Mum always used to tell us before we went to the dentist?"

"I'd prefer a fucking root canal to this," Charlie grumbled, but he got into the hot tub.

Gus tore open a pack of Durex and carefully removed the foil from one. "Right, I'll fill this up indoors," he said.

"Mind you use warm water," Charlie said.

"Don't drop it!" I said, when Gus emerged a moment later, carrying the water-filled condom.

"Shit, this is really heavy," Gus said. He stepped on to the edge of the hot tub and held the condom over Charlie's head. Charlie flinched. "For God's sake keep still."

They both started to laugh, and I found myself giggling too.

Gus addressed the camera. "Hi guys. You may or may not have seen the latest craze that's sweeping the internet. It's huge, it's hilarious, and we had to try it out for you. So, brought to you by the Berry Boys, with the beautiful SparklyGems assisting, here it is: the condom challenge."

"I'm going to count down," Gus said. "Three, two… oh fuck." The condom slipped out of his hand, hit Charlie's shoulder and landed in the water. "This is harder than it looks."

I was laughing so hard I could hardly breathe. "You should have got unlubed ones."

"Stop swearing," Charlie said. "Or Sloane will tell us off again. We should have thought of a different fucking idea for this week's vlog. Go on, try again, before I bottle it."

Gus repeated the performance, filling a second condom with water, carrying it gingerly outside, holding it poised over his brother.

"Three, two, one…" He dropped the condom. It landed on Charlie's head then bounced off, splashing water everywhere and, soaking both of them. The empty condom floated in the hot tub.

Charlie pushed his dripping fringe out of his eyes. "Epic fail."

"It was so close, though," Gus said. "It nearly worked. We'll try another – third time lucky, right?"

"Okay, but if you fuck this one up, we're swapping over."

"Fair do's."

"I'll try a new condom. This one doesn't work."

My sides sore from laughing, I watched Gus go through the process again. I heard the tap running in the kitchen, then he emerged, carefully carrying the swollen water-filled condom. He positioned it above Charlie.

"Oh, man," Charlie said, pushing back his hair and laughing. "Whose idea was this, anyway?"

"Yours, if I remember correctly," Gus said, and released his missile.

This time, it was a perfect, direct hit. The condom landed on top of Charlie's head, stretching and ballooning downwards. Charlie's face was left encased in latex, the end of the condom, still swollen with water, hanging down his neck like an absurd Father Christmas beard.

"Yes!" Gus launched into a victory dance around the hot tub, laughing madly. "We did it!"

"Oh my God," Charlie said, his voice muffled. "Someone get me out of here."

With difficulty, he stretched the condom off over his head, the latex sticking to his wet hair.

"That tasted so rank," he said.

"It looked immense," Gus said.

"Come on, Gemma," Charlie said. "It's your turn."

I looked at the pack of condoms and the two boys. I could think of nothing I wanted to do less than go through the ritual humiliation Charlie had just enjoyed. But I had no choice – it was that or look like a loser and a spoilsport.

"Okay," I said reluctantly.

Then Gus said, "Hold on, that's my phone." He pulled it from his pocket and said, "Sloane. I'll stick her on speakerphone. Hey, Sloane."

Charlie climbed out of the hot tub and switched off the camera. I passed him a towel.

"Hey Gus," Sloane's voice said, tinny but clear. "What's up? I just tried to call Charlie to talk about the shoot earlier, but he didn't answer so I thought I'd check in with you."

"We're filming," Gus said. "We've just made the most epic video, you're going to love it."

"Oh yeah? What video?"

"Condom challenge," Charlie said. "It's fucking skill."

"What challenge?" Sloane said.

"Condom challenge," Gus said. "We've just done Charlie and Gemma's next. Google it. It's hilarious."

There was a pause, then Sloane said, "Hilarious? Are you crazy? Do you know how dangerous that is?"

"It's not," Charlie protested. "It's fine. I could totally breathe all the way through."

"That's not the point," Sloane said. "You could, but when some nine-year-old tries it and drowns, and it turns out they were copying you – it doesn't bear thinking about. There's no way you're posting that video."

"Oh, come on, Sloane," Gus said. "It's all over the internet. Everyone's doing it."

"We could do a disclaimer," Charlie said. "You know: 'Don't try this at home, kids, unless you've got medical help at hand and adult supervision. We will not be held responsible for any drownings or damage to soft furnishings.'"

"That sort of thing isn't worth the paper it's not written on," Sloane said, "as you know full well. I can't allow you to put that video up on your channel, end of."

"We've got to put something up by tomorrow," Gus said. "It's in the schedule."

"Well, think of something else," Sloane said. "You two are never short of ideas – it's why you're so brilliant to work with. But I'm vetoing this one, I'm afraid."

"Oh man, you're no fun," Charlie said, but I could sense that they were going to capitulate.

"You'll thank me for it when you still have an income in a year's time," Sloane said crisply. "Now, Mia emailed me over some contact sheets from today and they look really great. I'll forward them for you to look at if you like, but our feelings were that the more informal shots…"

Charlie picked up the phone and turned off the speaker. Gus went inside and picked up his laptop again. I followed and stood for a moment, not sure what I was expected to do. Then I went to Charlie's bedroom and got changed back into my work clothes.

When I returned to the living room, Charlie had finished his call. He and Gus were outside on the balcony, looking down at the canal below. I joined them.

"Look," Charlie said. "Swans."

"And they've got babies!" I said. "Cute. How many – seven?"

"There used to be eight," Gus said. "We haven't seen the other one for a bit. We think…"

"We think that cygnet was the rebel cygnet," Charlie said firmly. "He's gone off to Manchester to join a rock band."

"He's jamming all day and gigging all night and shagging groupie swans, just because he can. He's living the dream," Gus said.

"And he'll come home for Christmas and the parent swans will be like, 'When are you going to get a proper job?'"

I laughed. "So what's the plan then? For your video, I mean."

Charlie said, "No idea, to be honest."

Gus said, "Fuck it, we'll think of something tomorrow. What's Sloane going to do, anyway – sack us? We're their second-biggest client. She's not the boss of us."

"Gus wants to go out," Charlie said. "Alto Club?"

"I'm bored of the Alto," Gus said.

"Nightjar?" Charlie suggested. "Wishy Washy?"

"There have been fans hanging around outside Wishy Washy every night since our launch," Gus said. "They keep asking on Twitter when we're going there again."

"Therefore, we aren't," Charlie said.

"And last time we went to Nightjar we couldn't get a table, remember?" Gus said. "They didn't even know who we were."

I didn't point out the obvious inconsistency in his argument.

"What's that new place Glen was going on about?" Charlie said. "They make their own bitters and do Peruvian street food, and they've got a popcorn menu?"

"The Clam and Cactus," Gus said. "Remember, Glen was wanking on about the ceviche martini. What if we bump into him there, though? We'd have to talk to him."

"He's in Singapore, remember? He posted that video about his first-class flight."

"Git," Charlie said. "When we went to Hong Kong in April they only flew us business."

"Not that we're bitter or anything," Gus said. "Right, Crayfish and whatsit it is then."

I said, "But Sloane said… and I've got nothing to wear."

"Wear what you're wearing now," Gus said.

"You look gorgeous," Charlie said. "You are gorgeous. Come on, Augustus, let's get some clothes on and go."

So it was settled. Charlie and Gus got dressed and I hastily slapped on a bit of make-up, and we headed out. I couldn't help noticing that there had been no discussion – no question

– about whether Gus was going to come out with us. But then, I thought, going out had been his idea, so really it was us who were tagging along with him, or me who was tagging along with the two boys.

Anyway, any misgivings I'd had about the evening were soon dispelled by the fabulousness of the Clam and Cactus. Once again, I couldn't help thinking of Jack – how impressed he would have been by the shelves laden with jars of mysterious cocktail ingredients (as well as less mysterious ones, like olives, but there seemed to be about a dozen different kinds of those); the exotic drinks on the menu, made with things I'd never even heard of; the beautiful waitresses gliding across the room with trays held above their heads, not spilling a drop.

Never mind Jack – I was impressed. I gazed around in the dim light, taking in the peacock-blue velvet banquettes, the shelves groaning with hardback books, the paintings on the wall of mountain scenery, which I supposed must be Peru. Where Jack was, or was going to be soon. Maybe now he was seeing the world, he wouldn't be so excited by a London cocktail bar. But I was – and then, when I looked at the prices on the menu, a bit horrified. Fifteen quid for a cocktail? That was more than Jack and I would have paid for a whole meal, when we were going out.

"What are you having, Gemma?" Charlie said. "I'm going for a pisco Old Fashioned."

"I'll try the ceviche Martini," Gus said. "It would be rude not to, right?"

"Um… I think I'll just have a glass of white wine," I said.

"Really? Why?" Charlie said.

Gus looked at me, and I saw a flash of understanding. "Don't be boring, Gemma, have a cocktail. Go on – it's my treat, since you two saved me from sitting at home editing videos and being bored out of my skull."

Gratefully, I let myself be persuaded, and picked something randomly off the menu, involving mezcal and champagne.

"And we'll have some chipotle popcorn, and a bottle of sparkling water," Charlie said.

The popcorn was delicious, almost burning the top of my mouth off, so I had to drink my cocktail really fast to put out the flames. Then Gus ordered another round, and I had something different, and then Charlie ordered a bottle of champagne and some food, and after that things all got a bit hazy.

Charlie and Gus kept up a constant flow of chatter, and I joined in, but I couldn't help feeling that I was interrupting a well-rehearsed performance. They made each other laugh all the time, and their laughter was so infectious I found myself laughing too, even though I didn't always understand their jokes. After the third or fourth round of drinks – like I said, things were a bit hazy by that point – the jokes became more obscure, and the conversation harder to follow. The food was gorgeous and I was very hungry, but Gus and Charlie kept ordering more and more things, until there was more on the table than we could possibly finish.

"Pudding?" Charlie said at last.

"I can't, I'm so full," I said, yawning hugely.

Gus looked at the plates scattered on the table, some half-finished, some barely touched. "This is all a bit last days of Rome, isn't it? I think I'll go out for a fag."

He stood up, wobbled, steadied and headed for the door. The two boys had had even more to drink than I had, I realised. Charlie signalled for the bill. I tried not to yawn again, but failed.

"I'm sorry," I said. "You're not boring me, it's just…"

"Poor Gemma, I keep forgetting you have to get up in the morning to do actual work," Charlie said.

"I know, right? Poor me."

"Can't you throw a sickie and sleep in?" I felt his hand caressing my thigh. For a moment I let myself imagine what it would be like to have no job to go to – then I remembered how frightening and boring the reality of that had been. For me, having no proper job had meant having no money; for the Berry Boys, it was quite different.

"I wish," I said. "I'd get sacked."

"You could make videos with me all day then," Charlie said. "Come on, let's find my brother and get you home to bed."

I don't remember the taxi ride back to The Factory; I think I must have fallen asleep. I do remember going up to the flat in the lift, looking at my face in the mirror next to Charlie's, and thinking how much I fancied him. I remember going to the bathroom and taking off my make-up and cleaning my teeth, and wondering which of the fluffy snow-white towels I was supposed to use. I remember putting on my satin camisole and knickers, and opening the door to Charlie's dark bedroom, and seeing the back of his blonde head on the pillow, and getting under the duvet next to him and snuggling up to his bare back, stroking his chest gently with my fingernails.

And then his voice shouted: "Oi! What are you doing in bed with my brother?"

I sprang away as if the skin I'd touched was red hot. Charlie emerged from behind the curtain where he'd been hiding. Gus rolled over next to me, shaking with laughter.

Then I saw the camera on top on the bedside table, its glass eye trained on the bed, and I understood what they'd done.

"That's tomorrow's video sorted," Gus said. "Thanks, Gemma."

"I'm sorry, babe," Charlie said. Then he started laughing again. "Oh my God, your face!"

I made myself laugh too, even though I didn't think it was funny. Not really.

Chapter Fourteen

On my way to work the next day, hungover and hollow-eyed with lack of sleep (because, of course, after Gus and Charlie had finished laughing and Gus had gone to bed, Charlie and I had resumed the sex I'd inadvertently initiated with his brother), I replayed over and over in my mind what had happened. And soon, checking my Twitter feed, I realised I was going to replay it online, too.

Pranking Charlie's bae, the Berry Boys' tweet read. *Check out our new video – sorry @sparklygems and thanks for the LOLs.*

Sorry, not sorry, I thought. And why should they be sorry? Pranking videos were what they did. By being Charlie's girlfriend – Charlie's bae – I'd signed up to be part of that. So why did I feel – I tried to get my feelings straight in my head – cheated, almost? Exposed. Humiliated.

I plugged my headphones in and pressed play on the video. I saw Gus and Charlie in Charlie's bedroom, giggling as Charlie took his T-shirt off and Gus pulled it on. I saw Gus peering into the mirror, rearranging his hair to look more like his brother's, before climbing into bed and pulling the duvet up to his chin. I heard Charlie say, "Shit, I think she's coming," and duck behind the curtain.

Then, before I could see myself coming into the room, see myself in the sexy lingerie I'd meant for Charlie's eyes only, not for hundreds of thousands of YouTube viewers, the train pulled into the station and I had to press pause, stuff my phone back into my bag and join the shuffling throng of commuters emerging on to Oxford Street to begin their working day.

And, I reminded myself, my working day was beginning, too. What happened in front of a camera, in the evenings, alone in my bedroom or with Charlie – that wasn't work. Work was brainstorming meetings with my colleagues, hoping my Clickfrenzy posts would get all the hits, making rounds of tea. Work was 'Why The World Would Be A Better Place With Cats In Charge'. Sometimes I looked back and remembered how thrilled I'd been about my new job, back in June, and wondered whether I'd have felt the same if I'd known that it was going to be wall-to-wall cats, every day. I wondered if there was any hope of that ever changing, but I made myself not think about it, because the idea that it might not, that I'd be stuck trying to think of funny things to say about cats forever and ever, was too depressing to contemplate. And I reminded myself that I was lucky – I could be unemployed, barely making ends meet on benefits or on a zero-hours contract somewhere, or scraping by with one waitressing job after another, still living with Mum. This was real life – this was what paid the rent.

Maybe, I told myself, glancing longingly into the window of Liberty as I walked past, my channel would get big enough for me to quit Clickfrenzy and vlog full-time. People did – not many of them, but enough for new people to start vlogs all the time, hoping that they, too, would make it. And I'd been extraordinarily lucky

– through a series of accidents, I'd already got bigger than I'd ever dreamed I would. I hadn't had another payment from YouTube yet, but I knew it would be bigger than the last one. Maybe a lot bigger, even with Sloane's commission taken off.

Then I thought of the hundreds of comments and tweets I still needed to read and respond to, and I remembered the jaded cynicism with which Gus talked about their channel and their fans, and I wondered whether I'd be able to sustain the real sense of connection I'd felt at first, with all the people who'd confided in me and consoled me about Jack.

And then I realised I'd been so deep in thought I'd walked right past the glass front of Clickfrenzy HQ, and I had to turn and hurry back, and I was almost ten minutes late.

The weird thing was, once I was in the office, sitting at my computer, combing through Tumblr for pictures of kittens that bore a passing resemblance to Miley Cyrus (surprisingly easy, given the twerking), it was hard to even picture Charlie's face. I couldn't channel the personality of the other Gemma, the one who made vlogs about make-up and healthy breakfasts and had a boyfriend who, if you were a certain kind of teenage girl, was, like, the most famous person in the world.

When I was with Charlie – as I was more nights than not, over the next week or so – my normal life seemed equally remote. He never asked me about work. He'd never had a normal job, and nor had Gus. I don't think he really understood what it was like to go to an office every day and sit behind a desk where you had to be by half past nine and weren't expected to leave before six. For Charlie, work meant lying in bed editing a video, going to a meet and greet and signing autographs, rolling his eyes when his mobile rang and he saw that it was Sloane.

It was almost as if there were two Gemmas, living two different lives, and I wasn't sure which one was really me.

I was mulling over this at my desk when, as if she'd been summoned from the ether by my thoughts in the manner of Lord Voldemort, I saw Sloane's name flash up on my own phone. I glanced around the office. Emily had said she had a dentist appointment and would be in late; Tom and Hermione were in a meeting with an advertiser. Sarah's office was empty.

I picked up my phone and slipped in, closing the door behind me.

"Gemma! How's it going?"

"Okay, thanks," I said. I wondered what she'd thought about the prank Charlie and Gus had played on me, and whether she cared how it had made me feel, then dismissed the idea straight away. It was still too raw, too intimate – and now, of course, too public for Sloane to do anything about it, even if she wanted to, which she wouldn't.

"I have got the most exciting news for you," Sloane said. "We have a new client, a young, fresh brand called Cantaloupe. You know them?"

"I think the name rings a bell," I lied.

"Great! Then you'll know that it's the brainchild of Ivy Savage, the model, you must have heard of her, and Colin Colbert, the celebrity aromatherapist."

What did that mean, I wondered? That Colin was famous for being an aromatherapist, or that celebrities smelled his… whatever things aromatherapists did.

"Cool," I said.

"Yes! Cool describes the brand perfectly. Cool, a little quirky, luxurious but affordable. They've been very exclusive until recently, very boutique, promoting the brand mostly through word of mouth. But now they're ready to take the next step in their marketing journey and reach out to a new, younger audience. And that's where you come in."

"Really?" I said. I often got the sense, when talking to Sloane, that I wasn't required to respond to her at all. She'd got her script all worked out and she'd deliver it regardless of what I said or didn't say.

"Yes! So here's the plan. I'm going to courier round some product – you're in the office, right? And maybe this evening you could have a little look, vlog about your first impressions of the brand – you know, all very informal and natural. And if you like what you see – and I know you will, Gemma, you and Cantaloupe are, like, the most totally natural fit ever – then we can organise some face time with them, and talk about how we can evolve you as a brand partnership."

"That sounds amazing," I said.

"It is! Totally amazing! The most rewarding thing about my work is finding opportunities like this, synergies that I know really have legs. But I won't keep you any longer. Look out for our delivery later, and I'll look out for your post in the morning."

"Thanks, Sloane."

"You're welcome. And by the way, I just adore your pyjamas."

She ended the call, leaving me flooded with fresh mortification.

*

"I'm sorry. I'm so sorry. Excuse me, please." With difficulty, I manoeuvred myself and the enormous box containing the Cantaloupe delivery on to the packed Victoria line train, a barrage of tuts and glares following me. The box wasn't heavy (okay, it was actually – my arms were trembling pathetically and I resolved for the millionth time to spend more time in the gym. Or any time in the gym) but its awkward bulk meant that I could hardly see where I was going, and I kept jabbing people with its rigid, high quality corners.

Maybe if I became their official brand ambassador, Ivy the model and whatshisname the aromatherapist would deliver my samples to my home. But then I'd have to fess up to Richard and Hannah about what I was doing in my bedroom at night, and while it wasn't like I was growing weed or sending abortion pills to women in Northern Ireland or any other overtly dodgy activity, I was fairly sure they would not approve.

Maybe Cantaloupe would love me so much that they'd offer me a massive, lucrative contract and I could resign from my job at Clickfrenzy and spend all my time filming myself playing with beauty products and hanging out with Charlie. That idea should have appealed to me massively, but for some reason it didn't.

I wrestled the box up the final escalator. *Nearly home*, I told myself. I was soaked in sweat and had scraped the skin off my knuckles and broken a fingernail. *I should film myself,* I thought – give my viewers an insight into the unglamorous side of being a vlogger. But I needed both hands for the box, so I couldn't even do that.

I was considering putting the wretched thing down and giving my arms a rest – or even, the way I was feeling, abandoning it,

Sloane, Cantaloupe and the whole vlogging thing entirely – when I heard a voice behind me.

"Hey Gemma! Need a hand?"

It was Raffy and Luke from the coffee shop.

"Hi," I said. "My God, a hand would be amazing. That's so kind of you. Are you sure…"

"We were just off to the pub," Raffy said. "I'll see you there in five, mate, I'll just help Gemma get this home. You're on your way home, right?" He took the box from me, lifting it easily. I stretched my aching biceps.

"Yes. I got this stuff for a video I need to film tonight. I was feeling quite excited about it, but I'm totally over it already. It's this road here on the left," I said, and then I remembered that of course he knew, having walked me home before.

"So where have you been recently? Luke says you haven't come in for your coffee for a couple of days. You haven't defected to Starbucks, have you?"

"Of course not. I've been… I haven't been home the last couple of nights."

"I see," Raffy said. He was wearing sunglasses, so I couldn't be sure, but I thought he raised one eyebrow just a tiny bit. I imagined his little niece watching the video Charlie had posted, maybe showing it to Raffy, and I died a bit inside.

I said, "But what about you? You haven't been there either. If anyone could be accused of defecting to Starbucks…"

"Oh," Raffy said. "I've moved on. The world of takeaway coffee is losing its brightest star. Luke's going to have to find someone else to screw up orders and piss off his customers. I'm just moving my stuff out of the flat, that's why I came today."

"Oh," I said. I wanted to ask him why he'd left, but I realised I didn't know why he'd been working there in the first place. "I'm sorry. I'll miss you. Where are you going? I mean, do you have another job, that's not making coffee?"

"I expect something will come up," Raffy said.

"Here we are," I said, stopping outside Hannah and Richard's front door, fumbling in my bag for my keys. "Thanks for helping me."

"No problem," Raffy said. "Want me to take this in for you?"

I imagined him following me up the stairs to my bedroom, putting the box down on the floor, closing the door – and shut the thought down before it could go any further. *You've got a boyfriend, Gemma*, I reminded myself.

"It's cool, I can manage from here," I said. "And, you know, thanks again."

"We'll be in the Prince George," he said, "if you fancy a drink later."

He took his sunglasses off and I saw again the extraordinary colour of his eyes – so pale a blue they were barely a colour at all against his tanned skin.

"I'd love to," I said. "But this is going to take me a few hours. I won't be done until midnight."

"Pity," he said casually. "Take care, anyway."

He touched my shoulder, leaned in and kissed me lightly on both cheeks.

"You too," I said, but I don't think he heard me, because he'd already turned away and was walking quickly and gracefully back up the road towards the station.

Hi everyone. It's been a few days since I've posted a video, so I really hope this one will be worth the wait. I think it will be, because I'm just so excited about what I've got to show you today. Now, first of all, in the interests of full disclosure, I'm going to tell you that I received these products from the company that makes them, as a gift. So they're all new to me, and I think they're probably new to you as well – this is a brand I'd never heard of until today, but I think we're going to be seeing a lot of Cantaloupe in the future.

Earlier in the evening, I would have been happy never to see anything of Cantaloupe ever again. But, once I'd manhandled the box up to my room, carefully slit open the tape securing its lid, and tipped the fragrant contents out on to my bed, I'd started to feel quite enthusiastic. I had a whole boxful of shiny, pretty things that smelled amazing – all for me.

So, first of all, let me tell you guys a little about Cantaloupe. I thought the name must mean something to do with wolves, but I googled and it turns out it's a kind of melon. Every day's a school day, right? And it was started by Ivy Savage, the Victoria's Secret Angel, and a guy called Colin Colbert, who has actually massaged Beyoncé. I know, right? So when I was offered the opportunity to try some of their range I was like, "Yes please!"

The first thing I noticed about these products was how totally gorgeous they smell. It's like a blend of something citrussy – lime, I think – and something floral. And it's just really fresh and feminine. I can imagine going out every day smelling like this and getting all the compliments. And the second thing I noticed was how beautifully packaged they are. You can see the colour scheme – everything's coral and rose gold, so it's kind of princessy but also really grown up and sophisticated. But you can't see the actual quality – how solid and expensive they feel. They even make the best noises when you open them. Listen.

I picked up a compact mirror and opened it. The case made a clicking sound that was undeniably satisfying. I pushed back my hair and looked at the camera. It seemed to be watching me expectantly.

The problem was, piled up on my bed was a collection of beautifully packaged, gorgeously scented things I couldn't imagine anyone, ever, actually wanting to use.

The mirror, for all its pleasing heft in my palm and jewel-like casing, was so heavy I couldn't imagine wanting to carry it around with me, and so pretty that if I did, I'd be constantly afraid of losing it. There was a lovely pink and copper lipstick caddy that suffered from the same problem – and the additional problem of being a lipstick caddy in the first place. I mean, who ever uses one of those? I'd had to turn once again to Google to find out what one even was. It was all I could do to remember to put a tube of lipstick in my handbag in the mornings, never mind remembering to put it in a special little case first.

There were hair masks and foot masks and things called pillow masks, which, confusingly, you wore on your face and not on your pillow at all.

There was a thing called a Himalayan salt lamp, which looked like a large, cumbersome tea light holder but apparently had magical powers and when lit would release negative ions or positive vibes or something into the atmosphere. It smelled wonderful, but – negative ions? Google suggested that the science was dubious at best. But I couldn't say that, of course.

I looked around me at all the stuff scattered on my duvet, and looked up into the waiting eye of the camera. I had to finish this video. I'd promised Sloane. I'd even bought a new ring light for my camera with money I didn't have, in anticipation of earning it back if Cantaloupe liked me.

"Come on, Stanley," I said. "Let's do this thing."

Two hours later, I was done. I'd picked out the least outlandish of the products and thought of nice things to say about them (and found some not too nasty critical things to say too, because Sloane had mentioned that that would add authenticity to my content). It was hard to imagine any content less authentic than what I'd just posted, but it was going to have to do.

"Stanley," I said, "if I say the word 'gorgeous' one more time, my tongue is literally going to fall out."

My teddy didn't say anything. I said, "And your eye's going to fall off if I don't get my act together and sew it back on, isn't it? And then where would we be?"

I kissed his threadbare head, then played the edited video one last time, just to make sure I wasn't obviously gurning at any point, and that the bit where I said, "What the fuck is the fucking point of all this fucking stuff, anyway?" had been removed in its entirety. Then I went online and posted it on YouTube and linked to it on Twitter and Instagram. I was done. I'd done my best.

I remembered how, just a few hours ago, I'd been envying Charlie his easy life, his ability to make an amount of money that was unimaginable to me without having a real, proper job. I was beginning to understand, now, why Gus rolled his eyes to heaven when he saw Sloane's number on his phone; why they'd been so annoyed when she had vetoed their condom challenge video; why Charlie said, "More fucking editing," when he reached for his laptop in the morning.

I could almost, but not quite, understand why any content for their channel, even making a fool of me, was fair game.

"That's that done, anyway," I said to Stanley. "I'm bloody starving now. I wonder if I've got any food in the fridge."

Wearily, I packed all the stuff back in the shiny Cantaloupe box. I'd have to get rid of it all somehow – I wasn't going to use any of it. I could put it on eBay, I supposed, but that felt like it would be compounding my dishonesty. I could take it to the charity shop, but the idea of carrying the box another step made me want to cry. I tried to push it under my bed, but it wouldn't fit, so I shoved it into the corner of the room under the window. I'd decide what to do with it tomorrow.

I thought about calling Charlie, but then I remembered he'd said he and Gus were going to yet another book signing. Amy was working a night shift. I looked around my bedroom, at the tasteful furniture and the white duvet and the fairy lights and the closed door, and felt suddenly claustrophobic. My phone buzzed with the first of the rush of comments and tweets that came, now, whenever I posted a video, and I realised I'd never felt so lonely in my life.

Then the solution came to me – it was obvious. I'd go out. I'd go down the road to the pub and see if Raffy and Luke were still there. It was only nine thirty – they'd probably even still be serving food. I could have a burger and chips and a glass of wine, and chat and socialise like a normal person. I didn't even need to change or put on make-up – I'd done my face before I started filming.

"Right," I told Stanley. "That's it. Decision made. You hold the fort here."

I laced up my Converse, picked up my bag and opened my bedroom door, giddy with excitement and relief.

"This feels almost like having a life," I said aloud.

But just as I started down the stairs, I heard the front door open and Richard's voice.

"… ever make a fucking fool of me like that in public again," he was saying – almost shouting.

I paused. *Shit.* I didn't want to go barging in on them in the middle of a row.

"Richard, I didn't. Seriously. I didn't mean to do anything…" Hannah sounded almost pleading, and definitely as if she'd been crying.

I retreated into my bedroom, pulled the door shut and sat down on my bed, trying not to make a sound.

"What, are you saying you can't control yourself? That you got drunk at a work event with my colleagues because you have no agency? Because if so, you need help, Hannah."

"I'm not drunk! I had three glasses of wine."

"You're lying. You look drunk, you're acting drunk. You embarrassed yourself and you embarrassed me."

I sat on my bed, frozen. Their voices were coming clearly up the stairs from the living room; either they didn't know I was home, or they didn't care. I simply didn't know what to do – interrupt them, and hope I could somehow defuse the situation? Somehow I got the sense that it was beyond defusing. And anyway, it was private. Normal couples didn't play out their relationships in public, like Charlie and I were doing. Normal couples had rows, didn't they? Probably one or both of them would apologise and they'd go to bed and have make-up sex and in the morning it would all be forgotten.

"I didn't mean to, Richard, honestly. I was just trying to be sociable. I was just…"

"You were fucking hitting on every man you spoke to. Jesus. It was sickening to watch. Even Lawrence, and he's gay, for Christ's sake. If you could have seen yourself."

"I know he's gay, Rich! He couldn't be more obviously gay if he tried! I was just chatting to him. I thought it would be okay to talk to him, *because* he's gay. After what happened last time, I thought…"

"What do you mean, 'last time'? Would that be the time at my brother's wedding, when you turned up dressed like you were going out on the pull in Liverpool on a Saturday night, and practically snogged my cousin on the dance floor and then fell over your own feet because you were so pissed?"

Hannah said, "It was a wedding, Richard! Everyone was pissed. I said I was sorry, afterwards."

Richard stopped shouting. His voice was very quiet now, so quiet I had to strain to hear him. "Yes, you did say you were sorry. You apologised and you promised it wouldn't happen again. And clearly you didn't mean a word of it. Either that or, as I said, you just can't control yourself."

"Please, Richard," Hannah said. "Don't be like this. I don't know what to do any more. It's like every time we're out with other people and I'm having fun, we end up having a massive row about it."

"Well, there's a simple and obvious solution to that," said Richard. "If you can't be trusted to behave decently around my friends, then I can't attend social events with you."

"But you don't like it when I go out with my own friends, either," Hannah said. "It's like you don't want me to have a life at all."

"What friends would those be?" Richard said. "That slapper Helena? Karen, or whatever her name is, who hasn't bothered to even get in touch with you for six months? You don't have any friends, and quite frankly I'm beginning to understand why."

"Karen only doesn't talk to me any more because you..." Hannah began, then she seemed to change her mind, and started again. "Rich. Darling, please. It's like we can't even talk about stuff we don't agree about without bringing up all this ancient history. I hate having rows like this."

"You bring it upon yourself," Richard said. "You're your own worst enemy. It's like you can't see how you're destroying our relationship with your thoughtlessness. Tonight was an important event for me. Senior management was there. I should have been networking, furthering my career, not having to leave early with my drunk girlfriend because she can't be trusted to behave decently in public."

Hannah said, "Richard, for God's sake, I'm not… Look, I'm sorry. Maybe I don't understand the way you do things in the corporate world. I had a couple of glasses of wine, I was chatting to your colleagues. I thought I was doing the right thing. If I wasn't, I'm really sorry."

No! I wanted to scream. *Don't apologise to him! Why the hell should you apologise when he's being a complete bastard and it sounds like you did nothing wrong?* But then I thought, *How do I know? I wasn't there. Maybe Hannah did get drunk and flirt with this Lawrence guy. Maybe Richard was embarrassed.* But still, somehow, I knew whose side I was on, and it wasn't his.

"This is what you say every time. 'I'm sorry, Richard. I won't do it again, Richard. Please be nice to me, Richard.' And then you go and do just the same bloody thing again and again. I'm tired of it, Hannah. You make me tired. I'm going to bed. You can sleep down here on the sofa."

I heard his feet thump up the stairs past my door, and found myself holding my breath as he passed. But he didn't stop; he carried on up the stairs and I heard their bedroom door close.

I sat in the dark and listened, but I couldn't hear Hannah at all. If I heard the sound of her crying, I'd go downstairs and talk to her, I promised myself. But I heard nothing, and I did nothing. It was too late now for me to go out, and I didn't feel hungry any more, so I waited for a bit, listening to the silence, and then I took off my make-up and got into bed. Even though every bit of me was thrumming with tension, I was so exhausted I fell asleep straight away.

In the morning, Hannah and Richard were having their tea and porridge at the kitchen table, just the same as every morning.

If I hadn't known, I might not have noticed that there were deep shadows under Hannah's eyes, and Richard didn't say a single word to her in the time it took me to eat two pieces of toast and honey, get my things together and leave for work – which, admittedly, I did as quickly as I possibly could.

Chapter Fifteen

"Good news!" Sloane said. "Cantaloupe loved your video. Really loved it. They're over the moon about working with you. They love you! So I thought we should have a quick catch-up about that, and then talk about some other exciting ideas I have for you."

It was lunchtime, and we were sitting in the snow-white meeting room at Ripple Effect. I'd practically sprinted there from the office in order to get there for the assigned time, and I knew from experience that the meeting was likely to take up my entire lunch break. I looked longingly at the jar of jelly beans on the table, but resisted. I had two huge spots on my chin and could feel an ominous tingling on my top lip that I was sure was going to erupt into a hideous, painful cold sore.

In the couple of weeks since I'd overheard Hannah and Richard's row, I'd been spending more and more time at Charlie and Gus's place. I told myself it was because I wanted to be with Charlie, and I did, of course. But there was more to it than that – after all, if all I wanted was to be with him, couldn't we just as easily hang out and sleep and eat takeaways and make videos in my bedroom in Hackney? Charlie's flat was more comfortable, I told myself. He had better cameras and decent lights. It made sense for me to be there – and besides, I didn't want Gus to ever think that I was somehow stealing his brother away from him.

I justified my decision to myself like that, but I knew there was more to it. Whenever I was in my own bedroom, I felt ill at ease, constantly listening for raised voices. I avoided the kitchen and the living room in case Richard was there. I felt awkward about having eavesdropped on their argument. I didn't want them to know I'd intruded on their privacy in that way, even though I hadn't meant to. And I couldn't get rid of a lingering sense of guilt – a nagging knowledge that I should have intervened to support Hannah. But I hadn't, and it made me want to avoid her as much as I wanted to avoid Richard. And so, gradually, more of my clothes and toiletries were making their way from my room to Charlie's flat – the previous week, I'd even tucked Stanley into my bag and moved him over.

"Now," Sloane said, "I know you think I'm a total old woman about this, Gemma, but it really is important that you maintain a presence across multiple channels. I noticed you were on Twitter yesterday and that's great, there was such cute interaction between you and Charlie – so adorable, honestly, I could just eat the two of you up – but it's important that you interact with your fans too, and that means spreading your wings – you need a presence on other social media too, and not just when you upload a new video. Your fans want to see as much of your life as possible, so tell them what you're up to, even if you don't think it's that interesting, and, more importantly, show them! And I know we've talked about this before, but we really do need to get a blog set up for you. We can get one of the juniors here to do most of the writing, but only with input from you. After all, you're the creative force behind SparklyGems!"

She paused for breath, and I stopped nodding in agreement, although my chin did rise and fall a couple more times from sheer momentum. I looked at the jelly beans again, then looked away. I fought the urge to yawn. I didn't want to make excuses, but Sloane always seemed to forget that I had a job – that responding to comments from my viewers and "interacting with other content creators" online as she had instructed meant that I hadn't texted Katie or Nancy for weeks (although, I realised, they'd pretty much stopped texting me, too). It meant rushing through things at work and then sneaking off to lock myself in the loo with my phone. And Charlie was the same – he texted me loads during the day wanting to know what I was doing and making plans to see each other again, or sometimes just sending me links to stuff he'd found online to make me laugh. Just that morning, he'd sent me a link to my own 'These Cats Hanging With Their Besties Will Melt Your Heart' post. I hadn't the heart to tell him to look at the byline.

Sloane had instructed me to post new content on my channel every day, which meant hours of editing, filming and a constant low-level worry that I was going to run out of ideas. It also meant I was permanently knackered.

I know, I know – I'm whinging about living a life I knew my viewers would kill to have. I was living the YouTube dream – I had a gorgeous boyfriend who was mobbed by fans whenever he went out, which meant I got mobbed too. I got regular deliveries of free products to try (redirected by Sloane to Charlie's apartment, so carrying boxes on the Tube was a thing of the past). I was making more money from my channel, and the payments, even though they were only a few hundred pounds a month, made me tingle with pride whenever I looked at my bank balance online.

But even that wasn't without its problems, because whenever I did log in to see whether a payment had arrived from YouTube, I was forced to confront the fact that I was haemorrhaging far more money than I was bringing in. Every night out with Charlie and Gus meant buying something new to wear, because I couldn't possibly pose for selfies with his fans in a top I'd bought from Primark three years before. Doing make-up videos meant buying new products to use in them. And even though Charlie always insisted on paying when we went out, I felt so guilty about it that I was forever buying random presents for him to make up for it.

So although I couldn't properly quell the doubts that kept surfacing in my mind – the feeling that I wasn't actually in control of the direction my life was taking – I was too busy to care.

"So I'm thinking we need to set up some collabs for you," Sloane went on. "Something around healthy eating, with Maddie, because I know the two of you have that in common." There went my last chance of grabbing a handful of jelly beans, I thought. "And maybe a shopping trip with Carly – we're talking with Bicester Village about some potential synergies, so you could spend a day there together and then post a haul video. How about that?"

"That sounds great," I said, my heart sinking slightly at the thought of spending an entire Saturday shopping with a girl I didn't even know, and then another Saturday taking back everything I'd bought, because I couldn't afford to keep any of it.

"And I see you were chatting with Lola on her wardrobe tour video – how about you follow that up with one of your own? Your viewers love to get the inside track into your fashion secrets, and of course they love seeing a little more of your home than you show in your regular vlogs."

"Cool," I said. "I'll do my best to film that tonight. I'm not sure whether Charlie…"

"Ah, yes, of course," Sloane said. "You might have plans together. Don't stress about it, Gemma, I know you need your ideas to flow organically, and it's so important to nurture your relationship as well. You two! So adorable!"

I smiled. She was right – well, about Charlie, anyway. He was adorable. Adorable, and hot, and funny. And there was a sweetness about him – almost a vulnerability. It was always Charlie who called me, Charlie who wanted to arrange to meet up, Charlie who texted me last thing at night when I wasn't staying over (which, to be fair, meant about three o'clock in the morning for him) to wish me sweet dreams and tell me he was thinking about me.

I know it sounds as if I was taking him for granted, and perhaps I was, a bit. But a huge part of me still couldn't actually believe that this man, who was not only breathtakingly gorgeous but an actual celebrity (at least if you were under sixteen) seemed to genuinely like me, to want a relationship with me. That was the part of me that held back just a little – the part that expected that it could all fall apart at any time; that Charlie would burst out laughing and tell me it was all a prank, another of his and Gus's elaborately set up jokes.

At last, I said my goodbyes to Sloane and hurried out, conscious that our meeting had overrun by almost ten minutes, so I was going to have to leg it back to work in order to avoid being late for a meeting with the promo team there. But as I hurried down the street, I heard a voice behind me calling, "Gemma! It's Gemma! SparklyGems!"

I stopped and turned around. Two teenage girls were following me, both brandishing their phones and smiling eagerly.

"We love your videos!" one of them said.

"We can't believe you're dating Charlie Berry," said her friend. "We're well jel. What's he like in real life?"

"You're so tall," the first girl said. "Even taller than you look online. I love your shoes."

"Can we take a selfie with you?"

"We've been waiting out here for, like, two hours and you're the first YouTuber we've seen."

"Someone said you're launching a make-up line. Is it true?"

"Are you and Charlie going to get married?"

I couldn't not stop and talk to them. It was important, obviously – it was part of my job – part of one of my jobs. But also, they were so sweet, their enthusiasm so infectious that I found myself smiling and chatting away for a few minutes, and taking selfies with them and even posting one on Instagram while they watched. That would keep Sloane happy for a bit, anyway.

By the time we said goodbye, I was well and truly, irretrievably late for the meeting, and had to make up a not-very-plausible excuse about getting caught up in a Hare Krishna parade on Oxford Street. And then, to make matters worse, I found myself nodding off while Tom was talking about choosing keywords that would keep us one step ahead of the Google algorithms, and Emily had to kick my ankle under the boardroom table to wake me up.

*

"Do you guys own a food processor?" I asked Charlie.

"A what?"

"A food processor. I'm making low-carb sushi for a video. Apparently it's a thing."

"Low-carb sushi?" Gus said. "That sounds gross."

"I know, right? But I need to post something tonight and this was all I could think of. So I need to make processed cauliflower."

"Cauliflower? You're totally not selling this to us, Gemma," Charlie said.

I said, "But it's packed with vital nutrients, including B-complex vitamins and essential fatty acids, and just think about it – when you eat regular white rice you may as well just be eating sugar."

"What's wrong with sugar?" Charlie said. "I had Frosties for lunch and I'm still alive."

"Why don't you ever make videos of nice food?" Gus said.

"Like mac and cheese," Charlie said. "Or pizza? You always do healthy stuff, and it's always rank."

"Like those boiled bones you made last week," Gus said. "The flat stank for ages afterwards. Who eats boiled bones, anyway?"

I chucked a tea towel across the room at him, and missed. "You don't eat the bones, you muppet. You drink the stuff they're boiled in. Bone broth. It's even more of a thing than low-carb sushi. And Sloane wants me to do healthy stuff. She says I need to be a role model for a healthy lifestyle."

"But you're not," Charlie pointed out. "You make all this paleo shit and then you eat toast."

I couldn't really argue with that. The bone broth experiment hadn't exactly been successful. I hadn't read the recipe properly before I started, so I hadn't realised that it needed to cook for eight hours, and then be strained multiple times, and by the time I'd filmed all that (not the whole eight hours of gentle simmering, obviously – that wouldn't have made for compelling viewing) and cleaned up the kitchen and edited and posted the video, I was so sick of the sight and smell of the stuff I hadn't been able to face even tasting it, and it was three o'clock in the morning anyway, so I'd tipped it wearily down the plughole and gone to bed.

Still, the video had been made – that was the main thing. And tonight's was going to have to be made too. I dug around in the kitchen drawers and eventually located a cheese grater, which didn't look as if it had ever seen active service, and set to work on the cauliflower.

"So here we have it," I told the camera, two hours later. "Crab and avocado rolls, spicy tuna rolls, salmon and cucumber rolls and egg and spring onion rolls. Delicious and so easy to make!"

I looked around at the kitchen. The 'easy to make' bit was a lie, obviously, and I wasn't even going to talk about the mess I'd made. Bits of cauliflower, salmon skin and rolls that hadn't ended up camera-ready were scattered all over the normally pristine white worktop – pristine, obviously, because nothing more complicated than a fish finger sandwich had ever been made in this kitchen before I arrived on the scene.

"I don't suppose you two want to try some of this?" I said.

"Thanks for offering, Gemma, but we're a bit busy right now," Gus said.

"Careful! Jesus, you almost crashed into that asteroid," Charlie said.

"Asteroid?" I said, looking more closely at the screen the two of them had been staring at all evening.

"It's a new game," Charlie said. "It's called *Elite Dangerous*."

"It's space exploration," Gus said. "There! Look, that's where we need to land."

"So, we've arrived here on Uranus," Charlie said, for the benefit of the camera. "After narrowly avoiding a black hole."

"Oo er, missus," Gus said, and they both started to giggle.

"So, what, you can land on actual planets?" I said.

"Correct," Charlie said.

"And the best thing is, there are four hundred billion solar systems to explore," Gus said.

"So we won't have to think about new ideas for gaming videos for, like, several millennia," Charlie said.

"God, I wish there was something like that for healthy eating," I said.

"Anyway, I've had enough for tonight," Gus said. "Are we going out? I want to go out."

I opened my mouth to protest, but said nothing. I had realised that staying over at Charlie's meant fitting in with his and Gus's lifestyle. Most nights, at around nine thirty, Gus announced that he wanted to go out. Often Charlie and I went too, which meant getting home at two in the morning; when we said no, Gus went on his own and got home even later.

I sometimes wondered where he went, setting off in an Uber on his own. He was always on his phone or his laptop first, so I guessed he must be arranging to see friends – other vloggers, probably, who shared his penchant for expensive cocktail bars with concealed entrances so their fans couldn't hang around outside wanting selfies. He never said anything about his nights out afterwards – but then, I didn't ask. My attempts to make friends with Gus were having limited success, to say the least.

On the nights when Gus wasn't home, Charlie would sit up all night listening to music, playing games and desultorily editing videos until the sun was coming up, and he'd want me to keep him company. If I insisted I needed to go to sleep, he'd wake me up when he eventually came to bed and we'd have sex, and then when my alarm went off at half seven, he'd reach for me again, amorously and sleepily, so I ended up being late for work.

So when Charlie said, "Want to head out somewhere, Gemma?" I genuinely didn't know how to respond.

"I don't mind," I said. "Whatever you guys want to do is cool with me."

Because, of course, I couldn't say what I really wanted, which was to go to bed, with or without Charlie, and sleep for ten solid hours.

"We could go to Fanny Nelson's," Charlie said.

"Nah," Gus said. "I'm bored of that now. It's totally over."

"Untitled?"

"I'm bored of that too. I'm bored of just sitting in bars drinking cocktails."

"We could go and get some food, then?"

"I'm not hungry."

I left them to their conversation, which I knew would go on for ages and involve much searching on Instagram to see where the people who mattered were hanging out this week, and endless digressions while they discussed whose opinion was worth bothering about and whose wasn't. It always left me feeling deeply conscious of my own cluelessness and lack of cool, and aware that, left to my own devices, I'd probably suggest All Bar One or the local Odeon or somewhere else where Charlie and Gus wouldn't be seen dead.

I took my make-up bag through to the bathroom and looked despondently at my face in the mirror. I knew I should take off the day's slap and start over, but it seemed like way too much effort. Instead, I rooted out a concealer stick and did my best to hide the blemishes on my chin and the shadows under my eyes before doing some aggressive contouring and sticking on a pair of false eyelashes, which for once went on straight. I brushed my hair and changed my top for a new one I'd bought a couple of days ago in the All Saints sale, vlogged about and meant to return. I could still return it, so long as I managed not to spill anything on it, I thought, but then guiltily dismissed the idea – my finances might be in dire straits, but they weren't dire enough to resort to what was basically stealing.

"Come on, Gemma," Charlie called. "Cab's on its way."

"So what's the plan?" I pulled off my trainers and rummaged through my bag for a pair of high heels. The polish on my toenails was chipped and my socks had left ridges on my ankles, but there was no time to do anything about that.

"Karaoke," Gus said. "Maddie and Lola and a few others are at this place in Soho – they say it's brilliant. So we're going to join them there."

"What?" I said. "But I can't sing."

"That's the whole point of karaoke," Charlie said. "No one can sing."

"I can," Gus said.

"Well, I can't," Charlie said. "And do I care? Hell, no."

"No, but I really, really can't sing," I said. "I sound like Cheryl Cole – or Cheryl whatever she's called this month – when the autotune goes wrong on *The X Factor*, only even worse than that."

"You couldn't possibly sound worse than that," Gus said.

I said, "Trust me, I can and I do."

I thought longingly of Charlie's bed, and of curling up with Stanley in my arms for the sleep I craved. Every bit of my body ached with fatigue – I felt like I had the one and only time Jack had persuaded me to go hillwalking with him, except that I wasn't wet or covered in mud. I imagined Maddie and Lola, Gus and Charlie and whoever else was going to be there listening to me sing, then starting to laugh with a mixture of horror and pity. I didn't want to look like a fool in front of Charlie – not again.

And then I realised that Charlie didn't care. He and Gus made fools of each other and posted the results online all the time. They didn't care – at least, they didn't seem to care. It was part of what being a YouTuber was about: casting aside inhibitions, filming yourself with no make-up on or making stupid faces for the camera, eating things you knew would be so disgusting you'd spit them out. I'd had no problem baring my soul for the whole internet to see after Jack and I had split up – why should I mind if people knew I sounded like a crow with a forty-a-day fag habit when I sang?

I needed to not care. I needed to learn to laugh at myself, and look like I was enjoying doing it.

"Coming, Gemma?" Gus said.

"Of course I'm coming," I said. "It'll be fun." *And if it isn't,* I told myself, *I'll just have to give an Oscar-winning performance pretending it is.*

Call me old-fashioned, but when I hear the word karaoke, I think of the pub in Norwich that Jack and I used to go to sometimes – but only once on a Saturday, because that was karaoke night and it was so terrifying we never went again. There was an old geezer who dressed up as Elvis and legit murdered croony ballads until someone dragged him off the stage. There was a woman who wore sequinned dresses so short you could almost see her knickers, even though she was at least sixty and her knees were all wrinkly and saggy, and rasped out Celine Dion in a tuneless smoker's croak. There were the girls and lads who were clearly only there to pull and went on stage in big groups and didn't bother to follow the words on the screen at all. There was generally a fight of some kind at chucking-out time, as we noticed whenever we went past on the way from somewhere else and said to each other, "We are never. Going. There. On. A. Saturday. Again."

This was nothing like that at all. Maybe it was London, maybe it was that karaoke had got all advanced in the year and a half since Jack's and my ill-fated night at the Bearded Clam, or maybe it was just that the only places Charlie and Gus ever went were the kind that had cocktail menus and served scotch eggs ironically (there was nothing ironic about the scotch eggs at the Bearded Clam. The night Jack and I were there, when the fight broke out, someone twatted one at someone else and it did serious damage).

Anyway, You're the Voice was karaoke, only posh. We were shown to a private room with purple velvet banquettes around the edges and gold lamé drapery covering the walls. There was a white baby grand piano in the middle of the room and a touch-screen controller for the music. There were ice buckets with bottles of champagne and shakers of cocktails in them, and trays of sushi that looked considerably more appetising than my earlier cauliflower-based efforts.

And there were YouTubers. About ten people, some of whom I recognised and some of whom I didn't. But all of them recognised Charlie and Gus, and fell on them with cries of, "Oh my God, it's totally amazing to see you! How are you?" And then they all returned to their drinks and their selfies and bickering about what song they were going to play next.

I poured myself a big glass of one of the cocktails and sat down to watch. Charlie sat next to me and put his hand on my leg.

Someone did 'Uptown Funk'. Someone did 'Love Me like You Do'. The beautiful girl I remembered seeing the night I met Charlie, whose I supposed must be Lola, did 'Hold My Hand'. Maddie's boyfriend did 'Bad Blood', and Maddie made Charlie go up and rap the Kendrick Lamar bits, and he was totally awesome. Then Gus sang 'Thinking Out Loud' and he was so good it made everyone cry.

"Uplifting!" Lola said. "We need uplifting and we need it fast!"

"We need a power ballad!" Charlie said.

"I'm on it," Maddie's boyfriend said.

And the next second, I heard the beginning of a song I knew so well I could practically sing it in my sleep, because it had been Jack's and my song. We'd discovered it when we started going out and talked about embarrassing things we were both into, and one of them was *Glee*. So basically, the first time Jack and I kissed, it was to 'Don't Stop Believin'' – the old-school Journey version, not the new one with all the edges smoothed away. And that was playing right now.

I'd had too many cocktails, obviously, while I sat there watching everyone else have fun and not look stupid, and now I didn't care if I looked stupid myself. I jumped up and grabbed the mic off Gus, and started belting out the lyrics I knew so well. And to my surprise, I didn't sound too awful. I felt okay, standing there on my own with everyone watching me and then joining in with the chorus. It was almost like singing this song – the song that had been our song – now, with these new people, might mean a new beginning. But I couldn't think about it too much, because I was too hazy from whatever ginny, lemony thing I'd been drinking and too focussed on not running out of breath and which bit I was meant to be singing at the end.

And so the whole thing seemed to last about thirty seconds, and it then was over and everyone was focussed on the next track, so I went to find the loo and fix my make-up, because inevitably the song had made me cry a bit.

The toilets – 'Divas', they were called, as opposed to 'Maestros' for the men – were just as plushy and fabulous as our private room, all purple and gold and white. I had a wee and then stood in front of the mirror taking in all the glamour and wishing I felt worthy of it, instead of being a bit shiny-faced and knotty-haired. I opened my bag and dug around for stuff to fix the damage, and just as I was reapplying my lipstick I heard a voice say, "Gemma! Oh my God, I thought it was you!"

It was Olivia's friend Shivvy, who'd defriended me on Facebook shortly after Jack and Olivia got together. In different circumstances, I might have found the strength to look through her as if she wasn't there and go swishing out, but now my head was full of thoughts of Jack, it felt so comforting to see a familiar face in this haven of over-the-top luxury, and anyway I still needed to dust loose powder over my nose to take the shine off.

So I tried to put on a puzzled expression, as if I'd just been reminded of a fragment of my distant past, and said, "Hi! It's Sherri, isn't it? How are you?"

She looked briefly disconcerted, then said, "Shivvy! Haha, everyone always gets it wrong. You look so amazing! I saw you last week in *Heat* magazine. Like, wow! Your boyfriend's, like, an actor?"

"Something like that," I said. "And how are you?"

She burbled on a bit about how she was teaching yogalates at a studio in Kensington, but I didn't pay much attention. I'd never been her friend really, on or off Facebook, and she hadn't been mine, as her speedy defection following Olivia's had made clear.

Then, after a bit, she said, "So, I heard from Liv the other day. Bless her, she's being so brave, even though it's like her heart is in tiny pieces."

I said, "What do you mean?"

"Oh my God, you don't know?" Shivvy said. She stopped brushing her curtain of impossibly shiny black hair, which hadn't needed brushing anyway, and turned to look at me. "It didn't work out with her and Jack. Everyone is, like, broken for them."

Funny how you weren't broken when he dumped me for her, was my first thought. But then I thought, *Hold on. It hadn't worked out with Jack and Olivia?*

"Oh no," I said. "That's just the worst thing. I'm so sad for them both. But what about their plans? They were going to see the world together and everything."

Shivvy shook her head, making her hair swish in the same way she'd always made it swish, which I'd always found incredibly annoying.

"Liv is so strong," she said. "Nothing, not even this, could destroy her dream. But Jack's coming home. I'm surprised you hadn't heard."

I don't know where I found the self-control, but I did find it. I finished dusting highlighter over my brow bones, and I said, "I don't follow him on social media any more. You know how you move on? Anyway, tell them both I said hi. Laters, mwah!"

And then I went back to our private room. Gus and Lola were at the mic, doing Echosmith.

"You're back!" Charlie said, as if I'd been gone for eight hours not eight minutes. I sat next to him and held his hand, and he leaned over and whispered in my ear, "I love you, Gemma."

I realised I'd been thinking about things that were nothing at all to do with him.

Chapter Sixteen

I was sitting at my desk as usual, drinking coffee and looking at pictures of cats, when a message popped up on my screen from Jim.

Hi Gemma – just wondered if you've got half an hour to spare for a chat with Sarah and me? Cheers, J.

I felt all the blood drain from my face and apparently fill my hands, which suddenly felt huge and clumsy on my keyboard. What had I done? I cast desperately through the past few days. I'd been ten minutes late yesterday, after the karaoke evening, and certainly hungover. But I'd kept my head down and posted not one but two cat articles, one of which had made it to second place on the content leaderboard, and I'd worked an hour late to make up for it.

I'd done my share of coffee runs. I'd participated constructively in the editorial team meetings, even though I spent every minute dreading Jim asking Callista what was happening in the world of celebrity gossip and Callista saying, "So, you know Charlie Berry, right? He's only got a girlfriend, and the internet is going totally cray about it."

But Callista hadn't, and gradually I'd stopped worrying – or stopped worrying quite so much. After all, although Charlie was incredibly famous if you were a teenage girl, he was also *only* famous if you were a teenage girl (or a certain type of teenage boy, I supposed). And there hadn't exactly been a shortage of gossip about proper celebrities (*Thank you,* Celebrity Big Brother *and* Strictly Come Dancing. *Thank you, Brangelina, for splitting up, even though I'm gutted for you. Thank you for having sex with your wife, Prince William, and thank you, K Middy, for taking seriously cute photos of your babies*, I said to myself in silent relief as each meeting came to an end with no mention of Charlie, Gus or me).

So I'd begun to feel confident that the two separate bits of my life would be able to stay separate, and that even if my relationship with Charlie was as public as a very public thing, it was of no interest to the people I worked with. But maybe I was wrong? Maybe I was going to get told off for bringing Clickfrenzy into disrepute. Maybe I was going to get sacked. I might complain about having to get up early in the mornings, I might roll my eyes about the cats, I might wish that Tom would stop making that incredibly annoying humming sound under his breath when he was thinking, but I didn't want to lose my job. The thought filled me with horror – I imagined walking out of Sarah's office, everyone turning to look at me, and carrying on looking at me as I packed my hand cream, my Panadol and my tissues into my bag and walked the long, lonely walk of shame to the lift, never to return.

"Gemma?" Jim had evidently got tired of waiting for me to message him back, and was hovering by my desk. "I know you're busy, but Sarah's got a meeting in half an hour, so maybe we could…

Or if now's not a good time, could we book something in the diary for tomorrow?"

"It's okay," I said, standing up and hoping that my trembling legs would support me. "Now's fine."

Jim said, "There's nothing to worry about – we won't bite, I promise."

Biting, I thought, was the least of my worries.

I followed Jim into Sarah's office and we sat on two identical white chairs facing the glass desk. Sarah was tapping intently at her keyboard. Her brow would have been furrowed with concentration if it wasn't Botoxed into immobility. Jim and I watched silently as she pressed the delete key a few times, then typed a bit more, then paused, stared at the screen for a bit, then clicked the mouse and looked up at us.

"Right! Sorry about that, minor crisis with a client. Thanks for dropping everything and dropping in, I know how stacked you are."

"That's okay," I croaked.

"We should really have had this meeting a few weeks ago," Sarah went on, "back in August. But of course, I was away on annual leave, and everyone's stretched so thin, housekeeping stuff tends to get overlooked."

Housekeeping? I remembered with a lurch of guilt that it had been my turn to clean the coffee machine the previous week, but I'd forgotten and even though I'd done it first thing the next morning, it had been too late to stop the milk clotting sourly on the frothing spout thing. Did people get sacked for that?

"Yes, so this meeting is overdue," Jim said. "We normally conduct a review after three months with the company – well, not a review exactly, as you know from the procedures section of the intranet, we don't really do formal performance appraisals here."

"We phased them out a couple of years back," Sarah said. "We did a survey and found that staff hated them and team leaders find them unnecessarily time-consuming. We prefer to have ongoing conversations with our colleagues, and of course, as you know, my door is always open."

Which was true, although mostly the office behind it was empty, because Sarah was so seldom there. But I didn't say anything – I just nodded and tried to look as if I was listening actively rather than gibbering with fear.

"Anyway," Jim said, "It's been three and a half months since you joined us. You're basically part of the furniture now, aren't you?"

I tried to laugh, and said, "I guess so."

"So we just wanted to catch up," Sarah said, "And get a sense of how you're getting on, whether there are any issues we should be aware of, and talk about how you see your career here progressing."

I felt the tight band of fear around my ribs relax slightly. I'd been sacked before, more than once, and in my experience the phrase "career here progressing" was not one that tended to be used.

I said, "I'm really enjoying it. I love the people, and I'm learning so much all the time. I'm still just so excited that you gave me this opportunity."

Hopefully, I thought, that would be enough to bring the meeting to a close, and I could go back to my desk and my status as the newest, most junior person on the editorial team.

But Sarah said, "You're having fun with the cats, then?"

Shit, I thought. Was there a right answer to that? If I told the truth and said that if I never saw another cross, whiskery face on my screen or typed the word 'cattitude' again, my life would be richer and fuller, would they tell me that in that case I could pack my bags and have a rich, full life elsewhere? But if I said yes, would they think that I'd found my vocation and consign me to writing about cats and nothing but cats, forever and ever?

I said, "I'm having loads of fun in my job. Coming up with new content that's fresh and shareable and has the Clickfrenzy edge is really, like, rewarding. And cats are cute. I've always loved cats."

Sarah laughed. "That was very diplomatic, Gemma. We all know the cat brief can be tough. Call it an ordeal by fire, if you like. But Jim says you've risen to the challenge."

"For sure," Jim said. "Gemma's stories are getting loads of hits."

"Almost as many hits as Gemma's vlogs," Sarah said, with another little smile.

I tried not to let the shock show on my face as I realised I'd been lulled into a false sense of security. I was being played. If this was Reddit, someone would post one of those memes that start, 'Only a fool would trust…' One of those gifs that only lasts a few seconds, and ends in bloody carnage.

"Obviously, your personal life is totally personal," Jim said.

"But we have been wondering," Sarah said, "at board level, whether there's potential for some sort of synergy."

Jim said, "You're the expert here, Gemma, of course. We know viral content, and how to monetise it. But your area is specialised, and it's got all sorts of rules of its own."

I thought, *It certainly does.* A whole book of rules, even more dense and specific than the bound document Hannah and Richard had presented to me when I moved in – except those rules were fixed, and even if they seemed petty and trivial, at least you could understand them, and choose to comply or break them and face the consequences. But the rules of vlogging were new to me – I was only just beginning to work them out, and try to understand how they applied to my own channel, my relationship with Charlie – my entire life. And now the bit that I'd thought was compartmentalised and safe, where all I had to do was turn up in the mornings and sit quietly looking at cats and making coffee, was being invaded by them too.

I remembered how I'd told Jack, over a glass of Prosecco that horrible night, that I'd impressed Clickfrenzy with my YouTube savvy. I wished I'd had the sense to shut up about the whole thing.

I said, "I'm not quite sure what you mean."

"We were thinking," Jim said. "Lots of YouTubers have second channels, right? Like, you have one where you post your formal vlogs, and one where you just chat about your life and stuff?"

"Yes," I said. "Lots of them – lots of us do. It's because doing haul videos and stuff like that takes a lot of time and planning, and viewers want more content than people have time to create. So, like, Charlie – my boyfriend – he and his brother post game reviews and pranks about twice a week, but they vlog every day about them just hanging out."

"That's what I thought," Sarah said. "So we wondered, what if you were to start a second channel, and include content about your work here at Clickfrenzy, and host it on our site as well as on YouTube?"

I had to bite my tongue to stop myself shouting, "No! I don't want to! That's a terrible idea!"

I imagined walking through the office with my camera, filming myself cleaning the coffee machine and trying not to fall asleep at my desk. I imagined even more details about my life being available for my colleagues to see – for Sarah and Jim to see. I imagined my fans, or Charlie's, waiting downstairs for me to go out for lunch, and asking me to sign things and pose for selfies with me. I imagined the fragile barrier that separated the two parts of my life crumbling and falling.

"Of course, we know you're short of time," Jim said. "But we could get you some help with the cat content."

"And we'd figure out a way of making it viable for you financially, as well," Sarah said. "Some sort of profit-share, we thought. But we wanted to get a sense of whether you actually liked the idea before we hammered out the details."

Great, I thought – they were offering me two things they knew I'd find it hard to refuse: more money and fewer cats. And I had to admit to myself that both were very, very tempting. But were they tempting enough? I thought about it for a moment and realised that they weren't – not even close. But then, how could I say no? I was still the newest member of the team. I was being offered an exciting opportunity to make my work more interesting and my vlog more profitable – after all, Clickfrenzy had millions of viewers and subscribers, far more even than the Berry Boys channel did.

I cast desperately around for a way to say no, or a way to say yes that was actually no.

"Of course, it would all take time to set up, and we'd have to have a launch plan in place," Sarah said.

"We don't expect you to make a decision straight away," Jim said.

Then I remembered. Those were almost the exact words Sloane had used when she signed me up to Ripple Effect. It was a lifeline.

I said, "Actually, the thing is, it's not really my decision. If it was, of course I'd love to – I think it's a fantastic idea. But I have a contract with my agent. Anything I do would need to be cleared with her first, and maybe even with their lawyers."

I thought of the dense pages of type that I hadn't even bothered to read before happily signing the rights to my content over to Ripple Effect. I had no idea which, if any, of the many clauses would affect my ability to host content on other platforms, but I was fairly sure that at least one paragraph would deal with the matter in dense, impenetrable detail.

"Of course," Sarah said. "There is that."

"Anyway," Jim said. "Have a think, talk to your agent. It would be great if we could work something out. And in the meantime, consider your probation over."

"And well done again, Gemma," Sarah said. "It's great having you on board and we hope you'll be with us for a long time."

Giddy with relief, I stood up, thanked them profusely and promised that I'd discuss their proposal with Sloane as soon as I could.

But in the event, that didn't happen. Because that night, something else did, and it changed everything.

*

When I got to Charlie and Gus's flat after work, I could tell as soon as I opened the door that something was up. For one thing, Sloane was there. This wasn't unusual in itself – she often dropped in for meetings or, I was coming to realise, just to check up on them and make sure that no alcohol or ashtrays found their way into Berry Boys vlogs. But she was normally a relatively unobtrusive presence, couching her instructions in the form of diplomatic advice and masking criticism with compliments.

Today, though, she was standing in the middle of the living room, doing what I can only describe as haranguing them.

"Honestly, sometimes I wonder what you boys think you're doing. Or rather, if you actually think at all before you do things. There's impulsive and then there's just plain…" She paused. I suspected she'd been about to say, "just plain stupid". "Just plain reckless. With your schedule, living here, this is really, really not a good idea."

"But I've wanted a dog for ages," Gus said. "We always had dogs when we were kids, we know what we're doing, and she's only small."

"And look at her," Charlie said. "She loves us already. We've called her Taylor."

"After Taylor Swift," Gus said. "Because she's a greyhound. Only a miniature one. An Italian greyhound. Swift – geddit?"

As I approached the sofa, I could see that the bundle on Gus's lap was a puppy. When it saw me, it jumped out of his arms and came scampering across the floor at speed, its claws slipping on the polished concrete. It skidded to a stop and looked up at me.

"Oh my God, she's adorable," I said. And it was true – the puppy was the soft, pale grey of an expensive suede handbag, with enormous dark eyes and paws that looked far too big for her tiny body. Her ears stuck comically out of the sides of her head. "She looks like Yoda."

"She might be miniature, but that doesn't mean she's going to be low maintenance," Sloane said. "Have you even thought how much care puppies need? You'll have to take her out every couple of hours during the night, you know."

"That's okay," Charlie said. "We're up all night anyway."

"And during the day," Sloane said. "And you're in bed all day."

"We'll take it in turns," Gus said.

"We'll do shifts," Charlie said.

"And you'll have to take her out for walks and to puppy classes and make sure she's properly trained," Sloane went on. "And she'll chew everything, and I mean everything. We've already replaced that sofa twice."

I felt blood rushing to my face as I remembered the first night I'd spent there, having sex with Charlie on the red suede, worrying that my wet skin and dripping hair would ruin it. I wondered if he'd told Sloane the reason for that most recent replacement, and what had happened the time before.

"We aren't completely irresponsible, you know," Gus said. "We've already bought her food and a bed and a load of toys."

I carefully picked the puppy up and stroked her silky ears. She made a little whining sound, then curled up in my arms and closed her eyes.

"See?" Charlie said. "She loves Gemma already, too."

I carried the small, warm body over to the sofa and sat down next to Gus. Despite the undeniable cuteness of the puppy, deep down I knew I agreed with Sloane. Responsibility was not a quality my boyfriend and his brother had in abundance.

"I can help," I said. "I can take her for walks before work, maybe."

"You have more than enough on your plate already, Gemma," Sloane said. "Look at you – you're exhausted. Although perhaps if this means the three of you will spend more time at home and less time out on the lash, it won't be such a bad thing."

"We can get puppy babysitters when we go out," Charlie said.

"Or take her with us," Gus said. "We can pretend she's an assistance dog. She can lead us home when we're pissed."

"She can do no such thing," Sloane said. "She's tiny – she needs to be at home, when she's not being appropriately socialised with other dogs. You're not hauling her around to clubs like Paris Hilton."

"I wouldn't mind hauling Paris Hilton around to clubs," Charlie said.

"Don't be obtuse," Sloane snapped. "Well, I reckon the first thing is to get her to the vet and have her properly checked out. You didn't buy her from some dodgy puppy farm, I hope."

"Of course not!" Charlie said. "We got her from a lovely woman who advertised on Gumtree. She was the last one left from the litter. Apparently she was the smallest and no one else wanted her."

"We basically rescued her," Gus said.

"From an ad on Gumtree!" Sloane said. "Christ, it's worse than I thought. You two just have no…"

Then she stopped. I could see her reining in her annoyance, remembering that these were her clients, and there was only a certain amount of telling off she could do without risking them flouncing off to another agent.

"I'm sure it'll all be fine, Sloane," I said. "Look how precious she is. Look at her little face. Imagine if they hadn't taken her – anything could have happened to her."

Sloane shook her head. "Anything could happen to her now," she said. "Poor baby. Well, it's done now, so we'll just have to make the best of it. Your viewers will love her, of course."

"They already do," Charlie said. "We put up a video earlier of us collecting her, and it's had fifty thousand likes already."

"Which is significantly more than you were getting from your *Elite Dangerous* gaming vlogs," Sloane said. Clearly, she hadn't managed to completely switch off castigating mode. "As I keep telling you, it's essential to keep your content fresh and creative. Losing subscribers is far, far easier than gaining them. There's no room for complacency in this environment."

"Yeah, well, we're bored of *Elite Dangerous* now," Gus said.

"We went to, like, fifty solar systems," Charlie said. "And then we realised they were all basically the same."

"Space is a bit shit, actually, when you think about it," Gus said.

Sloane rolled her eyes. "You got bored of virtual space exploration, so you bought a puppy. I see. Can't fault the logic there, boys."

Charlie and Gus were both slumped on the sofa, looking increasingly truculent. I could tell that they were getting pretty bored of being bossed around, too.

In an attempt at emollience, I said, "You can't get bored of pets, though. Not unless you're just, like, a really horrible person. The puppy – Taylor – will make amazing content. Look at her – she's got total star quality, even when she's asleep. The guys can vlog her whole education and growing up and stuff. It'll be amazing."

"Yes, thanks for that little tutorial on how to create successful content, Gemma," Gus said. "We have actually been doing this for, like, six years, as opposed to four months."

I felt myself physically flinch at his words. It hadn't occurred to me until now that Gus might resent my increasingly pervasive presence in his life – that he might, quite simply, not like me. But now that his words were out there, it was so obvious that I couldn't believe it had taken me so long to realise.

What possible reason did he have to like me, after all? I was his brother's girlfriend – he hadn't chosen me, Charlie had. And the whole world the two of them had created together, all their routines and habits, even Gus's own privacy, had been fundamentally disrupted by my arrival in their lives.

Charlie, I realised, hadn't mentioned any previous girlfriends. And Gus hadn't, either, apart from saying he'd been on a few dates with Maddie. I had no idea what Gus's private, internal life was like; he was just a sort of accessory to Charlie. No wonder he went off on his own while we stayed home, or at the end of our nights out together. He must hate not having his twin to himself any more. Perhaps he even hated me, and up until now he'd just been incredibly careful not to show it.

I said, "Okay, I'm sorry. I was just trying to be helpful. Next time I'll know to just shut the fuck up."

"Yeah, maybe you should do that," Gus said. "Maybe try sticking to your core skill. I can't speak for Charles so I couldn't possibly comment on how well you do it, but you certainly do it often."

Sloane winced. "Gus, that was completely uncalled for. I think you should apologise to Gemma."

I said, "Don't apologise. Please don't. Not when you don't mean it. I think it's probably best if I go back home tonight, to Hackney. You're right, Sloane, I haven't been getting enough sleep and these two want to bond with the puppy. And anyway, I was going to film a wardrobe tour, like you suggested, and I need my actual wardrobe to do that, obviously."

I stood up, still holding Taylor in my arms. She was fast asleep, warm, floppy and undisturbed by all the drama. Sloane took her from me and made some cooing noises.

"Precious baby, you're going to miss your mommy tonight," she said. "I'll email you tomorrow, Gemma. You guys, we should get on with our meeting, and let's try not to stray too far from the point now, right?"

I picked up my bag and started to walk towards the door. It seemed even further away than usual. A deep, tense silence followed me, which I knew would be filled as soon as I'd left the flat. I didn't say goodbye; I just kept going. I felt the time and the distance and the silence stretch out like chewing gum as I approached the door, then quiver and sag as I opened it, then finally give way when I heard the latch click shut behind me.

Charlie had let me go without saying a thing.

Chapter Seventeen

Hi everyone!

So, I promised you a wardrobe tour, and that's what I'm going to film tonight. One thing I've been doing a lot lately is reading about how organising your clothes properly can help you not only locate things more quickly when you're in a hurry, but also find new and interesting outfit combos you hadn't thought of before, and… Oh fuck, I can't do this now.

I didn't post a video that night. I tried, but whenever I looked at the camera lens and thought about saying my usual cheerful, "Hi everyone!" the words just didn't come out right. My voice sounded hollow and insincere; my face on my camera's screen looked tense and anxious.

And yet, I couldn't enjoy this rare evening alone, either. I thought of all the things I could be doing: going for a walk or to the gym, ordering a takeaway and finding something to watch on telly; having a long soak in the bath. I didn't really feel like doing any of them, but in the end I settled for the last.

I'd received a delivery of a load of bath products a couple of weeks before, and they'd been gathering dust in the pile of untested samples that was gradually taking over a corner of my bedroom. I rummaged through them and chose a scented candle in a glass holder and a huge, glittery bath bomb that smelled like the inside of a sweet shop. It wasn't my kind of thing, really, but the packaging said it had soothing and relaxing properties, and soothing and relaxing was totally what I needed right now.

I filled the bath with boiling water and, holding my phone ready so I could post a video on Snapchat, I dropped the bath bomb in. It fizzed and spun, shooting around like some sort of aquatic meteorite – like something Charlie and Gus would have seen on their virtual space travels, before they got bored of the game. I watched the water fill with sparkles, turning pink and then purple. Once it had completely dissolved, I took off my dressing gown and lowered myself into the hot, fragrant water. *This is me-time, Gemma*, I told myself firmly. *This is that pampering thing that everyone always goes on about – yourself included.* But even though I felt the tension in my shoulders ease as I sank down deeper into the water, even though the scent was much less sugary than I'd expected, more like violet cream chocolates and actually quite delicious, it wasn't enough to make my brain switch off.

I couldn't erase the memory of Charlie's face as he watched me leave the flat – first bewildered, then hurt, then accepting. I couldn't forget that he'd said nothing – made no move to call me back. And I could picture Gus's expression exactly, too – something that was almost triumph.

I didn't know if I was in love with Charlie; I didn't know if I was ready to be in love with anyone. Up until that evening, I'd felt confident that liking him, having a laugh and great sex with him, was enough. And, if I was honest with myself, the relationship gave me what I needed in other ways, too.

For years, I'd made YouTube content that had only been seen by a few thousand people – but I'd had a sense of real community with the small handful of people who commented on my videos, and whose comments I could read carefully and respond to. Now, I had more than five hundred thousand subscribers, the number was increasing in huge jumps every day, and it was all I could do to press Like on a few comments. Of course, what I'd posted about Jack back in August was part of that – the catalyst that had lifted me from total obscurity to being the girl who made that video about being dumped that went viral for a day. And Sloane had helped me to continue that process – her advice, her contacts, and above all her insistence that I work relentlessly hard at promoting my channel and myself.

But I knew that my success wasn't just about me. It was about me and Charlie. It was there in black and white every time I checked my stats: people didn't click on my videos by chance, they clicked on them because they were Berry Boys fans and I was Charlie's girlfriend. When people googled my name, they didn't just google 'Gemma Grey'; they googled 'Gemma Grey + Berry Boys'. When they watched me make some random paleo food thing, it wasn't because they wanted to know how to make tasty meals based on grated cauliflower – it was because seeing Charlie's girlfriend use Charlie's cheese grater in Charlie's kitchen made them feel they were gaining a deeper insight into Charlie and Gus's lives.

I knew that if I carried on as I was, I could be successful. I could make money – not the kind of money Charlie and Gus made, not for a long time, anyway – but enough that I could afford to rent a flat of my own, make vlogging my full-time job, maybe even have my own range of eyeshadows on sale in Superdrug. I could live the dream.

The problem was, I wasn't sure whether it was my dream. I wasn't sure whether buying clothes and trying them on, buying make-up and applying it, buying food and doing things to it before throwing it away, was how I wanted to make a living. But then, I knew for sure that writing clickbait headlines about cats wasn't, either.

And Charlie himself – Charlie had told me he loved me. He'd said the words and maybe, at the time, he'd meant them. But if he loved me, surely he would have defended me when Gus sniped at me? Surely he wouldn't have thought it was funny to see me getting into bed with Gus? Surely if the choice was between me and Gus, he'd choose me?

But Gus was his brother – his twin, for God's sake. Of course I couldn't expect him to make that choice, ever. It was unfair – it was impossible. The two of them had a bond that went back to before they were even born, whereas I'd just been sleeping with him for a few months. In relationship terms, I was the ultimate newbie.

I wished I had someone to talk to – a best friend to agonise with about the whole situation. But I didn't – until recently, that person would have been Jack, or it would have been Olivia, if the thing I wanted to agonise about involved Jack. *I could talk to Amy*, I thought – she was sensible, she'd give me good advice. But Amy was just my housemate – she'd think it was totally weird if I marched downstairs and sat at the kitchen table while she ate her instant noodles and asked her whether I should split up with my boyfriend because… Because what? Because I didn't love him enough? Because I thought he loved his brother more than he loved me?

I could ask the internet. I could go on to Reddit, on my phone, right now, and ask the relationships board for its collective wisdom. *WWYD – weird triangle with boyfriend, twin brother and YouTube?* But it would be impossible to give enough information without giving too much, and I knew that making myself and my situation identifiable would be fatal.

I couldn't talk to Hannah – I rarely saw Hannah without Richard, and the idea of Richard knowing anything private about me felt all kinds of wrong. I wanted to talk to Stanley, even though he couldn't talk back, but Stanley wasn't there – he was in Charlie's bedroom, probably face down under the bed where he'd fallen when we had sex the night before.

The bath water wasn't hot any more and the whole relaxing and soothing thing clearly wasn't going to happen, so I pulled out the plug with my toes and waited for the water to drain away before standing up. I blew out the candle and tugged the light pull, and heard myself gasp with horrified laughter.

I was covered in glitter, and so was the bath. And not only that, it was stained, too – a pink, glittery tide mark on the smooth white enamel, with a gap where my shoulders had rested. There was glitter on the bath mat, too, and on the floor, and even on the wall.

"Holy glittery shit," I said aloud. "So much for zen tranquility."

I stepped back into the bath and sluiced it and myself with the shower attachment, but it was no match for the stubborn sparkles. I imagined Amy having her shower the next morning and going off to arrest a drug dealer or whatever, covered in glitter – not so much 'It's a fair cop', but more 'It's a fairy copper'. I imagined the sticky note Hannah would leave: *Please refrain from using products containing glitter in this bathroom.*

It was no good – I was going to have to do a proper clean-up job, even though all I wanted, more than anything in the world, was to go to sleep. I pulled on trackie bottoms and a T-shirt and went downstairs in search of some serious housework ammo.

I opened the cupboard under the stairs and rummaged through Hannah's housekeeping supplies. There was all sorts in there – kitchen cleaner, glass cleaner, furniture polish, stuff for polishing stainless steel, stuff that apparently dissolved burnt-on grease from ovens, unopened packs of rubber gloves, sponges, dusters and scourers. I realised with a twinge of guilt that I hadn't done anything like my share of cleaning since I'd lived there – had barely done any at all, in fact, since the night of Amy's party. I hadn't really thought about it – I'd been too busy, too distracted, too not there. Too selfish.

I found a spray bottle of bathroom cleaner and a cloth and closed the cupboard. I'd give the whole room a good clean, I told myself, then make something to eat and go to sleep. It was only half past nine, but I was practically falling over with tiredness. My wardrobe tour video was going to have to wait for another day. But before I reached the top of the stairs, I heard the front door open and the sound of Amy's work boots on the floor.

"Hiya, stranger," she said. "You all right? We haven't seen you in ages. I was wondering whether you'd moved out."

I said, "No, I've just been at Charlie's. I came back here tonight because... I don't know. I just felt like having my own space for a bit."

She looked at me curiously and I could tell she was thinking we'd had a row.

"We didn't have a row exactly," I said. "But... you know."

"Spaces in your togetherness," Amy said, raising an eyebrow.

"Yeah, those," I said.

She grinned, and I thought again how good a friend she could be.

"I was meant to be working a night shift," she said. "But I think I'm coming down with something. There's this summer bug that's doing the rounds and we're all going down like flies. My sergeant told me to go home to bed and that was an offer I totally couldn't refuse. What's with the late-night housework?"

I told her about the bath bomb, and she laughed.

"Those things are fucking lethal," she said. "Seriously, Gemma, at your age you should know better. We'll be finding glitter everywhere for weeks – in our clothes, in our hair, in the cornflakes... I need to get out of my work clobber and then I'll stick the kettle on. Want a tea?"

She followed me upstairs and went into her bedroom, and I went into the bathroom and surveyed the task that lay ahead. But as I was half-heartedly squirting cleaning fluid on to the side of the bath, I heard the familiar sound of a key in the lock downstairs, and Richard's voice.

"Give me your phone, Hannah. Right now."

I don't know what made me do it, but I turned the bathroom light off again and hurried to Amy's room. She was sitting on her bed in the dark, her boots half-unlaced.

I sat next to her and whispered, "Listen. They're having a row. I've heard them before. It's weird. Scary."

Hannah's voice came up the stairs, quite clearly, as it had before. "No, Rich, I'm not giving you my phone. We've had this conversation before. You checking up on me all the time – it's ridiculous. You know I'm not… doing whatever you think I'm doing. We're together literally all the time."

"Not when you're at work," Richard said.

"But you drop me there in the mornings and pick me up in the evenings, for God's sake. What do you think's going to happen, when I'm surrounded by a bunch of eight-year-olds all the time?"

"Not all the time," Richard said. "Not at lunchtimes, to take a random example."

The tone of Hannah's voice changed. She didn't sound defensive and challenging any more. "So at lunchtimes I sit in the staff room and eat a sandwich. Or sometimes I have lunch in the refectory with the kids. Just the same as I've done for four years."

"Of course you do," Richard said. "And which did you do today?"

"Staff room," Hannah said. "No, I had lunch with the kids. I can't remember! I can't remember where I am every minute of every day!"

Richard said, "Maybe you need to try and remember a bit harder. Lunchtime today. Where were you?"

I could feel a knot of tension in my stomach, growing tighter and tighter. My mouth was really dry. I knew I should do something, but I didn't know what, or how. I looked at Amy. Her face was completely calm and still in the faint light that came from downstairs, but I could see the furrow of a frown between the perfect arches of her eyebrows. She looked like she was thinking really hard about something – a sudoku puzzle, or something like that.

"I… Okay, I remember now," Hannah said. "I had to go to Boots. I was running low on Sertraline, so I rang the GP and they faxed through a prescription for me. There was a really long wait, actually, so I didn't have time to eat lunch at all. I'm starving now, aren't you? We could order a curry if you like."

Richard said, "Which Boots did you go to? Because when I went past the branch on Mare Street earlier it was closed for refurbishment."

Hannah said, "Yes, that's right, so I had to go all the way to Homerton. It meant it took even longer, hence, you know, the no lunch thing."

"You went to Homerton? Are you sure you didn't go somewhere else? Like, maybe Liverpool Street, to take a random example?"

"Richard, what the fuck? Were you following me? That's completely bang out of order and I'm not putting up with it." Hannah's voice was high and trembly – she sounded furious, but frightened, too.

"I don't have to follow you," Richard said. I could hear that he was smiling, almost laughing. "Don't you know, there's an app for that? Now give me your phone. If you won't tell me where you went, it will. And then you're going to stop fucking lying to me."

His voice rose suddenly to a shout. I flinched. My nails were digging into my hands so hard it felt like I'd draw blood.

"Rich, please, please will you stop this now," Hannah said. "It's awful. You're frightening me. What if Gemma's home? What's she going to think?"

"She's going to think you're a lying, cheating bitch," Richard said. "Because that's the truth, isn't it? And anyway, if she's home she's shut up in her room with her headphones on and she won't hear a thing. And Amy's working, before you start about her too. Now. Give. Me. Your. Phone."

Hannah said, "No. I'm not giving you my phone. I'm not giving you anything. But I'll tell you where I was today. I went to see a solicitor, to talk about us selling the house and how we can split things up. I've decided to leave, Richard. I can't deal with this shit any more. It's not right. You're not right."

Richard said, "Say that again."

Hannah said, "I'm leaving. I've seen a solicitor. I'll leave tonight. I'll get a taxi and stay in a hotel."

"You won't," Richard said. "If you try and walk out of that door I'll fucking kill you."

I half-stood up, but Amy pulled me back down again. She'd laced her boots up again, I saw. I remembered how we'd joked together when she was planning her party, writing her polite note to the neighbours – "Don't call the police; I am the police."

Hannah said, "I'm going to leave now, Richard. Don't do anything stupid, for God's sake."

I heard the rattle of Hannah's keys, then an almost wordless shout of rage from Richard. Then there was a crash – I could feel the floor under my feet reverberate with it – and Hannah screamed.

Amy was on her feet so fast I barely saw her move – it was like one moment she was sitting next to me on the bed, and the next she was out of the door. I could hear her boots on the stairs as she sprinted down.

My knees feeling weak with fright, I followed her.

Hannah was lying on her back. When she'd fallen – or when Richard had pushed her – she'd knocked over a small glass table with a vase of lilies on it. The flowers were scattered over the floor, surrounded by splashes of water and bright shards of glass. There was blood on Hannah's face – lots of blood. Amy had Richard's arms pinned behind his back. He was struggling, but without success – Amy was small, but she was strong and she was trained.

"You're under arrest," she said. She sounded quite calm, but I could her gasping for breath. "You do not have to say anything…"

I barely heard the rest of what she said – I knew what it was, anyway, from watching crime dramas on telly. This was just like that, only it was real and it was happening to someone I knew.

Carefully avoiding the wreckage of the flowers, I went over to Hannah and helped her up. I put my arm around her shoulders. She felt tiny and frail – her whole body was shaking and I could actually hear her teeth chattering.

"Come on," I said. "Let's clean your face and make a cup of tea."

An hour later, colleagues of Amy's who she'd called had come and taken Richard away to spend the night in a cell at the police station, and Amy had gone with them to make a formal statement about what had happened. I'd cleaned up the living room while Hannah sat on the sofa, her feet up and her arms wrapped around her knees, huddled under one of the tasteful cashmere throws even though it was a warm night. I'd ransacked the kitchen and found a bottle of brandy and given her a glass, even though I was pretty sure sweet tea would have been a more proper way of dealing with her shock. While I cleaned up, she talked and talked.

"I swear to God, I never, ever thought he'd hit me," she said. Her words came out all jerky and stammery, because she couldn't seem to stop shaking. "I knew he was controlling, and I knew he was jealous, but I never thought he'd lay a finger on me. He scared me – I've been scared for ages – but in other ways, not physically."

I squeezed out the cloth I'd used to mop up the water into the sink and found the dustpan and brush.

"Are you sure you don't need a hand, Gemma?" Hannah said. "Why don't I just…"

"Don't just anything," I said. "You stay where you are. Keep talking, if you want."

"When we first met, I thought it was so romantic that he wanted to be together all the time," she said. "And it was – it honestly was. He'd come and meet me at lunchtimes and bring me random little presents, or a picnic for us to have together in the park. And before we moved in, when we weren't together because I was at work or whatever, he texted me all the time to say that he was thinking of me, and ask what I was doing – stuff like that. I thought it was lovely. I loved the attention."

I carefully carried the dustpan back to the kitchen and opened the lid of the bin.

"I wonder if we should recycle that glass?" Hannah said. "Or wrap it in newspaper, or something. I don't know what the best thing is to do."

So I found a copy of the *Independent* that Richard must have left in the kitchen that morning, tipped the glass into it, bundled it up and put it in the recycling.

"There, belt and braces." Then I went and sat next to Hannah and poured a bit of the brandy for myself, too. She sort of squished a bit closer to me on the sofa and I put my arm around her again. She'd stopped shaking so much, but when I touched her hand it still felt very cold.

"I always said I wouldn't put up with being treated badly in a relationship. My dad used to hit my mum – I spent my whole childhood being terrified of him. I always said I'd never, ever let that happen to me. That's why I thought Rich was different. He was so loving, so gentle, so thoughtful with the flowers and the gifts and telling me he loved me. It was such a relief – you know what I mean? Like, I'm not single any more, I won't have to worry about being good enough for someone ever again. I'll never be alone again."

I said, "Being alone isn't that bad. Not compared to being with someone who's horrible to you."

I thought, *What the hell do you know about that anyway, Gemma? You went from being with Jack to being with Charlie in about five seconds flat.* But I could tell that it didn't matter what I said, not really. Hannah didn't need advice – she just needed to talk. If I wasn't there, she'd probably be saying all these things to herself, inside her head.

"I can't even remember when it started," she went on. "It's like that thing about putting a frog into boiling water and it jumps out, but if you put it into cold water it won't notice the water getting hotter and hotter and will boil to death. I wonder if that's true, and how they found out. I hope it isn't. Poor frogs."

She shivered, and started to cry, and then cried harder and harder, occasionally sobbing something about cruelty to frogs. I ran upstairs to the bathroom and came down with a wodge of loo paper and handed it to her, then put my arms around her again.

"Poor frogs," I said. "It's awful, but I bet it isn't true. Who'd do something like that?"

Privately, I thought that in a world where people could do what Richard had done to Hannah, anything was possible, but I didn't say so. I just patted her back and waited for her to finish crying.

"I thought it was my fault," Hannah said, blowing her nose. "I thought if I could only be a better person, a better girlfriend, he'd trust me and it would all be okay. Because when he isn't being weird, he's lovely. He's funny and gentle and just... you know."

I didn't say that he'd always seemed a bit weird to me. I said, "I know."

Hannah said, "I thought when we bought this place he'd change. But then, it was so stressful having this massive mortgage and never enough money, and I was ending up in overdraft every month, and so he started asking to see my bank statements and making me tell him what I was spending money on – like, every single tiny thing, even a box of tampons. And I thought that was fair enough, because after all we're a couple – we were a couple – we had joint finances and we were struggling to make ends meet, and it was partly my fault, because I'm crap with money."

The thought of my own scary credit card debt pushed its way into my mind, but I pushed it back out again.

"So is that why you decided to rent out the spare rooms?" I said.

"It was my idea," Hannah said. "I thought it would mean that we could start saving up again, and that would kind of take the pressure off a bit, and also that having people other people around would mean that he wouldn't be able to... you know."

Except that hadn't happened, had it, I thought. I imagined Hannah carefully framing her argument for Amy and me as tenants, because Amy's shift pattern would mean that at least one of us was likely to be home a lot of the time. And then I'd met Charlie, and got freaked out by Richard, and basically abandoned Hannah to her fate. I hadn't known, it wasn't my fault, I doubted I could have done anything to prevent it, but the knowledge made me feel horribly guilty all the same.

I wanted to say sorry to Hannah, to tell her I hadn't meant to let her down, but then Amy came back from the police station and told Hannah that Richard would be kept there overnight, and that she could apply for an injunction against him in the morning, to keep him away from the house and keep Hannah safe. She explained a load of stuff about police bail and formal charging procedures, which I'm sure Hannah wasn't really able to take in – I know I wasn't. Then she asked, very gently, if she could take some photos of the bruises on Hannah's neck and the cut above her eye, and advised her to go to her GP to have them looked at, so there'd be medical records for when the case went to court – which it would do, she was confident, unless of course Hannah changed her mind and decided she didn't feel able to be a witness.

And then we all went to bed. Even though I was so tired, I didn't sleep well – I kept having horrible dreams and imagining I could hear footsteps on the stairs or raised voices coming from Hannah's room. At about five in the morning I pinged awake, suddenly certain that I needed to do something. I hadn't been able to help Hannah – I hadn't protected her from Richard – but maybe I could help other people like her, or at least tell them that there was help to be had. I googled and made some notes, and then, sitting on the edge of my bed in the morning half-light, without any make-up on and without even having brushed my hair, I switched my camera on and started to speak.

Chapter Eighteen

Cats that look like George Clooney. Cats that look like Amal Clooney. Cats that look like Kate Middleton. Cats that look like corgis. Cats with sideboob. Badass cats you wouldn't want to meet in a dark alleyway. Cats sleeping in awkward places. Cats sleeping anywhere…

My head jerked up and I realised I'd been nodding off over my brainstorming list. I yawned hugely. This was no good. I was meant to be working and I was literally asleep on the job.

Drink, anyone? I messaged to my podmates, and when the orders had come in I collected the empty mugs and went to the kitchen, taking my phone with me. I abandoned the tray and got the lift to the ground floor. I desperately needed some fresh air, as well as caffeine, if I was going to survive the rest of the day.

I walked around the corner, so I'd be out of sight if anyone came out for a fag, swiped my phone to life and went on to YouTube. My new video already had more than five hundred comments, and it had only been up a few hours. I felt the familiar tingle of excitement as I started to read them.

This is so brave, Gemma, thank you. Your friend is really lucky to have you. I hope she's okay. Love and kisses.

My sister is in an abusive relationship. I'm going to show her this vlog – we are all so worried about her but she keeps saying he's going to change. I cry every night thinking about her.

My boyfriend is really jealous too. I'm frightened of him but I've got nowhere to go. Maybe soon I'll be brave enough to click on one of the links you posted. I hope so. I don't want him to hurt me again.

I swallowed hard and blinked back tears. These were real women – women like Hannah, going through what Hannah had gone through. If even one of them could leave, call the police or one of the charities I'd found and recommended, it would be worth all the hard work, all the tiredness, all the saying what I was told to say about products I was given to review.

I scrolled down some more, reading more comments.

God, don't you just hate it when YouTubers sell out? Doing it for brands is bad enough, but shilling for a charity is just disgusting.

My finger froze over my screen. What did that even mean? Surely no one would think that the video I'd filmed that morning, unplanned and unscripted, was anything other than real?

They've got massive budgets, these not-for-profits. Loads of vloggers work for them. I think it's unethical, personally, but what can you do? It's her job, after all – she's got to pay the rent somehow.

Doesn't Gemma have a day job as well? She's always talking about going to work, and how knackered she is.

Yeah, she says that. But you never see her there. You might want to have a look at this thread.

And there was a link to a website I'd never heard of, called YouTruth.

My hand was shaking so much it took me a few goes to tap the link on my screen. It took me to a forum, where there was a whole thread about me with hundreds and hundreds of posts. The title of the thread was 'Gemma Grevytrain', and it had been started two months before.

So, who wants to talk about Gemma Grey? I know she's only recently got big, and I think she's been signed by Ripple Effect. I'm really interested to see what's going to happen with her vlog, and whether she goes the same way as all the rest of them. Discuss.

IKR? I've been following Gemma for, like, years – right since she started – I think I was one of her first subscribers. I used to really love her vlog – she was so fun and natural, and the way she talked to her teddy was so cute, and Jack was, like, hot! But since they split up her whole style has changed. Before, she was just like us – living with her mum, doing make-up looks with products she already had – I could really relate to her. But now she's completely changed.

She must be making loads of money now. All those new clothes and that house in Hackney – my brother lives near there and houses on his road cost like hundreds of thousands of pounds. And the way she does this whole, "Look how fabulous my life is," thing – she's become really annoying and fake.

There were lots more comments saying similar things. I didn't want to read them, but I couldn't stop myself. Feeling sick, I scrolled and scrolled, and then I turned over to the next page.

OMG OMG OMG! Have you seen the latest? Gemma and Charlie Berry are only an item!

Allegedly. I've heard that that's what Ripple do – when they've got a new client they really want to promote, they make sure they're seen with one of their established stars to raise their profile and make more of a story about it. Remember, there was that thing a while back with Gus and Maddie? That only lasted about five minutes, but it made Maddie's name for her. So I see this kind of news and I'm, like, hmmm.

I don't know, I almost want it to be true. I think they'd make quite a cute couple.

Yeah, they might, if it was real. But it's not. Seriously – look at that vlog they did together, with the picnic in the park and all that shit. You could just see how awkward they were together – they were like strangers. There's no way it's true.

Charlie's totally out of Gemma's league anyway. I mean, she's pretty and stuff, but have you seen her ears? Like, Dumbotastic. And her voice is really annoying.

I scrolled and scrolled some more, and turned over to the next page and the one after that. The comments kept on coming, horrible things about me, my face, my bedroom, my clothes, my life.

She's just become so false.

Her vlogs are all the same now. It's all just product placement.

Did you see that smoothie thing she made? God, it looked like vomit. I almost threw up watching it, but then I laughed instead. She's just tragic.

She must be making so much money. I wonder how Charlie feels, knowing he's being used like that.

I don't think Charlie cares. Their subscribers have gone up too, even though their channel's been shit and boring for ages. Why not pretend to be sleeping with some shallow wannabe if it makes you another quarter of a million quid a year?

It's Gus I feel sorry for. They used to be so funny together and now Gemma's there in the flat with them all the time and Gus just sits at his laptop with a massive face on him.

Yeah, don't feel sorry for Gus Berry. There are lots of rumours going round about him and they really aren't nice to read.

OMG, really? Link please?

Sorry, can't link here. This site's already threatened with being shut down. We don't want Ripple's lawyers on us again ;-)

I know Gemma in real life. At least, I used to know her. I feel like I don't any more. As soon as she got famous – if you can even call her famous – she basically dumped all her old friends.

That was followed by a crying emoji, and the poster was called TranceyNance – the name Nancy used on Twitter and Instagram. It wasn't exactly cast-iron evidence, but it was pretty close. And there was enough truth in what she said to really, really hurt.

That was it – I'd seen enough. I closed the window. I felt sick and somehow dirty, as if I'd been caught doing something wrong and shameful. The comments on the new video were bad enough, but all along, for months and months, people had been saying these things about me and I'd had no idea. It felt like a betrayal – like when I'd found out about Jack and Olivia, only in a way even worse, because although almost all these people were strangers, their vitriol was aimed directly at me. And they knew so much about my life – they watched my videos, they followed me on social media, they probably even interacted with me, and they came here, to this other corner of the internet, to talk about how much they hated me. I remembered the two girls I'd posed for selfies with just a couple of days before – did they read this stuff? Did they think these things about me?

I didn't know what to do. I wanted to hide away, to delete my vlog and every other trace of my presence from the internet. Then I remembered the contract I'd signed with Cantaloupe, the commitments I'd made to them with barely a glance at the impenetrable small print, which Sloane said was their standard terms and conditions. I remembered Hannah, and remembered how, just a few minutes before, I'd thought that no price was too high to pay for helping other women like her.

I called Sloane.

"Gemma! How are you doing? I'm so sorry about yesterday."

For a moment I couldn't think what she meant. Then I remembered – the puppy, Gus, Charlie. I couldn't believe it had only been the previous evening; it felt so long ago and so unimportant.

"That's okay," I said. "It really doesn't matter."

"Oh, what a relief, I was worried you were upset. Gus gets like that sometimes – he can be a bit temperamental. So talented, right? Anyway, I guess you're calling about your new video? You brave girl, I am so proud of you, I just love it when our creators embrace causes close to their hearts. Maybe something a teeny bit less hard-hitting – sorry, that probably isn't the best phrase to use – would have been more appropriate, but never mind. The point is, you're supporting something you're passionate about, and we love that. So well done."

"Thanks," I said. "But, Sloane, it's not that – have you seen what people are saying? Have you seen that other site?"

"YouTruth? Oh, sweetie, don't give that another thought. They've been around for ages. Most of the people who post there are unsuccessful vloggers themselves. So much jealousy, so much bitterness! We just let them get on with it, unless they overstep the mark into libel, and then we take action. It doesn't make for pleasant reading, does it? I mean, if you've got nothing nice to say, why say anything at all? But that's what the internet is like. Haters gonna hate, right? Hardly anyone reads YouTruth anyway, it's just a handful of spiteful trolls. I'm amazed you were able to get on it at all, actually – the build's so amateurish, it falls over all the time."

"But the comments on my channel – the things people are saying about me being paid for the video…"

"Gemma, I know how upsetting these things are. But you've done nothing wrong – we've always been completely upfront about your affiliate links and the products you're given for honest reviews, right? Maybe you could do a little post saying how hurt you are, updating people about how your friend's doing, and keep linking to the cause – it's a good one and you're a wonderful ambassador to raise awareness. And then rise above it! There's so much exciting stuff in the pipeline for you. I had a call earlier from *Elle* magazine…

But we'll talk in more detail about that later. And don't worry about what's happening below the line on your channel, okay? Interact, respond, build relationships, and ignore the haters. We've got it all in hand. That's what we're here for. I'm so sorry, I must dash into a meeting now but we'll chat tomorrow. You take care."

She ended the call and I looked at my phone, frustrated. She didn't seem to think any of it was that important. And the comments had been so awful, so hurtful and untrue. Masochistically, I opened YouTube to look at them again.

But they had gone. Now the only people posting on my channel seemed to be full of gushing support, saying how wonderful I was, how obvious it was that the video was totally natural and unscripted, how they trusted my integrity completely. How much they loved me.

I'd been away from my desk for half an hour, I realised. One thing was for sure, I didn't feel a bit tired any more. My heart thumping, adrenaline sizzling through me, I went back up to the office and made the round of teas and coffees.

"God, that took you long enough, Gemma," Tom said. "We were all, like, dying of thirst here."

It was only later that afternoon, once I'd finished writing my article for the day (Baked-Bean Paws, Pink Noses And The World's Fluffiest Tummy – 21 Cats That Have Smashed The Cute Barrier), that it occurred to me that there might be a reason why today was the first time I'd seen so many such negative comments on my channel. Sloane, or one of her minions, must have been moderating them all along.

*

Five thirty came, and there was the usual, almost imperceptible sense of anticipation in the office. I'd realised quite early into my tenure at Clickfrenzy that the advertised working hours were just that – advertised. In reality, everyone arrived early and worked late; I always tried to be at my desk by nine o'clock, but Tom was always there before me. Whenever I went out for lunch, I'd leave Emily eating a salad at her desk. Jim once got so engrossed in a story that he missed the last train back to St Albans, where he lived, and ended up sleeping on the sofa in the meeting room.

Still, at the official close of business, most of us began to look longingly towards the lift. Everyone wanted to go home, but no one wanted to be the first to leave. I watched Callista push back her chair, stand up and stretch her shoulders – I knew how she felt; mine were aching too – and thought with relief that if she was leaving on time, I could too.

But she said, "Anyone want a coffee?"

Tom said, "Yeah, go on then. Cappuccino, please."

Hermione said, "I'd love one, but I've got to go to a reception at Number Ten tonight; I need to be out of here in ten minutes."

I could almost hear the exhalations of relief around our pod. Hermione's thing might be work, but it was a jolly just the same and once she had gone, the floodgates would open.

Ruby said, "I really wish I could stay and finish off this story, but I'm way behind on my ClassPass round-up, and there's a yoga studio down the road I should check out."

Then I saw Jim come out of the lift, walk through the office, drop his laptop bag and sit back down at his desk.

"I thought you had a five o'clock off-site," Ruby said.

"Yeah, that's right," Jim said. "It finished a few minutes ago. Why?"

"Oh, no reason." Ruby looked defeated – as indeed we all were. By passing up the chance of heading home even five minutes early, Jim had officially won that day's round of passive-aggressive presenteeism.

"I'll have a decaf tea, Callista, if you're making," he said.

"I'm on it," Callista said.

I picked up my jacket and said, "Night everyone. See you tomorrow."

Someone had to end the evening stalemate, I told myself – it might as well be me.

It was only when I got to the Tube station that I realised I didn't actually know where I was going. Home to Hannah and Richard's house, or back to Charlie's? I hadn't spoken to Charlie all day – the usual flood of texts and WhatsApp messages from him had turned into a drought. We hadn't had a row – we just hadn't spoken, at all. Was he pissed off with me? He had no right to be, I thought, crossly. I, on the other hand, was perfectly entitled to be pissed off with him. The previous evening and the discovery of the horrible underworld of hateful comments about me had swept all thoughts of Charlie from my mind, but now, the more I thought about him, the more pissed off I became.

I'd done nothing wrong. I could have called Gus out on his rudeness, but I hadn't. Maybe I should have made the effort to get in touch with Charlie at some point during the day, but as he'd know from my vlog, there was a totally legitimate reason for my radio silence.

Stuff him, I decided. I'd go home. I'd see how Hannah was. I'd finish cleaning the glittery bathroom. I'd have something to eat – I suddenly realised I was starving. And maybe, before I went to bed, I'd call Charlie and find out what was up. Maybe.

When I emerged from the Underground half an hour later, I found myself automatically glancing into the window of The Daily Grind. Raffy didn't work there any more – I knew he didn't, and I didn't expect to see him there. But there he was. Not behind the counter frothing milk, or wiping surfaces with a spray bottle and a cloth, but sitting at a table – the table I'd come to think of as mine – working intently on a laptop.

I paused. Was it really him, or some other bloke with similar hair? Then he looked up, saw me, and waved.

I ducked into the coffee shop and went over to him.

"Hey," he said. "I haven't seen you in ages."

I said, "I haven't been around in ages. It's all been a bit weird. I've been mad busy, and… yeah. I haven't been around much. What are you doing here?"

He said, "What, I'm not allowed to sit in my mate's shop and catch up with some work?"

I blushed. "You know that's not what I meant. I meant it's great to see you. How've you been? Have you found another job?"

"Gemma," he said. "There's something I wanted to talk to you about. That's why I'm here, actually. I knew if I hung around here for long enough you'd come in for a coffee. I don't have your number and I could have contacted you on social media but that felt a bit…"

"Stalkerish? And loitering at the coffee shop at the end of my road isn't?"

He laughed. "I've got all the smooth moves."

Our eyes met and I smiled, and felt the strange lurching feeling inside me that I'd felt before when he looked at me. It lasted for a few seconds, longer maybe – me standing by the table looking down at him and him looking up at me, both of us smiling. I almost didn't want to say anything that would break the moment, the connection I felt – but then Raffy's phone rang.

"Hi Vicky," he said. "Yeah, I can talk. What's up? He did? Right."

There was a long pause. I could faintly hear a woman's voice, speaking quickly and excitedly, but I couldn't make out any of the words and I didn't want Raffy to think I was earwigging on his call. I moved away, but Raffy reached out and touched my arm.

He turned his laptop around. On the screen, he'd typed, *This could take a while. Here's my number – call me when you can.*

I hesitated, then I thought, what did I have to lose? He could find me on WhatsApp or Facebook or Twitter or practically anywhere else online if he wanted to – but I had no idea how to contact him. I didn't even know his last name. So I tapped the eleven digits into my phone, then checked that I'd got them right.

"Vicky, I know you feel strongly about this," he was saying. "But I'd question whether it's the right thing to do. I mean, these are people's lives we're talking about."

Then he mouthed, "Call me."

I said, "Okay. See you later," and walked out, feeling obscurely disappointed. I wandered aimlessly into the supermarket next door, trying to decide what I felt like eating – which was actually really hard, as it often is when you're ridiculously hungry – and trying to make sense of my feelings.

Raffy wasn't interested in me. He'd made that all too clear, all those months before, when I'd made my humiliating, drunken attempt to hook up with him. He'd asked me to call him – but it was probably something about my vlog. Maybe Zara, his little niece, wanted an autograph or something. Or he wanted me to go and deliver leaflets with him about the redevelopment of the estate. I barely knew him, I thought, staring blankly at the fridge full of ready-meals and throwing a lasagne, some sushi and a Vietnamese noodle thing randomly into my basket. Whatever I thought I felt – that connection, that thing – was probably not real. I wasn't thinking straight. Too much had happened in the past twenty-four hours. I was clearly experiencing some sort of emotional hallucination brought on by tiredness and stress, I decided, adding a block of cheese, a bottle of salted caramel sauce and a massive baking potato to my shopping. And anyway – can of sweetcorn, loaf of sliced bread, a bunch of pink tulips for Hannah – I had a boyfriend.

I had a boyfriend. At least, I thought I did. If Charlie had decided to dump me, I hadn't got the memo. Not yet, anyway. I needed to find out what was going on. I needed to speak to him – but first, I needed to check online for anything that might give me a clue to the reason for his silence.

I paid for my shopping, but before heading down the road for home, I glanced again through the window of The Daily Grind.

Raffy was gone; the shutters had been pulled half down and a girl I didn't recognise was wiping the tables.

The house was empty too. I opened the door cautiously, frightened that Richard might be there, even though I knew it was impossible. But when I called, "Hello?" I knew I didn't really need to wait for an answer – it had that silent, still feeling that places have when no one's home.

I put my bags down in the kitchen and found a jug for Hannah's flowers. She'd mentioned that she might go and stay with her sister for a couple of nights, until whatever needed to happen to get a restraining order against Richard had happened. Hopefully they'd still be fresh when she came home. Amy must be over her virus and back at work.

It was strange, but I realised that whenever I'd been alone in the house before, I'd felt a tension, a sense of apprehension, as if something was about to happen. It was why I'd got into the habit of going straight up to my room and staying there with my camera for company. I didn't feel that now. The house was very quiet, but it was a peaceful sort of quiet. I looked around the kitchen and saw again the room I remembered from my first visit – a homely, prettily decorated, tidy space that people could fill with happiness.

I tipped my groceries out on to the table and looked at them without enthusiasm. Then I put everything away on my shelf in the fridge, stuck four slices of bread in the toaster and put the butter dish on the table. *Please remember to use a butter knife*, said the Post-it note in Hannah's writing. For some reason, reading it made me want to cry.

"Snap out of it, Gemma," I said aloud.

When my toast had popped, I slathered butter and peanut butter on it and sat down with my tablet. Charlie and Gus had posted a video that afternoon. The title was 'Playing with our new puppy'. I pressed play.

"Hey all of you," Gus said.

"Hello!" said Charlie.

"We're the Berry Boys."

"As you know."

"And there's someone we'd like you guys to meet."

The camera cut to Taylor, sitting on the floor looking up expectantly. Gus threw a treat for her and she dashed across the floor to get it, skidding on the concrete and overshooting her target, then trotting back and crunching eagerly. She really was incredibly cute, I thought.

"So this is Taylor," Charlie said.

"Named after Taylor Swift, who we, like, totally love," Gus said.

"She came to live with us yesterday, and she is just the most adorable thing ever," Charlie said.

I felt a tiny twinge of resentment, then told myself not to be so mad – there was no way I could be jealous of a tiny puppy.

"So we'll show you some of the stuff we've got for her, to help her feel at home here," Gus said.

"We think she's been really missing her brothers and sisters, because she kept us up, like, all night, howling like a lunatic," Charlie said.

"That and peeing," Gus said. "Oh my God, the peeing."

"Puppies pee," Charlie said. "You heard it here first."

"So anyway, this is her bed," Gus said.

"And we've got a bowl for her water and a bowl for her food."

"And this cool harness and lead."

It was only a matter of time, I thought, before Sloane delivered a load of designer dog stuff for them to include in their videos, with affiliate links below the line. Then I told myself not to be so horrible and cynical – they were clearly smitten with her. It was really cute to watch. *That must be why Charlie hasn't texted today*, I thought – *he's just been busy, either puppy-sitting or catching up on sleep. Bless.*

"And lots and lots of toys," Charlie said.

"But she's already got a favourite," said Gus.

The camera cut to the puppy, crouched on the floor, determinedly chewing something.

"She's teething, the vet says," Charlie said. "He said we basically need to lock away everything we don't want destroyed."

"Charles here has put his trainer collection into a safe-deposit box in the Cayman Islands," said Gus.

Charlie threw a pillow at his head and the two of them wrestled briefly on the red sofa.

"No, but seriously," Charlie said. "Look at her! Seek and destroy!"

Gus threw the toy across the room and the camera shakily followed it as the puppy sprinted after her quarry and fell upon it. I watched as Gus went after her and pulled one end of it and Taylor, growling a tiny puppy growl, pulled back. I could hear Charlie laughing as he zoomed in on them.

The toy looked different from all Taylor's other new, brightly coloured things – it was greige and a bit shapeless, but the puppy was moving so quickly, shaking her head and struggling to get a purchase with her back legs on the slippery floor, that it was hard to tell what it was.

Then Charlie got the focus sorted, and I could see properly.

It was Stanley.

Chapter Nineteen

It was Friday evening, late opening at Brush, the swankiest hair salon I'd ever been to. The room was crowded, but the vibe was buzzy rather than frenetic. I'd been greeted by name and given a cocktail and a stack of glossy magazines, and seated at the colourist's station while I waited for her to finish with her previous client. And now, she was standing behind me, examining my hair with an expert eye that was rather more critical than I would have liked.

"So, I was thinking maybe I could go platinum," I said. "Not, you know, Gwen Stefani blonde, but properly silver. Or even blue, or indigo."

"I'm not sure I'd recommend that." Gentle, expert hands lifted up a lock of my hair. I could see them in the mirror, gold nails catching the light from the chandelier as they parted the strands, assessing and analysing. "Jesus. You haven't been using professional products, have you, Gemma? What have you been putting on your poor hair, Fairy liquid?"

"Just normal stuff," I muttered. "You know, from Boots? Are you saying you can't do it?"

"I'm saying I won't," she said. "Honestly. You have such beautiful hair, but you haven't been taking care of it, you've let it get far too long for its condition or your face shape, and now you want to bleach the hell out of it? I'd be doing both of us a terrible disservice if I allowed that."

She peered more closely at my hair, and her face in the mirror went from disapproving to downright accusatory. "Gemma. You've been using box colours, haven't you? I can see the product build-up – look. See the difference in the colour between the mid-lengths and the ends? Stripping all this out would take ages and wreck what little condition you've got left. We're going to have to take at least four inches off as it is."

"Hold on," I said. "I came all the way here because you invited me for a colour and cut, and now you're giving me a massive telling-off. Don't you know who I am?"

"I give all my clients the same advice," she said. "The right advice. And in your case, it's keeping the colour warm, with just a few foils – yes, I know that's totally 2014, but so is your hair. When you're tired of it, we can cut it off. And today, we're going to be cutting off lots already. Then we'll do a treatment to add some protein back. And you need to sort out your diet, because your hair is telling me it's not good, even if you're not."

"Can I have another French 75, at least?" I said.

"I don't see why not," she said. "But you should have a glass of water, too. Your skin's looking a bit dehydrated. Toby will get it for you while I mix your colour."

She gave my hair a final, despairing tweak between her fingertips and sighed. I'm pretty sure she rolled her eyes to heaven, but I didn't quite see, because I was rolling mine, too.

"Thanks, Mum," I said.

*

"So it didn't work out with them, then?" Mum said, twenty minutes later, folding foil around a section of my hair. I noticed, as I had so often before, how easy it was to talk to Mum in the salon while she was doing my hair, because all around us other clients were spilling the most intimate details of their lives to their stylists. I'd felt quite comfortable telling her what Shivvy had told me about Jack and Olivia. No one would even bother listening to what I saying, even if they could hear me over the roar of high-powered hairdryers and the Doors playing in the background. And also, with her standing behind me, I didn't have to look into her eyes and see whatever judgements she might be making; I could just wait for her wise, measured response, as hairdresserly as it was motherly.

"Apparently not," I said. "But I don't know – all I've got to go on is what Shivvy said. And I don't trust her; I never have."

"Mmm," Mum said.

"Jack hasn't posted anything on Instagram for a couple of weeks," I said. "Olivia's just wanking on about yoga and organic veganberries, same as usual."

"I never liked that girl," Mum said. "But she does know how to take care of herself. You could do with a few organic veganberries yourself, sweetie. You're very thin. But anyway, Charlie – are you having fun together?"

My throat closed up. I didn't know how to tell Mum how I was feeling about Charlie. If it had just been the misgivings I had about our relationship, Gus's resentful presence, the pressure from Sloane to model cheerful togetherness without any hint of actual sex – the chasm I'd felt opening between my online life and my real one, in which work happened, Hannah and Richard happened, Raffy happened... I didn't know if I could. But I could try.

But then there was Stanley. And I know exactly how silly and pathetic this sounds, but what had happened to Stanley was the single biggest thing that was making me think that I couldn't carry on going out with Charlie. Like I said – pathetic. As far as Charlie was concerned, Stanley was just a toy; just a shabby old bear who sometimes appeared in my videos, who I'd brought one day to the flat in my bag. I suppose he thought it was an affectation – something to make me seem more childlike and appealing to my viewers. He couldn't know just how important Stanley was to me. But at the same time, he *should* have known. And every time I thought of Stanley being mauled by the puppy, and Charlie and Gus laughing about it, it made me cry.

And Mum would get it – she totally would. Whenever I packed my bag to go back to uni after holidays, Mum would hover around asking me if I needed help folding my clothes and giving me samples of hair products from the salon and generally being a mum, and every time, when I was finally all packed and ready to go, she'd say, "Don't forget Stanley." (As if, mother!)

Because she knew. When I was little, I used to make her tell me over and over again the story of how when I was a baby and screaming the place down and no amount of shushing and bouncing from her (or even from Dad, when he was there) would shut me up, she'd stick me in my Moses basket with Stanley and go out into the garden for a fag, to get a bit of peace and quiet (and stop herself screaming the place down too, I realised when I was a bit older), and when she came back she'd find me contentedly sucking one of his ears. She'd seen me in floods of tears on my first day of school, because Stanley wasn't allowed to come too. She'd heard the endless conversations I had with him (one-sided, admittedly), in which I narrated out loud the adventures we had together, and she'd read the stories I filled numerous exercise books with about them (reader, I present that neglected classic *Gemma and Stanley Explore the Amazon*).

I knew she would understand how I felt, and I knew a part of her would feel the same. And so I couldn't tell her that Stanley wasn't part of my life any more.

Instead I said, "Charlie's fun. But I don't know whether it's serious really – not like I thought Jack and me were."

Mum said, "Jack's a lovely boy. I'm sure Charlie is too. You're sensible, sweetheart, you've got good judgement. But at your age, relationships are about finding out who you are, as much as about being with someone else. Does that even make sense?"

"Not really," I said.

"You see, Darren and me," Mum said, carefully folding another piece of foil around another strand of my hair. "When I met him, he seemed so glamorous. He had whole armies of girls after him, and it was me he picked. I was so thrilled that this older man – he was twenty-six and I was only twenty-one, so not a big difference, but it felt like lightyears – was paying attention to me. He knew everyone, he had lots of money, he took me to clubs and restaurants I'd never have been able to get into on my own."

Mum had told me this stuff before, but I'd never really thought about it in the context of my own life, other than to think that as soon as she heard Dad's name was Darren, she should have run for the hills. Now, though, I wondered whether Charlie's fame, his good looks and glamorous life were a part – even the biggest part – of why I was going out with him. I didn't think so – I never had thought so. It was his sweetness, his sexiness, his ability to make me laugh that I liked, I told myself. The rest was just gravy.

"Anyway," Mum went on, "of course if I'd taken the time to get to know him better, I'd have realised that he was completely wrong for me. But then I had you – which I don't regret one tiny bit, of course – and it was too late for me to change my mind, because even after he left, he'd always be your father. But if I'd been sensible about it – even a little bit sensible – I'd have realised that I was far too young to settle down with anyone, even if I'd met someone who was perfect for me, because you're changing so much in your early twenties it'll probably be about six weeks before they're not perfect any more."

I watched my refection in the mirror nod in agreement – although what I was actually thinking was that I was exactly the same now as I'd always been. It was my circumstances and the people around me that had changed, I thought, not my actual self.

"And there's nothing wrong with being single, you know," Mum said. "Look at me. I've been single for years and I'm perfectly happy."

"How come you go on all those Guardian Soulmates dates then?" I couldn't resist asking.

"I'm allowed to keep my options open, aren't I?" Mum said. "George Clooney and Amal might split up and he might come looking for love on Soulmates. Anything could happen. Besides, I like meeting new people, even if some of them are… not exactly every single woman's dream come true. But unless – until – I meet someone who I really, really feel makes my life so much better that I can't imagine it without him in it, I'll carry on on my own. And if no one comes along, I'll get a cat."

I took another sip of my fizzy cocktail, impressed by her pragmatism. But then, I reminded myself, Mum was old. She'd been married, she'd had a child, she'd done the whole romance thing. She and Dad has had a totally fabulous wedding with her in a white frock (hideous, admittedly, with a sweetheart neckline and a fishtail skirt). She could afford to turn her back on relationships and be super-fussy. I couldn't. If I was single now, who was to say I wouldn't stay single forever and ever?

"Right," Mum said. "I'll leave you to cook for twenty-five minutes, then we'll stick on a toner and a treatment, and then I am cutting off those ends, and nothing you can say or do will stop me."

An hour later, Mum whisked the nylon gown off my shoulders, gave my hair a final swish through with a paddle brush, and said, "There. Now that's a bit of an improvement, isn't it?"

When I'd arrived in the salon, my hair had been more than halfway down my back, way below my bra strap, and mostly a kind of streaky, dirty blonde that was meant to be a bit Cara Delevigne but, thanks to me leaving it way too long between colours, was more Cruella de Vil. Now it was six inches shorter, a coppery caramel colour, and seriously shiny in spite of being all sort of beachy and un-done. It made my eyes look really green, although they're actually a rather dull in-between hazel.

"What do you think?" Mum said.

"It's way too short," I said. "Seriously, I've got hardly any hair left."

"Nonsense," Mum said. "It looks longer than it did before, straggling down your back like that. It's got proper structure now, and movement. And more importantly, it's got a bit of condition back. Now I'm going to give you some products and you must promise to use them, and not leave it any longer than six weeks before you come and see me again. Right?"

"Right," I said. Then I gave her a massive hug. "I love it really," I said. "You're quite good at hair, you know. You could do it for an actual job."

"It helps to have such a pretty model," Mum said, glancing at her watch. "I've got another client coming in five minutes, then I'm done for the night. Shall I pick up a bottle of wine and some Wagamama on the way home?"

I was about to say that sounded like a pretty amazing plan to me, when the bell over the salon door pinged and a voice behind me said, "I haven't got an appointment, but is there any chance you could fit me in for a cut?"

I froze, then very, very slowly turned around. Jack was standing by the reception desk.

"I'm awfully sorry," Carly, the receptionist, said, "but we're closing in an hour and we're fully booked for the rest of the evening. Fridays are always so busy. Maybe you'd like to come in next week?"

"That's okay," Jack said, sidling back towards the door. "It's completely fine. Really. I'll ring next week, or drop in. I…"

But he'd reckoned without Mum. She descended on him like vultures would descend on dying antelope if they knew how to do it so casually that the antelope would think it was just going to be given a head massage, or something.

"Jack!" she said. "I hardly recognised you. You look so tanned, and your hair… How sweet of you to pop in. But we're rushed off our feet here tonight, so we can't… but Gemma's here…"

And she glided away, leaving Jack and me staring at each other.

Jack said, "Hi."

I said, "Hello."

Jack said, "I thought…" at the same moment I said, "I was just…"

Then our eyes met, and we both laughed. It was an awkward, uncomfortable laugh, but still.

Jack said, "Shall we go for a drink?"

I said, "Okay. That would be nice."

I looked around for Mum, to tell her that I was going to be late for our Sauvignon and udon rendezvous, but she'd disappeared discreetly off to mix a colour for her last client.

"All Bar One?" Jack said.

I remembered the last time we'd been there, the night that was supposed to be a celebration of my new job but instead turned out to be the beginning of the end of our relationship, and shook my head.

"Bearded Clam?" I suggested.

"But isn't it karaoke night?" Jack said.

"That's Saturday, remember?" I said. "We're safe."

It was really weird how, walking down the familiar street with him, our shoulders almost but not quite touching, going to the bar and ordering a glass of wine for me and a pint of Guinness for him, it felt like the past five months hadn't happened – like we were still together, my hopes for our future still intact.

We pushed our way to the last spare table and sat down, resting our elbows on its slightly sticky surface. Jack took a deep gulp of his drink.

"God, that's good," he said. "I've missed this stuff."

"Surely you can get Guinness all over the place?" I said. "It's a global mega brand, isn't it?"

Jack said, "Yes, but I – we – I mean, Liv, mostly, wanted to have an authentic experience. So we ended up drinking local drinks in little local bars and eating local food, and some of it was really gross. The first thing I did when I got home was go to the chippy."

Part of me longed to question him further about Olivia, but another, more tactful – or perhaps more cowardly – part shied away from the topic.

I said, "So what happened? To make you come back, I mean?"

Jack said, "We'd just arrived in Santiago from Sydney, and we got the bus from the airport. It's a twelve-hour flight and I was totally shattered. I was sat next to a woman with a baby on the plane and I swear it didn't stop screaming once. Oh wait – it did once, but that was to puke all over me."

"Ugh," I said. "Nightmare. Where even is Santiago?"

"Chile," Jack said. "Anyway, so we got the bus into town. All the blogs and stuff say to keep your bag with you, but we just weren't thinking, because we were so knackered. And we fell asleep on the bus, and only woke up at the main bus station when the guy told as we had to get off. And when we did – no bags."

"Oh my God, how awful," I said.

"I know, right?" Jack said. "There I was in the middle of this strange city, totally jetlagged, covered in baby puke, with no clothes to change into. And the worst thing was, I had no money either, and no passport, because like a total div I'd put my wallet in my bag instead of keeping it on me in my pocket."

"Shit," I said. "So what happened?"

Jack grimaced. "Liv went absolutely mental. Like, seriously, Gemma, I've never seen anyone so pissed off. So there I was in the middle of this strange city, covered in baby puke, with no money and no passport and my girl— with Liv screaming at me and telling me I was the biggest fucking idiot on the planet."

It seemed as if, in getting the story of Jack's travels, I was going to get the story of his and Olivia's relationship too, whether I wanted to hear it or not. I took another gulp of wine and said nothing.

"And the thing is," Jack went on, "I'd been starting to realise, about from when we got to Sydney, that this whole travel thing wasn't working out for me. I was missing home, and the flat, and my mates and my job, and you, and even the sodding rain. And now I was basically fucked, with no money to pay for a place to stay or even anything to eat, and I was starving but at the same time I was absolutely sick of foreign food."

I'd barely heard most of what he said, only the bit about missing me. I could feel my heart beating much faster.

"So what did you do?" I said.

"Liv still had her purse on her," Jack said. "So she wasn't as completely screwed as I was, and she had her passport too. But I'd had enough. Like I said, I was knackered and starving, and…"

"And covered in baby puke," I said.

"Exactly," Jack said. "Anyway, there was a McDonald's right there, so I said, let's go and get something to eat and I can get cleaned up in the toilet there, and then let's find the British Embassy and get ourselves on a flight home pronto."

"And?" I said.

Jack finished his drink and said, "I could do with another. How about you?"

I looked at my glass and realised it was empty. "Yes, please."

I watched him make his way through the crowd to the bar, tall and strong and familiar. He'd gone to the salon, not knowing that I'd be there, presumably to see Mum and ask her about me. He said he'd missed me. I thought of the nights I'd spent lying in my bed at Hannah and Richard's house, longing for him and later crying over him. I thought of the dreams I'd had for our future together – dreams he'd shattered so casually. I remembered how it had felt when I saw the photo of him and Olivia together on the beach, the heart drawn in the sand around their smiling faces. But before I could make sense of any of it in my head, he came back.

"There we go," he said, putting our drinks on the table together with a packet of cheese and onion crisps and a packet of pork scratchings. He ripped them open and crunched on a handful. "So good. Oh my God. Snack of champions. Anyway, where was I?"

"You were going to go to McDonald's," I said.

"Right," Jack said. "But Liv was like, did I think she'd travelled halfway round the world to eat a fucking Big Mac, and anyway, in case I'd forgotten, she's been a vegetarian for ten fucking years."

"Like anyone who's a vegetarian ever lets you forget it," I said.

Jack laughed. "I know, right? But anyway, I was starting to get pissed off too, and I started shouting back, and the next thing we were having this massive, screaming row right in the middle of

Santiago bus station. I said it wasn't my fault some random tea leaf had stolen our bags and she was being a total bitch to blame me for it. I said I'd had enough of travelling and I'd had enough of eating weird crap food that looked like a dose of campylobacter waiting for a place to happen and I'd had enough of sleeping in flea-pit youth hostels, and I wanted to go home."

"And what did she say?"

"She said I was being pathetic and how could I let a little setback (seriously, being stranded in South America with all my stuff gone – a little setback?) put me off, and had I never heard of travel insurance? And just because we weren't in the Castle fucking Mall didn't mean there weren't these things called shops. And that stuff is just stuff but experiences are irreplaceable, and she was going to head for the market because she'd read about this stall that did amazing fungus salad, and I could come or not as I pleased."

"So what did you do?" I asked, although I already knew the answer.

Jack sighed. "I said that if that was the way she felt, clearly she didn't give a shit about me and as far as I was concerned it wasn't going to work out between us, because I was sick of her moods and her selfishness. And she said she was sick of me being a deadweight and whinging about everything, and… well… that was it, really. I mean, we carried on shouting at each other for a bit, but there wasn't anything much more to say. And then she gave me some of her pesos and went off to wherever she was going."

"Poor you," I said, although I was beginning to feel a grudging admiration for Olivia.

"It wasn't too bad really," Jack said. "I got on the phone to my insurance company – they hadn't nicked my phone, thankfully –

and they sorted things out, and I booked myself into the Hilton and spent a few days watching *Game of Thrones* and eating ham sandwiches from room service, and then my new passport was ready so I came home. And I've been home for two weeks now and quite honestly it's the best thing ever."

"And Olivia?" I said.

"I guess round about now she'll be trekking in Patagonia." Jack made a face. Then he said, "Look, Gemma, there's a few things I need to say to you."

I nodded. "Go on."

"All this – basically everything I've done for the past few months – has been the most massive mistake. The travelling thing – I mean, bits were all right. But I'm just not cut out for it. I was miserable most of the time. I should have been really excited by it all but I wasn't – I was just homesick. And I guess that's why Liv and me kind of got together. I know it sounds stupid but I was lonely."

"Right," I said.

"And Liv – she's such a good mate. Well, she was. I don't know if she's going to be any more. But as a girlfriend – there was just no way it was going to work. She's so full-on. She's not like you – you're so… I don't know, so kind of restful to be with. Right from the beginning, me and her had rows. We never rowed, really, did we?"

"I guess not," I said. But I was thinking, *That's because I never disagreed with you, and I always went along with what you wanted.*

"I watched all your videos," Jack said, looking down into his glass. "Even the ones where you put on make-up. Even the one where you massively slagged me off. That made me feel like a pile of crap."

"I'm sorry," I said, then hated myself for saying it.

But Jack said, "Don't be sorry. They're really cool. You look really beautiful in them."

"Thanks," I said.

Jack said, "So, listen, this Charlie dude. Is he actually your boyfriend? Because I read on some forum that he wasn't really – that is was just, like, a set-up thing."

I said, "No, it's real. He is my boyfriend. Although I'm not sure whether he's going to be for much longer, to be honest."

Jack let out a long, heavy sigh that created ripples in the surface of his drink. Then he said, "So, do you want to come back to mine?"

It was the moment I'd longed for; the words I'd dreamed of hearing, night after night, lying in my bed nursing my broken heart. Just a few months before, there would have been no decision to make – I'd have fallen into Jack's arms, overflowing with relief that he and Olivia were over, that he'd come back, that he'd chosen me.

But my heart wasn't broken any more. And even if Charlie and I were still together – and I was far from sure about that – this wasn't about Charlie. It wasn't even about Jack, not really. Because I understood now that Jack hadn't actually chosen me – not in any meaningful sense. For Jack, this was just about a return to the way things had been before, back when he had his quiet, easy life – however frustrating he found it – his lucrative, easy job and his undemanding, easy girlfriend. Jack had seen the world, but it hadn't changed him. I'd stayed behind, but maybe I hadn't stayed the same, after all.

I said, "I don't think so, actually. Mum was going to get a takeaway for us. I haven't seen her in a while and we need to catch up. But thanks for the drinks. I'm glad you're home safe."

And I kissed him on the cheek and walked out of the pub.

Chapter Twenty

Hi everyone!

So, I'm doing something a bit different in today's video – but seasonally appropriate! Because at this time of year we all put aside our natural looks and can the contouring and go all-out... Whatever. All-out Goth, all-out witch – some of the other vloggers I admire, whose make-up skills leave me standing, have put together totally amazing special-effects looks, which I've linked to down below. But quite honestly, these are way beyond my limited ability, so I've gone for something quite simple, and, if I do say so myself, quite wearable. Yes, it's Halloween, and yes, I'm going to a party dressed as Wednesday Addams. Here's how I created the look.

There was a delicious smell of hot sugar and cinnamon drifting up the stairs. Hannah had been baking Halloween cookies, cut out in the shapes of bats, witches, spiders and cats and iced in lurid shades of purple, green and orange, as well as classic black, obviously.

I would have thought that, post-Richard, the last thing she would have wanted to do was revert to her domestic goddess ways, but she seemed to take comfort from cooking and housework. With Richard gone – he was staying with his brother in Dagenham, Hannah said – the house felt like a different place, a happier place. Even though we all knew that it couldn't carry on indefinitely, that Hannah was only managing to make the repayments on the mortgage thanks to the low interest rate and Amy's and my rent, Hannah had said nothing about needing to sell just yet. In fact, the only sign that her life had fundamentally changed was that, when I went up to her bedroom that morning to ask if she'd like a cup of tea, I found all the furniture dragged out on to the landing, and Hannah pasting totally gorgeous wallpaper, covered in lush green plants and pink flamingos, on to the walls.

"Because I can," she said simply. "Richard was all about the neutral decor and resale value, but fuck that. I don't know how long I'm going to be able to stay in the house, now, but I'm going to enjoy it while I can."

It was the first time I'd ever heard her swear. I would have given her a high five, except she didn't have any free hands.

Now she, Amy, Kian and a few of their friends were downstairs in the kitchen, bagging up Hannah's cookies in anticipation of groups of trick-or-treating children and concocting lethal purple cocktails. I wished I could stay in with them, but tonight was the annual Ripple Effect Halloween party, and the invitation had implied that attendance was not just expected, but obligatory.

I added a bit more chalk-white powder to my face, topped up my blueish-pink lipstick, and gave my pigtails a tweak. In the bottle-green gym tunic I'd found last weekend in Mum's loft (thank you, secondary school, for your utterly hideous uniform) and the prim, pointy-collared white blouse I'd spotted in a charity shop when I was dropping off a load of unwanted free samples, I was fairly confident that I looked the part.

Unfortunately, I didn't feel even slightly like going to the party.

I hadn't spoken to Charlie for more than a week. He'd texted, called, emailed and left loads of voice and WhatsApp messages, but I hadn't returned them. I didn't know what to say to him. But I was going to have to make my mind up sharpish, because there was no way he and Gus, Ripple Effect's second-most illustrious clients, weren't going to be in attendance tonight.

I put my top-up supplies of make-up, my keys, camera and mobile into my bag, checked my face one last time, and sighed. If Stanley had been there, I would have told him he was in charge of guarding my room for the night and I'd be back soon, but he wasn't.

Amy was frying chipolata sausages in the kitchen, Kian standing behind her inhaling their aroma and admiring her cleavage in her black batwing top. Hannah and her friend Karen were arguing about whether the cocktails needed more Ribena or more vodka – "More vodka, obviously," Hannah was saying as I walked in.

"My God, Gemma, you look amazing," Amy said. "Your legs in that outfit…"

"Have a drink," Kian said, passing me a plastic cup full of what was basically purple vodka.

"Group selfie!" Hannah said, and we all clustered round while she took one.

The door knocker crashed and a voice called, "Trick or treat!" as menacingly as you can if you're five.

I said, "I have to go. Have a fun night." And, my feet feeling even heavier than they should have done in my clumpy lace-up flatforms, I made my way to the station.

I remembered how I'd felt arriving at Charlie and Gus's launch party all those months ago – how out of place and apprehensive. Now, I was turning up at a different achingly cool cocktail bar in a different part of town, wearing different clothes. Then, it had been high summer; now, a raw wind was battering drops of rain against my face and the pavements were coated with a slippery layer of fallen leaves.

Inside, though, it was much the same. The room was crowded with people – not in normal party clothes this time, obviously, but dressed up as sexy witches, sexy vampires, sexy ghouls – you get the picture. My Wednesday Addams outfit, assembled as it was from random things I already owned or had bought at minimum cost, looked frumpy and amateurish by contrast, but I didn't particularly care.

I made my way through the crowd to the bar, stopping to say hi to a few of Charlie and Gus's friends who I'd met at the karaoke evening. Everyone was as casually friendly as they'd been then. Everyone still had their phones or cameras out all the time, filming themselves and each other. Everyone knew each other, although of course now I knew lots more of them than I had before, and even more who I didn't know recognised me.

"Gemma! SparklyGems!" said a sexy nun. "How are you? I just love your channel. Where's Charlie?"

"Not sure," I said. "I expect he and Gus will be along later. They've been really busy with the new puppy."

"Taylor," she said. "Oh my God, I just adore her. So cute!"

"Isn't she?" I said.

"Hi Gemma!" said a guy with glitter all over his face, who I supposed had come as Edward from Twilight. "I'm Perry, we haven't met but I just adore your vlog. I do make-up tutorials too, we should do a collab sometime."

"That would be great! I just love your channel too, I watch it all the time," I lied, hoping he wouldn't ask me about anything specific.

"Hi Gemma," said Maddie (sexy zombie). "Amazing to see you! Your channel's doing so great – congratulations!" She raised her bottle of fizzy water to clink against my glass, but I didn't have one.

"And yours too," I said. "I just loved that thing you did the other day, with the raw…"

"The raw brownies?" Maddie said, inadvertently coming to my rescue. "Oh my God, how good were they? It's amazing what you can do with dates, linseed and cacao. They're so filling, I could only eat, like, half a one and I was totally stuffed."

"I bet you were," I said, looking enviously at her tiny, toned frame and telling myself for the millionth time that I really, really must join a gym and go to it occasionally.

"Where's Charlie?" Maddie asked, and I repeated my line about the puppy.

Then I said, "Anyway, it's so amazing to see you. I'm just going to grab a drink – we'll catch up later, right?"

"Of course!" Maddie said. She took a selfie of us and so did I, and then I went off to find the bar. The effects of Hannah's vodka cocktail were wearing off, and I knew that my only hope of getting through the evening was to drink and drink, and then possibly drink a bit more.

The bar was draped in black netting, glinting with green and purple fairy lights. A flock of bats were suspended above it, lit by more fairy lights. The barmen were dressed as gargoyles, their faces and bare chests smeared with grey and green make-up. I joined the throng and waited to be served.

"Here you go," one of the barmen said. "That's one Bloody Mary, one absinthe sour and one Galliano Old Fashioned."

"Er… I ordered an Aperol spritz and a gin and tonic," said a sexy skeleton.

"You did? I'm so sorry. Whose are these… anyway. I'll get those for you right away. They're on the… Oh, wait. Everything's on the house anyway."

I started to laugh. Only one person in the world was that inept at serving drinks, and no amount of gargoyle make-up could disguise those brilliant aquamarine eyes.

"I'll have the Bloody Mary," I said. "And the absinthe sour. And the other thing, although it sounded totally minging."

"Hello, Gemma," Raffy said. He didn't seem at all surprised to see me – nothing like as surprised as I was to see him.

"What are you doing here, anyway?" I said. "How are you? Where have you been? You don't write, you don't call…" I hoped my face didn't give away how many times I'd scrolled to his number on my phone, my finger hovering over the green button – then changed my mind.

"I'm working, obviously," Raffy said. "Deploying my legendary service skills, as you can see. Here you go, one Aperol spritz, one vodka and tonic."

"But I ordered…" the sexy skeleton began. Then Raffy smiled at her, and she said, "That's brilliant, thank you."

I sipped the Bloody Mary, hoping its rightful owner wouldn't come and snatch it from my hands, and watched as Raffy took another order, got it right this time, then took another and got it wrong. The crowd waiting for cocktails was showing no sign of thinning. The Bloody Mary was finished, so I started on the Galliano Old Fashioned. I was right – it was minging.

Raffy said, over the rattle of ice in his cocktail shaker, "Look, it's crazy here. I'm on a break at nine – meet me outside?"

I looked at my watch and saw it was half past seven. "Okay," I said.

I spent the next hour shamelessly propping up the bar, like one of the old soaks who seem to be permanent residents in the Bearded Clam, watching Raffy mess up people's cocktail orders and drinking what seemed to be a bottomless glass of Prosecco – as soon as it was almost finished, Raffy would produce a bottle from the fridge and top it up, without me having to ask (which was probably just as well, I thought, because if I had asked I'd have ended up with Bacardi and Coke or something), and every time he topped it up, he'd smile at me and I'd smile back.

We couldn't talk much – he was too busy and it was too noisy. Someone had turned the music up and the lights down, so I could barely see the costumed figures moving through the gloom. Only the occasional camera flash illuminated the room, revealing the growing crowd. I strained to see, but I couldn't spot Gus and Charlie's identical blond heads anywhere. Perhaps they were in fancy dress so elaborate it had made them unrecognisable. Perhaps they weren't coming, in which case I would absolutely, definitely, have to call Charlie tomorrow.

"There you are, Gemma!" The voice made me jump, but it was only Sloane, in a sexy Day of the Dead outfit. Her hair was styled in snaky ringlets, she was wearing loads of red lipstick and a black lace mantilla, and bursting out of her corset top.

"Look at you – Wednesday Addams, right? So cute. You put all the rest of us to shame," she said kindly, making me conscious all over again of my amateurish outfit. "I've been hunting everywhere for you."

She leaned in close to me and whispered – although there was no need to whisper really, the room was so noisy she could just have shouted and I would have struggled to hear her, never mind anyone else, "I'm so sorry, Gemma, but Glen Renton is over there in the corner on his own. Would you mind terribly going over and having a chat? I've spent the past hour with him and I really do need to mingle."

I strained to see in the dim light, and eventually spotted Ripple Effect's most successful client, leaning against a black-shrouded pillar in the far corner of the room. Sloane was right – although everyone else in the room was chatting, laughing, gossiping, filming and snapping endless selfies, Glen was on his own. He wasn't dressed as a warlock or a werewolf or anything else – he was wearing jeans and a tweed suit jacket. I remembered Charlie and Gus telling me, the first night I met them, that everyone hated Glen, but I'd been too swept up in the confusion and excitement of meeting them to ask why, and I still didn't know. Professional jealousy, I'd have guessed, if I'd given it any thought.

But I hadn't. And now, looking at him all alone in the crowd, I realised I felt a bit sorry for him.

I made my way over. Glen was looking intently at something in his hands, which I could see glinting in the dim light. His phone?

But as I got closer, I realised it was a gold money clip in the shape of a dollar sign, holding a massive wad of fifty pound notes, and Glen was counting them.

"Hello," I said. "We haven't met. I'm Gemma Grey."

"Gemma Grey." He tucked his stack of cash in his jeans pocket and looked up at me. "Quite the hot property, aren't you?"

"Not really," I said. "This is all still really new for me – even though I've been vlogging for years, I never took it seriously until quite recently. I've got nowhere near as many followers as you, or even Charlie and Gus."

"You're still fucking Charlie Berry, then?" Glen asked.

I realised I didn't feel sorry for him any more. "Charlie and I are going out, yes."

"Smooth move," he said. "Shagging a Berry boy. Career-enhancing. Not that it's worked out that well for the others."

If it had been anyone else, I'd have asked what they meant – as far as I knew, apart from Gus's brief fling with Maddie, both boys had been single for ages. But I could tell that Glen liked putting me at a disadvantage, and there was no way I was going to give him the satisfaction.

"Have you come from far?" I asked.

"Brighton." Glen took the roll of cash out of his pocket, looked at it and put it back again.

"Oh, how lovely," I said. "How fab to live by the sea. Did you get the train up?"

"I drove," he said. "In my Maserati."

"How lovely," I said again, but this time I could hear that the tone of bright enthusiasm in my voice was significantly less bright.

"Do they do the Halloween thing every year, then?" I asked. "It's a great party, isn't it?"

"It's a waste of time," Glen said. "I only showed up because I had a meeting with some journalist. That was a waste of time, too. I don't normally do interviews unless I get a fee."

I felt a bit sorry for the poor journalist, and thought I was beginning to understand why Glen found himself alone at parties.

"So what are you working on at the moment, then?" I asked. My glass was empty – I glanced towards the bar and saw that Raffy wasn't there any more. He must already have gone on his break – I was meant to be meeting him and instead I was stuck here talking to a man who quite clearly didn't want to talk to me. I couldn't even offer to get him a drink, because he was driving. In his Maserati.

"Merch," Glen said. "That's where the money is."

I imagined teenage girls saving up their pocket money to buy Glen Renton T-shirts and beanies and mobile phone cases, with no idea that their idol was rude, arrogant and deservedly loathed by all his peers. I wondered what people said about Glen on YouTruth, and whether he knew or even cared.

I said, "Anyway, it was nice meeting you. I'm desperate for the loo, so excuse me."

As I hurried towards the door, I could see Glen pulling his money out of his pocket again.

The cold night air hit my hot face as I pushed open the door. It had been raining; the stairs leading down to the pavement were slippery, and I almost fell as I ran down them. A group of people I didn't know were standing around smoking, juggling beer bottles, fags and phones in their hands. I couldn't see Raffy anywhere. I wished I'd brought my coat, but I'd checked it in when I arrived.

I wrapped my arms around myself, shivering. I'd had loads to drink, I realised – too much. I needed to sober up and go home. But I also needed to talk to Charlie, if and when he arrived. And even more than that, I needed – I wanted – to talk to Raffy, to find out why he was here, what he'd wanted to say to me, and even more fundamentally, who he even was.

As I watched, he came round the corner with Maddie.

"God, it's Baltic out here," she said. "Hi again, Gemma, I didn't know you smoked."

"I don't," I said. "I just came out to get some air."

"Well, I've had enough air for now," Maddie said. "See you later."

And she ducked inside, leaving me staring furiously at Raffy. I had no right to be angry, of course – he and I weren't… weren't even friends, really. But the idea of him with Maddie – gorgeous, stylish, successful Maddie, who could have anyone in the world she wanted – made me feel suddenly bereft.

I said, "What the hell…" at exactly the same moment as Raffy said, "I thought you were…"

"Go on," I said.

"I thought you weren't going to turn up," Raffy said.

"I was stuck talking to Glen Renton," I said. If Raffy could go sneaking around corners with Maddie, I could damn well talk to Glen, I thought.

Raffy said, "Poor you. I tried talking to him earlier. He's not exactly a sparkling conversationalist, is he?"

"No, he's… hold on. What's this all about? You talked to Glen, you were having cosy little sessions with Maddie – what's going on? You're not just working behind the bar here, are you?"

"Glad you've worked that out," Raffy said. "Here, you're freezing – do you want my coat?"

He took off his leather jacket and wrapped it around my shoulders. The warmth was like an embrace, but I didn't want to be hugged.

"I want to know what's going on," I said. "You said you wanted to talk to me. I know I didn't call you, but… And now you're here. What the hell…?"

"Not here," Raffy said. "Come on, let's walk. I've only got five minutes – if I'm late back on my shift, they'll sack me. Not that it particularly matters."

I followed him back around the corner of the building, glad I hadn't refused his coat. It was starting to drizzle again. We walked past a bookie's, a launderette and a fried chicken shop, and I began to think that if Raffy and Maddie's tryst had been a romantic one, they'd picked a pretty dodgy setting for it.

He stopped under a bus shelter. I stopped too, glad to be out of the rain.

"So?" I said.

"So," Raffy said. "I'm sorry, Gemma, I haven't been completely honest with you."

"I'd worked that bit out, at least," I said.

"I make films," Raffy said.

"What?" I said. "Is there a single person in this entire city – on this entire planet – who isn't a bloody YouTuber?"

Raffy laughed. "Not those kind of films. Although they go on YouTube, sometimes. I made documentaries. I worked for Vice for a bit, but now I'm freelance. When I was working at The Daily Grind, I wasn't just helping Luke out – although I was doing that, too, he's my mate and he was short of hands. But mostly I was researching a film."

"About coffee?" I said, incredulously.

"Partly," Raffy said. "Coffee was kind of the jumping-off point. You know how people say they know a place is changing when an artisan coffee place opens? And then the dodgy fruit and veg shop goes organic and starts stocking quinoa and coconut oil, and then the pub gets a refit and puts pulled pork sliders on the menu and does vinyl nights, and then the property developers move in?"

I remembered a listicle Hermione had written a few days before: '12 Signs That You're A Victim Of Urban Renewal'. "You mean, like, gentrification?"

"That's the one," Raffy said. "And your area – with the plans to knock down the estate – well, it was a classic example. I wanted to talk about how it happens, and why it's not always a good thing. And then I got involved in the campaign to save the estate, so it ended up being mostly about that. It was shown on Channel Four," he added proudly.

"I didn't see it," I said. "I never watch telly."

"I know," Raffy said. "You watch YouTube, like everyone our age. Which is why I decided to make a film about that."

"A film about YouTube?" I said. Suddenly my lips didn't feel like they were working right – it might have been the cold or it might have been the booze, but smiling wasn't working for me. "Isn't that a bit meta?"

Raffy laughed, but I didn't join in. I was thinking about everything I'd told him about myself, and my channel, and why I'd stated making my videos, and Jack and Charlie and everything else. I imagined him watching my videos, not because he liked me, but with the appraising, thoughtful eye of a researcher.

"I tried to get your agent, Sloane, to talk to me and let me interview some of her clients," he said. "But she wasn't interested. So I had to find another way. Hence working at the bar tonight. It's a weird world you're in, right?"

I didn't say anything. I was trying to organise my thoughts, but I couldn't seem to get them to fall into shape – I was too shocked, and, if I'm honest, too befuddled by all the cocktails and Prosecco I'd drunk, to get past the idea that Raffy had been using me for material – had almost been spying on me.

"But it's kind of taken on a life of its own," he went on. "I've found out stuff. That's what I wanted to talk to you about. Your boyf—"

My thoughts might not be falling into shape, but my feelings were, and I realised I was absolutely furious.

"You know what, I don't actually want to know," I said. "How dare you snoop into my life? Who the hell do you think you are, 'finding out' stuff about me – about Charlie? Charlie's not perfect, right, but he's a decent guy and he's not hurting anyone. None of us are. Not even Glen. Okay, he's a dick, but if you were twenty-six years old and suddenly you're making loads of money and everyone wants a piece of you and you can't tell who your real friends are, wouldn't you get a bit defensive about it too? I told you why I started doing this YouTube thing – I didn't set out to make money, or be famous. I was just doing something I loved, that I thought

I might be good at. I've met incredible friends online, I've had amazing support from people who don't even know me, but who care about me anyway. And you do know me – I thought we were mates but you've just been… I don't know, *observing* me, like a lab rat in a psychology experiment, and not even telling me that that's what you were doing."

Raffy said, "Gemma, I know this must be weird for you. I'm trying to understand, but I…"

I hadn't finished. "And you know what? My landlady, who's a totally lovely, normal person, was in this horrible, abusive relationship and just trying to deal with it, with no one to tell what was happening to her. And I used my channel to try and help other people like her, and I got a massive load of flak for it. But that's not going to stop me. Okay, I mostly make videos about make-up, it's not like I'm the United Nations or something, but I can try and make people happier. That's all I'm doing. And I don't need you and people who watch Channel bloody Four analysing and judging me and the stuff I create."

Raffy looked as shocked by my rant as if I'd hit him. He said, "Gemma, it's not like that. It really—"

"I don't care what it really is! Make your poxy fucking film if you want to, but leave Charlie and me out of it."

And I dropped his jacket in a puddle and ran back to the bar, slipping and sliding on the fallen leaves in my high shoes.

The first person I saw when I got back inside was Charlie. He had his back to me, but I'd have recognised his shoulders in his trademark white T-shirt, his waxed golden hair and the tattoo snaking up his neck anywhere, even though it was dark; even though my eyes were blurred with tears. The way things were with us, I was tempted to duck away into the shadows. But if I went to get a drink, I'd encounter Raffy at the bar, and if I went the other way, I might get stuck in the corner talking to Glen again. Or I could reclaim my coat and go home – but I'd promised myself that I'd talk to Charlie tonight, to find out what was going on with our relationship – if we still even had one – and I was just going to have to pull up my big girl pants and do it.

And then he turned around, and any chance of escape was lost. I saw that, instead of a Halloween costume, he was just wearing a Berry Boys mask: the identical faces that were on the cover of their book, split in two down the middle and joined almost, but not quite, back together, covered his face to just above his lips.

"Gemma!" he said, more enthusiastically than I'd expected.

"Hello," I said. "Where's Gus?"

"Gus?" He paused for a second. "Oh, he's around somewhere. Probably getting a drink. We thought you weren't coming."

I said, "I got here ages ago. I was just outside for a bit."

He looked more closely at me and said, "Gemma? Are you okay? You look like you've been crying."

He put his arms around me and pulled me close, and I could smell the Tom Ford cologne he always wore. I breathed it in, relishing the feel of his arms around me, and started to cry properly. He held me close and waited while I sobbed and sniffed, not asking me what was wrong, which was probably just as well, because I was sure I wouldn't be able to find the words to tell him. But he just let me carry on until I was done.

I dug around in my bag for tissues, blew my nose and wiped my eyes.

"Sorry," I said. "I don't know… I was talking to someone I know outside, and we had an argument."

He didn't ask me what about. He just said, "Come on, let's get out of here."

"Can we?" I said. "The party's only just getting going. And you've just arrived. What will Sloane say?"

"We can do exactly what the hell we like," he said, getting out his phone and summoning a taxi. "Three minutes. I know what we can do with three minutes."

And he pulled me close again and started to kiss me. For a second I resisted, but then the urgency of his kiss – a hunger, a fierceness that was almost frightening and strangely unfamiliar – swept me up, and I kissed him back, on and on, not caring about my smudged eye make-up.

"Wow," he said at last. "That was a pleasant surprise."

Before I could ask him what he meant, he said, "Our driver's here. Let's go."

And he put his arm around my shoulders and led me out. The car was waiting outside, a silver Mercedes; Charlie and Gus only ever used Uber Exec.

"Hi, Mostak?" he said. "Great. We're going to Hackney, yeah?"

"Hackney?" I said.

"Of course," he said. "Back to yours."

He opened the door for me, and I slid on to the leather seat. Then, as he bent over to join me and the bright light shone on his face, I realised what was different.

In the same second, the driver said, "It's Gus, right?"

"That's right, mate," Gus said, slamming the door behind him. "Manwood Close, E9."

"Wait!" I said. "You can't do this. This is…"

But the taxi had already pulled off, its tires swishing on the wet road.

"Don't worry, Gemma," Gus said. "I'm not going to take advantage of you, as my nan would say."

I didn't point out that he already had – after all, I hadn't exactly objected.

"I don't understand," I said. "What's going on? Why did you…"

"Let you think I was my brother?" Gus said. "You must be pissed, Gemma, falling for the same prank twice. Look," he pointed to the tattoo on his neck. "We drew it on with a sharpie. Looks rather good, doesn't it? It was much harder covering Charlie's up – we had to order some special make-up off Amazon. Apparently it hides even the most unsightly blemishes. Glen Renton should use it on his personality."

I said, "What, so you went to the party dressed as…"

"As each other, yes," said Gus. "Part hilarious prank, mostly Charles helping me out. And then you helped me out even more. Anyone who saw us together would be sure I was my brother."

"Gus, if you think this is a clever way to pull me, it's not," I said. "One, I don't fancy you…"

"Really?" He raised a perfectly shaped eyebrow.

"Oh, for fuck's sake!" I said. "So, you can kiss. Well done. Clever you. I liked kissing you. But that means nothing at all. Just because you've got the tongue moves, doesn't mean I'd want to sleep with you! Jesus! Even if I wasn't still, kind of, going out with your brother, what you did back there is just weird and manipulative and… Horrible. And even if you hadn't done it, I wouldn't want to go to bed with you, because I don't feel like that about you."

"Just as well," Gus said. "Because I don't want to go to bed with you, either. And I shouldn't have kissed you. I'm sorry about that. You belong to Charlie."

"I do not!" I said.

"Whatevs," Gus said. "I'll leave it to you both to sort that one out." He pulled the mask off his head, and now that I could see his whole face, I realised how stupid I'd been to believe, even with the booze, the darkness and my distress, that he was his twin. He was so entirely different – not just physically, but in some other way that mattered much, much more.

I said, "Okay, Gus, you think this is funny. Ha ha. You've made a fool of me. I don't think that's cool – you do. Fine. But this isn't about you and me, it's about Charlie. You're meant to care about him more than about anyone else. And tonight, why I was crying – Raffy, the guy I was chatting to outside, he said…"

"Raphael Roden?" he said. "That fucker. He's been sniffing around us for weeks. But it's me he wants to bring down, not our Charles. Charles is pure as the driven snow."

"Gus!" I said. His flippancy was infuriating – it was impenetrable. "What's going on? What's this all about?"

"Gemma," he said. "Please don't worry your pretty little head about it. Your work here is done. Thanks for being so obliging tonight. You might not think so, but it's what Charlie would have wanted. And now I have my free pass."

Out of the window, I could see the shuttered windows of The Daily Grind, and the familiar trees lining the road where I lived. The taxi's indicator flashed amber in the falling rain, and the driver said, "Manwood Close."

I heard my voice saying automatically, "Anywhere here is fine, thanks. But, Gus…"

Gus said, "Out you get, Gemma. I'm going on to the Hoxton Hotel, please, mate."

Chapter Twenty-one

Amy, Hannah and I spent Sunday mooching around the house, licking our wounds (and our fingers, because Hannah made the biggest ever batch of pancakes, which we ate with mountains of bacon and maple syrup). I was hungover and remorseful, bitterly ashamed of my behaviour the night before: the way I'd ranted at Raffy, snogged Gus and failed entirely to have the Talk I'd promised myself I would have with Charlie. Hannah was hungover and anxious, because Richard had been in contact through her solicitor to say that, while he deeply regretted the behaviour to which he had been driven by pressures of work and Hannah's lack of understanding, he was not in a position to continue paying the mortgage on the house indefinitely and he awaited clarity on Hannah's intentions going forward, to be received within fourteen days. Amy was hungover and feeling guilty, because while Hannah's and my lives were such a mess, she and Kian were blissfully loved up and she'd played a pivotal, if small, role at work in smashing a particularly intractable skunk-dealing ring.

So the three of us were a pretty sorry sight. We lay around in our dressing gowns all day, drinking tea, stuffing our faces and painting our nails while binge-watching *Gossip Girl* and failing to do anything important or productive. I didn't vlog at all – in fact, I avoided social media entirely, not wanting to see everyone's 'Look how fabulous Ripple Effect parties are' videos, or Charlie and Gus's reveal of their latest pranking triumph.

The next morning, as if it was just another Monday and nothing untoward had happened, I set off for work.

The first thing I saw when I approached my desk, clutching my coffee and almond croissant, was that the empty workstation at the end of our pod wasn't empty any more. It was occupied by a guy with glasses and a wispy beard, who was clutching a bottle of water, staring at the company intranet, and looking every bit as lost and terrified as I'd felt on my first day, which felt like about a thousand years ago.

"Hi, new podmate," I said. "I'm Gemma, officially no longer the newbie here, I guess."

The guy jumped as if I'd poked him with something, spilled his water – narrowly missing his keyboard – and said his name was Harrison.

Trying not to sound pitying, I welcomed him, explained the drinks messaging system and made a round of teas and coffees, even though I didn't need any myself.

Then Jim emerged from Sarah's office, where the weekly management pow-wow was held at the masochistic hour of eight fifteen, and said, "Morning, gang. Team meeting time."

We all shuffled off to the breakout room clutching our spiral-bound notebooks and pens and looking somehow naked and incomplete without our phones and tablets. Team meetings at Clickfrenzy were tech-free zones, supposedly to stimulate creative thought. Actually, all it meant was that people displayed an alarming variety of nervous tics.

Jim introduced Harrison, who froze with fear at the prospect of having to say a few words about himself, then melted with relief when he wasn't asked to, just as I'd done.

"Right," Jim said. "What are we up to this week?"

"I'm thinking about starting a campaign," Tom said. "About plates."

"Plates?" Jim said. "What's wrong with plates?"

"Nothing, obviously," Tom said. "But restaurants and pubs don't seem to realise that. You know how everywhere you go at the moment food's being served in these ridiculous containers? Like, back in the day when chips in miniature frying baskets were a thing, that was cool, but there's been some serious mission-creep going on."

"Oh my God," Emily said. "The other day, right, I went out for lunch with my friend and my salad came in a flower pot. Seriously, a flower pot."

"Someone tweeted a picture the other day of a full English breakfast served on a spade," Ruby said.

"I got a bit of black cod in miso served on a roof tile last week," Callista said. "The fucking sauce ran right off it and over my lap. I was wearing my new turquoise suede skirt, too. I was, like, this close to sending them the dry-cleaning bill."

"You see?" Tom said. "I'm sure I've heard about somewhere that serves bread in a cloth cap, but it might just be urban myth. Anyway, everywhere's doing it. Wetherspoons are doing it, and that means it's long past its sell-by date. So #saveourplates is go."

"It's go," Jim agreed. "Right. Emily?"

Emily glanced down at her notebook. The page was blank. She always did this at meetings, I'd come to realise – arrived apparently unprepared, then nailed some genius idea that everyone loved. Either she had it all sorted in her head, or she was just really good at making stuff up as she went along.

"Yeah, I was thinking London property," she said. "Not the super-prime market, obviously – that's tanked since Brexit. But the rental market. You know – beds in sheds, people renting out the cupboard under the stairs, poor doors, no DSS – that kind of thing. I was going to have a look online and find the most barking mad ones and do spoof estate agent descriptions for them. Or even use the real descriptions and do a match the words to the pic thing, like an interactive quiz."

"Nice one," Jim said. "Everyone loves a good whinge about London property prices, right?"

I thought about mentioning Alethea Ayoola, and the campaign to save the Garforth estate from demolition, and its residents from losing their homes. But it didn't seem right, somehow – it would mean breaking the barrier I'd carefully maintained between my life at Clickfrenzy, my life on YouTube, and my real life – whatever that was. So I said nothing.

"God, yeah," Tom said. "My girlfriend I went to look at a place last weekend. The ad said it was a highly desirable North London location, but actually it was a twenty-minute walk through this fucking dodgy industrial estate. I thought we were going to get knifed on the way. And then the place was…"

"Why not send Emily the link?" Jim said. "Ruby, anything exciting in the world of wellbeing?"

"Barre fit," Ruby said gloomily. "I thought it was going to be all tutus and dancing bits out of *Swan Lake* with hot guys, but no. It fucking kills. I went yesterday and the instructor legit shouted at me. She was really scary. Worse than Sarah. So I'm thinking about doing something about wellness tourism. You know – retreats, and shit. Beaches. Coconuts. Stuff like that."

"I know someone who did a silent retreat at an old monastery," Callista said. "They weren't allowed to talk at all, not even during meals, which were all raw and vegan. She said it was life-changing. She doesn't even use a mobile any more, and she's gone zero-consumption: no buying anything new, ever. I really admire her commitment."

"Perhaps I could interview her?" Ruby said, surreptitiously tugging the price tag off her pearl-grey cashmere jumper.

"I'll let you know," Callista said. "It could be tricky, because she's living off-grid in a bothy in Stornoway. But I'm sure she'd love to have you to stay for a weekend."

"That sounds great!" Ruby said. "Really great! I'll… er… write to her. With a stamp. But the post there might be a bit unreliable, so maybe I should plan in something about athleisure fashion first."

There was a tiny ripple of laughter around the table. Jim said, "Right, Hermione, what's up in world affairs?"

Hermione flicked back through the pages of her notebook. The way her finger moved, it almost looked like she was trying to swipe left.

"So, I was thinking we need to do something about domestic violence," she said. "I mean, it was massive news earlier in the year with the whole Rob and Helen thing…"

"Who?" Tom said.

Jim raised an eyebrow. "As everyone knows, except Tom, who recently joined us from the cave where he's spent the past two years, *The Archers* had a long-running storyline about domestic abuse. It raised a huge amount of awareness, and money, too, for victims' shelters."

"Which is much needed," Hermione said. "Because there have been huge cuts to funding."

"And it's going to get worse," Emily said. "Here, because funding for everything's being cut all the time, but in the US…"

"Because the president-elect basically fucking hates women," said Ruby.

"I read somewhere that one woman in four will be a victim of domestic abuse in her lifetime," Callista said. "One in four. Think about it."

I thought. I looked around the table at Hermione, Ruby, Emily and Callista. One in four. I'd thought of what Richard had done to Hannah as an aberration – a sort of freak event, like being struck by lightning or something. But maybe it wasn't.

The atmosphere in the room had changed. Before, it had been energetic, light-hearted – everyone having fun with what were ultimately silly ideas for wasting people's time when they were meant to be working, or doing housework or whatever. Now, the faces around the table were all still and serious.

"What kind of story did you have in mind, Hermione?" Jim said.

"I think it's bigger than that," Hermione said. "I don't think it's just one story. I think we should do some video, talk to survivors, talk to the people working on the coalface, so to speak – refuges, police officers and so on. Maybe link it to a fundraising campaign."

"Okay," Jim said. "I'm down with that. I'll have to talk to Sarah and see if we can get the other teams involved. Marketing will need to have a say, and the ad guys. It's a bit of a shift from our usual content. But we could all get involved – make it a team effort."

"I'm running the London marathon next year," Harrison said, blushing furiously. "I got a ballot place, but I'm well up for raising money anyway."

"We could auction cakes in the office," Tom said.

I blushed almost as much as Harrison, and said, "I did a thing on my vlog, a couple of weeks back. It really seemed to hit a nerve. My housemate – well, my landlady, really, was in an abusive relationship. I didn't realise, even though it was happening right under my nose. I guess it's happening everywhere, right under lots of people's noses, and they don't realise either."

That was it. The barrier was down, and I didn't care.

"And that brings us to you, Gemma," Jim said. "What are you working on right now?"

"Um, epic cat fails," I said humbly. "You know, like being sat on by the dog and getting bits of kitty litter stuck in their whiskers and missing when they jump and stuff. I know, right?"

There was a moment's silence around the table, and then everyone started laughing, even Hermione.

"Think you might have a bit of spare time to give Hermione a hand with some research if this domestic violence campaign gets going?" Jim said. "We'll need to get a cameraman and a sound person on board – I'll have a word with the art department."

"Of course. I'd love to."

"Right. Harrison," Jim said, "you're on cats. Gemma will tell you all about them."

"Miaow," Tom said, doing the whisker thing again. I wondered how many times he'd done it before, and whether someone had done it to him on his first day.

"I'll send you the links I normally use," I said. "Cats are great, Harrison. You'll love doing cat content. It's really fun."

"Great. I think that's it then. Thanks, everyone."

I stood up, and it was the strangest thing – I felt as if I was almost levitating, such was the relief of knowing that the cat brief wasn't going to be my job any more.

We all went back to our desks – I almost skipped – and I spend a few minutes showing Harrison the various cat motherlodes of the internet.

Then I sent Emily a message, saying, *Hey – if you need someone to talk to for your London housing story, I know a woman who might be able to help.*

I stood in front of the orange door of Charlie and Gus's apartment, feeling at least as nervous as I'd done the first time I'd turned up there on my own. Tonight, though, there was no violin music pouring through from the flat. There was only silence. I strained my ears, but I couldn't hear anything at all. The door fitted too tightly in its frame for me to see if any lights were on. I took my phone out of my bag, but I already knew there would be no message from Charlie – the flood of texts, missed calls and WhatsApps had stopped on the morning of the Halloween party, and not started again. I scrolled to his number and looked at it for a bit, then told myself not to be ridiculous – I was standing outside his door, it would be daft to call him. I was going to do the analogue thing.

I raised my hand, knocked, and waited. There was no response. I listened harder, waiting to hear the scrabble of Taylor's claws as she dashed to meet me, but she didn't come. No one did. I knocked again, but I knew there wouldn't be any answer.

For the first time, I started to feel worried. Not about the difficult conversation I'd come there to have, but about Charlie himself. Charlie and Gus. I remembered how Gus had been on Saturday night – cool and off-hand as usual, but also… I tried to remember. I'd been so drunk, so bewildered by the events of the night. He'd been different, somehow. His normal insouciance seemed to be hiding something deeper – he wasn't pretending not to care, I thought, he genuinely didn't care. There had been a recklessness about him I'd never seen before.

And what was it that he'd said about Raffy – that Raffy wanted to bring him down? At the time, I'd thought it was just Gus being Gus, the starring actor in the drama of his own life. But now I thought, *What if it was real?* He'd called Raffy by his full name, Raphael something, but I couldn't remember what it was. What if Raffy – Raphael – had done something to harm Gus, or Charlie, or both the Berry Boys? Or, even worse, done something that had made them hurt themselves? If he had, I thought, I'd never, ever forgive him. And I'd find a way to hurt him, too.

I put my phone back in my bag and took out my keys. I'd never used the key Charlie had given me – I'd never needed to, because one of them was always there – mostly, they both were. They didn't do normal things like pop out to Sainsbury's or go to work. If they had a book signing or a meet-and-greet, it was planned ages in advance. When they went out, it was late at night, when their legions of teenage fans were safe at home.

Something was wrong. I needed to know what it was, and fix it if I could.

I fitted the key in the lock. It was a fancy, high-security lock, and I could feel heavy metal bars turning and releasing as I twisted it. The door swung open, and I stepped into the dark, silent apartment.

"Charlie?" I said, but my voice wasn't working properly and only a whisper came out. I tried again. "Charlie? Gus?"

But there was no response. I wasn't really expecting there to be.

I stepped inside, my heels loud on the hard floor. The lights from the canal towpath outside illuminated the room; no one had closed the blinds leading out on to the balcony and it was bright enough for me to see quite easily. I walked towards the kitchen where I'd prepared so many unwanted healthy meals, the glass dining table that was never used, and the sofa where Charlie and I had first made love – or its identical successor. As always, it felt like a very long way.

But something was different. It was only when I got to the end of the room that I realised what it was: all the lights, computers and camera equipment were gone. No trailing wires threatened to catch my heels as I walked. No LEDs blinked; no fans whirred.

I opened the door to the balcony and shivered as the night air rushed into the warm room. The hot tub was tightly covered by its grey vinyl lid. The water glinted darkly below; there was no sign of the family of swans Charlie and Gus had watched grow up.

Then, with no warning at all, the lights came on. I couldn't help it – I screamed. A high-pitched, girly shriek – and it was immediately echoed by another high-pitched, girly shriek.

"Who the hell's there?"

It was Sloane.

"Oh my God," we both said, our words colliding and jumbling together. "Shit, you gave me such a fright. Thank fuck it's only you. Jesus, I thought…"

"I came to pick up Charlie's mobile phone charger," Sloane said.

"I came to see him," I said. "But what… where are they?"

"I think we both need a drink," Sloane said. "But close that door, it's Arctic out."

I did as she asked, then sat down on the sofa, my legs feeling too rubbery and strange to support me. I watched as she opened the fridge, found two glasses in a cupboard and sloshed vodka into them. Sloane was wearing jeans and a checked shirt – it was the first time I'd seen her in anything other than the waisted fifties-style dresses she favoured. In trainers, she was much shorter than she was in my head. Her hair was scraped back in a ponytail and her face looked different – softer, somehow, and younger, but shadowed with fatigue. She bit her lip and I realised that I'd never seen her without her trademark scarlet lipstick.

She flopped down next to me, handed me my drink and took a deep gulp of her own, spilling some of it down her front and wiping her chin with the back of her hand.

"Sorry," she said. "I'm all over the place. It's been one hell of a day."

I said, "What's going on? Where are Charlie and Gus? Are they okay?"

"They're fine," Sloane said. "Honest. We just thought it would be best if they moved out. Just in case there's any… media attention."

"But there's always media attention," I said. "Social media, anyway. They have girls turning up all the time, wanting selfies."

"Tell me about it!" Sloane said. "This isn't that, though."

"What is it then?" I said. "Please, Sloane, you need to tell me."

"Oh God, I don't even know if I can," she said. "Our client confidentiality clauses… but I guess this involves you, too."

"How? What did I do?"

"You know Raphael Roden, right?" Sloane said.

There it was again – Raffy's name, being used by someone who until a couple of days ago I wouldn't have expected to even know of his existence. Hell, until a couple of days ago I hadn't even known his full name myself.

"He was just Raffy," I said. "The guy who worked in the coffee shop. I had no idea he was planning to do some massive investigative… thing… about YouTubers. I would never, ever have told him anything if I'd known. And what I did tell him was totally harmless, anyway. I just said stuff about feeling sometimes that I was recommending products I didn't really like, and that I wasn't sure where I was going with the whole thing, and… I'm sorry."

"You've got nothing to apologise for," Sloane said. "Well, apart from maybe not confiding in me if you were having doubts about where your career was going. Because that's what we're here for, right? I mean, we promote our clients and their brands, we broker partnerships, we manage reputations, but we also like to think of ourselves as friends."

"I know," I said. "I guess it was all just happening too fast, and stuff was going on with Jack – my ex-boyfriend – and I just needed someone to talk to. I'd had a few drinks, and…"

"Gemma, it doesn't matter. Seriously, this isn't about you."

"Then what… What's Charlie done?" The way she'd said "manage reputations", almost wincing at the words, filled me with dread. I imagined some horrible scandal enveloping Charlie – but what? Drugs? I'd have known, surely, if it was that. Charlie had never shown any signs of using any recreational substance stronger than a cocktail, not once in all the nights I'd spent with him.

"Not Charlie," Sloane said. "Gus."

Suddenly, things started to make sense. All the nights Gus had gone off out on his own. The times Charlie and I had come home without him, because he said the night was young and he wanted to carry on partying. The times I'd heard him come back to the flat in the early hours of the morning, or even passed him on the stairs on my way to work. The total lack of any girls in Gus's life since his brief, apparently totally unserious thing with Maddie.

"Gus is gay!" I said. "Thank God it's only that. I mean, poor guy, being closeted and everything, but it's no big deal, right? People come out on YouTube all the time. It's, like, a thing. People might talk about it for a bit, but no one cares. It's not like this is the 1980s. Boy bands don't even *happen* any more unless one of them's gay. Those girls who subscribe to their channel all have gay best friends. Half of them will probably come out as non-binary in six months' time, because just being gay is so over. It's…"

"Gus isn't gay," Sloane said. Then she added, almost under her breath, "I bloody wish he was."

"Then what…"

"When you went off with him the other night," Sloane said. "Where did you go?"

"Nowhere," I said. "I mean, we got an Uber, Gus dropped me home and went off somewhere on his own. He does that sometimes. I never asked, because, well, it's none of my business really, is it?"

"That's what I thought, too," Sloane said. "None of my business, he's a big boy, I can't nanny my clients 24/7. When I realised he did need nannying – well, they pulled that stupid prank at the party. For God's sake. How could I have been so dumb as to have been taken in by that? I've worked with those boys for years. I should have known."

"*I* should have known," I said, blushing at the memory of that all-too-public kiss.

"Yes, well," Sloane said. "So I spent the entire evening thinking I was keeping an eye on Gus, when really I was keeping an eye on Charlie, and how much of a fool did I look when he did his big reveal at midnight? But I thought it didn't matter, it was just another of their hilair pranks. Then just as I was leaving – I had to stay right until the end – one of the barmen accosted me and told me he was the guy who's been hounding me for months, wanting to know stuff about my clients for some film he's making."

"Raffy," I said. "Raphael Roden."

"Raphael Roden." Sloane practically spat the name out. "He told me he knew about Gus. He said he had evidence – video evidence. And he'd spoken to Maddie and Maddie told him she knew, too. And he'd told Gus he knew and Gus, the stupid idiot, went off anyway and…"

I waited. Sloane took another gulp of vodka, and so did I. I had a feeling I was going to need it.

"And what? What did Raffy know? Sloane, what's Gus done?"

"He's been meeting viewers," Sloane said.

Part of me wanted to protest, to say that wasn't a big deal any more than Gus being gay would have been – that meeting viewers was a thing that happened all the time. But I knew that wasn't what she meant.

"You mean, like…"

"Hooking up," Sloane said. "Sending messages on Twitter and Facebook and meeting girls in hotels for sex. Lots of girls. His fans."

"Jesus," I said. "Do you mean they were…"

"Not underage. Thank God. Christ, if he'd broken the law… But still, young girls – seventeen, eighteen, meeting up with him and… It's just so sordid. Sordid and irresponsible and – well, exploitative. Because even though they were throwing themselves at him – there's no question that anyone wasn't consenting to anything – it's an appalling breach of trust. If it were to come out – if people think he can't be trusted around his fans…"

I thought of myself at seventeen, of the huge crush I'd had on Tom Fletcher from McFly, and imagined what I'd have done if Tom had sent me a private message on Facebook and said he wanted to meet me. I imagined how giddily star-struck I would have been, how reckless, how utterly incapable of saying no to anything. I wondered how I would have felt afterwards – used, ashamed, dirty. Or perhaps not – perhaps just proud to have a story of spending the night in a hotel with a megastar to tell all my friends. Perhaps I'd have imagined I was going to be his girlfriend, and that I'd become famous too. And when I realised it would never happen, how would I have felt then? Used, ashamed and dirty. There was no getting away from it.

"That's awful," I said. "My God. I should have known. I should have…"

"Should have what? Grounded him? Locked him in his bedroom? Do you think I haven't been telling myself exactly the same thing? But there was nothing I could do, except hang around and just be there, because obviously even though he wasn't doing anything illegal, he didn't want me to know about it. I didn't know – well, I suspected, but what could I do? He's an adult, the girls are adults – in theory, anyway. And it wasn't… I mean, if he went on the occasional date with a girl I thought he'd probably met through their channel, it was easy to turn a blind eye. But in the last few months he's been doing it more and more. Since he broke up with Maddie, and since…"

Since I came on the scene, I thought. *Since Gus didn't have Charlie to himself any more.*

"And the girls talked, on those forums. No one believed them at first. People make shit up all the time about YouTubers. Everyone imagines they're much closer to you than they really are – it's how the medium works, why it's so powerful. But then the same stories started coming up again and again. About twelve girls, all saying the same thing. And that Raphael told me he'd met one of them, and she told him what had happened, and he filmed her telling him for his bloody documentary."

I said, "What's going to happen? When it comes out, I mean."

"It's not going to," Sloane said. "That's what Roden said, anyway. He said he's not going to release the film. He said it would hurt too many people. He said he didn't want to hurt you. I didn't realise he even knew you. But he said Gus can't be allowed to carry on, and he's right."

"But you said you can't stop him," I said.

"I can't," Sloane said. "But if there's no Berry Boys channel, there won't be any girls queueing up to meet Gus. Well, there might be for a bit. But it'll stop by itself. Our audience is fickle, as I keep telling you. So we're shutting it down, and the boys are going to lie low for a bit while they think things through."

I needed to think things through myself. My mind was whirring like a blender when you switch it on by mistake with nothing in. Raffy wasn't making his film – the film that would have ruined Gus, and by association Charlie, and perhaps also me. He wasn't making it because of me. The Berry Boys were over. What would Charlie do now? He loved vlogging. Even though he complained about his schedule, and about Sloane, he loved it. It was his life. It had been his idea, I remembered Gus telling me. "I'm just his bitch," he'd said. And I wondered whether, maybe, Gus had deliberately set out to cause a crisis that would bring it all crashing down – while having his own particular kind of fun at the same time.

I said, "I came here tonight because I was going to end things with Charlie."

"I figured," Sloane said. "I'm sorry. You two seemed so happy together – I really hoped it was all going to work out."

"I did too," I said. "But then… This is going to sound really stupid."

And I told her about Stanley being mauled by the puppy. About halfway through I started to cry.

"Oh, sweetie," Sloane said, wrapping her arms around me and patting my back. "It's not stupid at all. I totally get it. It's the selfishness. I love those boys, I really do, but we let them get away with murder because they're such big stars, and this is the result."

I said, "I'll call Charlie tonight. I've been putting it off for too long. But it's such a bad time…"

Sloane said, "I wouldn't be surprised if Charlie's expecting it. Bite the bullet, Gemma. There's never a good time for these things."

I blew my nose, and we both stood up. Sloane put the much-depleted vodka bottle back in the fridge.

"I'll lock up," she said. "I'll call you in the morning, okay?"

I turned to leave, then said, "Sloane? About my channel. I know it's not a big deal, especially not now, but do you think I'm going to have to stop vlogging, too?"

"Don't you dare!" Sloane said, then added hastily, "Unless you want to, of course. You're doing so well. We're all so proud of you. I was going to say, when we talk tomorrow, we need to discuss your strategy for Vlogmas."

"Great," I said. "That'll be great." But I wasn't thinking about Vlogmas. I was thinking, as I pressed the button for the lift and took my phone out of my bag, about what I was about to say to Charlie. By the time I got home, I'd made the call. Charlie Berry and Gemma Grey were over.

Chapter Twenty-two

"So, what happened next?" Hermione asked gently.

"He said he was sorry," the woman whispered. Her name was Siobhan, and she was in her mid-twenties, a couple of years older than me. She was pretty, with dark hair in a shiny bob and a scattering of freckles across her nose. But it wasn't the freckles I noticed when I looked at her. The crookedness, the slight mismatch between the left and the right side of her face, was slight but once you knew it was there, and why, you couldn't un-see it. Our viewers wouldn't see it though. Siobhan had asked not to be shown on camera, because she was too frightened. She was sitting by the window, silhouetted against the bright light.

The rest of the room was bright, too. It was sunny and warm, with mismatched cushions scattered on the beige sofas, children's art on the walls and their toys on the floor. I'd had to clear a space for the massive box of make-up and toiletries, which I'd brought because I'd read on the charity's website that things like that were desperately needed.

We'd been speaking to Siobhan for the past half-hour, in the living room of this sprawling 1930s house in west London that had been her home for the past two months. It had taken three weeks to set up the interviews with Siobhan and two of the other women who lived there. The charity had been reluctant to give us access at first, because its location was secret – and, from the outside, it looked entirely anonymous, indistinguishable from its neighbours, with its well-tended front garden and phalanx of wheelie bins standing outside the door. Hermione, the camera crew and I had walked past about three times before saying to each other, "This has to be the place, right?" and steeling ourselves to knock on the door.

The women were reluctant to talk, too, but once they began their stories were chilling. Martine had described how her husband first hit her on their wedding night, after a whirlwind romance that had felt like a dream come true.

"I lay there on the floor of the hotel room, and I thought I must be imagining things," she said. "I literally thought I was going to wake up and find that it hadn't really happened. And then I saw the blood on my wedding dress – the dress I was going to pack away in acid-free tissue paper and keep in case my daughter wanted to wear it one day. I thought, I need to soak that in cold water. Then I remembered it was meant to go to a specialist dry cleaner. It's funny how your mind works, isn't it?"

We never found out what happened to Martine's wedding dress. Instead, we heard how her new husband had begged for forgiveness, told her he loved her so much he sometimes couldn't control his feelings, promised her over and over that it would never happen again. The next time it did, he said the same things. And the time after that, and over and over again, until Martine stopped believing him – and stopped believing in herself, too.

"I knew it must be my fault," she said. "Because that was what he told me, and he was never wrong about stuff. He's a clever man, he's got three degrees, and I worked in a shop. After that first night, he never hit me where it showed. When he hurt me so badly I had to go to hospital, he came with me and told them that I'd fallen down the stairs when I was drunk. And they believed him, because I *was* drunk. I was drinking all the time. It was the only way I could get through the day. I tried to hide it from him but he'd always know, and then he'd punish me for it."

It took ten years for Martine to leave, and when she did, it meant uprooting herself and her children from their home in Exeter and moving to London.

"I still worry that he'll find me," she said. "I still worry that he'll get the kids taken away from me, because I'm an unfit mother. I must be, to allow my kids to see what he did."

Ann talked to us next. Her story was different from Martine's. Mark never hit her, she said. What he did was more subtle, more insidious – perhaps even more frightening.

"My mum passed away and left me some money," she said. "Not a lot, but Mark said it was enough for us to buy a house and for him to start his own business, like he'd always dreamed of doing. We couldn't afford to be here, near my sister and my friends, so we moved to a little village in Northumberland. Mark's a software developer – he could work anywhere. But there was nothing there for me to do. I cooked and cleaned and ironed his clothes, but nothing was ever good enough. He was just so angry, all the time. The work wasn't coming in and we were skint, and used to just fly into these terrible rages, blaming me for everything. He said I was lucky to have him, that no one else would want me – and it was true. He was all I had in the whole world, even though he terrified me."

Ann told us how, over four years, she'd become more and more isolated. "I couldn't drive, and the car was his anyway. He always promised to teach me but he never did. The one time he tried I stalled the engine and he went mental at me, so I never asked again. It just wasn't worth it. I couldn't even use the internet, because he said there wasn't enough bandwidth and he needed to work. There was no money for anything, so I couldn't even top up my phone to text my friends. One day I checked my diary and realised I hadn't spoken to anyone except him for six months. When the man came to read the gas meter I let him in and I couldn't think of a single thing to say, not even to offer him a cup of tea. I just stood there staring at him until Mark came downstairs and took over. It was like being buried alive. But I didn't know it was abuse – I couldn't put that name to it, because he never laid a finger on me, you see."

As I listened to Ann, I realised that although her story was so different from Martine's, in many ways it was the same. The same as Hannah's, too. And as Siobhan's would be. Although the details were different and the pain unique, the fear, the gradual erosion of self-belief, the sense of helplessness, were identical. I thought of Hannah's gourmet meals, her perfectly kept house, Richard's swings between affection, sneering dismissal and anger, and I began to see how Hannah's trap had closed around her, and I felt almost sick with relief that I'd been part of her release from it – even though it had so nearly been too late.

"I tried to leave," Siobhan was saying. "I went to Mum's, and he came and found me there. He cried and begged for me to come home, and Mum said marriage is for better for worse, and he was a good man really, he just had a temper and I should try not to provoke him. So I went back. Everything was fine for a while after that, even good – like when we first got together. Like a second honeymoon. Then I fell pregnant with my first, and it started again. Except now leaving was even harder, because I didn't want to break up the family. He was a great dad to her. Everyone said so."

I looked at Siobhan's face, her freckles and her poor broken cheekbone. Then I looked back down at my notebook and carried on writing the notes I'd use when I wrote the series of stories that would accompany the videos. My note-taking felt superfluous – I couldn't imagine that I'd ever forget anything I'd seen and heard that morning, in that warm and welcoming room.

"How old is your daughter now, Siobhan?" Hermione asked.

"She's four, and my little boy's two. There was another baby, but I lost it, after he…" Siobhan paused, and I heard her take a deep, trembly breath. I knew what she was going to say; I could hardly bear to hear it but I knew I had to listen.

"Summer found me," Siobhan said. "He'd gone out and left me. I was bleeding really badly. I couldn't ring for help because he'd smashed up my phone. When I didn't turn up to pick Summer up from nursery one of the staff brought her home, and it was her that called the ambulance. I'll never forget her face when she saw me. My little princess, finding her mummy like that."

"And was that when you decided…?" Hermione said.

"That was when," Siobhan said. "They told me, in hospital, how much danger I was in. I never thought that he might… that my kids would end up without a mother. Or taken into care, even, if

I stayed with him. And that was too much. I didn't care what he did to me but I couldn't have him do that to them."

She paused again. I could hear my pen scratching over the page; I could hear Hermione breathing. Somewhere else in the house, I heard a child laugh. I had a sense of relief – of entering the home straight.

The end of Siobhan's story was the same as Martine's and Ann's. The help, the escape, the leaving behind of so many important things but the salvaging of the most important of all. The realisation that, for the first time in years, she was safe. The slackening of tension; the fading of fear. The hope that now, perhaps, life could move on.

"Thank you, Siobhan," Hermione said at last. "You've been so brave and so helpful talking to us. We really appreciate it. And of course, you'll have the chance to see the video and make sure you're happy with it before anything goes live."

We packed up our things and said our goodbyes. There was a smell of soup and toast drifting through the air and I could hear children laughing again as we stepped out into the freezing afternoon. Once the door closed behind us, it became just another door in a quiet suburban street – there was no sign at all that this was a place where lives were transformed.

"You can see why it's called a refuge," Hermione said.

I nodded. We didn't say anything more, but I wondered whether she was thinking the same as I was – that, for all the peace, the warmth, the laughter and the food, this was a sanctuary no one would ever want to seek. No one would ever imagine that their life might take such turns that they needed to seek help from strangers because the person closest to them put them in mortal danger.

A taxi came and the camerawoman and the sound engineer loaded their bags into the boot and left. Hermione and I walked to the Tube station in silence.

"I know I shouldn't be, but I'm famished," she said as we stepped on to the escalator. "Want to grab a sandwich before we go back to the office?"

"I'm starving, too," I admitted. "I guess it's not the done thing to scrounge food off a charity, but I was totally desperate to ask if we could share their lunch."

We met each other's eyes and laughed. I felt some of the tension of the morning slip away.

"We did well, I think," Hermione said. "I'd forgotten how tough proper reporting is. Makes a change from cats anyway."

"God, I could do with writing a cat story after that," I said. "But I've got to head back to Hackney – I'm doing that interview for Emily about the housing estate campaign."

"Busy day for you then," Hermione said.

I said, "You're not wrong." But I had no idea how right she was.

For once in my life, I was early. Checking my watch as I stepped out of the station, I saw that I had almost an hour before I was due to meet Alethea Ayoola at her flat on the Garforth Estate. I was early, and I was hungry. I thought about popping into The Daily Grind for a salad, then I remembered the pizza Hannah and I had ordered for supper the previous night. It had a stuffed crust and loads of pepperoni and mushrooms on it, and it had been so filthy and so filling we'd only been able to eat about half of it. The rest was in the fridge at home, and it had my name on it. I quickened my pace and turned into Manwood Road. I'd grab some food, check the comments on my vlog, then it would be time to go and meet Alethea.

I opened the door quietly and carefully, in case Amy was at home asleep, but her bag and coat weren't on the stand in the hallway. *She must be back on a day shift*, I thought, *or at the gym or at Kian's.* I took off my own coat and hung it up with my bag, slipping my phone into my pocket, and shivered. The house was chilly – almost as cold as outside, which was weird, because it had been perfectly warm that morning. The heating must have gone off – I'd check the boiler, then have my lunch. I tried to remember if there'd been any instructions in Hannah's book of rules about how to reset the pilot light – there probably were, but I had no idea where my copy of that sacred document was now. I hadn't looked at in months. I stared at the control panel, perplexed. It seemed to be working – the green light was on, and that must be a good thing.

But something was wrong – something was different. I looked around the kitchen. Hannah's laptop was open on the table, its screen lit up. The curtains over the glass door to the garden were closed; usually Hannah opened them as soon as she came downstairs in the morning. I'd left before her that day – perhaps she'd forgotten. Perhaps she was ill and had stayed home. I pulled the curtain back and froze. The door was wide open, one of the panes smashed. There were shards of glass on the floor, and, dropped on top of them, a hammer.

We'd been burgled. It was a high crime area, I knew: Amy was always reminding us to lock up, to hang our keys on the hooks in the living room rather than leaving them on the dish in the hall, where a patient and enterprising thief could hook them out through the letterbox. But surely no intruder would have left Hannah's Macbook Air behind? He must still be in the house – upstairs, maybe, rifling through our bedrooms in search of jewellery or cash.

I stood perfectly still and listened. I couldn't hear anything. Not footsteps on the wooden floor, not the rattle of a wardrobe door opening or the thud of a drawer closing. I was sure I could hear my heart beating though – I could certainly feel it banging in my chest.

You know when you're watching a horror movie and someone – usually a woman – hears a noise and says she's going to investigate, and you're like, "Nooo! Don't do it!" and you cover your eyes with your hands because you know that in about five seconds she's going to get chopped up with an axe by a serial killer or have her heart ripped out by zombies or whatever, and you know that you'd never, ever be that dumb? Well, that day, I was that girl.

I don't know what made me do it. I know – I knew at the time – that the sensible thing would be to walk right back out of the front door and phone the police. But I didn't. My fear was suddenly overtaken by anger – that some thieving toe-rag had invaded our house, where Hannah had only recently started to feel safe again, and might still be there, going through our stuff. I'm not a brave person, but a surge of courage – or just plain stupidity – made me walk up the stairs instead of out into the street.

Amy's bedroom door was open. I could see her neatly made bed, her work boots on the floor and her uniform jacket on the chair. A burglar would have seen it too, and maybe had second thoughts about ransacking a house where the peelers could turn up unannounced any second. The idea reassured me – that was almost certainly what had happened, I thought, imagining the intruder muttering, "Fuck this noise," and turning round and legging it back out into the garden, over the fence and off to the pub as quickly as he could to tell his burglar mates about the almighty own goal he'd almost scored.

I opened my own door and looked inside. My room was just as I'd left it that morning: the wardrobe door open with a tangle of clothes spilling out on to the floor where I'd dropped them in my indecision about what to wear to interview victims of domestic violence. The jumble of make-up on my dressing table was undisturbed. My camera was still there on its tripod. I felt my thumping heart slow down, and realised I'd been holding my breath.

Then I heard the thump of footsteps coming down the stairs from the loft, and a voice said, "Where is she?"

I screamed. I couldn't help it. Not a proper scream, like the girls in horror movies do, but a sort of half-gasp, half-shout, and my hands involuntarily flew up to protect my face as I spun around.

"Oh my God. Richard."

"I came to find her," he said. "I need to see her. I love her."

It was the strangest thing: all at once, I stopped panicking and started thinking. I knew Richard was violent – I'd seen it, after all – but I also knew his violence wasn't, and probably wouldn't be, directed at me. I was an irrelevance to him. It was Hannah he wanted, and Hannah he wanted to hurt. I remembered reading, at some point in the hours I'd spent online researching domestic violence for the Clickfrenzy campaign, how common it was for men to stalk their victims after the end of a relationship, and how dangerous that period was for survivors. I remembered reading about women who'd turned their lives around, who thought that they were safe, only to be hunted down and savagely injured, or worse.

When I was reading about it, I'd wondered what went through those men's minds. How love turned to control, and when control was taken away, it turned to rage. I remembered one woman's story, how her attacker had said, "If I can't have you, I'll make sure no one else wants you," before he threw acid in her face.

Richard had brought a hammer to break into the house – I wondered what else he'd brought. He had a bag with him, the leather messenger bag he used for work. He was wearing his work clothes, too: the suit was much looser on him than it had been, and his face looked gaunt and shadowed. There was a plaster on his jaw where I guessed he'd cut himself shaving. I imagined him going about his life, going to work, going back to his brother's house, waiting for Hannah to change her mind, waiting for the date when he'd appear in court on charges of assaulting her – waiting, and thinking, and raging, and eventually deciding what he was going to do, and leaving his office on some pretext, and coming here.

I was scared of what he might do to me, but I was absolutely terrified for Hannah.

"Richard," I said, as calmly as I could. "Hannah's not here. You know she isn't. She's at work."

And she would be for the next two or three hours, I calculated. Safe at school, surrounded by high fences and other people. She'd be safe until she came home – so I had to warn her.

"I'll wait here for her," Richard said, as if he'd read my thoughts. "I know she wants to see me. That's why she sent me a key. I'll wait until she comes back."

He didn't know that I'd seen the broken window, I realised. He must have thought I'd walked straight upstairs. I didn't believe that he'd hurt me – I didn't think I was in any danger, not as long as I didn't try to thwart him, as long as I pretended I believed him. I forced myself to smile. "I'm sure Hannah will be really happy to see you. She misses you – she's said so often," I lied.

"I know she does," he said. "We're the world to each other. Without each other, we're nothing."

"I understand," I said. Then I said, "Look, Richard, I'm not feeling great – that's why I came home early. I think I've coming down with flu. I was just going to run a hot bath."

He and I stood there, on the landing, looking at each other. I knew, and he must have known too, that the only thing to do was to appear normal. He didn't want me to know what he'd really come for; he didn't want me to see the broken glass and the hammer, understand, panic and call 999. I didn't want him to know that I'd already seen, and that I understood only too well.

"I'll wait downstairs for Hannah," he said.

"Cool," I said, and I shot into the bathroom and locked the door.

I listened for a moment, but I didn't hear his footsteps going downstairs. I imagined him waiting outside the locked door, listening too, waiting to hear if I was going to make a phone call. And if I did – what would he do? I thought of the flimsy lock and the hammer, and I put the plug in the bathtub and turned both taps on full.

As quickly and silently as I could, I took my phone out of my pocket, gripping it tightly in case I dropped it with a clatter on the tiled floor. It was five past two – five minutes ago, I should have been knocking on Alethea Ayoola's door. I texted her apologising profusely, explaining that there'd been an emergency and I would be in touch to reschedule our appointment.

Then I texted Hannah. *Am at home. Richard turned up. PLEASE DON'T WORRY. I am fine but you need to let your lawyer and the police know, and stay safe until they've sorted it out. Don't come back until you know he's gone. And don't call me, just in case he hears.* Automatically, I clicked the emoji button and scrolled through looking for an appropriate one. A face blowing a kiss? No, of course that wouldn't do. Nor would a thumbs-up, a sad face, or any of the many, many cat icons that were in my most frequently used. I settled for adding a few x's, and pressed send.

I waited until I was sure the text had been delivered, and then I scrolled through my contacts and found another number, one that I'd looked at every day for the past few weeks but never dialled. And I sent another text.

Chapter Twenty-three

I sat in that bathroom for the longest time. I sat on the edge of the bath until my arse went numb, and then I moved and sat on the closed lid of the loo. I looked at the steaming water in the tub and considered getting in, and then I thought of Richard downstairs and myself, naked in the water, and thought better of it.

Hannah texted me to let me know she'd spoken to her solicitor, and that as Richard had broken the occupation order the court had imposed, the police would be sending an officer round just as soon as someone was available, but as long as I wasn't in any immediate danger it might take a little while. I texted her back and told her that was fine, I was safe, she mustn't worry. Then I went and sat on the edge of the bath again for a bit.

I texted Amy to tell her what was happening, and she eventually replied saying that she and Kian were at a parkour workshop in Milton Keynes, but she'd come straight back if I needed her, so of course I said there was no need at all, everything would be fine. Alethea Ayoola texted me back accepting my apology and saying she could meet up the following week. Sloane emailed me a draft schedule for my upcoming 25 Days of Vlogmas series of videos, and I told her I was a bit tied up but would look at it as soon as I could.

Then I moved back to the loo. There was no reply to the other text I'd sent. I read it over and over again, wondering if I'd been too casual, too dramatic, too needy – too something. But there was no way of knowing. I tried to look out through the window to see if Richard was in the garden or if the neighbours were home and had noticed the broken door, but all I could see through the frosted glass was a grey and brown blur of sky, roofs and trees. I stood by the door, pressing my ear against the wood, but I couldn't hear anything at all. I hadn't heard the front door opening or closing, so I had to assume that Richard was still in the house, and for the moment I was trapped, albeit voluntarily.

I wondered briefly how long I was likely to have to stay here for, and what I'd do. I'd stopped feeling hungry, at least, and of course I could drink water from the tap. But what if I got stuck here overnight? What if the police – overstretched as they were – only managed to send someone out tomorrow morning? Where would I sleep? How would I get ready for work in the morning and – more importantly – how would I get there? I imagined creeping downstairs and making a run for it, hoping that Richard was asleep or making tea or something. *Don't be ridiculous, Gemma*, I told myself – *of course they'll come, or Richard will give up and leave – there's no way you'll still be stuck here tomorrow.*

Then I did hear something. The neighbour's dog – Hannah had told me once that it was a cockadoodle and they'd paid a fortune for it from a breeder – broke into hysterical barking. I went to the window again, but I could see even less now, because it was getting dark. I undid the latch and pushed the window open, and peered cautiously out. A blast of cold air hit my face, and I realised it had started to rain. The dog was still barking – I could hear it quite clearly, but I couldn't see it. The neighbour's lights were off – they must still be at work and the dog shut inside. I knew how it felt: I was quite tempted to bark myself, or howl, or something.

I heard a sort of thumping scrape, and as I watched, a dark figure appeared on the fence, then dropped down into the garden on our side. The police, at last? But I couldn't see the neon flash of high-vis clothing, and surely a police officer would have knocked on the front door, not come sneaking over the fence like the burglar I'd imagined earlier. I could hear stealthy footsteps on the gravel, and I withdrew my head into the room, closed the window and waited, holding my breath.

I could hear voices downstairs. Men's voices. One of them was Richard's; the other I couldn't recognise, and they were both speaking too softly for me to make out any words. I listened intently, but it was no good – their conversation was no more than a rumble.

Right, I decided. I was going to go downstairs. This was ridiculous – I was an adult, I had my phone with me, I already knew that Richard was unlikely to hurt me. It was just a question of opening the door, walking down the stairs, and telling him that the police had been called and Hannah wasn't coming anywhere near the house until he was gone. I was being pathetic. I needed to confront my fears and get over them.

I put my hand on the doorknob, then took it away again. Then I went and sat back down on the edge of the bath and stared at my phone some more.

It sounds pathetic, I know. But I kept remembering Hannah's face after Richard had attacked her – the shock, the naked fear, the livid marks on her neck. I remembered reading, just yesterday, how dangerous strangulation is – how you can kill someone in seconds with your hands around their neck if you know exactly where to apply pressure, or even, accidentally, if you don't. I remembered the faces of the women I'd met that morning. I didn't want what had happened to them to happen to me. So I stayed in the bathroom like a big chicken.

A few minutes later, I heard a car beep its horn outside, and the unmistakeable sound of the front door opening and slamming shut, and then footsteps on the stairs and a voice calling, "Gemma? Are you there? Are you okay?"

I opened the door and stepped out, hoping that my trembling knees would keep me upright.

Raffy was on the landing.

"I came as soon as I got your text," he said.

I said, "Oh my God. How did you know? I mean, how did you even…"

"You were pretty cryptic, I have to say." He took his phone out of his pocket and read aloud the words that, over the past two hours, I'd totally committed to memory. "*Hey – sorry I haven't been in touch. I really wanted to. My dodgy landlord turned up at my house and I'm hiding in the bathroom. If I ever get out, shall we go for a drink?*"

I blushed. "Well, I didn't want to sound… you know."

"Gemma, you needed help. You could have just asked me to help you."

"But you did anyway," I said. "You came. How did you know what was going on?"

"I worked in The Daily Grind, remember? That place is a hotbed of local gossip. It's the Queen Vic of the hipster world. Someone told Luke what happened to your – to Hannah, and he mentioned it to me. So I knew what I was up against."

"What did you do? To Richard, I mean?"

"Oh, I bludgeoned him to death with an Ikea hammer," Raffy said. "I was hoping you might help me dispose of the body."

I gasped, and then laughed. "No, come on. Seriously."

"I just talked reasonably to him," Raffy said. "And now he's gone off quietly in an Uber to hand himself in at the police station – on my account, so I can make sure he gets there safely."

"You just talked reasonably to him?" I echoed disbelievingly.

"Well, mostly reasonably. I may have told him that I'd be watching him, and if he ever turns up here and frightens you again I'll hurt him so badly he'll wish he'd never been born."

"You what? You wouldn't."

"Well, no," he said. "But that's not the point, is it? The point is he believed I would. People like that – they understand violence, and threats. It's how they work. He's had lots of practice at intimidation, so it worked against him. Anyone else would probably have laughed at me."

I looked up at him. He was wearing black: black jeans and the same leather jacket I'd dropped in a puddle on Halloween night, black boots, a black and grey scarf over a charcoal coloured shirt. I noticed for the first time how broad his shoulders were. If he threatened me, I wouldn't laugh, I thought. The idea made me shiver.

"Gemma," Raffy said. "I studied drama in my first year of uni. I wanted to be an actor, but then I realised how shit I was, and changed my course to film-making. One of the shows I was in was this spoof gangster thing. All the lines I used on that bloke just now were from there. This isn't me, at all. I promise. I've never hit anyone and I never will."

"You're not some international man of mystery?"

"I'm afraid not."

"Not a leading figure in the Hackney underworld?"

He shook his head. "I'm just the guy from the coffee shop, remember?"

"Okay," I said. "Just the guy from the coffee shop."

Raffy took a step closer towards me, and I stepped closer to him. Then we were so close we couldn't step any further, and he put his arms around me and held me close. I was still trembling – I'm sure he could feel it. I reached under his jacket and put my hands on his warm, strong back.

"Now," he said. "What we need to do is get an emergency glazier out to fix that window, otherwise you'll all freeze. And once that's done, how about that drink you promised?"

"Trust me," Kian said. "It's the only way forward for mac and cheese. A splash of beer in the sauce. My mate's a chef and he gave me his recipe."

He was standing over the cooker, wearing Hannah's apron with the pink roses all over it, stirring intently. Amy and Hannah were at the table drinking tea. The emergency glass guy had just left and the room was starting to warm up again, and smelled deliciously of cheese and whatever spices Kian had put in the sauce. The hunger I'd almost forgotten about came flooding back.

"Twenty minutes in the oven and we'll be good to go," Kian said.

"Nice work, Jamie Oliver," said Amy. "Are you guys going to eat with us?"

"I should really…" Raffy said. "Unless Gemma…?"

For the first time since I'd met him, he sounded uncertain.

I said, "I promised to buy you a drink, didn't I?"

We put our coats on. Hannah hugged me and hugged Raffy, and kept thanking us, no matter how many times we told her not to worry, it was all part of the service. And at last, the door closed behind us and we were alone together in the cold, drizzly night.

"So, where to?" Raffy said.

I thought about all the places I'd been with Charlie – the clubs and cocktail bars and speakeasies. I could try to impress him with my encyclopaedic knowledge of London nightlife, but I sensed he wouldn't be impressed – that he'd know, just as I'd known on all those nights out with the Berry Boys, that those kind of places weren't my kind of places.

I said, "You remember, that night you and Luke were going to the pub and you asked me to join you?"

"And you turned me down," Raffy said. I felt a little thrill of pleasure that he remembered.

"I was going to come," I said. "I was literally just leaving, and then…"

"Excuses, excuses," Raffy said. "Right. The Prince George it is."

I found my umbrella in my bag and we sheltered together under its inadequate cover, our shoulders touching. After a few steps, Raffy took my hand. His fingers were warm and dry and felt entirely right twined around my own, and when I looked up at his face, half-smiling in the darkness, that looked right too. I felt the strangest sensation – like something clicking into place inside of me. We walked like that, close together, all the way to the pub, and once we were sat together on opposite sides of a shiny wooden table, he reached across to me and our hands found each other again.

We didn't talk about Hannah and Richard that night. We drank red wine and ate pulled pork burgers that were served on proper plates and chips that didn't come in a little wire deep-frying basket, and I told Raffy about Tom's obsession with serving implements. He laughed and said that the message had clearly been heard and understood, because everywhere was going back to plates now, and maybe for Tom's next trick he should expose the evils of kimchi.

He told me about the film he was working on, about refugee children in Dunkirk, and what he'd seen volunteering at the Jungle in Calais the year before. The way he described it was so vivid I could almost imagine I was there, surrounded by mud and smoke and despair and hope.

I told him about the gingerbread house Sloane had suggested I build for one of my Vlogmas videos, and how I was sure I'd mess it up, and he listened as if it was every bit as important, and said he'd tried to build one with his sister and Zara, and they'd messed it up totally, but that was surely the whole point of gingerbread houses.

We talked and laughed, and held hands again once we'd finished our food, and that feeling, that sense of things falling into place, didn't go away. We were so engrossed in each other that we didn't hear the landlord call last orders, and it was only when the lights were turned up bright that we realised it was midnight, and closing time.

"Come on," Raffy said. "I'll walk you home."

I remembered the last time he'd done that, after Jack had dumped me, and how embarrassed I'd been about getting drunk and trying to kiss him. I wondered if he remembered too. He didn't mention it, and nor did I – we walked back home in silence. The rain had stopped and I didn't need my umbrella, but we stayed just as close together as we had on the way.

At the corner of our road, we both paused. Raffy said, "Gemma?"

I thought, *He's going to ask if I'm okay to walk the rest of the way on my own. And I am, of course.* But I wanted him to kiss me – at least, I wanted him to want to kiss me, so I'd have the chance to say no, that it was too soon, even though it didn't feel too soon at all.

I said, "Thanks for a lovely evening. I really enjoyed it."

But then he said my name again, "Gemma," and when I turned towards him, he put his arms around me and kissed me. I wondered briefly if I had pulled pork caught in my teeth, and then, a second later, stopped thinking about that, because it was the most amazing kiss ever.

"I've been wanting to do that for so long," he said, when at last we came up for air.

"Me, too," I said, realising how true it was. "But not as much as I want to do it lots, lots more."

We walked rest of the way home – a short distance, but it took a long time, because we kept stopping to kiss each other again. And then when we got to our front door, I said I'd walk Raffy back up to the corner, and we kissed some more, then repeated the process outside my house, and by this stage we were both starting to giggle and I was worried we'd wake Hannah and Amy, so we stopped and reluctantly parted.

The house was in darkness. I wondered if Hannah was asleep, or anxiously listening for a key in the door and feet on the stairs. I hoped Kian had stayed over – with him and Amy there, she would surely feel as safe as she possibly could. And I felt safe, too – safe and cherished, but excited too, with the sense of something new and wonderful beginning and the memory of Raffy's kisses and his arms around me.

Chapter Twenty-four

So, it's Wednesday now – in fact, it's really really early on Wednesday morning – if you listen carefully you might hear the blackbirds that live in the tree outside my window – they go absolutely mental in the mornings and sometimes it wakes me up. It didn't this morning, though, because I was already awake. I was lying in bed for ages thinking about this video, and what I wanted to say to you all. It's a bit off the cuff, really, and I'm afraid there are no cool products or anything to show you, but I think it's important anyway – maybe the most important thing I've ever posted.

"So the charity we've been working with – they're called ADIVA, which stands for Against Domestic Violence and Abuse, which is a bit of a contorted acronym, I know – work with women throughout London and the South East. They've got a series of safe-houses where victims – survivors, they call them – can go to escape violent relationships. And it's not just about getting away from the person who's a danger to them – these women need huge support rebuilding their lives, accessing benefits, getting their children settled into new schools and so on.

"Often they've been prevented from accessing household money, so they've been made completely dependent on their abuser. That's one of the big things that prevents people from leaving – that and the threat of violence itself, of course. And after they've left, the danger doesn't stop, which is why many of them have to move to completely new areas, erase themselves completely from social media, things like that.

"As you can imagine, it's an expensive operation to run, and services in this area, like everywhere else, are being massively cut. So everything we as an organisation can do to help support them will also help save women's lives."

I looked around at the rapt faces. I was addressing not just the content team, but Clickfrenzy's monthly company meeting. Everyone had scooted their chairs up to one end of the office, and Sarah had asked Hermione and me to provide an update on how our story and campaign were developing. I was really nervous about it until I got started. It was strange how, when I was making a video, I could talk quite naturally and easily, even though I knew that far, far more people would watch me – but here, faced with a real-life audience, even though they were my colleagues who I saw every day, I still felt so self-conscious.

And of course, even though I talked them through as much as I could of what I'd learned over the past two weeks, and what I'd seen at the house in Acton, there were other things I wasn't able to talk about. Like how I'd locked myself in the bathroom for two hours waiting for Richard to leave the house, and how Raffy had come to my rescue. And how, the next night, Raffy had invited me round to his place. He hadn't said the words "Netflix and chill", but we both knew exactly what was going to happen. And when it happened, it was properly, unforgettably amazing – as amazing as kissing him had been, times a lot.

I felt myself blushing at the memory, and said, "But that's enough waffling from me. This morning we received the edited cut of the video, so let's hear Ann, Siobhan and Martine tell their own stories."

"Sandra at ADIVA has been incredibly helpful," Hermione said five minutes later, filling the silence the women's voices had left. "She's provided loads of facts and statistics, so we'll be able to put together infographics and animations to accompany the video and Gemma's article. And we all know how you guys in the art department love an infographic. The fundraising campaign is already going extremely well. Our readers have donated more than twenty thousand pounds so far, and that's only going to increase once this content goes live. We'll be linking to Gemma's vlog, too, and she'll link to us, so it's a great example of cross-pollination of content."

"Advertising sales are up, too," Sarah said. "Which isn't surprising, because our click rates have increased massively. We're leaving Boredcubed in the dust where they belong."

"And the bake-off made a couple of hundred," Tom said. "Emily's salted caramel brownies just pipped my lemon drizzle to the post. We meant to keep a slice for you, Gemma, but someone nabbed it from the fridge."

"I can't think who," Ruby said, and Tom went absolutely scarlet.

"We're all very proud of Gemma, Hermoine, Jim and the rest of the content team, as well as everyone else who's helped out on this campaign and, of course, all those who've kept our usual streams of business ticking over and growing," Sarah said. "Marina and Ian have had two great new business wins, we've got four new starters coming on board next month, and of course the events team have been hard at work organising the Christmas party – there'll be more details about that up on the intranet as soon as they're available. Any other business? No? Then let's all get back to work."

Dozens of chairs rolled back across the office to their desks. People picked up their phones and started tapping away of their keyboards. Callista did a tea run. Harrison asked me to look at his 'Have You Tipped Over The Edge Into Total Cat Craziness?' quiz before he sent it to Jim for approval. Sloane emailed me about a meeting with *Elle* magazine, and I put off answering until lunchtime.

It felt just like a normal day at work – and yet it didn't. Everything was different. It wasn't just Raffy, the sense of shivery anticipation mixed with soaring happiness I felt whenever I thought about him, or googled his name just to make sure that he was real. There was something else too, a new sense of purpose alongside the thrill of being – I was almost completely sure – in love.

My vlog wasn't going to change. I didn't want to change it, and Sloane would be seriously pissed off if I did. I love make-up and fashion just as much as the next girl – probably more, if the amount of stuff cluttering up my dressing table and bathroom cabinet is anything to go by. But I realised that I could talk to the audience I'd built up about other things, too – things that mattered even more to me and to them than the launch of the new Kat Von D palette, if such a thing were possible. My head was full of ideas, and I couldn't wait to get home, switch on my camera, and start recording. And at Clickfrenzy, too, now that the cats were in the past, I could work on new projects, learn new skills, become a proper journalist. The day – the whole world – felt replete with possibility.

I was startled out of my thoughts by an unfamiliar trilling sound. It took me a second to realise what it was – my desk phone. No one had ever called me on my landline at Clickfrenzy before. I picked up the handset and said, "Hi, Clickfrenzy content team, Gemma speaking. Oh, hi, Sandra."

On the other side of the pod of desks, I saw Hermione look up from her screen. The call didn't take long – just a few minutes – but I knew, watching her, how my own face must have passed from calm to shock, dismay to fear. By the time I replaced the handset, Hermione was hovering next to me.

"What's up?" she said.

I said, "It's Siobhan."

Hermione said, "Oh my God, she's not… He didn't…"

"No," I said. "It's not that. Sandra was just calling to let me know that Martine and Ann are happy with the clips we went them. She's going to confirm by email. But Siobhan isn't taking part any more. Well, she can't."

"Why not?"

"She's gone back to him – to Allan, her husband. Sandra didn't say very much about it, because confidentiality, obviously. But she's taken her stuff and left the shelter with her kids."

The knowledge of what Siobhan had chosen to do stayed with me – of course it did. Not just for the rest of that day, or the rest of that week: I knew that it would always be with me. I'd be doing something completely normal, like buying a coffee on my way to work or listening to music on the Tube on my way to work, when the memory of her voice and her story would come into my mind. In SpaceNK one lunchtime, when I was browsing new products for my channel, I caught sight of a woman's face in the mirror, smiling as the make-up artist slicked red gloss on her lips. The dark hair was the same as Siobhan's, and the freckles were too – but that telltale asymmetry in her face wasn't there.

I got into the habit of googling her name, almost every day, to see if there was a news item about her, but there never was. I hoped that Allan would have changed, as he must have promised her he would. Maybe he was having anger management therapy. Maybe the shock of losing his family had made him realise what was at stake. I hoped so, but I wasn't sure. I wasn't sure at all.

I talked to Raffy about it, one night when we were lying in my bed about to fall asleep, and he told me he felt the same about the things he'd seen in the refugee camps in France. He told me he dreamed about the children he'd met there, and woke up sure that he could smell burning plastic.

"Then I realise it's just some dodgy treatment thing you've put on your hair," he said, and I said, "Oi!" and poked him in the ribs with my elbow, and he tickled me, and then the play-fight turned into something else, and we fell asleep, comforted by each other's warmth.

In the next few weeks, I worked harder than I ever had in my life. The Clickfrenzy campaign rolled out and was hugely successful. I knew that if my vlog was about nothing but good causes, people would stop watching it, so I did as Sloane suggested and planned a daily Christmas-themed video for Vlogmas, which meant filming every evening after work, but at least I got to eat chocolates from my three different advent calendars for breakfast.

Although there was no reason not to go home to Hannah's house in the evenings after work any more, I still spent a few hours in the evenings at The Daily Grind, editing and posting my videos and doing what Sloane called "curating my social media".

Quite often, Raffy would leave the studio in Shoreditch where he worked and lived and join me. It was the strangest thing – sometimes, I'd be working away, so intently focused on what I was doing that I'd forget he was there, and then his ankle would brush mine under the table or I'd glance up from my work, and there he'd be, concentrating on his laptop screen until he sensed he was being watched, looked up at me and smiled the incredible smile that always made something shift and melt deep inside me.

When we weren't working – which wasn't a lot of the time, in those frenetic first few weeks – we did all the stuff normal couples do. We went to movies, and afterwards Raffy analysed and discussed them from a film-maker's point of view, and I told him off because we were meant to be having time off. We went to Winter Wonderland and rode on the Ferris wheel, and I filmed myself with the glimmering lights of London behind me for my vlog, and Raffy told me off for the same reason. We cooked random food together in his kitchen or Hannah's, with varying degrees of success.

It was, I realised, kind of like the life I'd imagined living with Jack. But in my daydreams it had always been summer, and now it was winter. I'd imagined Jack and me strolling along canal towpaths in the sunshine; Raffy and I hurried through the rain together, our gloved hands intertwined. So it was the same, but also very different – and it didn't feel like a dream at all. It felt like my life, like both my present and my future, and I knew it was a life that would make me happy.

I knew it because I didn't feel I had to pretend with Raffy. There was none of the anxiousness to please I'd felt around Jack; none of the sense of being not-quite-relevant that I'd felt with Charlie. We both knew that however big a part we played in each other's lives, we weren't the only thing in them, and that made each other all the more important. I knew that he loved me because I felt worthy of love, and that feeling was thrilling and reassuring, all at once.

One night in December, we were together at our usual table at The Daily Grind, surrounded by the familiar smells of toast and coffee. I wasn't working – not really, anyway. I was on my YouTube homepage, looking at the numbers. They were changing, and I was watching and waiting.

Then Raffy looked up from his screen and said, "Oh my God."

"What?" I said.

"I've just had an email from the RTS."

"The what?"

"You YouTubers! Honestly, it's like you've been living under a rock," Raffy teased. "The Royal Television Society. I've been nominated for an award. Best documentary, for *The Estate We're In*."

I jumped up from my chair, almost knocking over both our laptops and coffee mugs, and dashed around the table to hug him. Luke came out from behind the bar and joined us, and we did a bit of a victory dance around the shop.

"I won't win, obviously," Raffy said.

I said, "I bet you will."

"And even if you don't," Luke said, "it'll mean more great exposure for the campaign, and more funds. Maybe we'll even be able to afford a shit-hot lawyer to take on those bastard developers."

And the three of us headed out to the pub to celebrate, and in all the excitement I forgot to keep checking my phone, so SparklyGems' one millionth subscriber added herself without me even noticing.

Even though I'd known Raffy for what felt like ages, and been going out with him for more than a month (well, strictly speaking it had been thirty-two days since we first slept together, and that seemed like as good a day as any to think of as our anniversary), I was eager to make a good impression on my first official outing as his girlfriend, in front of all his friends.

So I spent ages getting ready for Luke's twenty-seventh birthday party the week before Christmas, although I knew that Raffy had fancied me even when I'd been wearing my work clothes and spent the afternoon hiding in the bathroom. I put my hair up in a messy bun with a sleek plait on one side and filmed myself doing it, because it was day four of Vlogmas and I seriously needed to multi-task to do if I was going to get a video uploaded before setting off for Luke's flat. I put on the black dress I'd bought for the Clickfrenzy Christmas do and a pair of ankle boots with seriously high heels, which I'd nicked from Mum on my last visit, because Raffy was tall enough for me not to have to worry about shaming him in front of his mates by towering over him.

I edited my video and uploaded it, and then I went downstairs, reminding myself to pick up the bottle of champagne I'd put in the fridge to chill. I was extracting a carrier bag from the designated drawer, which still bore a curling Post-it note (*We try to reduce waste by re-using bags*), when I heard the unfamiliar sound of heels treading carefully down the stairs.

Although she was so small, Amy never, ever wore high-heeled shoes. "You never know when you're going to have to chase a bad guy," she'd said once, with her usual indubitable good sense. And Hannah didn't, either. I'd never asked, but I'd assumed that it was because she was almost as tall as Richard, and he'd made it plain early on in their relationship that they were unacceptable.

Hannah was now, though.

Not just high heels – totally gorgeous gold cage shoes with her toenails painted gold to match – but a cherry-red drapey dress that clashed fabulously with her hair and made her skin look more porcelain-perfect than ever, and scarlet lipstick that made her lips look even fuller and her eyes even greener. It had genuinely never occurred to me before how pretty Hannah was, but it did now.

"Wow," I said. "Look at you! Big night out?"

"Not really," she said. "Just a friend's birthday party. Do you think this is totally OTT?"

"Of course not," I said. "It's December, so any party means being a bit OTT, it's the law. I'm going to a birthday party too, and look at me."

I took my bottle of fizz out of the fridge and noticed another, even posher bottle on the shelf next to it.

"I'll just grab that," Hannah said. She smelled as gorgeous as she looked, I noticed as she stretched past me.

"So where are you off to?" I asked.

Hannah was wearing blusher – a pretty, peachy coral with a hint of sparkle; I wanted to ask her who it was by, but finding out what her plans were for the evening took precedence – and I could see the natural flush of her skin under it.

"Just up the road, actually," she said.

"Really?" I said. "I'm going just up the road, too. Looks like it's birthday party central round here tonight."

Hannah said, "It's a friend's place – well, more an acquaintance, really. I met him when I was delivering leaflets for the Save the Garforth campaign. A few of us at the school have been helping out, because so many of the kids live there and it's just so awful to think that they might have to move away when they're doing so well and we just got rated Good by OFSTED. Anyway, my colleague Alice and I went for a sandwich and a pint with a few of the other volunteers afterwards and we got chatting, and one of the organisers invited us all to his birthday party. I kind of feel I need to expand my social circle again, so I said yes. Are you sure the dress doesn't look stupid?"

I told Hannah that she looked about as un-stupid as it's possible for a person to look. And, as we left the house together and I explained how it had happened that we were going to the same party, I found my imagination running away with me a bit. I thought how kind Luke was, how he always made sure that any food left over at the end of every day was delivered to the local homeless shelter and how he paid his staff the London living wage instead of minimum wage, even though he didn't have to. I remembered what Raffy had told me about Luke's wealthy background, and I knew that, even though Hannah didn't really care about money – who can afford to, if they're a primary school teacher? – she'd been fretting about having to move into key-worker housing once her lawyers and Richard's finished their negotiations and the house on Manwood Close was sold. I even tried to recall what I'd learned about genetics in GCSE biology, and whether it meant that Luke and Hannah would have adorable red-haired babies.

And then, just as we turned the corner on to the high street and saw the multi-coloured Christmas lights sparkling in the window of The Daily Grind, my imagination suddenly hit an insurmountable barrier.

I said to Hannah, "But you don't like coffee."

Hannah said, "Correction. Rich made me stop drinking it when he did, because it made him even crankier, and plus it gave him the most awful bad breath. I, on the other hand, totally love the stuff."

And she did a little twirl under a streetlight, looking just like the dancing lady emoji in her red dress, and the two of us hurried on down the road as fast as our shoes would let us.

Chapter Twenty-five

Hi everyone!

So, this is my second-to-last post of Vlogmas. I can't believe how it's flown by! A video every day of December – I never thought I'd manage it, but it's been so much fun and I've loved having all of you along with me on this journey. I'm going to show you a gorgeous, simple festive make-up look in just a minute. It's sparkly and glowy with red lips and heaps of glitter – basically, it's Christmas, only on your face.

But before I start, there's some stuff I want to say to all of you, because this year has been made as incredible and exciting and special as it has been because of you. When I started this channel, I never thought it would get this big. I never thought I'd have a million subscribers. I'm just totally overwhelmed by how much support and encouragement I've had from so many amazing people.

And it's because of all of you that I've been able to make SparklyGems about far more than the stuff I started posting about. Don't worry – I'm still going to be showing you amazing beauty products, fashion, even some cooking. I'm getting a bit better at that now! But it's about other things too – things that matter even more (and make-up matters to me, like, a lot!). Thanks to

"So let's all raise a glass to our outgoing Head of Content."

Everyone drank and cheered and sang, and I joined in, even though I could hear I was singing out of tune. Jim said a few words, and shed a few tears.

Then Sarah went on. "Of course, when someone is as big a part of the team as Jim, they leave big shoes to fill. And although she only takes a size four, I know that Hermione will do a formidable job heading up the content team. She's already been at the forefront of some incredible changes here, including setting up the fledgling campaigns section. I'm sure you all share my view that today, more than ever, it's vital for us to stand up for what we believe in and produce fearless, compelling content that moves hearts and changes minds. Gemma will be taking that over from Hermione and I'm sure taking Campaigns from strength to strength.

"Congratulations to you both, and if you know of any turkey activists who want Christmas to happen more often, have a word with Gemma."

There was another burst of laughter, and this time Harrison joined in.

"And in the meantime," Sarah continued, "enjoy the food and fizz, but please don't let the festivities spill into the next-door room, or get too raucous, because I've got a client meeting at five, for my sins. I hope you have a wonderful Christmas. And thank you all so much for all the hard… What's that noise?"

She paused. We could hear a bit of a commotion outside, and suddenly the whole of Clickfrenzy was gathered around the windows, looking out. I joined them, hearing high-pitched shrieking coming from the street below.

"What the hell's going on?" Hermoine said.

I was right at the back of the little crowd, so I couldn't see anything.

"My God, it's like a riot out there," Jim said.

"A riot of teenage girls," Ruby said.

"There must be, like, five hundred people outside our office," said Callista in bewilderment.

"It's worse than when Five Guys opened," said Tom.

"It's worse than when some idiot tweeted they'd seen Beyoncé shopping in Hollister," Ruby said. "I mean, as if. That was totally insane, remember, Tom?"

"They closed the Tube station and everything," Tom said.

"Someone's phone's ringing in the office," Jim said.

I said, "I'll go and see. Shit, it's mine."

I legged it back to my desk and snatched up the handset.

"Gemma?" It was Martin, the downstairs receptionist, and he sounded narky as hell. "There's a gentleman here to see you. And a mob of young women following him. I've had to call the police."

I said, "Oh my God. I'm so sorry. Is it Charlie?"

"Mr Berry, he says," Martin said. "Shall I send him up?"

"Yes, please." I put down the phone, my face flaming with mortification, and hurried to the lift. What was Charlie doing, turning up at my work? He'd never been here before. As far as I was aware, he didn't even know the address.

The lift doors slid open and out stepped the familiar blond figure. He was holding a large white box and a bunch of roses, except the cellophane wrapping was all crumpled and torn, the flowers were squashed and several of them had been decapitated. When he handed them to me, a shower of red petals drifted down on to the carpet.

"God, Gemma," he said. "What a fucking nightmare. I went into Liberty to get you these and I was browsing the Bigelow counter and I put a pic up on Snapchat, and then I wandered round some more and tried on some shoes, and then when I came out there were all these girls waiting. Bloody hell. That was actually quite scary. It took me half an hour to get here and it's only just round the corner. Sorry about your flowers."

Except it wasn't Charlie. It was Gus.

I said, "That's okay. I guess we'd better sit down."

He followed me through to the smallest, empty meeting room and I gave him a glass of water. He looked a bit pale and I could see streaks of lipstick on his white T-shirt. This, I realised, was why he and Charlie had never, ever got the Tube, never gone out anywhere without a draconian door policy… quite often, for days at a time, never been anywhere at all. This was why Sloane planned their signings and meet-and-greets with such military precision – except, of course, when Gus escaped and went off on his own, to do his own thing, which had meant the end of the Berry Boys.

This was what it meant to have eight million followers on YouTube. This was what my life might be like, one day. I looked out of the window. The crowd was still there. I could hear the furious beeping of many cars' hooters and the distant sound of a siren.

"It doesn't look like that was much fun," I said.

"No," Gus said. "It wasn't. It was horrible, actually. Next time I want to buy someone flowers, I'm getting them delivered."

I laughed, then I remembered how furious I ought to be with him about what he'd done, and stopped.

I thought about my faltering attempts to make friends with him, and whether it would have made any difference to what happened if I'd succeeded. I wondered whether, if Gus had apologised for what he'd said to me the day they got the puppy, Charlie and I would have carried on being together and everything would still be the same as it had been three months ago. Before the Halloween party. Before Raffy. I wondered whether, if I hadn't been home and seen what Richard had done to Hannah, I would ever have found the courage to vlog about things other than make-up and scented candles.

I couldn't be sure. Thinking about it, about the whole complex tangle of possibilities and what-ifs, made my brain go all funny, like when I read about alternate realities, quantum interference and the nature of causality in Terry Pratchett novels when I was a teenager. But I was as sure as I could be that the way things had turned out was the right way.

And I supposed that, in spite of everything, I was quite grateful to Gus.

So I reached out and touched his hand, and said, "How are you? Where have you been?"

"Wales," Gus said.

"Wales?" I said, as incredulously as if he'd said the planet Neptune, although given his and Charlie's brief passion for virtual space exploration, Neptune was actually quite a bit more likely. "What's in Wales?"

"Mountains, mostly," he said. "At least, in the bit where I am. And sheep. And our nana and grandad."

I gawped at him a bit more, and then said, "But what are you doing there?"

"Well, mostly, right now, I'm thinking. And playing the fiddle. There's no broadband where our grandparents live and hardly any mobile reception. They only got satnav in their car a year ago and they listen to Classic FM all the time. Nan plays the violin – it was her who got me into it. I expect we'll do duets in the village hall. It's boring as fuck and I'm loving it. Coming up to London today was so weird. I'd forgotten how crowded the Tube gets. I literally got lost changing at King's Cross."

It had been a lot longer than just a few weeks since Gus had been a regular commuter on London Underground, but I didn't want to remind him of that. "It is kind of busy," I muttered.

"It's great for Taylor, too," Gus went on. "Grandad is obsessed with dogs. He's teaching her manners and about chasing rabbits. She loves it there."

I finally untied my tongue from around my tonsils, where it appeared to have got stuck, and said, "But what about vlogging? I mean, don't you miss it?"

Gus said, "Gemma, we're going to be twenty-five next month. I did the YouTube thing for seven years and I'm getting a bit too old to spend my time playing games and pranking my brother. Don't you think?"

I thought. I thought about the condom challenge and the food fights and the Korean sweets, and the feral, studenty lifestyle they both lived. I thought about Hannah and what had happened to her, and about how different the way I felt about Raffy was from the way I'd felt about Charlie, or even about Jack, and I understood exactly what he meant.

I said, "Yeah, I guess so. But what about the flat? What about Charlie?"

"Sloane managed everything," Gus said. He sounded a bit angry, and very tired. "She told us what to do. She set Charlie up with a shiny new channel all of his own, and he's signed up to be a brand ambassador for Topman. Apparently she's talking to MTV about him fronting a show. Our Charles isn't finished with celebrity, not by a long shot. But I am."

I looked at him. He looked just the same – a duplicate of the hot blond boy I'd fallen for, only slightly different. But the difference now was more pronounced – under his bright blue eyes there were shadows I couldn't remember being there before. There was a loose flake of skin on his lip, as if he'd been biting it and not using chapstick. He looked tired – not in the yawny, up-all-night way I was used to seeing, but a different kind of tiredness, one I suppose would take a long time for a person to notice, and a long time to get better from.

I said, "You hated it, didn't you?"

"Not at first," Gus said. "At first it was all a bit of a laugh. And once I realised I was never going to be a famous classical musician, it was another way of getting what I'd wanted from that, I guess. The adulation. But getting that from a bunch of teenage girls is a whole lot different from getting it from an audience at the Barbican, like I thought I would when I started college. And I hated them, Gemma. I hated the fans. I couldn't get past it. I couldn't get my head around why they loved us when what we were doing was so totally pointless."

"But you…" I began, but I couldn't bring myself to finish saying it.

Gus did it for me. "Shagged them anyway? Yes, I did. And believe me, I'm not proud of it. It's the shittest thing I've ever done – even shitter than snogging you that night, and that was a shit thing, too. I guess I thought that if they were making me live this life I hated – and I know they weren't, not really – then they could pay for it in a way that gave me some pleasure, at least. And afterwards, every time, I hated myself so much. So I focused on hating them, and that justified doing it again."

The shock I felt must have showed in my face, because Gus said, "Like I said, I'm not proud. You know, one day, I'm going to meet someone special, and I'm going to have to decide whether to tell her about what I did. If I do, and I lose her, maybe that will be my payback. And if I don't, I'll always know, and I'll always worry that somehow she'll find out."

But that wouldn't be Gus's only payback for what he'd done, I realised. Whatever happened, even if he fell in love with a girl and found a way to make her feel okay about this short, grubby series of events in his past, there was one thing that had changed forever: he and Charlie would always be twins, always be brothers, but them being a double act, perfect reflections of each other, was over. The mirror they'd been able to look into and see each other had smashed and it could never be repaired.

Gus knew that, I realised. I wondered whether Charlie did too, and whether he understood that he was partly responsible for it.

"Don't worry about me, Gemma," Gus said. "I'm okay. The book's still selling loads, so I won't starve. I'll be happy, somehow, I guess. I've got Taylor, and music."

I turned towards the window again. The noise outside had died down, and when I looked I could see just a handful of girls waiting on the corner.

I said, "It looks like the coast is going to be clear soon."

"Thank God for that," Gus said. "Listen, Gemma, I need to say something else before I go – and I'm going to get an Uber this time, don't worry. I won't make your man downstairs call the peelers again. How mental was that? He's one hard bastard, though. I thought for a bit he might be going to arrest me, but then I told him I was here to see you and he backed off."

I said, "Martin is kind of terrifying. But when you get to know him he's a real softy."

"Maybe he is," Gus said. "But he scared the shit out of me anyway. Post-traumatic stress disorder, here I come. But anyway, I was saying…"

"You were saying?"

"I was jealous of you," Gus said. "Charlie fell for you, big time. You two were good together."

I said, "I guess just because something's good, doesn't mean it's meant to last."

Gus took a deep breath, as if he was inhaling a fag, and blew it slowly out again. He said, "I know that, now. And I should have let it run its course. But I didn't. I wanted it to end, and I helped end it."

I said, "I know how hard it must have been, me suddenly being there, like, all the time. When the two of you were used to it just being you."

Gus said, "Yeah. And now it's just me."

I reached across the table and gave his hand a squeeze. "It's going to be okay. Whatever's happening, you'll be okay."

He brightened, and said, "And I'm staying over at the flat tonight. It's way too late to get the last train back to Bangor. Charles will probably want to go out on the town, now he's free and single again. Shoreditch House maybe."

I said, "Gus…!"

He laughed. "Don't worry, Gemma. That chapter in my life is over. We'll stay in and get a takeaway. I expect Charles will be glued to his laptop all night, editing videos. Anyway." He pushed the white box across the table towards me. "I nearly forgot. You need to open this. Merry Christmas."

I'd almost forgotten about it too, even though it had been on the table between us the whole time we were talking. It was a plain box, tied with a blue ribbon. I thought about what might be inside, and I wasn't sure I wanted to find out.

But he said, "Go on, open it."

I said, "Gus, I don't want to hurt your feelings or anything, but I don't think you understand."

He said, "I think I do."

He had sort of half-smile on his face, the look people have when they desperately want to have got something right, but aren't sure they have – a look of almost puppyish eagerness. But I definitely, definitely didn't want to think about puppies at that particular moment. I didn't want to know what Gus might have brought me to make up for the loss of Stanley.

But then I looked at him again, and saw his tired eyes and knew that even though the Berry Boys were finished, even though it was all over between me and Charlie, he needed me to do this one last thing for him, to pretend he'd got it right even if he hadn't.

I untied the ribbon and lifted up the lid of the box. There was a layer of crisp white tissue paper inside, and I lifted that up too.

And then I gasped.

There, lying on his back as if nothing had happened to him, was Stanley. Not another teddy like him. Not a replacement. Stanley. His fur was worn away in the same places it had been for as long as I could remember. His smile was still a bit wonky, although the loose thread at the corner of his mouth had been stitched back into place. The dangly eye I'd kept meaning and forgetting to sew back on was now securely attached to his face. And his arms and legs, which I'd watched the puppy chewing off, were reattached as good as new.

I lifted him out of the box and held him close to my chest. He smelled a bit different, but not in a bad way – even I had to admit, he'd become a less than fragrant bear over the years.

I said, "Oh my God. Gus. I can't believe you did this."

Gus said, "I didn't, Gemma. Come on. Sloane took him to a special toy repair place, after she'd given us the mother of all bollockings for letting the puppy chew your stuff. They took ages to fix him, but they did. I haven't said sorry to you about that. But I am sorry."

I said, "Thank you."

And then we had the longest, most massive hug, which only stopped when Sarah turned up at the door for the meeting with her clients and alerted us to her presence with a discreet cough. I jumped like someone had chucked icy water over me and so did

Gus, and we gathered up the box and the flowers and Stanley and hurried out, apologising profusely.

As we were leaving, I heard one of the clients say, "Was that…?"

I kept walking, knowing that the rest of his question would be whether one of the famous Berry Boys had graced Clickfrenzy HQ with his presence, and that Sarah would find a way to make it sound like he'd been there on official business.

But the client must have thought we were out of earshot, because he went on, loudly enough for me to hear quite easily, "That's Gemma Grey, right?"

A letter from Sophie

I want to say a huge thank you for choosing to read *Out with the Ex, In with the New*. If you did enjoy it and want to keep up to date with all my latest releases, just sign up at the following link. Your email address will never be shared and you can unsubscribe at any time.

www.bookouture.com/sophie-ranald

Writing a novel is like having a baby, or so the cliché goes. Now I've never gone through pregnancy, but if I were to extend that analogy to my experience writing this novel, it would involve morning sickness, swollen ankles, varicose veins, stretch marks, and then a doctor hacking away at my nether regions with a scalpel before saying he'd changed his mind and I'd have to wait another four months to meet my baby.

Okay, who am I kidding – writing is *nothing* like giving birth! Nonetheless, the process of gestating *Out with the Ex, In with the New* was a long and arduous one. The novel was first published in 2017 as *The Truth About Gemma Grey*, and now, more than two years later, I'm absolutely thrilled to be bringing it to you in its shiny new incarnation.

Out with the Ex, In with the New is the first in what was to become a series of four novels based around The Daily Grind, a coffee shop/café/restaurant/cocktail bar in trendy Hackney. Over the course of the four books, the place, its customers and the people who work there took on a life of their own. It sometimes feels to me like The Daily Grind must be positively Tardis-like in its ability to accommodate parties, food preparation, bicycle repairs and used vinyl sales – not to mention all the dramas played out inside its extremely stretchy walls and in the world beyond them!

If you've enjoyed this book, I hope you continue with the not-quite-a-series by reading *Sorry Not Sorry*, *It's Not You, It's Him* and *No, We Can't Be Friends*. And if you're coming to *Out with the Ex, In with the New* having read one or more of the other novels set in this world, I hope you've enjoyed finding out more about some of the characters you've met before!

Over the page, I have some words of abject gratitude for the many people who've helped me bring this novel to life in both its editions. But first of all, I wanted to say thank you to the most important person of all – you. I know how many wonderful books there are out there, and I feel privileged and grateful when you choose mine. I read every single review you post on Amazon – long or short, good or bad – and I respond personally to every reader who contacts me on social media or email. So please do get in touch and tell me what you think – I'd love to hear from you.

Love, Sophie

✉ sophie@sophieranald.com

🖥 www.sophieranald.com

🐦 @SophieRanald

f SophieRanald

📷 @SophieRanald

Acknowledgements

The world of vlogging was completely new to me when I started writing *Out with the Ex, In with the New*, and my research involved countless hours spent glued to YouTube, immersing myself in the channels and lives of Zoella, Tanya Burr, Estée Lalonde, Jim Chapman, Alfie Dayes and others. It's left me with the greatest possible respect for these creators, who share often highly personal and sensitive aspects of their lives with their viewers, expose themselves to some seriously brutal sniping and trolling, then come back the next day, smile for the camera, and do it all again. It's also left me with a much-increased make-up collection, some killer contouring skills, and a Christmas jumper I never knew I needed.

But there's more to YouTube than Minecraft and make-up, as I discovered. Many content creators are passionate about raising awareness for causes they care about: politics, HIV prevention, online bullying, mental health – the list is endless. For Gemma, it was a realisation of the huge scale and insidious nature of domestic violence that inspired her to vlog about more than just cosmetics and clean eating. Women's Aid, Refuge and a host of other charities do incredible work to support people in abusive relationships and help them to rebuild their lives – and do it in the face of ever-diminishing funding. We should all be thankful for the work they do. I'd also like to thank Clare Smith, who gave me some pointers from a police officer's point of view about the process of reporting and arresting an offender.

My research then took me to Google's palatial London HQ, where Tom Price and Thea O'Hear were kind enough to show me around and bring me up to speed on the practical and financial aspects of being a YouTuber. Any deviation from reality in Gemma's experience is either poetic licence, or simple error on my part resulting from information overload! The writer Matt Whyman also provided invaluable insights into vlogging and introduced me to the strange online underworld where YouTubers' fans and ex-fans gather to discuss their idols in minute – and often malicious – detail.

To find out more about how new media companies work, I visited Buzzfeed's offices just off Oxford Circus. Although I named a character in the novel after him, I have to emphasise that Jim Waterson is a highly skilled journalist who I'm sure has never posted a cat meme in his life. Thanks for your help, Jim!

I am lucky enough to be represented by The Soho Agency, where an amazing team of people have held my hand throughout my journey as a writer. Araminta Whitley, Jennifer Hunt, Alice Saunders and Niamh O'Grady have my eternal gratitude for their expertise, kindness and ability to deliver a good shake when it's most needed. Becca Allen deployed her ninja proofreading skills and spared my blushes.

I'm also unbelievably fortunate to have the best people in the business supporting me at my publisher, Bookouture. If Carlsberg did editing, they'd be putting Christina Demosthenous in a can for sure. And Noelle Holten, Kim Nash, Peta Nightingale, Alex Holmes and Alex Crowe are just a few of the others in the dream team who've supported me over the past two years. Thank you all.

At home, my partner Hopi has been by my side and had my back all the way, providing contacts, advice, kisses and gin with unstinting generosity. I love you very much. My darling Purrs has been the best companion any writer could want, making me laugh when I'm on the brink of despair and shouting at me when it's time for an afternoon nap – and now little Hither has added another grumpy-faced literary critic to our family. I couldn't have done it without them all.

CPSIA information can be obtained
at www.ICGtesting.com
Printed in the USA
BVHW030246190421
605284BV00015B/320

9 781838 882488